TURTLE

TURTLE

Gordon Folkins

Writers Club Press
San Jose   New York   Lincoln   Shanghai

TURTLE

All Rights Reserved © 2001 by Gordon L. Folkins

Writers Club Press
an imprint of iUniverse, Inc.

For information address:
iUniverse, Inc.
5220 S. 16th St., Suite 200
Lincoln, NE 68512
www.iuniverse.com

ISBN: 0-595-20218-7

Printed in the United States of America

"Sometimes at night, when it's very late,
I can almost believe there is something outside my
closet…waiting for me…
but I keep on dancin' anyway."

—Boogie Man

"I just need it, man."

—Bobo, the Junkie Donkey

"I never got it, Denny. I never understood. See you there."

—the poet *Rice Ternbal Mazel's* last words to his brother, *Dennis Mazel*, before leaping thirty-two stories to his death.

Contents

ONE

10...

It felt like wading into a lake on a cool summer morning; you teased yourself with the chilly water, excessively conscious of your body and the water's effect on it. Goose bumps spreading in an instant upon first touch; a breeze ruffling the surface of the lake, urging the chill on.

He stood on the rocky bank of this desolate, acrid lake, looking patiently across to the opposite shore. With a virginal wonder he realized he could stop—it wasn't too late. In a shunned and unspoken corner of himself, he wanted to put an end to it before it was too late. He settled on waiting, at least awhile, just to see what would happen; tease it a little and see if it would blink. Besides, it wasn't all bad...

Lane White sat at his computer terminal in his cubical and typed with mechanical, bored efficiency. Thick hands and beefy arms contradicted the fluid, almost graceful casualness with which he typed. Long healed scars marred an otherwise handsome face. On the rare occasion he would be asked about the scars he would say it was from acne, and some of the scars were actually from that teenage torment. The majority of the damage was from another torment.

The thick, disarray of black hair that sprang from his head only caused his light, gray eyes to stand out; white stones in a black pool. Gray eyes and dark hair ran in his fathers' side of the family, as did the athletic build. The light, fair skin came from his mother.

He paused in his typing, removed the sheet of paper from the pressure sensitive holder and placed it in a wire basket on the right side of his desk. From an identical basket on the left side of his desk he plucked out the next page of instructions, slipped it in the holder with familiar ease, and began entering the information.

Twenty-six employees and one manager were cozily stuffed into the maze that was Hubbard Electronics Data Entry Department. They were as friendly as any clan can be with a high turn over. There was a core group of eleven that had been at it as long as Lane and they tended to guide the new recruits in the how's and what's of the job, but there really wasn't that much to it.

He had been writing well. *Night Vision*, his current work in progress, was turning out better than expected. Though maintained and expressed as a work of fiction, he had infused the book with the chaotic violence of his dreams to create a work that evoked more reality than an imagined world. It had begun with the idea of a collection of short stories that would be spun from his dreams. Now the short stories had somehow merged into a beast of a tale that may soon get out of hand.

Night Vision had a quality that he liked. It was smooth, ethereal, dark, slick—it was the best work he had done in his too few years of writing, at least he liked to think it was. It bolstered him and gave him something to grasp.

Writing began to hold a serious interest for him during the equivalent of his freshman year in high school. It wasn't until then that he actually thought he could pull it off. He had started slowly with a few articles and short stories on the side just dabbling and experimenting with the feel of it. Occasionally he would send off an article, coupled with the vague hope of the beginnings of a professional writing career.

He had never published.

During his brief stint in college he'd read somewhere that if you wanted to earn a living writing fiction (by that time his chosen genre') you wrote Novels. So he gave up the short story and article bit and began his first Novel.

Sweating it out a word at a time, encouraged by his foster parents, Henry and Linda McAlester, to stick with it, he completed his first book. It wasn't really a Novel, more a Novelette at only two hundred thirty-seven manuscript pages. But it had felt good to finish it. The act of completion had given him a shot of confidence that he had needed at the time.

He had completed a book.

The contents of that first book were another matter.

Night Vision would be his sixth complete Novel. There were countless others he had begun then abandoned because the story had simply run out. The closest he'd come to publication was with his fourth book, *Sleep Talk*. He had received a letter from a small publishing house in California stating the book held "great potential" and would be "reviewed further". He'd never heard from them again. Yet, even that brief whispered kiss of success was a tremendous encouragement.

By now, at age thirty-three, he had hoped to be publishing on a regular basis. After the years of struggling, still holding fast to the writing ship, Henry and Linda helping as much as he would let them, he landed with Hubbard. It paid enough to give him the feeling of earning his own way and it wasn't a distraction from his writing.

Two promotions had been offered during his six years of employment and he had turned them both down, not wanting to distract himself from his writing.

"Count?" someone called from the front of the room. There was a daily betting pool on who could enter the most information sheets. Everyone tipped in a dollar that wanted to play. It helped stave off the boredom. Numbers and jeers began to be called out in response to the request. A five-minute warning was called then the keyboards were finally silent as the five o'clock chimes rang out the hour.

Sheila Nelson won the pool. Lane watched as Foster Estorga congratulated Sheila on her winnings. Foster was, as it has been said, One Strange Dude. At five feet nothing and weighing in at maybe a hundred pounds fully clothed, he wasn't a physically imposing figure. He kept his shoulder length black hair covered by a tattered, faded, blue baseball cap. He had dark, Hispanic features and pallid, lifeless eyes. His lips were always wet and he gave you the feeling that he wanted to touch you and do nasty, dark things to your body when those eyes turned your way.

The clatter of keyboards died completely as musical chimes over the Muzak system rang out the five o'clock hour. Chairs rolled across low-shag wear-dated carpet and heads began to appear above the cubicles in the room. Mr. DeAwn—Red to his friends—lumbered out of his glass enclosed office at the front of the room.

"Who gets it?" he asked the casual parade of Hubbard Data Input Employees cleaning up to leave. Though it was against corporate policy to gamble, most office pools were overlooked.

"Who do you think?" Sheila gruffly asked. "The fastest keys in the valley!"

"Yeah, and you'd better enjoy it while you can," David Sumner said, only half joking. "Tomorrow, biker lady, tomorrow, it's mine!"

Lane continued clearing his desk while several people milled around the front of the room gossiping and razing Sheila on her winnings. Mr. DeAwn handed her the number ten white envelope that contained the pooled money. She shook it in the air triumphantly; some of the loose change clinked together, muffled by the bills.

"Later," she said, and turned to leave.

Lane finished clearing his work area as the group began to break up and leave.

"Lane, gotta' minute?" Mr. DeAwn asked from where he stood in front of his office.

He was one of the few people that Lane took care to avoid whenever possible. Nothing against him personally, you understand. It was just easier to avoid the man than to fake it. It was rumored that Red was the individual that had drilled a peephole into the woman's bathroom and had been watching the goings on.

"Sure," Lane said, as he shut down his terminal. With his worn, green canvas briefcase in hand, he followed Red into his office.

"Come on in and sit down," Red offered. Lane smiled, thanked him, then sat, laying his bag next to the chair. The bag didn't contain anything more than extra pens and pencils along with several legal pads for note taking, but he was used to carrying it around and felt awkward without it.

The office stank of cigar smoke, sweat and old food. Red's desk was a confusing jumble of papers, order blanks, thick print outs on computer paper, at least three paper weights, pens with teeth marks on the ends, pencils, and other assorted trinkets. If Red's brother wasn't sitting on the Hubbard Board of Directors, Lane couldn't imagine Red being able to keep his job beyond the time it would take a supervisor to view his office.

Pictures of a much younger and thinner Red lined one wall; Red as National Wrestling champion in nineteen sixty-three and nineteen sixty-four, heavy weight division, during his college days. Red was quick to tell anyone that would listen, that if it weren't for that sum'bitch Dell Thomas from Syracuse, he'd have won again in nineteen sixty-five.

Red on the cover of the college sports magazine "The Collegian" stiff arming a blocking dummy, looking with confidence off into the distance. On the cover, in the lower right corner, a faded, out of date print read, "Red 'Tank' DeAwn—Burkett's Iron Man!" and below that in smaller print, "Red talks about his future in football."

Lane had to stifle a laugh as he read this last statement. The vision of this past athletic hero, standing tiptoe on the back of a toilet in the men's bathroom, with his pants around his ankles, spanking his monkey as he strained to see through the peephole, was almost too much.

It had been Rachel Simpson a small, mousy woman that Lane would guess was around forty years old who had spotted the hole. She bolted from the bathroom in time to catch a glimpse of Red lumbering around the far end of the hall. Nothing had been proven, nobody was singled out, the hole was patched and the matter ended.

Lane squelched another laugh at the thought of it as Red moved to his chair behind the cluttered desk.

"What's the joke?" he asked, settling his bulk, the chair creaking in protest.

"Oh, it's not really that good. I heard it today from a guy over at the Davy Chicken place on Lindsey during lunch."

"Well, let's hear it," Red offered, as he picked a cigarette from a crumpled package on his desk and began searching for a lighter.

"What do you do with an elephant with three balls?"

Red stared at him blankly for a moment, shrugged his shoulders, lighted his cigarette and said nothing.

"You walk him and pitch to the Rhino," Lane finished. Red continued staring, wheels turning in his meaty head, then a bulb, with the shattering brightness of nearly four watts went off and he got the joke. He laughed casually around his cigarette, took a thick drag, and flicked ash in the general area of the overflowing ashtray.

"Told you it wasn't that good," Lane said, smiling. His eyes seemed to shift in color when he smiled, the gray going more to silver or white, the depth increasing.

Red grinned around the cigarette and nodded his head.

"So how long have ya' been here, Lane?" he asked, already knowing the answer.

"A little over six years," Lane responded, wanting him to get on with it so he could leave. The smell of sweat and cigarettes was beginning to make him nauseous.

Red nodded, sucked on his cigarette some more and said, "Six years, hmmm. Long time."

"Yeah, it is."

"How's that writing going?" he asked, with what Lane thought was just the slightest hint of superiority that said writing was beneath real men. Real men were athletic, bigots and sexual predators, though Lane doubted Red would have been able to describe his own personal philosophy with such detail.

"Great. It's going very well."

"You getting paid?" he asked, a broad grin spreading across his thick face. Lane felt a sudden burst of anger toward good 'ole Red. He hadn't felt it coming on, which was the part that scared him the most. One moment he was fine, though a little impatient to leave, and with four words and a smirk Red had been able to stir something Lane hadn't felt for a long time. He was totally focused on this pre-dawn man that had begun to tread rather heavily on ground Lane considered to be, if not sacred, then something quite like it.

He felt the warm glow of some black, living thing beginning to breathe deep within himself. He could smell reeking, spoiled fish and taste its bitter, sharp fragrance. It was familiar, this dark thing, and there was a time Lane was almost sure he had been rid of it. But that wasn't really being honest, now was it? No, it wasn't. Turtle would always be with him. It was just a matter of keeping Turtle asleep.

Red's eyes drew slightly wide and he slowly dropped his sloppy grin, letting his mouth move to its natural position—a horizontal slit framed in thick, chubby lips. His right check began to twitch. He moved to wipe a trickle of sweat that suddenly appeared down his left temple with the palm of his hand. It was an unconscious motion that Lane and everyone that knew good 'ole Red was quite familiar with. He wiped the sweat from his hand onto his pants.

His eyes began to feel hot. Somewhere he was crying. Cowering in a corner was a boy trying to become a man. Just a little over twelve years old, the first tiny bursts of acne that would soon rage over his troubled, confused face beginning to appear.

Turtle was slowly waking. It was happening again. He could feel it beginning to get out of control. Like playing at the wheel of a monster diesel tractor, starting it up just to hear it run, then it slips into gear and you're off on your ride to nowhere. It was going to happen again and he wasn't going to make it back this time. Not again. It was too much. Not again. He couldn't handle it. The mess...the mess and the blood and the...the meaty flesh torn and disfigured.

Blood splattered across a bedroom that was musty with age and time. Soaking through a mattress that was so full of blood and torn flesh that it could hold no more; releasing a dark, tiny river of blood to a sagging, marred hardwood floor. A wall peppered with blood and bone.

His thoughts turned briefly to Kristy, but he shoved them hard and she was slipped back behind mental fortifications.

Turtle paused. Lane could feel him hesitate, unsure, listening. A new contender entered the arena that was the workings of Lane White.

Today is a new day the past is gone. Today is a new day the past is gone. Today is a new day the past is gone. Today is a new day the past is gone.

The mantra began and continued to grow. The voice was familiar and he grasped onto the mantra with renewed hope. The boy in the corner lifted his head and bolted for the safety it offered. The caress of a cool, feminine hand that was soft and smooth. One that didn't offer only pain and harsh, brutal force.

Turtle withdrew into a tentative silence.

Lane leaned forward in his chair and began to rub his temples. His head had begun to hurt. His eyes started to cool. He felt sick to his stomach. Red's plain face showed only curiosity and an odd hint of amazement. Thirty seconds had passed since he'd asked his potent question. Red leaned back in his chair as Lane leaned forward.

"You Okay?" he asked the hint of superiority and bravado seeping through.

"Yeah, fine. Just getting a headache." Lane listened for the darkness within him, praying he would hear nothing.

He didn't.

Sighing deeply to clear his thoughts, he rubbed the back of his neck, then folded his hands across his lap.

"No. Nothing published yet. But the work is going well," he replied, forcing his face into the shape of a smile. The mantra continued, though now it was small and distant.

Today is a new day the past is gone...today is a new day the past is gone...the past is gone...new day...gone.

"Want an aspirin?" Red offered.

"Yeah, that'd be good. Thanks," Lane said as Red casually dug into the top desk drawer and removed a small tin of aspirin. He tossed it toward Lane across the desk. Lane dry swallowed two of them, thought about it a moment, then took a third, tossing the tin back to Red. He thought he felt a little better.

Red drew on his cigarette and began to look more relaxed, though Lane could tell something was causing that steel-trap mind of Red's to work hard. He could almost see tiny, cartoon puffs of smoke coming out of Red's ears as his brain was slowly turning over.

"Lane, I think you're doing a great job for Hubbard and so does everyone else." By which Red meant his brother, Bobby, who, because he sat on the Hubbard Board of Directors, was really calling this meeting.

"I enjoy the work," Lane said, keeping the smile on his face.

He watched as Red began to struggle with whatever he was working up to saying. Watching Red B. DeAwn struggle with an intellectual problem was a little like watching a chimpanzee figuring out how to stack crates to reach a suspended banana.

"I got a call today from an old friend of yours," he said, pausing as if he had finally placed the first crate and was looking for the next one.

"Oh?" Lane said. A slight twinge of fear pricked into him, just in the back of his neck, right where his head latched on. He smashed it immediately, not giving it the slightest bit of edge on him.

"I would've told you sooner, but I didn't have time to catch you at lunch."

"Oh," Lane said, nodding with repressed agreement.

"You have to understand that I'm just doing my job, here. Looking out for what they tell me to…you know, look out for," Red clumsily plunged ahead. He absently wiped a new trickle of sweat from his temple. It was hard to believe that a person could sweat so much, especially in an office that was so cold.

"Sure," Lane responded dryly. His mouth felt too full, as if someone had slipped up on him and stuffed it full of cotton candy that wouldn't dissolve.

"Look, can I be straight with you?" Red asked, the old Iron Man himself finally coming out.

"No problem."

"I, ah, could get in a lot of trouble asking you about this and I don't want you to misunderstand. So can we just say that this conversation is from one friend to another? Not an employee-employer, ah, position?"

He found it hard to consider Red a friend. Friends were people you hung with, went out for a beer, watched Monday night football with. He couldn't quite picture he and Red taking turns peeping through holes in bathroom walls, trading racial jokes and razing the feminine gender together. The throbbing in his temples began to ease up as the aspirin kicked in.

"All right. Just you and me then."

"Stuart Hill called and said the he needed to talk with you," Red blurted out. His right cheek twitched quickly and his eyes blinked rapidly, as if expecting something strange and perhaps dangerous to happen.

"Oh?" Lane asked. The prick of fear was back, only this time it wasn't fucking around. It slammed him with the heaviness of a meat cleaver instead of a needle. He wasn't able to get on top of it in time and it steadily hummed in the back of his neck; a formula-one car throttling, whining in the pits, tuning up for the big one. He could faintly taste the fuzzy smell of spoiled fish.

"What did he have to say?" Lane asked, struggling to remain calm. He began to drift.

Today is a new day, today is a new day, today is a new day.

"He didn't have anything to say, only that he wanted to talk to you. I guess it was important or he wouldn't have called here."

"I guess so," Lane said, not knowing where to go from here. The usual chatter and blur of his thinking seemed to slow down as he drifted further.

"He said he'd be working late and you could call him at the office. Here's the number." Red handed him a yellow sticky-note on which he'd scrawled in his rough penmanship the name Stuart Hill and a phone number.

"Thanks," Lane said, taking the piece of paper.

Today is a new day the past is gone. Today is a new day the past is gone. Today is a new—he crushed the mantra and stuffed it down far enough to reach the black, smoldering cinder that wanted out. Slammed shut tons of steel and rock over the whole mess and left that part of himself to fight it out with Turtle on its own.

Yeah, Okay, the day is new, but the past wasn't gone. Not by a long shot. No way, no sir, huh-uh. The past was here and now looking at him in the form of a sweaty, meaty overweight man named Red.

He couldn't remember the last time he had spoken with Stuart, the attorney who had handled his case. He was twelve at the time, still a child-boy-man struggling to find a foot hold in the world of foster homes, therapy, psychoanalysis, and court appearances he had suddenly found himself in after…well, after things had been taken care of.

The memories didn't want to leave him. The years of therapy had slowly cracked open Lane White to discover what he was repressing, what he was thinking, how did he *really* feel. Then more therapy to handle the Post Traumatic Stress as Lane White was lain open for the world to see, poke and prod.

Then the drugs, oh boy, the drugs. He couldn't remember how many, how much, or how long, it was blurred at best. Through the guidance of his therapist, Marilyn Duran, and the continual, unconditional support of Henry and Linda, he had come back from the dark, eternal edge of what had been.

Then the addiction recovery, hadn't that been fun? Here Lane, swallow this, it'll help with the dreams. Hold still Lane, it's only a little needle this time, it won't hurt and it'll make you feel better. Before long he'd become a system supported junkie.

More therapy, more institutions, more pain and then…and then he began to find some solid ground. Not all at once, nothing overnight. But slowly he began to struggle out of the squelching, stinking, wet muck that was his past onto some drier territory.

At the age of nineteen he was ready to finish high school through a program arranged with Burkett High. He breezed through the work, hungry for something to do, something to give focus to his life. Henry and Linda, retired and never having had children of their own, were completely accepting of Lane for what he was and, perhaps more importantly, for what he was not. They understood, they told him, about what he had done. Though he doubted, despite all their love and sincere honesty, that they really could understand what he, Kristy and his mother had had to endure.

College was something different. After he discovered his thirst—his need—to write, nothing else seemed to matter. He couldn't get into the groove of college. It didn't seem to make any difference to him. He had his Dictionary, his thesaurus, his Little, Brown handbook, what more did he need from college? Dour, old, worn professors encouraging him to ponder the question of why Bluebeard's beard was blue and not maroon or plaid? Lane was sure Bluebeard didn't give a tin shit. He had some throats to slit and some dying to do of his own keeping him plenty busy. He didn't make it through his first year of college.

A job at Hubbard was suggested. Marilyn Duran and Stuart Hill put the deal together with Bobby DeAwn, Hubbard board member and Red's big brother. Lane would be given a job as long as it wasn't made public. It didn't really matter by then. Lane was twenty-six at the time and the press attention had died down many years before.

Red had asked him a question.

"Sorry?"

"I asked if there was anything going on that you think I should know about?"

"No, not that I know of," Lane responded, coming back a little and wondering if that wasn't exactly the truth. He didn't know why Stuart would be calling. The brief thought that his legal case would be opened again crossed his mind and set his fear rocketing out of the pits. It hit the track with a full tank; tires smoking, the engine red-hot and scream-ing, throttle wide open.

"Well, if there was, I hope you would let me know," Red managed to get out without the slightest bit of sarcasm or belittlement in his voice.

"Sure," Lane said. His fear was on its second lap of a solo bid for the lead and showed no signs of slowing anytime soon.

"I'm not trying to pry, or anything. I mean, we're both, ah, aware of the, ah, circumstances Mr. Hill helped you with and I think that, ah…I…or I mean, Hubbard, needs to know if there may be something going on that would change your position here." Red finished his crate stacking and settled back in his chair with his banana reward, visibly strained from the effort.

Something going on that would change my position here? Like what? Like the possibility of getting sucked back into the system that, though well intended, nearly killed me? Is that what you mean by that oh so tactful statement, Reddy-Wetty?

He wanted to let the thoughts run on, wanted to slam and lock the throttle to the floor of his fear and let it roar out of control in the next corner, ending it in a bright, white-hot flash of twisted metal and burning high-octane fuel.

His fingers itched to be working over his Brother typewriter, setting in motion the only activity he knew that allowed him to be gone from this patched together world that was his life. He wanted to answer the voice of that somehow sinister womb of creation beckoning him to write, to create, to live in other worlds and times where the rules were anything he wanted them to be, where he had the ultimate control. Worlds where he could one moment be a God and the next a Demon, where he could run outside of that old box and see what there was to see.

He'd read somewhere a quote by an author that considered writing to be something of a childlike, self-serving activity. He couldn't argue with that. But if a childish, selfish activity was the only thing that kept you walking around and breathing, so be it. He had clutched it like a falcon blasting a pigeon out of the sky, and he didn't have plans on letting go anytime soon. His writing was fresh meat and the dinner bell was ringing.

"Yeah, I can understand," Lane responded. "I appreciate everything you and Hubbard have done for me. I don't know where else I could have gone. I wasn't really in a position to move out of state," he paused, not wanting to lay it on too thick. Red may be dumb but he sure wasn't stupid.

"I haven't spoken with Stuart for quite a few years. I honestly can't imagine why he would be calling, but if something is happening with my…situation, I'll let you know right away."

Lane smiled and wished that it felt as good as it had less than an hour ago.

"Well, I certainly would appreciate that," Red said, firing up another cigarette and not believing him.

"Is that it?" Lane asked, not really caring much if the statement was out of line. He just wanted to get out of his office and to a phone so he could find out what Stuart wanted.

"Yeah, sure, that was it. I sure hope you aren't taking this the wrong way. Hell, I don't give a shit what you did, Lane. I'm sure you have your own reasons. I mean, the past is gone, right?"

Lane slid up to the edge of his chair, nodded his head in agreement and fought the urge to ask if there was an echo in the room. He was hoping that Red would take the not very subtle hint that he was leaving now and it was time to say good-bye, see ya' later, nice visiting with 'ya, I'm outta here.

"So, are we okay on this? You don't look very well."

"Sure, fine. I still have a bit of a headache. I may be coming down with something."

"Hmm," Red said.

Lane stood and stuck out his hand.

"Thanks, Lane. I sure do appreciate you taking the time," Red said, standing with very little grace and taking the offered hand. He pumped it twice then let go. The rapid movement made Lane feel strangely like a rag doll, and then thoughts of the bathroom peephole made him want to wash his hands.

He left Red's office, exited the data input offices and marveled at how fresh the air smelled outside the confines he had been in. He headed for the bathroom. The nausea had abated somewhat and a splash of cold water on his face should help the matter even more.

A little after five-thirty, walking slowly across the parking lot, enjoying the surprisingly warm breeze for this early in March, he left the Hubbard complex. Washing his face had helped him feel better. Not only physically, but also in some far away place he had warm and secure feelings connected with the act.

The memories of his mother were fragmented, yet he felt the connection was with her. A little riff of nursery rhyme played briefly in his thoughts. He couldn't quite remember it all. The memory was distant, but comforting, soft, like a well worn quilt. In his past a little boy was standing on a stool in a bathroom with his head leaning over a sink. Small hands braced a fragile body on the front edge of the sink as a soothing hand poured cool water over his head.

He had been crying. His face and eyes still puffy and strained from the effort.

*Hush little baby don't say a word, Mama's gonna buy you a mocking-bird…*the thought paused, wanting to continue, but it couldn't on its own and he didn't want to try and force it.

Mama was gonna do a lot of things that she didn't. Mama was gonna leave and take him and Kristy with her. They were going to live some-where—anywhere—to get away. Then Mama was going to call the police and end the abuse. But she never seemed to be able to get around to doing either.

"It'll get better. He's been drinking, that's all. It'll get better," she would tell them as her lip or the side of her face began to swell. It would calm down for a few days, or maybe even a week, then it would happen again.

It never got better and all Mama was able to do was die. He was seven at the time and Kristy was eleven or twelve, he couldn't quite remember, or rather, as Marilyn Duran had told him, didn't *want* to remember.

Somebody was yelling. He looked up to find he was standing by his car, a late eighties Oldsmobile Cutlass. Red was yelling something and waving to him from the front of the building. He could feel the quiet tears of his past on his face and was glad for the distance between them.

"See you tomorrow!" drifted across the expanse of the lot. Lane lifted his arm in response then watched Red drive out of the parking lot.

He slipped into the car and started it, turning on the radio and vent air. He was drifting too much. The mantra started up, pulling him back, anchoring him to what his life was. Not had been, but what his life *was*.

The classic rock station sounded sharp and acidic and reminded him of spoiled tuna. He turned it off.

Today is a new day, today is a new day, today is a new day…on and on it ran, buoying him and giving something to which his anchor could be tied. He took a slow, deep breath, clicked from vent to A/C and listened to the engine growl at the added strain.

Henry and Linda had offered more than once to support him completely whilst he plied the sometimes rough and always unknown waters of the budding novelist. He had refused most of their help for the sole reason that he didn't think it would be as satisfying a success if he had been carried the whole ride by Henry and Linda.

Slipping the car into gear he began pulling out of the mostly empty parking lot. The activity seemed to help him feel better, though the fear of what Stuart may have to say was still alive and well. He pulled out of the parking lot, turned right onto the State Highway nine service road, then turned left a mile down and crossed back under the highway. The crush of five o'clock traffic hummed along the highway above him as he waited with the anxious knot of cars under the overpass for the light to change. After what seemed a small eternity the light changed and he quickly shot through the light and pulled into the Pit-Stop convenience store on the corner.

He parked a few slots down from the pay phones.

It was nearly six. Maybe Stuart had already left for the day. He dialed the number and listened as the phone rang in the offices of Billings, Stallworth, Finch and Hill once, twice, three times. As he was beginning to hang up on the fourth ring a pert female voice answered.

"Billings, Stallworth, Finch and Hill, how may I help you?"

"I'd like to speak to Stuart Hill," he said in a quiet whisper.

"Pardon me?" the pert voice responded in a flat professional tone. Lane cleared his throat and spoke louder.

"Stuart Hill, please. If he's still in," he quickly added.

"May I ask who's calling?"

"Lane White."

"One moment please and I'll see if he's available."

The pert female voice was cut off and replaced with light rock music. Maybe he was in a meeting and couldn't be disturbed? Maybe she had *thought* he was in but he really wasn't? Maybe the sky would fall? Maybe there would be a nuclear strike and he wouldn't have to worry about much of anything anymore?

He wished he could get off it and let it go. After all, if something had changed with his case, two or three tough looking characters in shabby suites with big, evil bulges poking through the sides of their jackets probably would have met him back at Hubbard.

"*Lane White?*" they would have asked. He would have stood up from his desk at this point.

"*Yes?*"

They would have introduced themselves, flashed some badges, and asked him to come with them.

And then…well, he didn't know what would have happened then. Would he have run? Ran *where*?

A dark chuckle began erupting deep inside him. Turtle began to come out of his rank and putrid shell.

No, old buddy, we would have made a stand. Right then and there. Made a grab for some of that hefty cop shooting iron—

"Lane?" the phone suddenly asked. Turtle clamped up.

"Yeah?"

"Hey, how've you been? Haven't spoken with you in…a long time, buddy."

Lane realized suddenly how long it had been since last they spoke. Years, how many he wasn't sure

As their relationship had grown over the years of legal battle, Stuart had become a legal champion, father figure and big brother rolled into one.

He had spent many Saturdays at Stuart's house shooting baskets, swimming, sitting around letting their barbecue settle. Henry and Linda would usually come along and occasionally Marilyn Duran would also. He hadn't minded much. She was always low key about the process of putting Lane White back together. He never would have guessed that the seemingly trivial act of going over to a friend's house to hang on a Saturday was the best kind of therapy he could have. If he had known at the time that it *was* therapy he might have whistled a different tune.

After the culmination of the case and the non-guilty verdict—coupled with what Lane thought to be an infinite number of stipulations including five years of supervised probation, periodic testing of his inner workings, and weekly visits with Marilyn, to name but a few—their relationship had begun to drift. Stuart went on to other cases and Lane began to get his house in order.

"Still there?" Stuart asked on the other end of the line.

"Yeah, I'm here," Lane said, choosing not to elaborate on the past. "You've just got me a little worried about what you need," he said, letting a nervous laugh escape. He wanted to run down the phone line after it, being careful not to trip over the tops of the poles in the process.

"Sorry about that. I should have thought about it before I called. You've got some tough boss in that Red DeAwn. I tried to get through to you but had to settle on leaving a message."

Lane felt himself relax a little. He let himself begin believing it wasn't as cryptic a call as he'd thought. The day seemed suddenly brighter, despite the slightly overcast sky. He took a deep breath and exhaled with relief.

"You had me wondering," he added.

"Sorry about that. Nothing to worry about. I just had something to go over with you. Do you remember how we handled your parents property after the case?" Stuart asked, shifting into lawyer mode.

The house they had lived in was turned over into some kind of trust that Stuart was handling for him. Since his mother was gone, Kristy had died and his father had been taken care of, not to mention the fact that there was no will, there was nobody left to inherit it. His father had no extended family that he was aware of. If he did, they hadn't written to date and probably never would. He never knew why his mother's parents didn't step in and try to help their grandchildren. He only remembered meeting them once and then only for a few hours. He hadn't seen them since. The state had wanted to take the property, but Stuart had done some shuffling so that Lane could one day legally take advantage of the assets that were left. Financial dealings were something he'd never had much patience for.

The house was fully paid for at the time of his father's death and what little Duane Trammel White did have in assets was turned to cash and invested by the trust for Lane. All by Stuart. Henry and Linda had hired Stuart at the onset, after they had read about Lane in the *Burkett Daily*. Most likely they were paying him still. Even though Stuart was a great guy, he still had a business to run. Lane didn't know how much money was in the trust, and wasn't sure he really cared at this point of the game. Relatively speaking, he had much bigger fish to fry. He had never been lacking in the money department and never really thought about it that much.

Though the house was where the major turning point of his young life had taken place so long ago, he had gotten over any aversions to the house. Marilyn had seen to that. They had spent countless days and nights walking through the house, room by room, as she calmly (sometimes not so calmly) forced him to see that, after all, it was just a simple wood frame house. Everything else was tied up in that gushy stuff between his ears, just behind his eyes.

"I believe it's in some kind of trust," he said, as a flash of memories washed through his thoughts like pale, dull confetti.

He was seventeen or eighteen the first time Marilyn took him back to the house. She had been preparing him for six months for the big event. Henry and Linda hadn't agreed with her on the therapy, but that was really all they could do. Marilyn had been assigned by the state to handle Lane White and she could recommend putting him into a quiet room with rubber walls for the rest of his life if she deemed it necessary. There had been some heated arguments on this point as Marilyn struggled to make his adoptive parents see that she was on their side. Especially with Linda. They had finally relented their position and hoped for the best.

Marilyn had chosen the brightest, sunniest May day she could possibly predict for the big event. When she came to pick him up around midmorning, Linda had again pushed for attending the event if she couldn't prevent it. Marilyn had said no, knowing that the scene might get ugly. She mentioned that she had brought some assistants from the hospital. Seeing Lane stir at the mention of assistants, she quickly moved to put him at ease.

"You know Ronnie and Blake, don't you?" she asked. They were two young men in their early twenties, which like Marilyn, were under paid and over worked by the state. Yet they wanted to help the mentally crippled just the same. Lane had seen them around the hospital grounds and spoken to them on several occasions.

"I wouldn't have brought them along," Marilyn continued, "if I didn't have to. The State requires it." This last was said with a slight shake of her head. Lane nodded his understanding and they left, leaving Henry and Linda tense and worried, standing in the driveway, seeing them off.

Ronnie and Blake were all smiles, asking him how his studies were going, and generally trying to get him to talk it up on the twenty minute ride across town. Lane couldn't help but notice that Marilyn didn't take the quicker route on the Highway, but stuck to the main roads through town.

"We don't have to go in this time. Only if you feel like it, okay?" she'd said as they turned onto Cherokee Place.

He'd nodded and didn't feel much of anything as they turned and slowly began to make their way down to the house. He noticed that the neighborhood had improved dramatically since he had lived there. While he'd been off getting his head back on it had apparently become the fashion to move into homes that were built in the thirties and forties and bring them up to date. It was no longer a blue-collar neighborhood.

As they drove along—Marilyn quietly smiling and trying not to watch him too closely—he had a hard time seeing the houses for what they had been. Lawns that had only been mowed out of absolute dire need in the past were now spreads of deep green grasses of exotic origin mowed and edge to perfection. Not a dandelion one could be found in those lawns. Flower beds, sapling Oak and Maple trees lined the grounds, framing houses that were once mottled with chipping white paint. The paint was now firm, crisp hues of green, red, lavender, yellow and a myriad of other shades.

Broken glass formerly covered in plastic to keep out the weather was now pristine and secure behind new window frames and storm glass. Architecturally pleasant low brick walls and dirt berms covered in dozens of different flora and fauna surrounded some of the homes. Infinities, Volvos and Jeep Cherokees sat in driveways long ago replaced or cleansed of oil stains from rusty, leaking Fords and Chevys.

Marilyn stopped on the side of the street two houses down from 711 Cherokee Place. Here was the home he remembered. Though the lawn was being maintained, the house wasn't. Here was the chipped paint and plastic covered windows he had remembered, complete with oil stained drive.

They sat quietly, Marilyn's aging little Honda hummed and waited for movement. Lane looked at the house he grew up in and could only feel a dull, numb void. Nothing was being said, though he could feel

Ronnie, Blake and Marilyn watching him. Waiting, perhaps, to see if he was going to start getting out all that icky repression stuff.

"Do you want to go up to the house? Would you be comfortable with that?"

He'd nodded and the car slowly moved along until they were sitting across the street from the house. He remembered wanting to feel something; rage, sorrow, anything. The memories were there, but muted, as if wrapped in miles of cotton. The low wooden front porch with the four wide wooden steps leading up to it was sagging with age. He remembered falling and cutting his head while playing some game with Kristy. The rattling window air conditioner unit that had sat sullenly in the window to the left of the front door had been removed and the warped window forced closed. He could still see the outline of dirty, old paint framing the place where it had been.

He had gone no further that day. Choosing instead to sit quietly in the car across the street, remembering. Over a period of time—he couldn't remember how long it had actually taken—with Marilyn's patient encouragement and steady insistence, he had gone up on the porch, then into the front living area. From the living area it had taken a few weeks to progress into the kitchen at the back of the living room. Off the kitchen there were two doors, one lead to the garage and the other to the basement.

He had eventually made it through the entire house, including the three bedrooms in the back and the basement. It had taken a great deal of effort and encouragement to deal with his father's room. The flashbacks and dreams kept him from it for nearly a year. The hardwood floor was no longer stained, the rickety chest of drawers long gone and the sagging, tired bed frame along with it.

Now the house at 711 Cherokee Place was just that—a house. A piece of real estate that only the older residents of Burkett, Oklahoma knew the history of. He had never come to the decision that he was over the incident, but he had come to a balance with it.

"That's right. It's in a trust with the rest of your parents' assets. There wasn't much to start with, but now you have almost thirty-thousand dollars, in addition to the house," Stuart said.

"Thirty-thousand?" Lane asked, suddenly realizing what he'd been told.

"Not bad, eh? But there's more to it. I've taken the liberty of trying to sell the place. I spoke with Henry and Linda about it and they thought it might be a good idea to do it. I've not gone so far as to list it with a realtor, but I have put the word out and the house has been shown several times."

He was selling the house? *His* house? Then he wondered why he would care what was done with it. There was no longer anything there for him. He had no memories that couldn't be dealt with on his own terms. Nothing but slowly rotting wood and peeling paint to sell to the highest bidder.

"Oh?" Lane asked.

"I hope you don't mind. I guess I assumed that you'd want to sell it eventually. Anyway, we have an offer and I wanted to run it by you. It's substantial and I think you should consider it."

"I don't know. I never really thought about selling it. Do you need a decision today?"

He didn't want to deal with this. Not today. Not now. He was tired of thinking about it. It had been too long. His head began to throb again and he could feel himself beginning to reach the end of his emotional track.

"No, not right now," Stuart said, hearing the strain in Lane's voice. "But as soon as you can. They're anxious to take possession."

"Okay. I'll let you know. When are we going to get together? I've got some big money that says I can take you two out of three," Lane chided.

"You got it buddy. As soon as things settle down here we'll have everyone over for a day of it."

Lane could hear a voice in the background. It sounded like the same pert voice of the receptionist. Stuart replied in a muffled voice then came back on the line with Lane.

"I've got to run. Busy day. Let me know as soon as you decide on the house."

"Sure, talk with you soon."

He hung up the phone, realizing that they would never get together. Stuart's invitation had been sincere, but their relationship had grown apart and Lane could feel that it was going to stay that way.

The frantic hustle of rush hour traffic had died down. He got back into his car. It was nearly six-thirty. He pulled out of the Pit Stop meaning to get back on the highway and head east to his apartment. At the last minute he decided to go by the house on Cherokee. Fifteen minutes later he was slowly easing the Olds down Cherokee Place.

The street and houses looked the same as they had the last time he and Marilyn had been there. After the first initial surprise at seeing the neighborhood so dramatically changed, it was no longer new. The only exception being some of the houses had been re-painted in different color schemes and the sapling trees were now much bigger.

The last time he had been here was after he had been given the job at Hubbard. It was Marilyn's idea that they celebrate his future success at the house. Lane had thought it a morbid idea at the time, but had come to trust Marilyn, due to his own—albeit youthful—recovery.

They planned to have a picnic lunch in the dining area but the stifling heat of that long ago August day drove them out to the front porch. Lane moved the rickety card table and two lawn chairs Marilyn had waiting for them to the front porch. They had enjoyed a leisurely afternoon eating pasta salad, French bread and bottled water.

After that day some six years ago, he had begun to see Marilyn monthly per the court order. Four years from that time he was released from his commitment and probation and wished the best of luck. They still stayed in touch. Lane still needed her even if it was just to keep up to date. He sat in the car looking at the house and thought he would give her a call tonight, before he wrote. The episode with Red had scared him. It had been a long time since he'd had to deal with Turtle.

The house had changed very little since the last trip. The fence was still gone, the porch sagged a little more and the paint was peeling a little more. He noticed that the wall on the south side was missing a board or two and what appeared to be rotting wood hung like moss from a vine near where the boards were missing. The lawn hadn't been mowed in what Lane would have guessed to be about a month. Maybe the lawn service wasn't working it this summer, or hadn't gotten to it yet.

The window to the left of the front door had been boarded up with plywood. The matching window to the right side of the porch was still intact. He could see what had once been white curtains, yet were now yellow and sickly looking with age, hanging loosely behind the window.

He turned off the car and got out. He didn't want to stay sitting in the car with such a warm March day to enjoy. Leaning against the driver's side door with his arms akimbo, he faced off with the house.

Did he really want to get rid of the place? Today was a new day, by now he'd gotten that. But as Red had so kindly pointed out, the past wasn't gone. It felt as it there was still something here for him, but he didn't know what it was. Maybe it was the only time in his life he was a part of a family. All the pieces were there—Mom, Dad, Sister—even though they didn't work properly, they had still been there, together.

A gusting wind drew him out of his thoughts and he looked to the gathering clouds in the southwestern sky. The dark boiling sky held more than a little rain. The first storms of spring were on the way.

Maybe he shouldn't sell it. After all, it wasn't costing him anything to keep it. Stuart had seen to that. He might even spend a few weekends fixing up the place. Nothing major, just a little carpentry work, some paint. Hire a new fence built.

"What 'cha doing?"

He jumped at the voice and turned to see a thin boy, about eleven or twelve years old sitting on an expensive looking BMX bike. The kid was eyeing him curiously. He was wearing a blue short-sleeved shirt that was much too large and bright green shorts smeared with grass stains and dirt. He slowly rolled a sucker in his mouth and kept a tight grip on the handlebars of his bike, incase Lane took too much interest in him.

"Just looking at my house," Lane said, turning back to face the house. He looked over his shoulder at the kid.

"That your house?" the kid asked, removing the sucker with a dirty hand and pointing.

"Yeah, it is," Lane said, not sure if he was proud of the fact or not. "You live around here?"

"Why?" the kid asked, replacing the sucker he gripped the handlebars, ready to ride.

"Just thinking that it's going to rain soon. If you live very far, you're going to get wet.

The kid gave the sky a quick scan, then looked back at Lane.

"I live over there, one street over," he said, pointing in the general direction with his sucker. Lane noticed that his right knee had an ugly, dark scab clinging to it.

"Why're you lookin' at your house?"

"I'm not sure. A friend of mine wants me to sell it and I'm not sure if I want to."

"I wouldn't want to keep it if it was me," the kid said, slipping the sucker back into his mouth. He removed his hands from the handlebars and sat up on the seat, a little more secure. Lane turned from the house to face him and the kid's hands shot back to the handles; legs tensed on the cement. He pretended not to notice how high strung the kid was. He was a jumpy little guy and had an odd look about him. He seemed to shimmer and move in the air, like badly copied videotape looks on a television.

"Why's that?" Lane asked.

"It's haunted, man,"

"Haunted?" Lane asked, smiling.

"I'm not shitting you, man!" he said. "That's the house where that guy got killed. He's still in there, man, and he's pissed," he said, as he looked at the house. "At night he walks around looking for the other half of his head…but he'll take yours just as easy," he looked back at Lane when he said this with the manic face of a true believer.

The day suddenly became very heavy; the sky darker; the coming storm oppressive instead of cleansing and nourishing. The smile dropped from Lane's face and somewhere Turtle was beginning to stir. Though the facts were a bit screwed up with time, enough people had remembered to pass it on to the next generation.

"Blake went in there once and Halfhead came after him. He said his head was all mashed up, like he'd been run over by a car."

Or shot close range with a shotgun? Lane thought. He couldn't believe he was actually hearing what the kid was saying. Unable to respond for the moment, he looked back at the house. The house wasn't haunted of course Lane knew that. The history of what had happened in the house had just hung around long enough to become yet another urban myth. Though there was the occasional claim by a family that some kind of evil force was terrorizing them. In most cases those evil forces seemed to be coming from their wallets, not from any kind of spiritual source.

"Who's Blake?" Lane finally asked.

"My friend. He lives over there," he said, thinking that Lane would ask him anyway so he might as well get it out of the way. He pointed in the same direction as his own home.

"Why'd he go in the house?"

"Had to. He wanted to be in our gang. You got to do what we tell you if you want to hang with us," he said, proudly tipping his head back. Lane smiled at the irony and wondered how long until the kid and his buddies were into drugs and gang beatings, or if they were already.

"You're not going to tell on Blake, are you?" he asked, suddenly aware of what he had told in a moment of bravado.

"Did he break that window?" Lane asked, pointing to the plywood covered space where the window had been.

"No! Huh-uh! That piece of the roof that fell broke it!" the kid shot back, desperate to save Blake from an unknown fate.

Lane looked at the boards that had partially fallen down. He could see how one of the longer boards from the wall could have been hanging from its last nail and with the help of a well timed breeze, swing free and break the window.

"Did you see it happen?" he was curious as to the details of the kid's story about the house and was trying to work the conversation around to it.

"Nah, we figured it out. The board was sticking in the window," the kid said, leaning back on his bike again.

"Oh. Obvious then, huh?"

"Yeah."

"Is that how Blake got into the house?"

"Yeah, through the broken window. He cut his knee on some of the glass. We told his parents he wrecked his bike."

"Look, I don't care if Blake was in the house, as long as he wasn't going to wreck the place."

The kid shook his head from side to side and rolled the sucker in his mouth.

"Tell you what. I won't tell his parents if you tell me a little more about this big man he saw. Deal?" Lane asked, banking that the kid wasn't going to figure that Lane had no idea who Blake was much less his parents and where he lived.

"Sure, I guess."

Lane saw the kid was beginning to get nervous and tried to lighten up.

"I'm Lane, by the way," Lane said, still just turning his head so as not to frighten the kid away.

"Oh. Tim," he said, nodding his head, the sucker rolling. Tim absently twirled the pedal of his bike with his right foot and waited for Lane to begin.

Lane plunged onward feeling mildly like an asshole.

"Thanks, Tim, for your help," Lane said, trying on a winning smile that he hoped didn't look lecherous.

Tim nodded and continued twirling the pedal.

"So Blake went in through the window and Halfhead came after him. Is that right?"

"Yeah. That's what he said. We were waiting for him right over there, in front on the Wilkerson's shed." He pointed three houses down from where they stood, on the opposite side of the street.

"How long was he in there?"

"I dunno. Not very long. He fell back out of the window and ran back. That's when he cut his leg. He was too scared to talk, so we just took off on our bikes. We thought he was lying about it, but he told me later that it really happened. I believe him." Lane saw the real fear in his eyes and felt sorry for him.

"So when he got into the house, what happened?"

"I just told you. He went in and—."

"I know, Halfhead chased him out, but *where* was Halfhead?" he asked, trying to remain calm and detached but not doing a very good job of it.

"Blake said after he got in the window he turned on the flashlight we gave him and looked around the front of the house."

"The living room?"

"Yeah, I guess so. I've never been in there," he said, looking over at the house, then back to Lane. Thunder clapped with a muted rumble in the distance and the wind kicked up a little more, rustling the tops of the taller trees around them. They both looked to the approaching storm.

"I've gotta go. My mom'll be wondering where I am," he said, nearly pleading.

Lane pressed on, ignoring his plea and trying not to feel like an asshole. There was something wrong with Tim. Something he couldn't quite place. He tried to look closely at him while trying to remain casual and detached. It didn't work very well and he gave up on it.

"When he looked around the living room, where was the man? Did he just sort of appear, or did he walk into the room?"

"Blake said he was…he was going to walk down the hall to the back of the house and the—I mean he—heard something behind him and he turned around and saw the man."

"So he came up behind him, like from the kitchen?"

"I told you I've never been in there! Please, can I go now?"

Lane gave up, thinking that this could go on for hours.

"Sure. Thanks for your help. I won't tell on Blake."

With that Tim shot off down the sidewalk at full speed; a blur of flashing blue bike and pumping youthful energy. Lane watched him go until he had disappeared around the end of the block.

The wind blew hard again through the trees and the air cooled. He stood watching the house and listening to brittle memories, as the storm threatened to crash in on him at any moment. He had the beginnings of an idea he wasn't sure he wanted to develop, yet was equally sure he wouldn't be able to stop. The air faintly reeked of some familiar dead thing.

He wondered about the kid Tim.

He wished it were winter.

TWO

9...

It was cold.

He walked slowly across the sharp rocks of the lake bottom until water lapped at his knees. Looking to the growing dawn he wished the sun would show more of itself and give of its warmth; just a hint of security.

The opposite bank invited him with a silent siren call. There were trees over there; big, green, lush trees. They looked like pines, the kind you see in the Pacific Northwest. The wide, clear beach looked sandy with only the occasional rock: easy on the feet.

He rubbed his shoulders, thought warm thoughts, and took another step. The dark water welcomed him, hungrily washing half way up his thighs.

A flash of light followed by a much closer clap of thunder made him jump. The sky was no longer cloudy, but had now taken on a deep, ominous boiling blackness as the storm began to rumble in from the southwest. He got back in his car as the first heavy drops of rain began to hit the car with loud, brittle pops.

He supposed Marilyn Duran would be able to explain his sudden change of opinion concerning the house. There was probably some kind of deep seeded need to try and put his life back to what it had been. Back to when the pieces of family were still there.

The heavy rain gave way to the storm as the wind kicked up another notch and the sky began to dump in earnest. He started the car, clicked on the wipers and headlights and wondered if the kid made it home before the storm started. The rain hit the roof like marbles and the wind rocked the car. His headache had finally given up. Turtle was, thankfully, silent. The mantra started and he let the words soothe through him even though he could only get half of it out. It ran on as he sat watching the house through the thick blur of rain.

Today is a new day, the… Today is a new day, the…

He gave up on it and settled for *today is a new day, today is a new day, today is a new day.* The mantra flowed easily and seemed to be much more content with this partial affirmation. The rest felt like a lie.

The house sat quietly, silent, dark. He thought it looked lonely next to the freshly painted and cared for homes on either side. In those homes the lights burned brightly. Through the heavy rain he could see people in some of the windows; televisions on, kids playing, parents preparing to finish the day, looking forward to the next.

He missed his mother and wondered briefly if Kristy would miss her, if Kristy were alive. A darker thought wondered if the freak that had been growing in her would have had such feelings of longing. The question would never be answered. She had taken it with her in her own escape from the cold, brutal world she had known. The freak never grew long enough to breathe the air of this world. Had in fact only made a brief appearance in the form of a small, hard lump in Kristy's young womb.

A flash of light coupled with a tremendous rumble of thunder shook the car. The rain that had been falling as hard as Lane thought rain could fall began to fall harder. He pulled away from the curb and turned around in the street. Looking at the glowing digital clock set into the dash he was surprised to see it was past eight.

The storm was comforting in its rhythmic pounding of rain and brash rumblings of wind and thunder. He reached the end of Cherokee Place and turned right toward the highway and his apartment. He made his way through the rising water and the occasional stalled car, his thoughts now syrupy and slow with the chaotic past of the day.

He smiled at how enveloped he had become in the kids' story of the house being haunted. He could see, outside of the kids fearful, believing influence that it all must have sprung from an adrenaline induced imagination. Blake, anxious to prove himself to his brothers in arms, coming up with the story to guise his own short comings and fear of the dark, shadowy house.

He pushed the thought aside. Forty minutes later he arrived home, the storm having slowed what would have normally been a fifteen-minute drive. After a bowl of soup and crackers he quickly showered and prepared to write. It was nearly ten, but the time didn't matter. This was the reason for his being, the only thing that he had in his life that provided him with an anchor. He could always catch a nap during his lunch break, as he'd done on many previous occasions.

He read through the last ten pages of *Night Vision* and settled into his high-backed executive chair. Slipping a clean sheet of paper into his Brother AX-22 typewriter he quietly waited for the story to open up.

The small office in the two-bedroom apartment was the only room he spent anytime in. He did have a television in the living area but only used it to watch rented movies and the occasional morning news. One complete wall and most of another was a maze of bookshelves crammed full with hardback and paperback books. Old magazines hung lazily from the tops of most of the shelves. At the desk he used as a work station a complete set of encyclopedias, several dictionaries, a Thesaurus, a grammatical reference book and other off beat reference books such as "The Encyclopedia of Word and Phrase Origins" held solemn vigil over his writing. He liked to keep them close at hand, so as not to interrupt the flow when he got it going.

Fifteen minutes later a blank page still looked back at him. He read the ten pages again then put them back on the pile of preceding pages on the shelf above the typewriter, absently adjusting a book that fell over in the process.

If there was one thing he had learned very clearly after so many years of writing, it was this: You cannot push the story. If you pushed, you ended up with crap. More often than not wasting time in the process and sometimes kicking off a series of days that would bring nothing. So he waited, patiently, for the story to begin.

He adjusted himself in the chair and looked out the window at the storm. The initial fury had abated, leaving behind a steady, light rain that might last through the night. In the lower right hand drawer of the desk he removed four yellow legal pads that represented his Journal of dreams, hoping to find inspiration. He thought briefly about calling Marilyn to talk over the incident with Red, but it was late and the thought was gone as soon as it had appeared.

The entries in the journal didn't follow any systematic order, only the dates they had been recorded were noted at the beginning of each entry. Reading through them was a bit like looking through a photo album as he remembered old dreams and brief snatches of prose that had come to mind. Some of the writing he didn't remember, but most of it was familiar.

By eleven-thirty he was beginning to doze off, the soft rain and light wind rustling the trees next to the balcony adding to his exhaustion from the long day. With a start he realized he had fallen asleep with the notes scattered on his lap and across the small, open space of his desk. He reluctantly decided to give up for the night and removed the blank sheet of paper from the typewriter, placing it back in the pile on the right side of the desk.

He had desperately wanted to find the escape hatch this evening, losing himself in the story. Apparently the story had other plans that didn't include him. He shut down the office and made his way to the bedroom, not bothering to turn on any lights, and lay down. Sleep came immediately and with it a dream that was vague and hard.

Outside the storm wore on, trickling away a few hours before dawn. Lane slept, knowing that six years of waking promptly at seven would again wake him without the need of an alarm.

His mind quietly, carefully adjusted to the turmoil of the past day. Filing, shutting out, and tabling the events so Lane would continue functioning as he had. All that was left to him was his writing, his job at Hubbard and dull, sporadic memories of what had been. He had lived through it and come out not untouched, but whole, in a gelatinous way.

*   *   *

"They dropped the offer," Stuart said.

"Any particular reason?" Lane asked. Wondering if the buyer had run into the man in the house that the kid had told him about. Not that he believed the kid on the bike, but the similarities couldn't be over looked, especially by a mind that was by nature tuned into the details.

"Not that they mentioned. Want me to keep trying?"

"No. I don't think so. I may want to keep it," Lane said, then paused, waiting for something to happen. He hadn't come out and stated this in the open and now that he had, it felt awkward, but he wasn't sure why.

"That's probably a good idea in the long run. The market over there is booming. If you hold out for another year or so, you could probably get another ten or twenty thousand," Stuart said.

"Yeah, that's what I was thinking," Lane said, though the financial gain was the furthest thing from his mind. Stuart hadn't faltered or questioned his decision to keep the house and his unstated approval gave him a shot of confidence.

"I was thinking about cleaning it up. Nothing major. Just getting the roof fixed, some paint, new glass for the broken windows, that sort of thing. What do I need to do to get the money out of the trust?"

"It's already yours. Your probation is up and you've kept your agreement with the court so I can release it at any time. I never mentioned it before, I didn't think you needed it."

"I didn't…but I think I could now."

"Drop by the office. I'll leave the paperwork with Susan. You'll just need to sign some things. I'll call the bank Monday and arrange it. There may be some penalties, I don't remember all the details, but it shouldn't be much."

Lane spent the weekend in a jumpy mood. The thought that he actually was going to get the trust money and fix the house at 711 Cherokee filled his thoughts. Resigned to the fact that he was going to do it didn't seem to help matters much. He'd tried several times to reach Marilyn Duran to talk it over but only got her answering machine during the day Saturday. Henry and Linda were out of town on vacation in the Pacific Northwest. By Sunday morning, after a thankfully dreamless sleep, he felt somewhat better about his decision.

As he sat down to begin a writing session, the phone rang.

"Hello?"

"Hey Lane! It was good to hear from you. How are you doing?"

He smiled at hearing her voice and the memories it stirred.

"Great, Marilyn. Work is still there. I'm writing well."

"That's wonderful. How's the book going? It's about your dreams, right? The latest one? What was the title? Something about seeing?"

"Close. *Night Vision*. It's going well. Always taking off on some new tangent, but I'm able to keep it fairly well centered. We'll see how it turns out in the next couple of months."

"Have you gotten an agent yet?"

"No, nothing yet," Lane said. Though he hadn't pursued getting an agent for over a year. Tired of getting rejected, he opted to bury himself in his work, until he had written "The Book" that would break him into the industry. *Night Vision*, he felt, was turning out to be such a book.

"Keep it up. It'll happen sooner or later. It's really great that you're still using your gifts so well."

"Thanks," he said, wanting to say more but not sure what. He was silent.

"So, what else is going on in your life?"

"Stuart Hill called last week about the house," he said, pausing, feeling his way along emotionally. "He had a buyer for it and was wondering if I wanted to sell."

"Oh? Do you want to sell the house?"

"Well, the buyer backed off yesterday. Stuart said he could probably find another buyer if I wanted him too. I'm not sure that I want to sell the place. And I'm not really sure why."

"Then don't sell it," Marilyn said with her usual tactfulness.

"Well, there's more to it," Lane paused, trying to get a feel for the situation and to keep up with the turmoil of emotions he was feeling. He wasn't sure why he was so confused by the idea he had, but it just seemed to be almost perverse. Moving back to the house in which he and his family had become so thoroughly fucked up that his mother and sister died and he had…had taken care of his father.

"I'm thinking about moving back into the house."

There was just the briefest hesitation on Marilyn's part. Nothing more than a few seconds, but long enough for Lane to notice.

"Oh?" was all she said.

"Well, maybe. I'm just thinking about it now. I've made arrangements to have the trust released so I can use the money for repairs. But I'm not really sure why I want to do it. You know? It just doesn't seem to make sense."

"Why?"

"The obvious reason."

"Why don't you come over this afternoon and we can talk about it? Are you free?"

"Sure, that'd be great. What time?"

"Give me an hour to get something together."

"All right. See you soon."

Lane hung up the phone and felt better. He didn't realize how much pressure he'd been putting on himself until now. Marilyn would have some answers for him. If she didn't, she would help him to find them.

*   *   *

"I think I already know why, Lane. Let's see if I'm right," Marilyn said.

He arrived fifteen minutes early and helped Marilyn finish slicing fruit for the salad. Though he hadn't seen her for longer than he could remember, she hadn't changed. She still dressed the part of the older and wiser flower child that she was. Still wore her long blonde hair drawn back into a simple bun, and adorned herself with silver and turquoise jewelry.

Her house sat on five acres east of Burkett. It was a small house cluttered with antique furniture, off beat sculptures and landscape paintings. They now sat on the back porch beneath a lattice covering overlooking what had once been a thriving garden in the backyard. The garden was now choked with weeds. Marilyn explained that she didn't have the time to tend it, but planned to when she retired, whenever that would be. She was in her early fifties and by the looks of some of the weeds in the garden, hadn't given up all of her flower child habits.

The first thunder storms of spring had backed off for the moment and the day was warm with a hint of the high humidity that would soon drench them all. They were comfortable in the shade of the latticework, sipping herbal iced tea with fresh spearmint leaves as the day stretched into the afternoon.

"Okay," Lane said, ready to hear her answers.

"Do you remember talking about focusing? How focusing on something can affect your life in ways that you cannot initially imagine or connect to your original intent?" Lane thought back to their innumerable sessions.

"Yeah, a little. Something to do with life bringing to you what you most desire, even if it is in a form that you may not recognize."

"Right! Whatever you most desire will eventually, somehow or another, come to you. Within reason, of course. You will get that which you truly desire, not what you may *think* you desire." She paused to sip her tea.

"What has the focus of your life been since the death of your father? What is it you truly desire?"

"To be a professional writer," Lane said, not following her train of thought, but trusting her from years of experience.

She leaned back in her chair, sipped at her tea again, then leaned forward, a slight smile crossing her lips.

"Notice that you didn't define a genre'. Just that you want to be a professional writer."

"Yeah, but you know that I—."

"Yes, *I* know and *you* know but your statement of wanting to be a professional writer will be returned to you just as you've thought it. A *professional writer*. Not any particular area, just a professional writer. That being your true desire, that is what life will bring you," she said, smiling broadly.

Lane wondered if she hadn't been playing with the funny weeds in her garden this morning. Marilyn saw that he wasn't getting it.

"Okay. Let's try another thought," she said, looking off toward the woods, thinking. Lane drank his tea and waited.

"Have you seen the movie Papillion with Dustin Hoffman and Steve McQueen?"

"Yeah, that's a great movie. I read the book, too. Henri Charriere. What a story."

"Yes, it was. What do you think was his desire? What motivated him?"

"Freedom. He wanted to be free."

"Did he find it?"

"Eventually, yeah."

"Why do you think he wrote the story of his life? Have you heard about that?"

Lane shook his head.

"Once he reached freedom, he settled in Venezuela, then wrote the story of his life. He sent it to a publisher with a simple note explaining that the book was his life's story and, with some editing, might be able to be published. I'm not sure if that's a true story or not but it sure is good PR." She stirred her tea and took another long drink.

"Do you think he received an income from that book and movie?" she asked.

"If he didn't, someone screwed him really bad!" Lane said, laughing. He'd missed Marilyn more than he knew. She always had an interesting and intriguing way of explaining things. She laughed with him then came around to the point.

"I think it would be safe to say that he did receive some monetary compensation for the story. But what would that money mean to him at that point in his life? Working odd jobs for very little pay, he was free from the prison, but didn't have financial freedom."

"What would that mean?" Lane asked, more to himself than to Marilyn.

"Yes. What would that money—however much it was—mean to him?"

"Freedom," Lane said, smiling with understanding. "It would mean *financial* freedom to him."

"Exactly," she said, pointing at him for emphasis. "Freedom. He'd spent almost his entire life focusing on his *physical* freedom. Once he had that, the force of his desire for freedom kept on producing in his life. He was moved to write the story of his life for whatever reason and that, in turn, produced for him financial freedom, or at the least a lot of money."

Marilyn smiled and drank the last of her tea.

"So you're saying that his focus of freedom was carried out no matter what that freedom might be?"

"Yes."

Lane nodded.

"Anyway, it makes sense to me. I've seen it happen when a person will really focus their energy. So what you need to do is look at your focus and relate that to your desire to move back to the house. What do you think might be there for you?" she asked, her brown eyes twinkling with the answer she was leading him to.

He felt as if they had just started the conversation from the beginning. He thought about his desire of becoming a professional writer. Not, as Marilyn had pointed out a professional writer of fiction, but just a professional writer. It had never occurred to him that he might have to be more specific with reference to his style or genre'. He'd always assumed it was understood by whatever forces were out there that he wanted to publish works of fiction.

Turtle began to laugh quietly, but Lane couldn't hear it.

The thoughts began to gel in his mind. With writing you did the best if you dealt with subjects that you knew not something that you've guessed at. Use your own experiences in your work, those that you had actual first hand knowledge with. He'd read that in a writer's handbook at some time or another and couldn't remember the author of the essay, but that didn't change the truth of the statements.

You always told the truth.

Always.

If you didn't you would lose the reader in the first few sentences.

He'd strived to do that. *Night Vision* was the most complete and honest novel he'd worked with to date. How could you be more truthful that to turn your dreams out for the world to see? Sure, the book wasn't considered to be a work of non-fiction since he was placing the dreams in a fictional format, but that didn't discount the reality of the honesty and truthfulness. In fact—

He drew a sharp breath as he suddenly saw what Marilyn apparently already knew.

"You could help a lot of people understand themselves better," she quietly said. "I think it would be great for you also." She reached across the small patio table and took his hand smiling warmly.

"What do you think?" she quietly asked.

"I think you might be right."

He felt a cold numbness come over him, as if he were being charged with low voltage power. Why it had never occurred to him before he couldn't understand, but it was there. Marilyn was right. The reason he was drawn to the house and his past was to rid him of it once and for all the best way he knew how. To write it out.

He wondered what this new direction would do to *Night Vision*. Maybe he could intermingle the autobiography with the dreams of *Night Vision*. Maybe use them as preambles to the chapters, something like that might work. He would have to see where it went once he started to lay it out. The year and a half of work would be a waste to shelf.

"I think you might be right," he said again, stumbling around new thoughts and ideas the project was beginning to produce. And, as Marilyn had said, it may be good for him. It would be the final act of therapy that would, hopefully, release him from his past for good. The image of the little boy standing on a stool in front of the bathroom sink came from the flow of ideas. The cooling water soothing him, calming him. He missed his mother again. Even more so now that he saw a way to put her to rest.

"What are you thinking?" Marilyn asked, her voice low, comforting, therapeutic.

"About my mother…and how…just thinking about her," he said, then began to cry. The tears slowly streamed down the face of a thirty-three year old man, who was, after all, still a scared little boy struggling to understand himself and his life.

Marilyn slid her chair next to his, without a word, and put her arm around his shoulders until he regained his composure.

"It is a frightening thing to think about doing," she said, brushing his black hair from his forehead. Lane nodded, not wanting to speak and risk the possibility of his voice cracking.

There was a rustling in the garden and the weeds began to shudder with the passing of something beneath them.

"Look," Lane said, pointing to the shifting weeds. Whatever it was, it was coming closer.

Marilyn smiled and winked at Lane. She pursed her lips and made a soft burring sound. The movement in the weeds stopped. Lane heard what sounded like a cat's purr in response to Marilyn, then a large raccoon appeared through the weeds. It sniffed the air tentatively and waved a paw in their direction.

"Come here, Bob. Say hello to Lane," Marilyn said. She stood and walked to the back corner of the patio. There was a collection of rusted garden tools, planter boxes, several piles of clay pots, boxes overflowing with old flower bulbs and several bags of peat moss. After a moment searching she produced a half-full bag of stale marshmallows. Bob the raccoon was watching her movements from the edge of the garden with interest, but didn't move any closer until he saw the marshmallows.

He slowly lumbered across the remaining distance to the porch and climbed into the chair Marilyn had been sitting in.

"Hello, Bob. Have you been a good raccoon?" Marilyn said, handing Bob a marshmallow. He took it and began to munch, burring and smacking with satisfaction.

"I found him last spring wandering around the garden. The little guy was nearly starved to death. I don't know what happened to his family. He's been wandering in and out of here ever since. Haven't you, Bob?"

she said, petting him. Bob burred in response to the attention and reached for the bag of marshmallows. She handed him another.

"Do you want to feed him?" she asked, handing the bag to Lane. He wasn't sure if he wanted to or not, but Bob answered the question for him by following the bag of treats. He climbed across the table and into Lane's lap, reaching for the bag.

"He isn't one for social graces," Marilyn said, laughing at the antics of Bob. Lane handed him a marshmallow and petted the big animal that was happily sitting in his lap.

He left Marilyn's house a little after seven that evening. Bob had stayed around long enough to eat his fill of marshmallows, then lumbered back into the woods. On the drive home, Lane felt as if he'd left one theater and was entering a new one. The day marked a dividing place in his life, a point of departure. It was a familiar emotion. He'd always felt the same when hitting on a story line for a new book. The world seemed more intense, brighter, sharper. His senses more alive to colors, sound and smells.

Marilyn's "Papillion" metaphor had merit and he understood it as it related to his life. Whether it was true or not didn't really seem to matter. It made sense. That was all. He wanted to be a professional writer. Now he was given the material with which to reach that goal. It had been so obvious, he hadn't seen it.

After filling nearly three legal pads with notes for the autobiography, he finally laid down to sleep around two Monday morning. He dreamt of dark, closed tunnels and hot, burning fumes.

∗   ∗   ∗

He pitched in his dollar on the office pool on Monday morning, but his thoughts were elsewhere. Sheila wasn't working today. The word was that she'd spent the weekend partying and was just now getting around to realizing she had a hangover.

William gleefully plunged into his work. Now that his main challenger was gone, he sensed victory at the end of the day.

Chris was unusually quiet and withdrawn. His seemingly unending chatter and jokes were silent. Trisha informed Lane, as she walked past his cubical with an arm full of new data, that she and Rachael had spoken with him before work.

"His boyfriend left him," she whispered, leaning down conspiratorially and distorting her face into a pinched look of disdain.

"Oh," Lane said, turning back to his work, not willing nor wanting to play her game. Trish stood a moment longer, somewhat confused, then opted for stalking away.

He could hear a babble of conversation in the back of the room. Trisha was beginning the long process of relating the details of their short conversation to Rachael. Probably throwing in that Lane was gay and secretly in love with Chris. As the stomach churns.

He promptly forgot about it and fifteen minutes later hit his stride. The couple of hours until lunch passed quickly. As he was leaving the office Red asked him if everything was going well. Lane smiled brightly and told him everything was going great.

Trisha and Rachael gave him a sour look as he walked past them in the hall. He smiled at them and continued walking to the parking lot. On the drive over to Stuart's office he thought again about asking Henry and Linda to help him so he could quit working at Hubbard, but the old feelings of being given everything surfaced again and he pushed it aside. He'd persisted this long and decided he could deal with it until he published.

The idea of writing his autobiography was now seeded. He thought it would be easier than fiction. All he would need to do is recite his story. It shouldn't take more than six months at the most. He'd seen enough "true story" books to know that the public would eat it up. Then, once he had his foot in the door of the professional literary world he could get back to the fiction. It made perfect sense.

The receptionist he'd spoken with introduced herself as Susan, told him Stuart wouldn't be in all day, then quickly handed him a yellow envelope. She pointed to a door adjacent to the reception area and told him there was an empty desk in there that he could use, then went back to answering the phone.

The office was a large conference room with a long oval desk set in the middle surrounded by chairs. He sat in the one closest to him and opened the envelope. He quickly completed the forms, signing where someone had highlighted and placed little Xs. He handed the proper copies to Susan on the way out. It was a little past twelve when he pulled out of the parking lot. He'd hoped to get by the bank today but wouldn't have the time. By one he was back a Hubbard punching keys and wishing he'd stopped for lunch.

*　　　*　　　*

He spent Monday night wrestling with the autobiography. A stack of yellow legal pads began to grow on the floor next to his desk as he remembered and re-remembered his tattered youth. With bold, thick printing and a firm hand he worked in a therapeutic ecstasy he had never known, the words and thoughts flowing effortlessly from the pen to the page. He embraced the work completely, able, somehow, to detach his emotion from it, as if he were working on yet another fictional novel.

The vague fear that Turtle might return with a vengeance should he begin to prod it by searching out his memories piece by piece, vanished quickly as he plunged into the work.

It never occurred to him that he might already have been taken.

*　　　*　　　*

"Look, man," Tim said, lazily weaving around broken bottles, dead wood and trash. "There's nothing to it. Just wade out and dunk under the water. That's it."

Tim and Blake were riding down a cement overflow ditch. Blake Morrow looked pensively at his comrade and nodded his head, thick legs pumping. There was an ugly, healing cut about two inches long on his right leg, just below the knee.

"If it were up to me I'd let you in 'cause I believe you about the house and Halfhead, you know? I mean, you cut your leg and all. But the guys, man, you know, don't want to make it too easy. We gotta' be careful who we let in, you know?" Tim said.

"Sure, yeah," Blake said, thinking of his father. Today was the Anniversary. His Mom always lighted a blue candle that would burn all day and she sat or lay in her room watching television and eating cake on the Anniversary. Blake didn't do much of anything on this day except wait for his mom to come out of her room. If he could have asked his father one question—just one last question—what would that be? He wasn't sure what he would ask, but *why'd you check out?* would be close to the top of the list. *Why'd you fucking leave us?* would be there also. Maybe *what were you so afraid of chicken shit?* would be in there also.

He was reminded of what his father had hoped for every time his mother sent him to the basement to get a can of frozen juice, or, on special occasions, steaks from the big freezer humming quietly to itself in the corner. Stacked in the back of the basement his dad's dream of flight slowly molded and decayed in the form of model airplanes.

One Saturday morning Blake had gone to the basement in search of the broom. He found his father quietly sitting in a rusting deck chair, holding one of the jet models.

The model was very old. The silver paint scratched and marred. The emblems and insignia pealing and dull. His father had looked up in surprise at the sudden arrival of his son and Blake realized that he had accidentally stumbled upon something that he wasn't meant to see.

Instead of the yelling he expected to hear, his father called him over to where he sat and embraced him. He felt warm, slick tears trickle down his neck. He was scared for his father. After what seemed to be a very long time his father released him and set the model carefully back into one of the boxes, then took Blake's arms and looked him in the eyes.

"You're a really good boy, Blake, and I love you very much. Do you understand?" he'd asked. Blake shook his head, unable to speak. His father had rarely bestowed so much affection in one swoop. His Dad had nodded, satisfied with the unspoken answer, then abruptly stood and walked briskly up the stairs.

Three weeks after their chance meeting in the basement, Blake's father committed suicide. Blake was nine.

He remembered two things about it. The first was that Rich Tomex said his father had committed *pussycide* because he'd taken pills and hadn't used a gun. And that he was now "getting it up the ass from the man downstairs." The second was that something in Blake changed. A part of him simply turned off, winked out. Like a dying star, that part of him seemed to be gone forever. Maybe it was hope that died that day, or maybe the little boy that he never had the chance to be died in him. Whatever it was, from that day on, it always hurt where that part of him used to be.

So he would endure whatever Tim and his cohorts came up with as an initiation. Though he had wanted to be part of the gang, the novelty was beginning to wear thin. They had decided he hadn't stayed in the old house on Cherokee long enough to pass the test. All but Tim had believed he lied about being chased out by a monster, and so they'd devised a new test. He had to wade into the middle of the snake pond and dunk his head to complete his initiation.

The concrete run-off creek they now rode in ended abruptly. From there the water dropped ten feet to a natural creek bed. It was here that the pond was created. It was full of water year round, even at the height of summer. The banks of the small pond were littered with trash. Chunks and slabs of old concrete took the place of boulders and rocks in this citified version of a creek. A small trickle of water ran through the drainage ditch that cascaded down to the pond.

They left their bikes at the top of the drop-off and, with familiar ease, nimbly climbed down the bank, balancing on the concrete slabs. On their way down, Blake tried to peer through the murky water to gauge its depth. The recent rains had churned it up and made it impossible to tell. The day was hot and his shirt was sticking to him, though he knew that not all of the sweat was from the heat. The scabbed over cut on his knee itched.

"How deep do you think it is?" he asked, trying his best to be casual about the whole affair.

"Greg's brother waded across it once and it came up to his chest," Tim said, working his way to the bank. Blake calculated that since Greg's brother was almost a foot taller than he was, that meant the water would just about cover his head, if he went to the middle. He took a deep breath and tried not to worry too much. Besides, he was a good swimmer.

They stood on the bank and looked across the surface of the pond. A slight skim of algae coated the surface. Here and there frogs leaped from the bank with croaks of protest at the intrusion, then surfaced in the deeper water of the pond to eye them suspiciously. They both watched as a snake slid smoothly from a overhanging branch into the water. It floated momentarily, then with a quick whipping-splash, disappeared beneath the dark water.

"Think it was poisonous?" Blake asked, still committed to the task.

"Don't know. If their head is shaped like a diamond then they're poisonous."

"Did you see its head?"

"No," Tim said, looking across the water.

"Look, man. I told the guys not to come because this was just between you and me. I believed you about the house, man, so if you don't want to do this, that'll be cool. We'll just say you did it and you can be in. Okay?"

Tim casually took a crumpled pack of cigarettes from his back pocket and offered one to Blake. Blake shook his head and tried not to look surprised as Tim took one of the bent cigarettes straightened it as best he could, then lighted it with a match. He took a deep drag then stifled a cough.

"I stole them from my dad," he said, as if this explained everything.

"Oh," Blake said, looking back to the pond.

"Well, what'd 'ya say? Deal?"

"No. I don't think so. I'll do it. Thanks anyway."

Tim looked momentarily surprised, then quickly hid it by shrugging and taking another drag on the cigarette.

"You gonna take your shoes off?"

"No. I wore my old ones," he said, then turned and began to wade into the pond.

THREE

The sun hadn't moved.

He thought it would never come. Summer mornings could be that way. Behind him the bank was farther than he thought it should have been. The distance he had covered hadn't felt that far. It had something to do with time. It moved differently here, though he wasn't sure just how.

The slope of the lake bottom was deceiving. It felt as if he'd walked only ten or fifteen yards into the lake from the bank, but it looked more like fifty from where he stood.

The sun could have moved. He told himself it had and took another tentative step. His penis and scrotum shriveled away from the cold water, drawing closer to his body. He wanted to unfold his arms and let them drag in the water at his side, but didn't. He wasn't quite ready for his arms to hang in the dark water.

He waited, watching the growing light.

He wanted to take them both, but couldn't. The big one was being protected. He didn't understand the protection as a thought only as an emotion or an instinct. The big one was protected. By whom or what didn't matter. Even in the new life Duane Trammel White had found in death there were other forces greater than he.

He pulled back to watch for his opening.

The bottom of the pond was littered with accumulated debris that the creek had carried down. Blake stepped carefully in the water, not wanting to fall on the slick, slime covered branches, bottles and other ill-defined things he slipped on. His imagination made them into the smooth, algae covered skulls of dead people, limbs were transformed into the skeletal remains, bits of moss, entrails. He quickly changed his thinking.

"Is it slippery?" Tim asked from the safety of the bank. He had discarded his smoke and now looked anxiously as Blake slowly made his way to deeper water. He hadn't really wanted to hang with Blake. What had first been meant as a joke to see how far they could push him, had, for Tim, turned into something else. He knew about Blake's father killing himself. As he watched Blake perform whatever antics they could think up, he'd begun to feel sorry for the fat kid.

He didn't expect Blake would actually go through with this last rite and it caught him off guard. He was sure Blake would say yes to his offer of letting him off the hook. That he hadn't made him admire Blake that much more. Shit, he wasn't even sure he would get in that stinking, crappy water for the guys, or anyone else for that matter.

"Yeah," Blake answered, not looking back. He was now up to his stomach in the thick, stinking muck and going deeper.

"Just dunk your head there," Tim said, anxious for him to get out of the water. "That'll be good enough."

"Okay," Blake said across the small expanse that separated them. He stopped walking and settled his tentative footing as best he could.

He slowly lowered his head to the water. At that moment something grabbed his ankles—something that was *alive* had grabbed his ankles— and he opened his mouth to scream. His feet were jerked out from under him and as his balance went south his head was plunged into the dark water nearly head first. The vile, putrid water rushing to fill his open mouth choked his scream from him.

Whatever had grabbed him let him go just as quickly and he sputtered and stumbled in the thick, swampy water gasping for air and trying to stand. He could smell the stink of water on his body and taste its acrid, putrid essence in his mouth. His eyes stung and there were things stuck to his face. Most were leaves and chunks of algae but some of the things seemed to be *moving*. There were things in his mouth some were hard and some were soft. He had enough time to wonder why the soft things were moving.

"What happened?" Tim asked, his face twisted into an odd expression that was an attempt to hide genuine concern.

"*Something grabbed me! Something's in here!*" Blake had time to scream, before he was grabbed by the ankles once again and pulled beneath the water. He fought for the surface.

"*Help me! Help me!*" he screamed, his face smeared with mud. He struggled to stand in the slippery mire. His eyes stung from the water and his arms were scratched and cut from hitting the rough bottom of the pond. The water tasted like sour pudding and lumpy milk.

Tim crashed into the water toward Blake who was only ten yards away. As he reached him, Blake was pulled under again.

"*Ahhhhhh!*" he screamed in a panicked wail as he stumbled into the dark water and fought the slick, metallic fear that was telling him to run the other way.

He turned at the sound of something breaking through the surface, expecting to see Blake. Instead he was met by a figure covered in pond scum and dead leaves. Its head was disfigured. Tim had time to see that the thing had one good eye glaring from its broken face. He watched in pale horror as it opened its mouth, spilling forth leeches and thick, white worms.

"Now you can be in my gang, Tim," the thing croaked, then embraced him in its cold, dead arm. There was a brief moment of pain, nothing more than a wasp sting, then a warm, dark silence enveloped him as he felt the last beat of his heart, the final rush of blood through his body, and the cold, dead arms of his captor hold him tighter.

In a daze and more than half drowned Blake scrambled to the bank of the pond. He'd heard the thing getting Tim and he didn't wait around to find out anything else. Tim was beyond any help that Blake could give. Bleeding from a dozen small cuts and covered in pond scum, he began to run for home. A part of him wondered why he didn't take his bike and that it might be stolen if he left it. But that part of him he left to wonder as he ran as fast as his overweight body could carry him.

He wasn't able to convince the police that there was something in the pond that had pulled him under. His mother had better luck with them because she did believe her son. At least to the extent that *he* believed there was something there.

Water rescue crews from the Burkett Fire Department station 16 recovered Tim's body later that afternoon. The next day, at the suggestion of the police, and Blake's mother's prodding, a crew from the city dug a trench at the back of the pond and drained it on the off chance that there was some kind of animal in it big enough to overpower a child. A representative from the zoology department at Burkett University was on hand, just in case. The one idea that took hold and was taken seriously was the possibility that a pet python may have been lost and grown fat on turtles and rats. After a considerable effort of time and money, the pond was drained.

Nothing was found.

*   *   *

Wednesday morning, he tipped four quarters into the office pool out of habit more than any burning desire to kick somebody's ass. He quickly slipped into that strange hypnotic state of work mode. Now that he had made the commitment to move back to the house and write an autobiography he began to lose some of his adrenaline induced courage. Just what, exactly, was this going to accomplish?

Well, if all went well, it would hopefully cause all his earthly worries to go away and it would set him on the road to a plush, lucrative future as a professional novelist. Yes, and if this weren't enough, he would then be able to shit gold as way of a simple by-product of his radiant success and great skill as a writer.

Yeah.

"Oh, *Mr.* White, how could you go back to that *awful* place to write about what happened?" Leslie so and so from such and this primetime entertainment show would ask. He would smile with great confidence and knowing then respond with...he paused in his data inputting, shifted his seat, scratched an itch on his arm and...nothing. Nothing there. No response. Or was...was that just a whisper of something there? Yes, that right...*there.*

It sure was, wasn't it? Let's be honest, now, Lane. There was a wee-small something calling softly way down deep. Something beyond the beatings and the abuse Kristy endured, not to mention his mother. Yes sir, there was a little small something down there and he didn't think it was going to come out anytime soon.

Today is a new day, today is a new day, today is a new day.

He stopped the mantra and waited, listening for that small, sharp memory to die or hide or just go away.

"Well, Leslie, it was just something I had to do to get on with my life. I wish it had all been different, but it wasn't and I had to deal with that as a reality." He would then smile knowingly and with great confidence as millions upon millions of viewers shook their collective heads in amazement.

He began typing again, a thin smile on his face, glad for having buried it once again. Yet, above all of that little secret, quite a few layers above it, was Turtle. Turtle the Avenger, Turtle the Destroyer, Turtle the Great and Turtle the Fine.

As part of his recovery Marilyn had urged him to give a name to the vile, festering pain and anger that had been planted and blossomed years before. He'd always thought that Turtle was not a part of him. That Turtle was an entity all his own that was comprised of bits and pieces of Lane White yet didn't come directly from him.

When the therapy sessions had begun to get a little on the rough side—with the screws really beginning to bite deep, with all the crap out of the way and his soul skinned alive for all the world to see—he would let go of whatever last bit of rational self he may have been clinging to and allow himself to be totally consumed by the anger. Anger at his father, anger at his mother for not doing more, anger at life for having him live it. So on and so on and Boo-hoo and Big Whine.

As part of the process of piecing himself back together she would have him draw pictures of his anger and give detailed explanations as to the contents of the pictures. Most of the pictures looked like the lumpy, thick shell of a Turtle, with a beak protruding slightly. Thus, Turtle had been named. As the Therapy progressed, Turtle had slowly disappeared from his life. Yet, now it seemed, Turtle was making an attempt for a come back tour.

He hoped that the incident with Red several weeks ago and the brief stab of Turtle since then was from simple stress. It had been over seven years since he'd had to deal with his past of such an immediate basis. Now he was aiming to chronicle the majority of the events in an autobiography. Record all the chaotic peaks and valleys, the pain, the healing and hopefully, the eventual closure. Turtle was just coming up as a part of his past. The old guy didn't want to be left out of the picture, that was all. Had to get his piece in. Shit, buddy, if it weren't for Turtle, none of this fun shit would be happening. Let's give the credit where the credit is due.

He decided it was as simple as that and forced his thoughts into another direction. If it happened again, and Turtle showed up to say howdy, he would tell Marilyn and then she could work her magic on him.

Chris was happy again and joking up a storm. Twice Red had to come out of his office and tell him to keep it down and get to work. The gossip was that his long lost boyfriend had returned. Trish and Rachael kept away from Lane and would throw dirty looks his way when he happened to catch their eye. They paraded back and forth loading up or unloading hard copy data from the tables at the front of the room.

Sheila and William were back at their daily game of who could be the fastest and loving every minute of it. Sheila had come back to work Tuesday with tales of a weekend's indulgence at Wallace Lake.

David Sumner was as studious as ever, and would tell anyone that would listen that he was moving up in the world of Hubbard. There was an opening for a research assistant, and with his B.A. in Computer Science, he was sure he would get it. And from there, it was a short hop to becoming an actual, cast-in-steel research and development technician.

With work at Hubbard back to as normal as it ever got, the remainder of the week passed quickly.

*   *   *

He woke early Saturday after going to bed late Friday and set right into the autobiography. The legal pads filled with notes were scattered around his desk and stacked on the floor like mutated tree stumps in a somewhat organized fashion. The piles of notes would have easily filled a two-volume edition of his autobiography at over a thousand pages each. Add to that the incorporation for the "Night Vision" project and he was looking at another half volume. He had never been short with his words. He smiled at the pages of words and paragraphs and scribbled notations for changes he'd made during a read through.

By six that same night he had the general working idea for the chapters. There would be twenty-three, if he stuck with his plan and the work cooperated. He doubted that it would. It never did. Even though this was non-fiction, he could feel the autobiography and already knew, as with fiction, if would come to life and direct the writing.

He finally gave in as his brain had turned to jelly and his fingers were sore from pushing a pen around all day. Suddenly not wanting to be alone with the small towers of paper that contained his life, he called Henry and Linda to invite himself over for dinner.

He remembered the first time he saw their house. It hadn't been a year since his life took that really momentous turn that landed him in the town of the seriously fucked when Henry and Linda had entered his life.

At the time, having become numb with the attention over what he'd done, they were just more people in the blur of faces. After meeting them several times with Marilyn firmly at his side, they began spending time together without Marilyn, then he was staying at their house periodically, very soon after that it was as if he had never lived anywhere else.

The exterior was a sandstone and cedar contemporary design and the interior was done up in what Lane liked to think of as rural Oklahoma hell. Linda had that bargain store, cheap mail order touch that was the gift of so many. He'd forgotten about the seven o'clock dinner rule as he was arriving. Linda opened the front door before he reached it.

"Well, I guess we'll take you in anyway," she said, greeting and scolding as only a mother can. They hugged and she began to turn into the house, then stopped. She looked back at him.

"Are you feeling well?"

"Yeah, fine. Just a little tired. I've been working on something."

"Oh?" she asked, folding her arms akimbo across her ample bosom and tilting her head back slightly.

"Yeah. It's really going to be…big. I think. Yeah, I think it could be really big."

"A book?" she asked, arms still crossed, but her face softened a little.

"Yes, a book. *The* book, if all goes as planned," he said, smiling at her.

"You coming in or leaving?" Henry called from somewhere in the house.

"Coming in," Linda called back over her shoulder. "I can't wait to hear about it," she said to Lane, taking his hand and leading him into the house. Lane thought she still looked like that Aunt something character from that old sitcom with Ron Howard in it. Henry, on the other hand, with his bright red hair and green eyes could have passed for an older Ron Howard any day of the week. He was sitting at the set table waiting for them.

"Lane," he said, offering his hand. Lane took it and was suddenly very happy he'd come over for dinner.

They had a sedate evening during which Linda chided Henry about their upcoming trip to Israel. She said he wanted to see the Holy City to make amends for his life, now that he was getting old. After their appetites had the edge taken off Linda asked about his project. He explained what he was planning to do and why. Both Henry and Linda listened quietly and attentively.

"Well, you need to slow down some and pace yourself, you look too tired. There really isn't a need to rush. Slow down some." He told her he would, though they both knew it was just a courtesy statement. He'd wanted the success of a professional writing career far too long. Now that he saw a bit of light, a possible way to get there, a few hours of missed sleep was a small price to pay.

The pork chops had been perfect topped with a spoon full of applesauce, the new potatoes just right. Around ten Lane left, hugging Linda and shaking Henry's hand. He promised to keep them updated on the move. They offered to hire the moving company when he was ready. It was the least they could do, Linda said. He told them he would consider it.

As they watched Lane drive away, Linda turned to Henry, her face heavy and dark. It wasn't the superficial concern she usually carried.

"What is it?" Henry asked.

"I don't know. Something's not right with this autobiography he wants to do. And moving back to that house. I don't know what it is, Henry, but I'm worried about him."

She looked out the foyer windows to the dark and empty street.

"Do you want to call Marilyn? See what she thinks? Lane said he spoke with her," Henry said, standing by her side. Though he hadn't felt anything was wrong with the situation, he knew Linda well enough to respect her intuition.

"I don't know. Maybe I should," she said, still looking out at the street. It wasn't the biting, sarcastic answer he'd expected she would give. Usually any reference to Marilyn would be followed with a swift reply that was not flattering.

Henry knew that the animosity she felt toward Marilyn was due to jealousy. She could have helped Lane just as much as Ms. Marilyn Duran could have if the state had given her a chance, or so she thought. However, the reality was much different, and deep down she knew it. That this other woman could provide her son (she never referred to Lane as being anything other than her son) with something that she could not was forever grating on her.

But now, as she stood in the bright lights of the foyer in their spacious, comfortable home looking out to the street, her concern for Lane overrode her feelings for Marilyn and she seriously considered calling her for help. She would not be calling for personal help, of course, she would be calling to speak about Lane. And she would ask for an explanation as to why she had encouraged him to return to the house and write an autobiography, of all things, about what he had done.

"Maybe I'll call her tomorrow afternoon," she said.

*   *   *

Sunday morning and most of the afternoon was spent working the notes, trying to capture the new found voice that was to be the voice of the autobiography. It was a hard thing to do, capturing your own voice on paper, but he thought it was going well enough. By five he was ready to call it a day. He drove over to the house on Cherokee Place and killed an hour wandering around. Chasing his own demons and finding others he didn't know were there. Such a very long time ago and yet it all seemed like it happened yesterday.

"Sounds like a line from a novel," he said to the empty living room. The house smelled badly, as if something had died in it and hadn't finished the major part of its rotting. He would have to do something about that before he moved in.

Without realizing it, he had come here to make a decision. And he had in fact already made that decision before he realized that there was even a decision to be made. He would not renovate the house. Nothing would be changed. Only the basic necessities would be added. Just enough to get the heat and air going, running water and safe electrical. The atmosphere would be much more conducive to the autobiography, the memories clearer, the pain just as sharp as if he left the house just the way it was. Covering it all up would be just the opposite of what he was setting out to do. He wanted to uncover it and share it with the world. This is why and this is how I feel about it now.

He had a brief vision of the picture that would grace the hardcover edition of the book. He would be standing on the porch of the house, dressed in worn jeans, boots and a short sleeve work shirt. The shot would be enough to encompass the house, but not so far that you couldn't make out his personal features. He smiled again and let the vision play on.

He would camp out in the living room, right here where he stood. Turn on the utilities, put up a couple of light bulbs, get the bathroom working, but that would be it. Maybe patch that leak in the roof, but not much more. He could live on restaurant food and use a hot plate if the old stove wasn't up to it anymore. Hell, he had over twenty thousand dollars to put into the project, he could easily eat out every meal if he wanted to.

It was nearly six and the sun was beginning to glow with the oncoming evening. Diffused light splayed across the roof of the house, plunging the porch and side street into premature darkness as Lane watched. The memories were there but controllable and secure. He felt the twinge of excitement at the prospect the autobiography held. The macabre aspects of writing it in the house that it all happened so long ago only seemed to add to the allure and mystic of it all. It was almost, but not quite, fun.

Visions of interviews on television morning shows ran through his thoughts. What would he say in response to their questions? Better yet, what would they ask? How would the book be received? Would it sell well or would it be stuck in with all the other countless writers who shared his vision of writing glory? And, worse yet, was this just a self-delusion vision he was having? Not if Marilyn was suggesting it was a good idea also. He trusted her judgement, if only because he was unable to trust himself.

There really wasn't anyway he could be sure that it was the right thing to do, but it *felt* right. At least for the most part, it felt right. And that had to be good enough, folks. 'Cause when that old dead horse yer kickin' is powdered bone and there wasn't shit on the horizon but more of the same, you took what you were given. If what you were given tasted like elephant leavings then, buddy, you choked 'em down and asked for more.

He drove away from the house thinking of the autobiography and the next tedious process of piecing together the chapters. Though he had been working at a frantic pace, he could no longer push it. Now came the time to coax the story into moving, then trying to keep up when it ran screaming ahead of him. He decided that Marilyn had been right. This idea might just work.

As Lane drove away, Duane Trammel White chuckled deeply and smiled his twisted, rotting grin into the glowing night. Playtime was over, now it was time to get down to business.

The boy was almost home.

*   *   *

She decided she would hang up on the fourth ring. On the third ring, the phone was picked up.

"Hello?"

"Marilyn?" Linda asked, trying her best to be pleasant.

"Yes?"

Linda remembered the voice, cool, confident, a hint of curiosity as to who was calling, but no worry, no concern. She could handle anything. She was a *therapist*.

"This is Linda McAlester," she stated, reminding herself that though Lane was not their biological child, he was their son legally. There was much more to being a parent than being an egg donor to some man's sperm. They had done their best, and it was a testament to their efforts that Lane had been doing as well as he had. Oh sure, Marilyn had had *something* to do with it, but without her and Henry's consistent support, she doubted he would be doing so well.

"How are you, Linda? I haven't heard from you in quite some time."

Did she sound just a little *too* nice, a little *too* pleasant?

"Yes, it has been awhile," Linda said. She had sent Henry on an errand, giving him a list of six items she didn't need, two of which were not available at the store she had sent him to. It was in the late afternoon on Sunday and Lane was still looking over the house on Cherokee Place.

"How's Henry?" Marilyn asked.

"Oh, grumpy as ever. We're planning to go to Israel as soon as he makes the arrangements."

"That sounds like it will be exciting," Marilyn responded.

"Oh yes, it does. We're looking forward to it."

The silence began to grow.

"How is—?" Linda began.

"Did you know that—," Marilyn began.

They both stopped and waited for the other to continue. Linda laughed lightly and Marilyn joined in.

"I guess I'm a little uncomfortable," Marilyn said. "I know that we haven't gotten along very well over the years we've both come to know Lane, but that's all over now. I think we can work through it, can't we?" she asked.

"I wanted to talk with you about Lane and what he is planning to do," Linda said, ignoring Marilyn's suggested treaty.

"Okay," Marilyn said. She quietly sighed and moved with the cordless phone into her small, comfortable living room. She sat on the couch facing the large bay window that overlooked the backyard. The overgrown garden was to the right side of the scene the window framed; the rest was lawn and distant woods under a clear, cloudless sky. She waited for Linda to begin.

"First of all, he told me you said it was a good idea for him to move back to the house and write an autobiography. Is that *right*?"

She knew instantly that Lane had been careful not to tell Linda it had been her idea in the first place. Actually, it *hadn't* been her idea, she had just pointed out what Lane was missing. He had made the decision. Linda would be twice as mad and screaming by now if she knew that.

"Yes, I did. And I still do," she said, keeping her voice even and low, her words short and to the point.

"What makes you think that by going *back* to the house he *suffered* so much in to *write an autobiography* about all the suffering he had to endure could be *helpful*?" Linda asked through clenched teeth.

"Why don't we get together and talk about it?" Marilyn asked.

"I can hear you just fine," Linda said.

Marilyn sighed silently again and shook her head in frustration. If it weren't for Lane, she would hang-up now and Linda could take her paranoid behavior elsewhere. She cared for him and didn't want to see his adopted parents screw things up anymore than they had to.

"I know that it is hard for you to understand, but the human mind and body is very complex."

"*Oh?*"

Marilyn backed off and let the silence build. "I would much rather meet with you, if you don't mind. We could get together over a late lunch. I've not eaten yet, have you?" she finally asked, still hoping for a face to face.

"No, Marilyn, I don't want to meet with you. I've already had my lunch. Now, are you going to answer my question or should I call Doctor Litchfield at the State Psychiatric Board and tell him what you are doing to Lane?"

"Linda, Lane called me. I didn't call him. Further, I'm not *doing* anything to him. He called me for advice and I gave it to him. That's all. If you're having trouble with the decision Lane has made, you need to discuss it with *him*. In fact, why don't we all get together and discuss it?" She knew Linda would never do it and would do her best to keep this conversation away from Lane. She had obviously gotten rid of Henry because she couldn't hear his usual grumbling in the background.

"I know he called you. That's why I'm calling," Linda said, her confidence growing. Maybe she would finally be able to win one over the hippy. "To find out why you are encouraging him with this crazy idea."

"Linda, it's not a crazy idea."

"Well, it certainly sounds like it to me! Why in the world would you think that this could possibly be good for him? You're the one who's the psychologist and suppose to know everything about how people think, can't *you* tell me?"

Marilyn shook her head. She was tempted to tell Linda to go ahead and call Doctor Litchfield and tell him all she wanted to. Stan would catch on right away. They had been friends for over twenty years and trusted each other completely. Besides the fact that there were no longer any legal requirements binding her to Lane or to his adoptive parents. Her work had been completed with the case several years ago; the legal system had been satisfied. Now, she and Lane were no more than friends. She wanted to see him continue to grow, and to help him when he needed her.

"Linda, I will do my best to do so, Okay?"

"That's all I want."

"Lane has to come to terms with what he did in that house and, more specifically, *why* he did it. Was it for his sister? Was it for his mother? Was it for himself? I don't know. I can only speculate that it was for all of those reasons, and perhaps something more that we will never know," she said, pausing for Linda to begin razing anew. She didn't respond.

"In all the years I've know Lane and worked with him and treated him, he has never given one specific reason why. Lane, Kristy and their mother, while she was alive, suffered terrible abuses by his father, but is that reason enough? To actually take a life; pull the trigger? I don't know, Linda, I just don't know. And I think that Lane is trying to come to a final understanding with that question. Do you know what happened to his sister, Kristy?"

"No," Linda said, not really having expected to get the answers she was getting.

"I'm violating about 16 court orders and my patient confidentiality by telling you this, so if you repeat it I will deny we ever spoke. Understand?"

"Yes," Linda said, in a quiet whisper.

"The trauma of losing her mother had been severe. Lane told me that she would do nothing but sit in her room. He had to bring her meals and encourage her to eat.

After about a month she slowly came out of it; started back to school and was doing her best to deal with the situation. Duane didn't care one

way or the other if they went to school or not, Lane told me. He just
wanted them out of the way when he was home. If they were around he
would start in on them. Since he was home all weekend, and they had
no where to go, didn't have anyone they could trust, they stayed in their
rooms and hoped that he would get drunk enough to pass out before he
found them.

"Most of the time he would drink himself to unconsciousness. The
times he didn't, he would beat them. You've seen Lanes scars. After several months of beatings, he changed tactics. He would beat Lane into
leaving the room, or into a stupor and began molesting Kristy. She
became pregnant."

Linda let go a small, involuntary gasp, horrified at the thought. She
had known of the beatings, everyone did. During the trial it had come
out that his sister had been molested. But there was no mention of her
being pregnant.

"Why didn't it come out in the trial?" Linda asked meekly, forgetting
her anger.

"Because nobody knew at the time. Lane didn't tell because Kristy
asked him not to."

"Oh God, that's so...so..."

"Yes, it is. But that's not the worst part. She killed herself when she
was four month pregnant and beginning to show."

"I never knew," Linda quietly said, gasping silently, clutching at her
mouth. "Why didn't I ever *know*?" she asked, more to herself than to
Marilyn.

"Because she was a minor and Lane never wanted it revealed."

Linda remembered Kristy from the trial. She hadn't taken the stand
in Lane's defense and only made one appearance in the courtroom. Her
testimony was given to another state assigned psychologist. The psychologist had taken the stand for her and described his views as to the
extent of the abuse for the benefit of those involved.

The one time she had made an appearance was at the sentencing. Lane had sat with her at the defense table and was consoling her, keeping his arm around her most of the time. Linda remembered her as being a rather dumpy child, with ill-kept medium length black hair. She had worn a blue dress with a matching top covered in brightly colored bows. Linda didn't remember seeing her speak, or smile or relate to anyone other than Lane.

"We still don't know how she did it, but she managed to find several bottles of pills and took them. Lane found her the next morning."

"Oh my...Oh my."

"They were both in the custody of the state at the time. I think you can understand why nobody ever knew what happened to Kristy."

"But Lane always told us she was living with their aunt somewhere?"

"Can you blame him?"

Linda couldn't. Even if it was a lie, there was more than enough reason for him to tell it.

"No. No, I can't," she said, trying to digest all the newfound information. "I suppose there really isn't an aunt anyhow," Linda said, more to herself.

"Not that I am aware of."

"I feel so awful. We always asked about her. But we never pushed it, you understand? Maybe we should have...asked more often. He would tell us things that she was doing, up there in Indiana, or Ohio, wherever she is, or was, I mean isn't. Well, I—. Why would he lie to us about it? I don't understand *why*? I mean, we never really wanted to push him that much, but I just don't understand."

"Because he would have to tell you the whole story. She was pregnant. By her father, Lane's father and she asked Lane not to tell. And so he hasn't told anyone other than me. And only after the years of therapy did he trust me enough to tell me the whole story. Of course, I knew from the autopsy that she was pregnant. But I didn't tell Lane. Kristy getting pregnant was the proverbial straw that broke the camel's back. For whatever reason, Lane had decided for them that they had both had enough and ended it the only way he knew how."

"We used to ask him to bring her down for a visit. He said he would mention it to her, but then we would never hear anything. Henry said not to press it, and I didn't. We just never knew," Linda said, remembering and not liking the feelings it gave her now. She felt guilty, as if she had violated Lane in some way.

"Linda, you understand the need to keep this conversation between us? Besides the legal ramifications, there is what I consider to be the more important factor of Lane not finding out."

"Oh yes, completely. I won't say a word. I just feel so awful having asked him about her all these years."

Marilyn felt confident she could trust her and hoped that her show of confidence in Linda's ability would help to create a warmer relationship between the two of them. Linda would tell Henry, she had no doubt, but it would go no further.

Though she had given up her patient confidentiality, it was for the greater good of all involved. Henry and Linda would have a better understanding of Marilyn's motivation and a little more insight into Lane's world.

"Well, you couldn't have helped but to ask. As far as Lane is concerned, it's resolved."

"Yes, but it still worries me."

"Linda, Lane still has to come to a point of finality with the situation. There is no better way to do that than to face if head on. To take it apart piece by piece, moment by moment, emotion by emotion and study those individual aspects for himself. He needs to be able to reach a point of resolution with this. He may never be able to do so but that he is trying says a lot about his mental state. All we can do to support him is to be there and hold his hand the best we can. We can't point it out for him. He has to find it himself."

"I understand," Linda said.

"I'm glad to hear that. He needs your support in this decision. He hasn't mentioned anything in particular, but I think that he is having a harder time with this move than he wants to admit."

"But doesn't that mean that he shouldn't do it?"

She had lost the hard edge in her voice. The question was honest and asked in a tone of wanting to understand instead of wanting to disrupt.

"No, not with this situation. It just means that he is striving to reach a point of finality. He hasn't had to deal with the situation in many years. Of course it will be hard at times, but the end result will be a positive, empowering experience."

"Oh," was all Linda said.

"Has he begun plans for repairing the house?" Marilyn asked, purposefully changing the subject.

"I'm not sure, he didn't say anything about it. I suppose he'll have to do something," Linda finished, lost in the confusion of thoughts the newfound information had brought.

"Yes, I suppose so," Marilyn said.

A comfortable silence set in. There really wasn't anything more to say. Linda wasn't going to invite Marilyn over for dinner and a game of cards, and they both knew that their relationship would never be anything more than mutual respect, if not just tolerance, for each other. The gap in belief systems was just too great.

"Do you understand now why I feel it is a good idea for him to pursue it?"

"Yes. Yes, I think I do."

"Good. I'm so glad that you called and we had this chance to speak."

"I am too. I hope you understand that I'm just trying to help Lane," Linda said.

"I do, Linda. You and Henry have been tremendously supportive of him and I know that you will continue to be."

They finished their good-bye, both promising to keep the other informed.

*   *   *

Blake had given up his attempts to convince anyone about the…the *thing* in the snake pond. They told him that Tim must have gotten his foot caught between a crack in the maze of debris that was the creek bottom and drowned. That his struggle to free himself may have *looked* like he was being dragged under the water by something. When Blake protested and told them the monster had grabbed him, that *he* had actually felt hands quickly twisting around *his* ankles—even had the bruises to prove it—they calmly told him the same thing. The slick, rough rocks and branches may have *felt* as if he was being grabbed, but he really hadn't been, after all.

The policeman that had spoken with him explained that they were going to drain the pond and see if there was anything in it. Blake didn't think that that would do any good. The monster would just hide, or go away. When they reported back to his mother that the pond was empty, he wasn't surprised. He would have to be careful of where he went, because he knew it was out there, and now he had a good idea of where it slept.

Their minister just *happened* to drop by for a visit and his Mom just *happened* to leave them alone in the living room. Taking *way* to long to get the drinks she said she was going after. Blake fidgeted and listened to the man. He'd never been very comfortable with church. He told Blake a lot about life and death and Heaven. Blake had a hard time understanding what he was being told. It all seemed just a little too neat a package. Almost as if it was easier to believe what he was saying instead of the reality behind the apparent façade. Besides, the minister hadn't been in the pond with him. And he hadn't been in the house with him either. Blake didn't think that the preacher understood the whole picture.

He'd listened politely, nodded in all the right places, said all the right things, and looked appropriately fearful when he'd talked of Hell and damnation. He thanked his mother for the drinks, patted Blake on the head then left.

"Did you have a good talk with Mr. Kybett?" his mother had asked, closing the door behind the minister.

"Sure."

"Do you feel better?"

"No, but I think that Mr. Kybett does."

That had earned him a full hour of "quiet time" to "think about what he'd said." He didn't mind it though; it was nice to be alone with his thoughts.

Later, by way of apologizing for the quiet time, they went out for ice cream at the Ice Cream King. She was trying her best to keep up a happy front for the both of them, but wasn't doing a very good job. Blake knew that Tim was being buried today, but didn't want to attend the funeral anymore than his mother wanted to. He'd been there for the real thing, and that was enough for now, thank you very much.

When they returned, ice creams in tow, they settled at the breakfast table in the kitchen.

"Aren't you hungry?" she asked for the umpteenth time as he poked and prodded his hot fudge sundae.

"No, not really. I think I'll save it for later."

He went to the freezer and placed the barely touched sundae in it.

"Do you want to talk about it?"

"No."

"Are you thinking about your Dad?"

He winced. He had been watching her face as she asked this and could see the pain he felt in it. Though his pain was always there, in the same spot, he hadn't gotten used to it. Not yet. Probably not ever.

"What was his funeral like?"

"He was cremated. Do you know what that means?"

"Yeah."

"Yes," she corrected out of habit.

"*Yes*," Blake responded, equally out of habit.

"There wasn't a viewing."

"Oh."

"Honey, I know how you feel about everything and I've done my best to tell the police what you saw. They just don't believe it. But I do," she said, laying down her spoon. There was nothing left of her banana split, except for the dredges of sweet chocolate and melted ice cream. He knew that if he left the room she would begin to pick at the remains, even lick the plastic tub clean. But she would never do it in front of him. It was bad manners.

"You do?" he asked without much belief.

"Yes. I do. If you say you saw a monster, then I believe you."

He could tell that she did, even though she believed that the monster was in his imagination. He could tell from the way she didn't look him in the eye when she said it. But she hadn't been there, so he couldn't expect her to think differently.

"Thanks, Mom. I think I'm gonna go change."

"Going to go change."

"Yeah, *going* to go."

He turned to leave the kitchen and she called him back.

"Can I get a hug?"

"Sure."

He hugged her and kissed her cheek.

"Let me know if you want to talk some more. All right?"

"Sure."

He left her in the kitchen to finish off the ice cream in private and for the sanctuary of his room. He quickly took off his church clothes and hung them neatly in the closet. Then he dressed in his favorite jeans, the baggy ones and a Burkett University T-shirt that his Dad had given him.

He lay on his bed and watched his dad's model airplanes hanging by threads attached to the ceiling. They slowly turned and twisted in their captive sky. He'd kept them together as best he could, touching up the paint, gluing on bits and pieces that fell off over the years. He could feel his dad was up there, looking down on him from one of the cockpits, watching, waiting, ready to take control if a thread broke.

Closing his eyes he slipped into a familiar fantasy. His dad was at the controls and Blake was riding shotgun in the cockpit of a jet. Side by side they flew, the ground a distant mosaic of blue, green, concrete gray, dirt brown, clouds flying by, the sky opening and closing around them. A spin just for shits and giggles, nosing up and hitting the afterburners, punching through into a darkening sky, diving back down to the earth, pulling out just off the wave crests of a rough sea. A distant voice in the headset calling off distances, altitudes, headings, weather reports. His dad laughing, offering up a high-five after they cruised through Mach One, the jet bucking then smoothing out.

The sky darkened, a thick boiling mass of clouds towering in front of them. Blake moaned and twitched where he lay asleep on his bed, his eyes squeezing tight, his hands becoming fists. He looked over at his dad, a patch on his shoulder said, "Captain Stephen Morrow, Angel First Class," his face was calm, collected, but he was no longer smiling. The plane pulled hard to the left and the storm clouds moved with them. He pulled again to the left and the clouds were closer.

"*Morrow, Morrow, pull around to heading One Eight Five! Repeat! Heading One Eight Five!*" shouted through the headset. The jet banked hard right, their speed increasing, decreasing, the plane fighting the edge of the storm as they searched for a way out.

"*Heading Two Three Zero! Heading Two Three Zero! You've got a wind shear condition one mile ahead! Repeat! Wind shear one mile ahead!*" The plane pulled back around again, the engines whining from the strain, G-forces crunching them down in their seats.

"We're going down, Blake! We're going down! You have to take control! Grab the stick!" Stephen shouted above the roar as he let go of the control wheel.

Blake reached out and felt the cold, black plastic of the wheel in his hands. He gripped it tightly, felt the power of the plane through it and the calm terror in his heart settle to a dull, screaming roar. Red and amber lights flashed across the instrument panel, a buzzer was sounding, a mechanized voice was repeating, *"Pull up, pull up, pull up."*

"Just keep it level, you'll do fine!" his dad shouted. Unbuckling from the pilots seat he stood stooped over in the cockpit.

"I love you very much! Don't ever forget that!" he shouted in his ear. A fierce, sharp wind thick with the darkness of the coming storm cut through the cockpit and stung his face, and then his dad was gone and he was left alone in the cockpit, flying into the heart of the dark clouds.

"Bail out! Bail out! Bail out! Bail out! Bail out!" shouted the voice in the headset, the wind whipped through the cockpit, but Blake held the plane level and pointed the nose straight into the storm. A thick, heavy hand settled on his shoulder.

"Your *Daddy* forgot these," the voice choked out through its ripped, violated face. He could smell the rotten-death of the monster and felt its hot maggot-thick breath on his neck despite the roar of the wind. It held out a brown quart sized medicine bottle filled with blue triangle shaped pills. He could read the prescription on the bottle. *"For pussycide. Take entire bottle one time. No refills. Dr. Duane Trammel White."*

His eyes banged open and he rolled off his bed, a thick sheen of sweat covering his body, a chill setting in. He stood up in his room and tried to catch his breath, the dream still strong on him. Who was Duane Trammel White? The monster? Yeah, but the name didn't matter. The name was something that the monster no longer remembered, no longer was. His father. The blue pills. Pussycide. The monster had killed his dad. Killed him? No, not killed him but somehow caused him to commit pussycide. Tim the monster had outright killed.

His mom was coming down the hallway. She didn't stop at his door but continued down the hall to her bedroom. After putting his sneakers back on he went down the hall to his mom's room.

"Mom?" he asked, knocking lightly on her door.

"Yes, honey?" she said, her voice was muffled and echoing. It sounded like she was in her bathroom.

"I'm going out back for awhile and maybe for a ride."

"*What?*"

"I'M GOING OUT BACK AND FOR A BIKE RIDE!"

"Just a minute," she called back.

He waited by the closed door. The toilet flushed in her bathroom and he could hear her heavy steps coming to the door.

"What did you say?" she asked, as she opened the door, hoping that he wanted to talk.

"I'm gonna go for a bike ride."

"Are you sure? Don't you want to stay here? You could play in the backyard on the swing?" she said, hoping that he would stay near the house.

"I feel like riding around."

"Well, Okay. Just stay on our street. All right?"

"Yeah, Okay."

"Are you feeling sick, honey? You don't look well."

"No. I just got up from a nap, that's all."

"Oh. Well, Okay."

Since all the streets were connected, that sort of made his street all the streets, Blake calculated as he punched the button for the garage door opener. He jumped on his bike and rode onto the driveway. It was only two-thirty in the afternoon. The day was warm and almost hot. The air didn't seem to be moving. Warmth radiated up from the driveway pavement in small waves he could feel caressing his face.

He rode quickly down Arapaho and cut through the alley next to the Chim's house, peddled across the drainage ditch he and Tim had ridden through just a few days ago, then rode slowly down Cherokee Place.

The Stein's shed made a great hideout. Mr. Stein was a million years old and hardly ever came outside. Mrs. Stein was even older and Blake hadn't seen her in a long time. He could easily park his bike in the back of the shed and watch the house from around the corner without being seen. He rode up the Steins' driveway, across the side yard to the back of the shed and slipped off his bike.

He was sweating from the effort the ride had taken and from the excitement. He slowly walked down the side of the shed and stood in the shadow of the eve, watching the house. Even from across the street Blake could feel the presence of the monster. The house seemed to be alive with the darkness the monster brought with it. A distant voice was telling him to bail out. He rubbed his face where the wind had bit into him in the dream.

A car turned onto Cherokee Place and slowly drove down the street. It parked in front of the house and a man got out and walked up the lawn. He had black hair and was what his Mother called stout. He walked up the lawn and stopped half way to the house then stood looking at it. Blake could feel the monsters' excitement build as the man began walking again up the lawn to the porch. He stood, silently staring at the door. After a moment, he dug around in his front pockets and pulled out a key ring, unlocked the door and pushed it open. Blake could hear the monster sigh with pleasure as the door opened. The man stood at the door, and then stepped inside.

Blake waited, tense and fearful for the screaming he was sure would soon follow, as the monster began to break up the man. He began to breathe again not realizing that he had been holding his breath. Maybe it had choked him and was at this very moment eating his heart? He sat down in the tall weeds next to the shed and watched eyes wide and alert.

Five minutes later he was picking up his bike and riding out into the street. He was just going to take a quick glance in the windows on the way by, just to make sure the man was still in there. The thought that he would see the monster, covered in blood, gnawing on the guy's bones stopped him from riding on the side of the street the house sat on.

Coasting down the Stein's driveway he slowly peddled into the middle of the street and, as casually as he could, peered at the house. He could see the silhouette of the man standing in the back of the living room. He rode slowly past three houses, and then turned back toward the Stein's. The man was still standing where he had been before and didn't seem to be in any trouble. Blake rode back to the shed dumped his bike then sat in the shade to watch.

The monster couldn't get him here. It liked dark places where people couldn't see it. It was scared to come out into the open. He didn't know how he knew it, but he did. His father used to call it having a hunch. He had one now and didn't doubt it.

The man with the dark hair came out of the house, locked the door then drove away. Blake got back on his bike and road into the street, watching the house.

The monster was still dangerous, of that he was sure. But now that he was beginning to understand its rules, he wasn't afraid. It was there now, watching him. It wasn't there when the man was in the house, but now it was back. He stood his ground and closely watched the windows of the house. There was a crack in the board that had been put over the broken window he'd fallen through. He scratched at the scab on his knee. He felt the monster watching him through the crack, felt it reaching out to him to come on down and take a twirl on the dance floor of *its* life.

Then it was gone. With a sudden surge of confidence that it had backed down, he stuck his middle finger up in the air at the house then rode away. He rode back through the drainage ditch and thought about Tim. Looking down the creek he and Tim had ridden through gave him

the creeps. He wondered if Tim was cold and if the monster had followed him after he had died. He didn't think so. The monster was from
a different place.

The car was gone when he got home. His mom had left a note on the
refrigerator that she had gone to church and that he could fix himself
some potpies for dinner. Glad for the time to spend alone, he quickly
put two chicken potpies in the oven, then took a quick shower and
changed his clothes.

He sat at his desk and carefully began to reconstruct the event of the
day on the pages of a spiral bound pad. He wrote slowly, carefully printing the words, remembering the dream and writing down what happened at the house.

Satisfied with his scouting report for the day, he checked on the potpies, set the timer for another ten minutes, and then sat at the kitchen
table. He turned back to his notebook and wrote at the top of the next
page in thick, bold letters, ATTACK, then began to make his war plans.

FOUR

...7

If the sun had actually moved, it was hard to tell. The shadows the trees cast seemed to be growing shorter. He wondered if the lush scene across the lake would disappear the moment he drug himself onto the bank.

He hoped not.

Shivering from the cold he steeled himself to plunge fully into the brackish water and make the swim for the other shore. Thirty feet in front of him something broke the surface of the lake, creating a wake as big as a small boat. Some large thing was moving under there. Some very big, large...thing. He froze and stared at the small waves washing toward him from Its passing.

The following Wednesday was a typical March day. It was cool not quite cold and raining lightly. The water, gas and electric had all been turned on. The electric guy had just left, shaking his head in wonder.

"You ain't gonna do nuthin' to it?" he'd asked through tobacco stained teeth.

"No, not yet anyhow," Lane answered, thinking it sure did sound like a sane question. Was this what he wanted to do?

"Well, I guess it's yer' house," he'd stated, then left, leaving no doubt as to his true feelings on the matter.

He moved slowly, tentatively, but not fearfully. For some reason he found himself trying to remember what the house had been like so many years ago and found he was having a hard time doing it. He could feel the house, though. He may have changed but the house hadn't. He could feel the old anger, confusion and pain vibrating around him. Standing where he was it didn't seem that old, and it still felt just as painful.

He found himself standing in the doorway of what had been his father's room, yet would now be his office. The wood was darker where the bed had been, and the same dank, musty curtains still hung loosely around the window. The air in the room was old and he found he had to force himself to stand in the doorway. Marilyn's little instructions and encouragement flickered through his thoughts, overlaid with the mantra.

Today is a new day, today is a new day, today is a new day.

The irony of writing the autobiography in the room that it had happened in was almost perfect. He smiled and let the vision of book deals, interviews and success play out again in his thoughts.

'How could you do that?' they would ask. 'In the very room where it happened?'

What would he say? He didn't know. But something would come out. Something if not particularly wise, at least authored would flow from his vocal chords and the public would eat it up.

Then the fiction books would begin to flow. No splash in the pan, one hit wonder would Lane White be. No sir. One after another they would come, like a mill slicing lumber, they would be written and stacked in thousands of bookstores as his reading audience grew. He watched the fantasy of his future play out in his mind. He surveyed the space in which his past had been so fucked up and in which his plush, lucrative future would unfold.

He stepped across the hallway to what had been his bedroom. Three cardboard boxes were sitting on the dusty floor. Two were about two foot square and the third was slightly larger. Stuck with clear tape to the large box was a note from Henry and Linda. Lane recognized Linda's handwriting before he could read what was written.

Surprise! We thought you could use this for the autobiography! We love you!

He carefully inspected the boxes and wasn't surprised to see the familiar Hubbard Electronics logo on them. The larger box contained a Hubbard DX-II Laser printer. The other two contained a CPU, keyboard and a color monitor, according to the labels on the boxes.

It was the gift they had been trying to give him for years and he had been denying it just as long. The poetic aspects of his typewriter not withstanding, he knew on a practical level that it would make the work much easier and faster to complete. The quicker he could complete the autobiography, the sooner he would publish. He let the vision of his future begin to roll again.

Torn between wanting to get the computer set-up and going home to work on the autobiography, he chose the autobiography. He turned out the few lights that were on and double checked the pilot lights on the aging hot water heater and stove.

After checking the doors and windows were locked as well as they could be he left the house. He marveled at how fresh the air was outside the house. He would have to remember to crawl under the house and drag out whatever it was that had died. It was not something he was looking forward to doing.

*   *   *

He took the day off Friday to finish packing for the move. Henry and Linda came over to help out. Despite Linda's protests, Henry hired a moving company to come by Saturday morning and finish the job. Lane was relieved when they finally left late Friday night. He was tired of fending off Linda's attempts to "take a peek" at the autobiography.

The movers showed up at nine the following morning. Lane had been pushing around his notes and worrying the boxes waiting for them. Once the loading was complete he stopped at the apartment complex office and dropped off the keys and a forwarding address. With the moving truck following behind, he drove over to the house.

He parked in the street in front of the house then stood on the porch watching the mover's back the truck into the drive. A small sprout of panic began to grow in the base of his neck. He slammed it immediately with the mantra—*Today is a new day, today is a new day, today is a new day.* Marilyn had thought this was a good—no *great*—idea. By confronting the past he would not only be helping himself, but many other people as well. He tried to fill his thoughts with images of the effect that reading the bio would have on others; trying to stick with positive ones. Would they then be able to go back to their lives and confront their own memories, dark or otherwise? He didn't know and didn't really care at this point. Writing the autobiography was for him as an individual and as a writer. Not as an exercise on how to get your shit together and get on down the road.

Though Marilyn had made that point, it didn't seem to matter that much. Standing in the kitchen that was exactly as it had been when he was a kid made him feel dizzy and the rest seemed to matter very little. Marilyn had had a cleaning crew over that had gone through the entire house. They'd even found whatever had been slowly rotting away and smelling up the house. The floors were still marred and stained, the walls in need of paint and patches, the linoleum yellowed and peeling, it was now just all *clean* stains, spots and peelings. She'd left a note on the refrigerator that they would be by later that evening and would be bringing dinner.

After the movers left he cranked the new window air conditioning unit down a couple of notches. It was much quieter than the old rattling unit that would freeze up in the middle of the night, leaving you in a fuzzy heat for a couple of hours until it thawed. He went back to his father's old room, now his office, and began to unload boxes. He'd had the movers put his desk on the back wall so that the one window in the room was on his right as he wrote. He went back to his old room for the computer boxes and suddenly smelled the rotten stench that he had the first day. It wasn't that strong, but it was enough to drive him out of the house soon if he didn't find the source.

He went through the house and garage, vainly hoping it would be this easy, then ended up at the basement door in the kitchen. He opened the door on the same dimly lighted, musty smelling basement that he remembered. It hadn't changed in all the years he'd been gone. The maze of old pipes clinging to the ceiling of the basement, looking like the web of some gigantic, metal-spinning spider ready to catch you across the head if you didn't duck at all the right places. The loose mortar in the brick foundation dropped a steady stream of dust and the occasional chunk of brick or concrete onto the floor. It was maybe sixteen feet across by ten feet deep, and most of that was taken up with the old gas furnace, drainage pipes and the staircase that led down to it.

Before he had the door open an inch the smell nearly knocked him unconscious. It was the smell of some hapless coyote killed by a car and left by the road for a week in high summer; the smell of an elephant of a road kill splattered a mile or more. It made his eyes water and he began to gag on the thick stench trying to crawl down his throat.

He remembered the time he had gone fishing on an outing from the hospital. They had caught twenty or thirty small perch and cut them up for catfish bait, storing them in glass mason jars, the lids screwed down tight. The jars had sat in the hot sun for another hour or so until they were ready to fish for cats. When he had opened the jar, he'd thrown up from the smell. That same heavy stench now choked him as he stood, holding the door open.

Pulling his shirt up over his nose, he pulled the door fully open until he could see into the basement. The same rickety stairs led down to the dusty floor. Cobwebs ran across the stairway in thick, dusty trails, light from the small, mesh covered basement window lighting them from behind. The basement looked as if it hadn't been entered in a hundred years. The steps were covered with a thick layer of dust.

Standing in the doorway, choking on the stench, he tentatively reached out his foot and tested the first step. The wood was solid underneath the dust. He tapped it a few times to make sure. A small, ineffective puff of dust rose from the step. The cobwebs shimmered in the slight breeze that was created by the opening door. The stench became stronger. He let his shirt drop from his face, as it didn't seem to be making any difference and decided against venturing any further. Closing the door, he then went to the kitchen window above the sink and opened it.

The odor vanished with the closing of the basement door. He could smell nothing but fresh air. There was no scent of the putrid essence that had only moments before assailed him.

"Must have blown out already," he said to the empty house.

Standing in the kitchen and looking at the basement door, he tried to rationalize the situation. Marilyn had always told him that some things were not always as they seemed. The mind was a powerful machine that could so some amazing, inexplicable things. With that thought he went back to the basement door and slowly opened it just a little, his shirt in hand to bring back up to his nose.

There was no smell. Letting go of his shirt, he slowly descended the stairs. They creaked and wobbled, threatening at any moment to give way and send their host tumbling down to the cement floor as they once had. At the base of the stairs he stopped and surveyed the basement. Nothing had changed since he'd hidden down here twenty-plus years ago.

Breathing deeply through his nose, he smelled nothing but the usual musty odor and dust of an old, unused house. He went back upstairs to his new office.

*   *   *

Brenda Morrow stood at the edge of the front porch, looking anxiously up the street in the direction Blake would be coming from any moment. She hoped. It was nearly dark. Blake was always home by dark. He had been staying out late every day and it seemed she was spending more and more time on the porch waiting for him.

She'd been struggling with the idea of getting some kind of counseling for him. After Stephen had died, they both had gone to a therapist for several weeks, but it hadn't seemed to help either of them very much. The guilt she was carrying would always be there. She had pushed Stephen too hard.

Can't you ask Mr. Dill for another raise? It should be time now, shouldn't it? Brenda had always thought that their financial struggles would all be solved if only Mr. Dill would come forth with the raise Stephen always seemed to be due.

When the raise would finally come through, it never seemed to go as far as she thought it would. A year would pass, and then she would be after him again. *Can't you put in more overtime? Isn't it time for another raise?* On and on it would go.

Movement in the street caught her eye and she quickly squinted at it, hoping to see Blake. She had lost her glasses the day before. It was only a stray dog, a mangy looking little mutt that was sniffing along the lawns.

She went back inside and poured herself a large glass of grape punch. If it became fully dark and he wasn't home, she would call the police, officer so and so that had helped them when Tim had drowned. She began to rummage in the clutter of papers and junk by the phone for his card when she heard Blake slam down his bike in the garage and, seconds later, burst through the side door.

"*Where* have you been? Do you know that I was getting ready to call the police?" she said, trying to sound stern and forceful. Her relief at seeing him was tempering it.

"Sorry. I got busy and didn't know it was so late," he said, brushing by her side and walking toward his room. He didn't think that he'd make it far, but it was worth a try.

"Sorry? Is that all I get for being so worried about you? *Sorry?*" she said, wiping grape punch from her mouth with a dirty napkin she picked from the cluttered table.

"Well…" Blake said, looking at her blankly.

"I think we need to talk about what you've been so busy with. Come here and sit down."

"Oh, Mom. It's nothing. I'm just out doing some stuff for school," he said, hoping he could follow it up with something that made sense.

"School?"

"Yeah. I've been working on a science project for Mr. Brickman's class," he said, getting himself in deeper than he had wanted. He just hoped that she didn't ask to see any paper from Mr. Brickman.

"Oh," she said, sipping her punch and wiping her mouth.

"Well, let's talk about it," she said, brightening.

"It's nothing."

"Blake, Honey, let's talk about it, Okay? I don't want to argue with you. I'm just worried that you may be working too hard, that's all."

"Let me put my pack up," he said, beginning to move toward his room.

"No, just lay it by the couch and come sit down," she said, motioning to a chair at the table. She watched as he slung his pack to the floor and walked to the chair. He looked tired. No, he looked exhausted. His eyes were puffy and underscored with dark smudges, and his pants seemed to be fitting a little loose. She could tell he wasn't eating right. Even though he may be a little heavy, he still had to eat to keep up his strength.

He sat heavily in the chair and looked at his feet.

"Do you want some punch? It's your favorite, Grape."

"No."

She took another sip from her plastic cup and wiped her mouth with the same dirty napkin.

"Honey, are you feeling all right? You look a little tired. Do you feel sick?"

"No," he said, staring at his feet. There wasn't any need to explain everything to her. She hadn't believed him before, why should she now?

"Let me feel your head."

He leaned forward and allowed her to place a thick, chubby hand on his head.

"Well, you don't feel hot."

"I'm fine."

She sipped some more from her cup and looked at him, trying to decide what to say.

"Tell me about this science project."

He stopped shuffling his feet and looked up at her, jockeying for time.

"Well, it's about watching people," he stumbled forward in the growing lie. If he kept it close to the truth, it might not be that bad, he thought.

"Oh?"

"Yeah. We're just supposed to *observe* as many different people as we can and write down what they are doing. The time of day, stuff like that."

"This is going to be your science project, watching people?"

He paused long enough to be suspicious, but not to be caught.

"Yeah, sorta'. You know how on nature shows they have were these people are watching animals and figuring out all that stuff. Mr. Brickman says that since I can't go to Africa I can start here, with the human animal." He looked up, amazed at his own story. It sounded good. Really good. He wondered if it was too much. He tried to look calm and plaintive about it and waited for her to say something.

"So that's what you've been doing? Watching people?" she said, suddenly relieved that it was just her son's determination to do well in school and not smoking and running around with bad kids that had kept him away from home.

"Yeah," Blake said, now completely confident in the lie.

She sipped the last of the purple drink and watched him, wondering if he was telling the truth and then wondering *why* she wondered if he was telling the truth. He had never lied to her or Stephen. They always tried to maintain an open and honest relationship with him and it seemed to work.

"You're not spying on them, are you?"

"Oh, no," he said, doing his best to muster a *gee whiz Mom* look on his face. "It's nothing like that. I've been sitting down at the Quick Mart most of the time, just watching people and taking notes about what they do." He caught the slip up too late. If she asked to see his notes he didn't know what he would do.

"Like what?"

"Just stuff. Mr. Brickman said to pretend like you were in Africa and that the people were like, you know, the animals. I just write down what they're doing," he said, silently praying she wouldn't ask to see the notes.

"Well, Okay. Just take it easy and don't over do it. I don't want you staying out late. If it happens again…," she said, letting him think up his own punishment for being tardy.

"Thanks, Mom," he said, standing and hugging her.

She watched as he grabbed his pack and quickly walked down the hall to his room. If Hubbard hadn't come though with Stephen's benefit package she would have to be working now. Insurance companies, she'd found, didn't think very highly of suicides. Stephen's lawyer, somebody Blankenship, was still fighting them. He called periodically to give her an update. It wasn't costing her anything, unless by some miracle he got them to settle, then it would cost her thirty percent.

For now, she had Stephen's retirement for her and Blake to live on and it was more than enough. She couldn't imagine working. Leaving Blake alone all day during the summer and to come home to an empty house during the school year. She stood from the table, got a quart of Strawberry Ice Cream from the freezer, and then slumped on the sofa in the living room. Using the remote control she clicked on the television.

Blake quickly showered then returned to his room. Hearing the television on he knew that he'd pulled off the story for the time being. He didn't feel any better about it but knew that for now it had to do. He settled down at his desk and began the now familiar process of reviewing his notes. It was a heavy exercise for an eleven-year-old but he'd set a goal for himself and he wanted—*had*—to see it through.

Carefully thumbing through the pages, he quickly scanned over the past weeks activity. There really wasn't much there, only the comings and goings of the man and Blake's eleven-year-old thoughts on the matter. The highlight of the week was when he'd felt the monster leave the house. In a moment of bravado brought on by so much sitting he'd ridden up to the house and gone up on the porch to peer in the window. It looked like he'd remembered it the night he'd broken in. He'd gone to the back yard and looked around, adrenaline pumping to be doing this in the bright daylight. He knew the man's schedule by now and knew he wouldn't be back for hours.

There was a small window imbedded with a metal grate at the base of the house. It probably lead to the basement and it had given him an idea. He'd drawn a picture of the backyard at the time so he wouldn't forget what it looked like. His idea wasn't fully formed yet, but he thought if the *house* wasn't there, the *monster* wouldn't have a place to stay and it would leave for good, or be taken away by something else. He had an idea of how to make the house go away, but didn't dare write it down in case his mother somehow stumbled onto his journal.

He smiled to himself, feeling more confident in his plans, and tucked the journal carefully in the bottom of his homework drawer.

*   *   *

He woke to the beating of a drum. No, not a drum, a knocking on a door. Opening his eyes he found himself staring at a pile of boxes, pushing him further into confusion at his surroundings. After a moment of groggy waking, he remembered where he was and quickly began stumbling for the door.

"Did we wake you? I'm sorry. You must be exhausted from the move," Linda said, moving into the house past Lane, her arms full of brown paper bags.

"No, no that's all right. Come on in," Lane said, rubbing his sleep puffed eyes. His face was still stamped with the imprint of the mattress, and his hair stood up at odd angles.

"What time is it?"

"Well, if I could see my watch I'd tell you," Henry said, jiggling the sacks he was balancing.

"Sorry, here let me take some of that," he said, grabbing a few sacks from each of them.

"It's six-thirty," Henry said, twisting his wrist to look at his watch as they all walked to the kitchen. He'd been asleep for almost two hours.

"Didn't you get my note?" Linda asked, beginning to unpack the sacks.

"Yeah. I just laid down for a nap. I guess I was worn out."

"Must be the new mattress," Linda stated, fishing for a thank you.

"Must be," Lane said, kissing her cheek

"You're welcome. Is that where you're going to be sleeping?"

"I'm not sure yet. I haven't had time to think about it much."

"Well, go get cleaned up and Henry and I will start dinner," she said, shooing him away. Henry began to unpack sacks of groceries.

"Go on, Lane," she repeated.

"What is all this?" he asked, really seeing the bags and the shear volume of food that was beginning to spill out onto the cracked, old linoleum kitchen counter.

"We thought you wouldn't have had time to go by the store, so we did a little shopping for you," she said, patting him on the cheek.

"Wasn't my idea," Henry said, winking at Lane.

"Yes, dear."

"Spaghetti and Meatballs, boy-oh-boy!," Henry said, mimicking an excited, hyperactive six year old. Linda pinched his arm and motioned to the bags of groceries.

"Lane, out," she said, pointing out of the kitchen.

He left them both and went to the bathroom to shower. The only difference between this bathroom and the one he had grown up with was this one was clean and smelled of bleach and soap instead of sewer and mildew. The familiar stains by the tub drain and chips in the porcelain were still there. Why he thought they should be gone he wasn't sure.

After showering he dried himself and looked in the mirror above the sink. It was the same mirror and he had a brief flash of the little boy he had been standing on the small, cracked wooden stool as his mother soothed his pain. He broke the chain of thoughts before they could take him much further.

Not bothering to dry his hair, he searched through the boxes piled in the corner of the bathroom for his toothbrush and shaving gear. Finding it, he rummaged some more for his Burkett University sweats that Linda had gotten him when he started his brief stint in college. He quickly dressed, brushed back his wet hair and went back to the kitchen.

"Hi, honey," Linda said, busy with the boiling spaghetti and simmering, thick red sauce on the stovetop.

"Smells great. I guess the stove still works," he said, opening the old stove and peering in at the sizzling golf ball sized meatballs she'd laid out in a deep roasting pan.

"It'll be about ten minutes. You want to find out what Henry's doing in the basement? I've heard some banging around."

He remembered the little shift of though he'd had with the basement. Shift of thought? Yeah, that sounded good. It had simply been a slight shift of his thoughts that caused him to believe he smelled that dank, putrid decay. Just a slight twist of thought. That was all. It hadn't been real, just something his mind made up to relieve some stress. It had been a simple shift, like a daydream.

He realized that the only flaw with that theory was that he could still remember the thick, pungent smell of rotting flesh.

"Are you all right?" Linda asked, spoon in hand, carefully swimming it through the bubbling sauce.

"Yeah, still a little tired. I guess," Lane said, looking at the basement door. "What's he doing in the basement?"

"I don't know, but I wish you would find out. I haven't heard anything down there for awhile."

She went back to her cooking and Lane moved toward the basement door. It was still opened, but only a little. He stood before it and drew in a deep breath through his nose, trying to smell something. The only thing he could smell for sure was the tangy garlic and onion spaghetti sauce, and very faintly, the dusty smell of the damp basement, but that was all.

"Are you sure you're all right, honey?" Linda asked, as she cut slits in the huge loaf of French bread. She paused in her cutting and looked at him.

"Yeah," he said, smiling at her. "I was just thinking about how it used to be...here," he said, looking around the kitchen.

She lay the knife down and turned to him.

"You're not comfortable being here," she stated, placing a hand on his arm.

"No, not at all. Well, maybe a little, but it's nothing to worry about," he told her, adding a little laugh to show her he was indeed fine and dandy.

"I'm just tired from the move, that's all."

She began to speak when Henry began coming up out of the basement, a beer in hand. He smiled at them both as he opened the door all the way and stepped through.

"Yes?" he asked, smiling at them.

"What are you doing?" Linda asked.

"Just poking around," he said, turning to go down the hall to the back rooms.

Linda nudged Lane to follow him and shook her head.

"Hey, what's this?" Henry said to himself as he entered what was going to be Lane's office.

"Lane, come on in here and I'll give you a hand," he called down the hall.

"I'll call you when dinner's ready," Linda said, patting him on the arm and returning to the bread.

"It looks like you need some help getting set up here," Henry said, pulling boxes around, looking for a place to start. They began to work together in a comfortable, known silence.

"How do you like it here so far?" Henry began, then laughed at himself. Lane laughed with him, wondering how many beers he was into.

"Haven't really had much time to adjust, but I'm excited about the project. I think there will be some good things come out of it."

"Good. You sound like you're set on it. I think that's good," he said, pulling open another box. He began to empty the contents onto the floor. Lane had begun to organize the bookshelves. "Well, I'm behind you with this Autobiography idea. I know that Linda is having a hard time with it, but I think you can understand why."

Lane nodded.

"It was her idea, you know, to clean-up the place. She wanted to do a lot more but I managed to talk her out of it. I think I can understand why you wanted to leave it the way it was," he said, taking a long drink of his beer.

"But I would still be glad to do more if you want," he quickly added.

"Thanks for the offer, but I need to leave it the way it was, for the most part, I'm not sure just why, though," he said, smiling and shaking his head. "I just appreciate all you've done for me. I don't know how to thank you enough."

"You already have, Lane. You already have," he said, sipping at his beer. Apparently not wanting or not thinking that the statement needed an explanation. Henry had never been long on words. Linda seemed to be able to handle most of the explaining. Now that Henry was trying to tell Lane something, he wasn't doing a very good job of it.

"What do you mean?" he asked, trying to prime Henry's pump.

"Well, I mean, that, ah…this is very hard for me," he blustered, sipping at his beer again. Lane watched as he drained the last of it.

"This is just between you and me, Okay?"

"Sure," Lane said, leaning against the door jam.

"Not that Linda doesn't know everything I'm going to tell you, well at least most of it. I would just rather you keep this to yourself. It'll save us both a lot of unnecessary trouble."

They could hear Linda busily shuffling around the dishes in the kitchen and setting the small table.

"Sure."

"When we first read about your story in the paper, Linda immediately wanted to help. You didn't have any family left, that the paper mentioned, and we have always tried to share our success with other the best we can. Within reason, of course." He smiled and winked at Lane, beginning to get more comfortable with the situation.

"We've never had any children of our own. I don't know if you know this or not, but it's because of me."

Lane nodded, wondering what had brought Henry to this point.

"I've got a problem with my sperm. I guess I don't have enough of the little guys to get the job done," he said, laughing slightly. Lane smiled with him and tried to look comfortable. It had taken a lot of work for him to be able to share his feelings with Marilyn over the years. But it hadn't gotten any easier. He didn't think that it ever would be.

"Anyhow, we tried everything the Doctors recommended. Shots, pills, boxer shorts, you name it and I tried it. Nothing worked." He shrugged his shoulders and looked at the now empty beer bottle in his hand.

"I was really upset over it all. You know, not being able to become a father. We talked about surgery and implantation in a surrogate, but I never was very interested. It just didn't appeal to me." He twirled the bottle in his hand and looked at it with feigned interest.

"Linda wanted to keep trying. I just got more and more upset over it. After awhile we didn't talk about it anymore. My work at Hubbard started taking off and I guess I was just focusing my anger on my work. Trying to prove that if I couldn't be a father, I sure as hell could make a lot of money. Sounds like a screwy kind of motivation, but it got us where we are today."

"Yeah," Lane said, wanting to say more but not sure just what that should be.

"I guess what I'm trying to say is that I'm proud of you. And that Linda and I feel that you are our son. I've had to learn a lot of things over the years about family some were hard to take. Even though we aren't your biological parents, we both love you as if we were."

He looked up at Lane, his heavily lined face showing the frank honesty of his feelings. Lane realized that this wasn't any easier for Henry to be saying and his own emotions caught him by surprise. He wished that they *were* his biological parents and that his whole past had never happened. But it had and they weren't. He didn't love them both any less for it, though.

"I don't know what I would have done without you," Lane said, trying to keep back the sudden rush of emotions. He couldn't even begin to describe the feelings of being needed and cared for felt like. His mother had cared for him, but her love had been tarnished by the circumstances of her marriage. It hadn't been a full and complete acceptance. She had struggled with her own failings to get herself and her children out of the situation, until it had been too late and her struggles had ended. Then his Dad had bailed out with a little help. Then Kristy had ended her own tormented life. Now here he was, finally making it out of the dark past into a future that was turning out to be a little brighter than he'd have ever thought possible.

Today is a new day, today is a new day, today is a new day.

"Are you two going to come in for dinner or stand there all night?"

His body jerked at the sound of Linda's voice breaking off the mantra. Henry didn't seem to see the involuntary motion.

"Why? The kitchen on fire?" he asked, winking at Lane. Lane noticed his moist eyes.

"Yes, dear. The kitchen is on fire and I thought that you'd both better come up and eat before the fire department gets here."

"We're on our way," he called after her.

"Thanks, Henry," Lane said, clumsily reaching for him. They hugged awkwardly and quickly ended the embrace.

"You're welcome."

Lane turned for the hallway and Henry held him back.

"One more thing."

"Yeah?"

"Finish it. If you can. Just finish it. All right? Get it all behind you and get rid of it. You've got the talent to really make something out of your writing. I mean that," he added as Lane smiled slightly with embarrassment. "Get out there with this autobiography thing…then let it go. I know you can do it."

"Thanks. I'm planning on it working out." It came out sounding a little harsh and quick-mouthed. But Henry just smiled and clapped him on the back—the coach sending in the star player.

The table was set and Linda was dishing out the spaghetti when they made it to the kitchen.

"Looks great," Lane said, sitting at the small table.

"I hope we're stocked up on the Malox," Henry said.

Linda ignored it and they dug in. They ate in silence for a moment, taking the edge off their hunger, twirling spaghetti and munching crisp, buttery French bread.

"How is the autobiography going?" Linda asked between bites.

"Good. It's going very well. I've lain out the chapters and now just have to fill in the blanks."

"When can we see it?" Henry asked.

Over the years he had willingly shown them everything he wrote, the outside input helped him hone his craft. But now, he just didn't think that it would work well that way. The book was a little too close to home for that. He had planned on avoiding this conversation until a little later in the game, when the book was much closer to that magical time of publication. He didn't expect them to ask so soon.

"I'm not sure. I've still got a long way to go. I'll let you know," he said, brushing the topic aside with as much tact as he could. They didn't question him any further, though Linda wasn't hiding her feelings very well on the subject. She glanced at Henry, urging him with her eyes to continue pushing the subject, but he either failed to notice the plug or was faking it.

"Besides, with that new computer in there I won't need you to correct my spelling." He smiled at Linda and took another big bite of spaghetti. She smiled back, still wanting to see the book.

"Oh, you found that, huh?" Henry said, working with Lane to get Linda off seeing the book. After their talk in the back they both felt a renewed sense of kinship. Linda went back to her meal and said no more on the topic.

"Did you get a chance to look at it?"

"No, I was hoping that you would be able to help me get it up and running. If it's here, I may as well use it. No use putting off the technology any longer."

They finished the meal in relative silence. Linda contributing with the occasional yes or no or small comment. It was obvious that she felt a sense of exclusion from Lane. As if he had now grown to the point where he no longer needed her.

The meal finished, they all cleared the table and began cleaning the kitchen.

"Why don't you get that computer out and we'll get it together," Henry said.

"Sure," Lane said, getting the hint. He went to the back room that would be his office and began moving boxes around. Their muffled tones floated down the small hallway over the clatter of dishes being rinsed and put away. Linda's voice occasionally rising enough for Lane to catch some bits of the conversation.

"...just want to know..."

Henry responded in a low voice and Linda's raised a little.

"...worried that this isn't..."

Henry again, too quiet to hear clearly said something.

"...feel better about it if I knew what..."

He began to focus on the computer and after a time, Henry came down the hall with another beer in hand.

"Well, what have you done so far?" he asked, coming in the room. Lane looked up as Henry walked in and saw him looking at the floor where the bed used to be. Did he see the darker wood? The stain that looked like a pool of something dark had been spilled there? Maybe a few quarts of oil, or, oh, I don't know, somebody's blood perhaps? Or was Lane the only one to see the stain? He didn't want to ask.

"I think I've just about figured out how to unpack it," Lane said, burying his thoughts behind the mantra.

Today is a new day, today is a new day, today is a new day.

Henry had the system up and running in twenty minutes and they spent the next couple of hours going over the software. At ten Linda interrupted them.

"We'd better get going, Henry."

"Okay," he said, without looking up from the screen. Lane looked at her and smiled. "Think you can handle it from here?" he asked Lane.

"Yeah, I'll call if I get stuck."

They left the room and Lane walked them both to the door.

"We might drop by after church, if your going to be around," Linda said, adding the last bit as Henry gave her a severe look not to push.

"That'd be great." He hugged her and shook Henry's hand, thanking them both again.

Standing on the porch he watched them drive down Cherokee Place. Long after they had gone he was still on the porch, watching the night and remembering. The feelings and emotions seemed to be stale, or else he wasn't opening up to them all the way. The newness of being in the house seemed to damper most of the feelings, but they were there.

Just stale.

Old.

No longer painful.

It had been a long time ago.

The kid he had spoken with the day he'd parked across the street, trying to decide what to do with the house, had been right about the house being haunted. But not in the way the kid had thought. The haunting was in Lane's head, not in the house. At least he didn't think so, as the memory of his time here came back.

A strange ringing sound began to pulse intermittently. Lane looked around the yard and to the street, trying to see what was ringing. Then he looked back at the house and realized that it was his phone; his new phone that went with his old house and old furniture but not with his old memories.

"Hello?" he said, grabbing it on the fifth ring.

"Lane?"

"Yes?"

"Well, how is it?"

"Hi, Marilyn. I'm fine, how are you?" he said, happy to hear from her.

"I know you're fine, or I would have asked. How is the house?"

"It's a little more than I thought it would be, but I'm holding my own."

"Oh?" she asked, urging him to continue.

"Nothing too tough."

"Are you sure?"

"Yeah. I'll let you know."

"Can I come by tomorrow?" she asked.

"Why don't we do it Monday evening? I'm starting back to work on Monday and I'd like to finish unpacking before then."

"Great. It's a date then. What do you want me to bring?"

"Surprise me."

"You're on. What's the main course?"

"Chicken? Maybe throw some halves in the oven?"

"Sounds good? So you're comfortable there?"

He knew that she wouldn't give up that easily.

"Yeah. So far. There was one thing that caught me off guard."

"Tell me about it."

"It's nothing really. I just have smelled this rotten smell every now and then. It just struck me as odd."

"When was this?"

"Once a couple of weeks ago and then just the other day."

"What did it smell like?"

"Something dead, like rotting fish, or something like rotting fish. Not quiet rotten but definitely on it's way there. Real bad. And then it's gone, just like that."

"Did you find anything dead around the house?"

"No. Nowhere."

"Had you ever smelled it before?"

"What? Before today?"

"Yes."

"I remember thinking that it smelled like the fish bait we used on that outing to the lake. Do you remember? We all went and those two guys you used to work with took a few other people and us from the Hospital? We caught a bunch of perch and cut them up for bait. They sat in a jar in the sun for too long. I remember opening it and nearly throwing up from the smell!"

Marilyn started, but quickly caught herself.

"Do you remember anything else?"

"No. Not really. I went to lie down."

"How long did you sleep?"

"Couple of hours."

"Anything else happen?"

"No."

"What about when Henry and Linda got there?"

"No. We just ate dinner and visited."

"Did you smell that odor again?"

"No. Nothing. Just the usual old musty smell."

"What did that smell like?"

"Like old musty smell. What are you getting at?" he was beginning to feel he was back in the Hospital.

"Nothing. I was just curious, that's all. You think that it was some kind of daydream?"

"Maybe. I'm not sure."

"And you feel all right with this?"

"Sure. I've had a lot worse dreams," he said, silently shrugging to the empty room.

"Good. Well, as long as you're comfortable with it. I won't keep you. I'll see you tomorrow night, Okay?"

"Yeah, Okay. I guess I'll see you then."

Lane hung up and wondered what that was all about. Probably just worried about me being here, he thought.

The kitchen had been thoroughly cleaned by Linda and he shut off the lights and went to his room to begin unpacking boxes of clothes. It was almost eleven, but he wasn't tired. He still had most of Sunday to catch up on his sleep.

*   *   *

Marilyn hung up the phone and stood looking at it in a silent moment of thought. She slowly turned to the living room and sat on the plush couch. Going over the conversation in her mind, she remembered her notes and went back to the kitchen for them. With the note pad in hand, she returned to the couch. No matter how she chose to think about it, no matter how many times she read through the notes, she still came to the same conclusion. It was nearly eleven, but she couldn't wait. There was too much going on. She went back to the kitchen and dialed Stan Litchfield from memory. It rang only once.

"Yes?" a voice heavy with sleep asked on the other end.

"Stan? Marilyn. Did I wake you?"

"What time is it?"

"Almost eleven. I wouldn't have called so late but this is very important to me."

"Can it wait until morning, Marilyn?"

She could hear Stan saying something to his wife, Kara.

"No. I don't think it can. It's about Lane White."

"Okay. Okay. Can I call you back in ten minutes?"

"Sure. Thanks, Stan."

She hung up the phone and sat on the couch. Five minutes later he called back.

"I hope you realize that I have a six am meeting with the board," he said, sounding fully awake.

"No, I didn't. Stan I wouldn't have called if it wasn't important."

"I know, I know. What is it?"

"You remember Lane White?"

"Of course. It was only the largest criminal case in Burkett in the last fifty years."

"Stan, come on. I need your help."

"Okay. Sorry. Let's hear it."

She told him about the move Lane had made to the house, the background of the move, the autobiography Lane was writing and why she had supported him in it.

"Sounds like good therapy to me. Is he having any unusual reactions to the move?"

"Maybe. That's why I called."

She told him about the rotten smell.

"He told me it smelled like rotting fish or something like that."

"Nothing else? Just a rotten smell?"

"Yes."

"Did he check around for something dead under the house?"

"Yes, Stan, he did."

"Sorry. How about any other smells? Oranges perhaps?"

"Nope. Just the smell of rotting fish."

"Well, it could be something physical. Maybe he should be checked out physically," Stan said.

"I'm afraid that the move it doing more harm than good. I'm worried. I've got a feeling about it, Stan."

"Any mood swings?"

"Just the usual reactions that you would expect from making such a change. He's decided to take it head on. I think that it could be the final break through for him."

"Yes, it could. But you're wondering which way he will break."

"Yes. With these new developments, I'm not so sure anymore."

"It may just be a temporary reaction to the move. You said he's writing an autobiography?"

"Yes."

"How far along is he?"

"I don't know. The last time we spoke he was still just writing notes, laying out the work. He's very disciplined when it comes to his writing. I'm sure he's well into it by now."

"I think, for the time being, you should stay close to him. Will he notice it if you do?"

"No. We stay in touch. I'm going over Monday night for dinner and to see the house."

"Good."

"Anything else you can think of?"

"Yes. Considering his history with writing, the Autobiography should give you some insight into his current condition. Is there anyway you could get a glimpse of it?"

"Probably. I used to help him edit his work. He really is very good. I hope he can do something with this project."

"Great. Good for him. I hope he makes it."

He was winding the conversation to a close and Marilyn didn't want to push it any longer. She had the answers she was after. He hadn't really told her anything she didn't already know, but it was good to get confirmation of her own conclusions.

"I'll keep in touch."

"Okay. But unless something big happens, don't call so late. Kara needs her sleep."

"Ha. Ha. Goodnight, Stan. Thanks again."

"Bye."

She hung up the phone and slowly read through her brief notes and let out a small gasp. She had forgotten to tell him the most important fact of her conversation with Lane. When she had asked him is he had smelled the same odor anywhere else, Lane had told her he had on a fishing trip to a lake during an outing from a Hospital. But the problem with that was she had *never* taken him to a lake and had *never* been fishing in her entire life.

FIVE

...6

The thing under the brackish water hadn't returned. He thought he had seen a ripple off toward the far end of the lake, but couldn't be sure. He hadn't moved and didn't really intend to do so. The thought of that big thing in the water was pervasive. Maybe it was some harmless animal, like a manatee or a porpoise. Yeah, but what it wasn't? What if it was something that more resembled a shark? Which was probably more likely in this place.

It could have gotten him by now if it had wanted to. Unless it was too big to come in water this shallow. An ill-colored sun had just begun to peak over the mountain-studded horizon. He crossed his arms, rubbed his shoulders and waited, unsure.

It was seven o'clock on Sunday morning and the house was quiet. After two hours of unpacking boxes the night before, he had pushed the mess aside and pulled out the autobiography notes. With the tablets and sheets of paper spread around him on the floor, he had worked on the structure of the book until sometime well after midnight. Ending the night by forcing himself to stop.

He didn't remember going to sleep, and he didn't feel like he'd slept that much. Standing in the bathroom, he finished at the toilet, flushed it, then leaned over the sink and splashed cold water on his face. The mirror reflected his puffy, blood-shot eyes. It was still early and he decided to go back to bed. Thirty minutes later he was back in the bathroom running the shower having been unable to sleep.

After a quick shower he grabbed an apple and went out the back door to explore the yard. The steel lawn furniture Linda had purchased didn't look very inviting, but when he sat in one of the chairs it was surprisingly comfortable. He ate the apple slowly and looked out at the yard. The grass was getting long but it didn't really matter at this point in the game.

The memories had begun to come back. Not in a rush, but slowly. The old Mimosa tree where he and Kristy used to play was still there, but the tree looked dead for the most part. It had never been properly pruned and the branches were twisting into one another, choking themselves off it a strange suicide.

He might prune it this winter to see if it would come back. There was still the mark of the rope swing he had rigged for them to play on. A few nails were all that were left of the fort they used to hide in more than play.

During the summer it hadn't been that bad. It was even peaceful in the halo of the Mimosa, away from the noise of their father. They would quietly sneak back in the house after they were sure he had fallen asleep. In the winter, when it was too cold, they sometimes hid in the basement, near the broken down, clunky old furnace to stay warm.

He felt his head beginning to spin and he closed his eyes. The memories were coming faster now; a video on fast-forward. It was as if he had removed his finger from a hole in his memory dam. Kristy crying, his mother crying, he was crying, his father yelling, his face bright red and spit flying from his mouth.

"Get the *fuck* out'da here!" followed by a fist in the face to whoever was in reach.

Finding his mother at the bottom of the basements steps, her eyes blank and her head twisted at an unnatural angle. Going to the funeral, his father already drunk. Saying something about having to keep up the right look. Telling them to shut the *fuck* up with the crying and get over it. Then listening to Kristy crying through the walls of the house telling her father to please stop that it hurt.

But he never did stop. Not until Turtle had come along. He remembered the thick, oily smell of the shotgun and the weight of it in his small hands; the metallic click of the three shells sliding into the belly of the cold machine, opening the door of his father's room, lifting the heavy gun and bringing it in line.

His head shot up from the back of the chair. The bright sunlight hurt his eyes. He rubbed his face with both hands and sat upright.

"Today is a new day," he said aloud to the yard, trying hard to forget.

"This day is new," he altered the mantra, trying to bolster some kind of conviction behind it. Turtle was quiet. Or gone. Though he didn't think that he would ever be rid of Turtle completely, he thought he could keep him quiet most of the time.

The memories began to recede again. The feeling left him heavy. It left him thinking that his...*plan* may turn out to be much harder than he had thought.

The phone began to ring in the house and he quickly stood, dropping the apple into the yard, and hurried back into the house.

"Hello?"

"Honey? We're just leaving church, can we come by for a little while? We thought we'd treat you to lunch."

"I'd really love to but I'm really right in the middle of the autobiography. Can we make it another time?" he said before even thinking about it.

"Well, sure, honey, if that's what you want to do."

He knew he was pushing her away but he just didn't want to leave, not now. He felt something and he didn't want to walk out on it. Not yet.

"Thanks. I'll call you later this afternoon."

"Well, all right," Linda said, either sorely pissed or hurt, Lane couldn't tell.

He hung up the phone and looked at it, thinking about nothing in particular. Shifting gears, as Henry would say, wool gathering, Linda would say. He went to the bathroom, washed his face, and then wandered back to the living room. The memories had receded. They were best when they were distant. He wanted it that way. Most of them were dark, if not all, and though the Autobiography was just going to scratch the surface of them, that would be all that was needed. It would be enough to get the ugly, painful task over with and out of the way.

Things were beginning to get a little slippery in his thoughts. The idea of the rotten smell being there one minute and gone the next was suddenly not sitting well. Was he beginning to falter? Slip a little? Trip? Had Turtle come back a little stronger than he had thought? He wasn't burning black candles, wasn't burying bodies under the house, not yet anyway.

It just didn't feel right. He felt…he wasn't sure how he felt. Just that he didn't feel right. If the stench in the house was a dream, fine. That would have been that. But he knew, he *knew* that it wasn't a dream. He went into the kitchen and opened the door leading down the steps to the basement. Nothing there. Just the basement. Dust, mold and cobwebs. No putrid stench. Nothing. Not even any bugs or spiders dancing in the corners. He paused, staring down the steps, and then closed the door.

He dug into the autobiography, pushed through the rambling notes, defined the chapters, sharpened them and piled up more legal pads.

*   *   *

He woke Monday morning promptly at seven, showered, dressed and ate a quick breakfast. He was exhausted and wanted nothing more than to go back to sleep, but he had had his time off from work. Even though he didn't need the money, he needed the boost to his moral. The work at Hubbard gave him a center point to focus on; a base in reality to work from. He couldn't explain it further than that.

He fired up the trusty, aging Olds and made it to work with ten minutes to spare. Red gave him a slap on his back and asked if everything was going all right, but Lane didn't see anything that he would have been able to label as sincerity in his eyes. He smiled and told him everything was going great. Yes, the move went fine and, no, he didn't have any trouble.

"Well, that's good to hear," he said, pausing oddly and just looking at Lane. "Well, good to have you back," he finally said, then turned back toward his office. Lane had time to wonder when Red's movement would move from the *slow* category into the somewhat more critical area of *ponderous*. Thirty more pounds should do the trick.

He stopped staring at Red when he realized that Red was staring back at him as he slowly walked to his office.

Lane chatted up the group of early arrivals in the room that were milling around, drinking coffee and get warmed up for another thrilling, no holds barred day of data input.

Scattered welcome backs came from throughout the room. He sat his lunch beneath his desk and began arranging the few personal items he had. The cleaning staff had managed to completely re-arrange his desk during the weeks he was gone. Lane noticed a few new faces in the crowd as he watched Chris walking from desk to desk collecting the dollar entry fee from everyone that was participating. He was explaining the rules to a very heavy girl of about twenty. She was nervously looking around as if there was some joke about to be played on her.

With another nervous glance around the room, she plucked up her purse, opened it, and gave Chris a dollar bill. He handed her the clipboard he carried and pointed to it. She took the pen Chris offered and quickly wrote on the paper. As she moved behind her desk, and started to pull up the chair, Lane saw what was about to happen. It had happed before, but never to somebody of this poor girl's bulk. Even Lester

Hollie had managed not to be a victim of the vanishing chair. Lane quickly stood and began moving toward the girl, though he already saw he was going to be too late.

Lane watched in silent horror/amusement as the girl carefully pulled the chair up and began to sit down on the front edge. As she began to settle her bulk, just as Lane had feared, the chair whipped out from beneath her and zipped across the hard plastic mat, crashing into the portable wall behind her. The wall began to fall back onto Lester Hollie's desk. Lester came out of seemingly nowhere and bullied his equally considerable weight past Lane and managed to grab the wall as it met the desk. The girl hit the floor. It knocked the air out of her and she said something that sounded like, *Haaauuummm*, as the air escaped her.

Lane wondered about the odds of Hubbard placing these two exceptionally large people next to each other being a fluke. He then began wondering if Lester and this as of yet unnamed girl would find some kind of romantic interest in each other.

A whirlwind of people from all over the office clattered around, asking her if she was hurt and trying to help. Lester was in the thick of it, having propped the wall sufficiently against his desk for the time being, and taking up large volumes of space trying to help the girl up. Lane thought that love might be in bloom soon.

Her face was red with embarrassment as Lane pushed past several people to help in the effort to right her. He took her right arm while Lester did his best to hold her left arm. They heaved mightily but couldn't get her up. She shook them off, her face now fuming with anger.

"I can get up," she said, very quietly in a tiny voice completely out of place in that large body.

The group around her backed away and watched, a few faces trying to hide embarrassed smiles, as she turned over on her stomach and slowly rose to her knees.

"Now you can help," she said, raising her right arm out to her side.

Each arm was grabbed and she slowly rose.

"Thank you," she said, looking fiercely at the floor.

"Everything all right here?" Red asked, walking up the aisle.

"Yes," the girl said, trying to smile. Her face was blood red. Sheila was suddenly at her side, putting an arm around her. It was a gesture that Lane thought to be overtly motherly and one he didn't think Sheila was capable of. The crowd began to break up; giggles and smothered laughter followed part of it. Red looked confused and unsure, so he went back to his office.

"Don't worry about it, we've all done it at least once. These chairs are tricky. You have to sit down on the back or you'll do it again," Sheila said, pulling the chair up as Lester pushed the portable wall back in place.

"Okay."

Lane watched as Sheila helped her into the chair.

"I'm Sheila," she said, offering her hand.

"Tina," she said, taking Sheila's hand briefly.

"There you go, no problem," Sheila said, settling Tina in the chair, which groaned for mercy under the weight.

"If you need anything, or have any questions my desk is in the back by that wall," she pointed in the general direction.

"Okay," Tina said, her face beginning to come back to a more normal shade of pasty white.

Sheila patted her on the back and turned to go to her desk as the nine o'clock chimes rang over the Muzak system.

The small clot of people grouped around the room immediately broke up and spread out to their respective desks. Red came out of his office and watched as keyboards began rattling. He surveyed his domain until he seemed satisfied with it, and then returned to his office.

Lester managed to slip in and introduce himself to Tina before he began work. There did seem to be something going on there, or at least the hint that something might be going on there. She seemed to get into the rhythm of the process after about thirty minutes. He didn't think she would last long. There was an air about her that didn't seem to fit with long-term employment.

When the lunch bell's chimed, he grabbed his bag and walked up the aisle to her desk.

"How are you doing?"

"Oh. Fine," she said, her face was no longer flushed, but she seemed uncomfortable with the attention. She glanced at him in quick flashes.

"Don't worry about your spill. Like Sheila said, we've all done it a time or two."

She laughed, a strange kind of tittering laugh, and looked back at her keyboard.

"Thanks."

"I'll see you later, then," Lane said. He walked out to the plaza, leaving Tina with Lester getting to know her.

The day finished quickly and he was back at the house by five-thirty. Marilyn had left a message confirming their dinner. He put the chicken halves in the oven, and then sat down work the autobiography until she arrived.

SIX

...5

He was sure he hadn't moved. The water still reached to his crotch. He couldn't feel much below that, except for the sharp rocks of the lakebed pressing into his bare feet. Though he had not moved—was sure he hadn't—the opposite bank was closer.

He'd been watching the thing emerge from the water for the past couple of hours. At least it had felt that long. Time had no business in this place. Like air in a vacuum, it just wasn't done. The thing was about forty feet long and looked like an alligator turtle that was too large to have ever been. It lurched it's bulk across the sandy beach, its rough shell making crunch sounds on the sand as it slowly moved from the dark, black water.

He could still see it's misty breath exhaling. His fear of it was overridden by relief that it was out of the water and in the open where he could see it.

Humping along, it drug itself up to the tree line, then slowly turned to face the lake. He was reminded of those bull walrus you saw flopping around the beaches of some remote wilderness on National Geographic specials. Once it had made the turn, it lay still.

He took another tentative step and felt the water tickling his belly button.

"Look at it, Benny! Look at 'er fly!"

"I'm not blind or deaf yet, Walsh. I can see the damn ball."

At sixty-eight years old Ben Morrow was sitting in a golf cart, pretending to see the ball his friend of nearly fifty years had just hit. They were on the second tee box at the Hillcrest County Club, a long, straight par four. By the excited way in which Walsh Teter was cavorting on the tee box—wiggling and shaking around in a bad pantomime of a dance—Ben could see it must have been a good shot. Well for someone their age. Ten years ago a tee shot of around two hundred twenty yards would be a fair shot for him. Nowadays if he got it over a hundred and fifty he was pleased as punch.

"Must be at least three hundred yards out!" Walsh said, lumbering back to where Ben sat in the cart. He was wearing loud plaid pants, a lemon-yellow short sleeve shirt through which his T-shirt could be seen and didn't carry much of a spare tire for a man his age. He was built like a retired lumberjack and had the face of a range cowboy. A straw Panama hat topped his six foot five inch frame and completed his outfit.

Ben tended to stick with his favorite beige work pants and much more earthy toned short sleeves shirts. To protect his balding scalp he had an odd assortment of Baseball hats advertising everything from *Bill's Auto Parts* to *Dottie & Ed's*, a fishing outfit in Victoria, British Columbia. Though he liked to say he was as tall as Walsh, he was actually a couple of inches shy. He couldn't compare to Walsh around the middle though. He had to admit that he did have just a little more of a spare tire, but not much. He wasn't as stoutly built as Walsh either and he looked more like an accountant than a cowboy.

"Uh-huh. And I take a crap everyday," Ben offered, getting out of the cart to set up his shot. He had always hated it when Walsh called him Benny, sounded like a little kid.

Walsh laughed by way of politeness and took a hard look at his friend.

"Benny, you're turning awfully sour these days," he said, looking after his friend. He seemed to be considering something, shrugged his shoulders as if deciding on some internal conversation, then asked: "Is it about Stephen?"

Ben leaned slowly over and placed his peg in the ground, slowly stood, produced a ball from his pants pocket and leaned back down to place the ball on the peg. It took him two tries to stop his shaking, slightly arthritic hands before the ball would stay in place. He stood and adjusted his hat.

"Not really, but maybe. I'm not sure, Walsh. I'm just not sure," he said, slowly lining up the shot he was fairly sure wouldn't go much beyond a hundred yards.

It was the best answer he could give Walsh. He honestly did not know how to explain everything but that he would have to do some talking was beyond consideration. Walsh was the only person he could trust. He would either explain everything to him or go careening off the edge of sanity, giggling, slobbering and wetting his pants.

Stephen had committed suicide, what? Two, three, four years ago? He couldn't be sure. His mind had begun to get a little soft, though he wouldn't have ever said that out loud. It never settled in him that Stephen was gone. He had never been close to his son, but they hadn't been enemies either, like some fathers and sons become. They never really did all that much together. Stephen was kind of a bookish boy and Ben was more of an outsider. Not really a sportsman, he didn't hunt, but he preferred to be outside doing something than inside, no matter the weather.

Stephen had left his grandson, Blake and his daughter-in-law, Brenda, behind. They were getting along well enough, though. Stephen had had a good job out there at Hubbard and his pension was taking care of most of their financial needs. Stephen's life insurance policy wasn't paying up, saying Stephen hadn't had his policy long enough, or some such happy crap. He supposed that when that law firm Brenda had hired got greedy enough they would really put the squeeze on and Brenda and Blake would get their settlement, less a large percentage of course.

Carly was always pushing their relationship. 'Why don't you take Steve with you? Maybe he could drive the cart?' she had asked on more than one occasion. The one time he had offered and Stephen had taken him up on it (both of them uncomfortable with the idea, but willing to give it a shot) had been a disaster. Stephen had been unable to grasp the simple mechanics of driving, even at the age of thirteen. They had had to wait for the course sheriff to run back to the clubhouse for the groundkeeper and a tractor to pull the cart out of the water hazard on the seventh hole. Fifteen hundred dollars later he vowed not to bring Stephen back to the course unless and until he had his divers license.

Thinking back on it now, it had actually been a fun day. Something they had ended up laughing about over the few Sunday afternoon dinners they had shared.

Yeah, it was about Stephen, his foul mood as of late. For almost two months now the dreams had been getting worse and now this…the explanation for the dreams had become clear and he wasn't sure he liked it. But that didn't matter much, because it didn't change the facts.

"Well? Are you gonna tee off or just stand there all day, Benny?" Walsh said from where he stood by the cart.

"Hold your water, Walsh, I'm swinging." He took a deep breath, exhaled slowly, went through his back swing and followed through with almost everything he had. He topped the ball and it flew thirty yards nearly parallel with the ground. It hit and rolled another forty yards down the left side of the fairway.

"You want a mulligan?" Walsh asked, settling himself in the cart.

"Nope. I'll take what I got," Ben said, searching for his peg. He found it unbroken and picked it up, returning it to his pocket. The shot wasn't that bad, he had gotten nearly the distance he had wanted, and besides it wasn't how, but how many that counted in golf. He settled in the drivers' seat of the cart and punched the accelerator. They rolled off down the fairway.

"Isn't that something about old man Hubbard's son-in-law? Colby or something?" Walsh said, making conversation to try and ease Ben into talking.

"I think it was Corbin."

"Yeah, Corbin. What a way to go."

The morning mist had just begun to burn off the grass and the tracks of the golfers and their carts that had gotten out earlier than they had were fading. They could feel the humidity coming on already. Their three-day weekly sessions would get earlier and earlier as the summers heat came in. By August they would be down to just one or at the most two games a week. The heat would be too much for either of them no matter how early they started by then.

The cart trundled along the path as they slowly made their way to Ben's ball.

"So, what's the deal, Ben?"

They pulled up a couple of yards behind Ben's ball on the fairway.

"Walsh, this is something I've never had to deal with. I swear, as long as we've known each other, this has got to be the craziest thing you've ever heard. But I have to have your word on this. You hear? I've got to have your word that this won't go beyond you and me."

"Who the hell else am I gonna tell?"

"Walsh."

"You're right. Sorry. You've got my word."

Ben got out of the cart and began rummaging through his clubs that were ridding on the back of the cart. Though he knew he should use a fairway wood, he settled on a three iron, painfully admitting he more than likely wouldn't be able to get the wood to lift the ball from the turf. He stood by the cart and eyed his ball. In the great distance he could just make out the red flag on the green. When had they begun to make golf courses so long?

"Walsh...," Ben started, then paused, looking a his ball, then the ground, the head of his club. This was going to be hard, but he didn't see any other way of doing it.

"Do you remember back when Carly died?"

"Of course."

It had only been five years ago, just a little longer than Stephen's death. He'd always thought that Carly dying had sent Stephen on his way toward suicide, though he couldn't be sure. Nobody could be sure why someone killed himself or herself. Like that rock star kid from Seattle that had knocked his self off. For what? It didn't make sense. Having seemingly had so much to live for.

If Carly had been alive when Stephen had killed himself...he didn't like to think about what that would have done to her. Hearing that her only son had killed himself. At least there was that. What did they call it? The lesser of two evils? That sounded right. Carly dying before Stephen killed himself was the lesser of two evils.

"I had...a bad time, for awhile. You remember?"

Walsh nodded, now silently listening to his friend. He was thinking about how he would feel about losing Jennie. Both of them were, thank the Lord, in good health.

"I think that the worst part of Carly dying was after I really understood that she wasn't coming back. Does that make sense, Walsh? Once you really understand that they aren't coming back, no matter how much you cry and mope and wish and pray—they are not coming back—a deep set...pain sets in," Ben said, looking up at his friend. Walsh nodded, urging him to continue.

"But it's not exactly a pain. It's more like an itch that you can't reach. And it *never* goes away. That was the hardest part for me, Walsh. Long after Carly had died and I had finally gotten it through my thick head that she really was gone, there was that itch."

Walsh nodded again and waited patiently for his friend to continue. Ben glanced back toward the tee box and saw a foursome waiting for them to get moving. He waved them through and walked off the edge of the fairway.

"You mind sittin' for a minute or two?" Ben asked.

"Not a bit." He slid over to the drivers seat and pulled the cart off the fairway under the spread of several large oaks in the rough. Ben had a thought, and quickly walked back to his ball and picked it up.

"I marked the spot," he said with a wry smile.

"Yup, and my drive was a little over three hundred yards," Walsh said, returning the wry smile.

Walsh had pulled the cart perpendicular to the fairway and they had a clear view up and down it. They sat watching the foursome teeing off. From where they were sitting at about a hundred yards out there was very little chance of getting hit.

"About the time that itch started to lessen a little, Stephen went and...died," Ben said, looking hard up the fairway. He pressed his lips tightly together against the pain. "Then that itch started along with Carly's itch. Can you understand that, Walsh?" he asked, turning to look at his life long friend.

"Yup, sure do."

"Then I just wasn't sure I was going to make it. You know? You start to think some crazy thoughts. I was really put out about how I never did seem to connect with Stephen. Maybe there was something I could have done when he was younger. Maybe something that would have helped him get through whatever tough times he was having that caused him to do what he did." Ben looked up at the soft *thwack* of the first of the foursome teeing off.

"Uh-huh," Walsh said, thinking of his two daughters.

"So this went on for awhile. Thinking about how he wanted to fly jets. Always building models and reading books but never getting out and *doing* something about it. Like joining the Navy or taking flying lessons. I don't know. Maybe I should have pushed him a little in that direction. It was something he always wanted to do, he just never seemed to do it. Maybe if I had pushed harder he would have gone ahead on his own. Like pushing a big rock off a hill. Just give it that little start and it'll do the rest."

"You can't know that, Ben. Not for sure. What if you had pushed him into the Navy and he'd been killed in Vietnam or the Middle East or from just falling off a ship? How'd you feel then?"

"Yeah, maybe. But I still think that I should have done more. Made more of an effort to build some kind of relationship with him. Instead of just being around not saying much either way."

The metallic *dink!* of a metal driver announced the second of the foursome teeing off. They both turned to watch, neither of them seeing the ball.

"Hell, my Dad was never around. Maybe that's why I never pursued a closer relationship with Stephen. But I still don't feel like it let's me off the hook. You know? Just because my Dad and I didn't get along that well. We didn't fight or nothin' like that. We just didn't ever talk about anything that really mattered when he was around."

They watched the third and fourth of the group tee off, comfortable with the silence as only good friends can be.

"Want to tell 'em about your ball?" Ben asked as the group began making their way up the fairway.

"Nah, got plenty more where that one came from."

They waved back to the group as they drove past them on the other side of the fairway.

"Anyhow, it was just about all I could take. Carly dying, then Stephen a couple of years later. A real double whammy."

Walsh remembered. Ben had been sickly and aloof for more than a year. It had worried him, but he couldn't do anything more than what he was doing now. They were both grown men and had to work out their own problems. Just being there when he wanted to talk seemed to be what he needed the most. Someone to bitch too and bounce your problems off.

"I got through it and I guess I've got you to thank for most of it." Ben looked out over the course, not looking at, but not looking away from Walsh.

"Ssssh," Walsh said, waving his hand and chuckling deeply. "You're going to get me all excited and there's nowhere we can go," he said, diffusing the weight of Ben's statement. But he didn't let the point get by him. He knew he had been a part of keeping his friend alive during that time, but it wasn't until now that he knew just how large a part he had played. Ben chuckled with him and turned to face him.

"I mean that, Walsh. I don't know where I'd be now if you hadn't been there to help me."

Walsh smiled and nodded his head, accepting the compliment graciously. The leaves in the large oak rustled in a gust of warm wind. A crow called out somewhere in the distance.

"I kept thinking about what I could have done to maybe save Stephen, but I never did get anywhere. It's an endless circle. Like you said, what if he had gone on and flown like he wanted then died in a crash? What would I have felt like then? Probably fairly much the same, but not quite. He still wouldn't have done it himself," Ben said, looking back out to the fairway. "Shit, maybe I would have wondered if he had nosed one in for whatever reason. See what I mean about the circle? It never ends."

Walsh chuckled and produced a red handkerchief from his back pocket. He removed the straw Panama and mopped his shiny, nearly hairless head with it.

"After awhile I got better at it. Almost to the point of where I could put it away—accept it for not being reversible. Except for that small itch. I've never found a way to get rid of that."

Walsh nodded, returned the handkerchief to his pocket and the hat to his head. He watched in silence as Ben's eyes began welling up with tears. Ben swiped at them, maybe a little embarrassed. After a silent couple of minutes, Ben continued.

"About two months ago I started having these crazy dreams, Walsh. I mean…crazy," he said, shaking his head and staring down at his feet.

"Walsh, I've really got to have your word on this. No fucking around. We've been friends a long time and there've been more than a few times you shared some things with me that don't need to got any further, you with me?"

"Yup, I'm with you, Ben. You got it. Scouts honor. Hope to die, stick my finger in a pie," Walsh said, holding up his index finger. They both laughed in an odd, boyish way that didn't seem to fit two old men sitting in a golf cart in the middle of a golf course *not* playing golf.

They quit laughing after a moment and Ben's face drew down. It looked like the shades being drawn closed on a very old rustic home.

"Nobody, Walsh. I mean that. Nobody."

"Ben I wish you'd quit dicking around and just get to the point here. I got it. Nobody knows."

"Not even the authorities?" Ben asked, not too sheepishly.

"What? You mean the Police?"

"Yeah, I mean the Police."

"Just what the hell are we talking about, Ben?"

Walsh scooted up in his seat, leaning forward slightly in the cart. Though he was putting up a front of being alarmed, Ben didn't see any real surprise in his friends face. After all, they had done more than their share of shaky business deals and maybe just a couple that were a little more than shaky. That was good. He didn't doubt that he could trust Walsh. He had, in fact, stopped doubting he could trust him almost forty years ago. He was a good and dear friend and Ben thought that he was going to miss him terribly when this was all over with. At least, if it turned out like he thought it would and from where he was standing he couldn't see any other way it would end up.

"It's about these dreams I've been having…and I think it's about—," Ben paused, wanting to be as clear as he could so there would be no misunderstanding.

"I think it may also be about...redemption. You know Walsh? Reaching back to a time when I had a chance to make a friend of Stephen. Back to a time when I could actually sit him down and really talk with him. Talk with him about life, or just to shoot the breeze without worrying what he was thinking about me."

They both turned as the sound of ladies voices carried across the small expanse from the tee box to where they sat. A couple of women were preparing to tee off. They watched with a feigned, distracted interest for a moment.

"So, I guess I'd better get around to telling you everything."

"I guess you'd better, now that you've gone and made me an accomplice," Walsh said with a wink.

"About two month ago I started having these dreams about... Stephen and Carly. Now, I know that you'd think it was probably some kind of remorse for them triggering it, but it's not. At least I don't think it is."

Walsh slowly drew his index finger in the shape of a circle and smiled.

"Yeah, yeah, circling again. So I started having these dreams. They weren't much at first. I could only remember little pieces of them. But when I realized I was having these dreams, I started to try and remember. I gave myself an autosuggestion that I would remember. Don't look at me like I'm nutty, Walsh or I'll stop right here. It works; I'm here to tell you. It works.

"At first I didn't think that it was, though. But then I began to wake up right after the dreams and found I could remember more and more about them. Like I said, they weren't much at first." Ben looked up at the ladies walking slowly up the fairway toward them. With a twinge of regret he watched as they walked well beyond where his own drive had landed. When had they teed off? Was his hearing going now as well as his physical mobility?

He shook his head slightly as if to clear his thoughts. Circling. He was circling again. Well, if there was such a thing as destiny, he sure as hell was beginning to get a good picture of what his might be. No, now wasn't the time to bullshit. It had gone much too far for that. He had been given a rare prize. He had been allowed to see his destiny with a clear, bright intensity that maybe a handful of people had been given. The thought sounded lofty enough, but the reality tasted like a cup of warm crap touched up with cinnamon and cream.

His life had taken on a bright, steely edge as of late. Half the time he was terrified, unable to believe what was happening and the other half he stood looking out on the forty acres he lived on, thinking about nothing in particular. Just being amazed at the life all around him.

Birds. Something you never really took a good look at, he now found himself spending hours just watching. Not really caring if he was watching a Titmouse or an English Sparrow. It was a small, living being. Something he wasn't going to be for very much longer if he had read everything right.

But was that such a bad trade off for atonement of the sin of being a shit of a father? Hell, he hadn't even worked hard enough at it to be called a father. He had just been the sperm bank from which Stephen had emerged to blossom in Carly.

The real miracle of the situation was Stephen then married Brenda, the now widow Morrow, and Blake had blossomed in her. Not Stephen by no means, but still a living route through with he now hoped he could redeem himself. If not completely, then at least something for making the effort.

How many old men wish they had done things different? How often did they—.

"Ben," Walsh said, poking him in the arm slightly. "You want to come on back now? I'm getting kinda' lonely here."

Ben smiled and tried to pick up the conversation where he'd left off.

"Sure, sorry. I get caught up in it." He thought back to where he'd left off.

"Anyhow, the dreams began to get clearer. Now, I'm not talking about clear as in fuzzy I-can-sort-of-remember clear. I'm talking about clear like you and I are sitting here right now."

Walsh folded his arms across his chest and leaned back in the cart, trying to get comfortable. If he was still worried about the Police, he didn't show it. Ben was very glad for that. He might need Walsh to help him out before this was over.

"Now this part is a little bit hard for me to say. I've known you for a hell of a long time, Walsh, and you've just got to take my word for it that I'm not crazy. I've already given that Litchfield fellow a call over at the hospital. We sat down for a couple of sessions and though I didn't tell him nearly what all I'm telling you, I told him enough just to see what he thought."

Walsh nodded and smiled slightly at the thought of Ben seeing a shrink. Ben let the smirk slide only because he hadn't wanted to laugh about it at the time.

"And?" Walsh asked.

"Well, I'm still not locked up so that should tell you something."

Walsh cupped a hand to his ear and tilted his head as if listening to something. All Ben could hear was the grasshoppers and cicadas gearing up for another day.

"Those sirens I hear? Sure they aren't coming for you?"

"You're a regular riot today, aren't you Walsh?" Ben said, trying not to smile.

Walsh smiled back and shrugged his shoulders, scooting around on the cart seat, trying without much success to get comfortable.

"In these dreams I'm sitting out back of the house up on the deck, the one up at the edge of the cinderblock barn, by the barbecue. I'm just sitting there and I can't really tell what time of day it is. It's still light out, though."

Ben looked back to the tee box as another twosome set up to tee off. Walsh waved them on through.

"So I'm sitting there on the deck. Just sitting. Then Carly and Stephen come walking out of the woods just beyond the pond. You know where the hill just starts to rise? There's that big sandstone outcrop there?"

Walsh nodded. He'd been out to Ben's place almost as often as he was at his own home.

"If you look at it just right it looks like a small cave. At least in my dreams it does. So, they come walking out of the woods and say hello, just like it was another Sunday afternoon sitting around the place."

Ben looked carefully at Walsh, looking for signs of rebellion or humor. He saw none. Once again he had not heard the tee off. The twosome drove by in the fairway, waving at Ben at Walsh. They waved back.

"At first we didn't seem to talk about much of anything. Carly would go on about the garden or what her friends were up to and Stephen… well, Stephen would just sit there and nod his head as if he were right in the middle of the conversation. Like when he was alive. Both of us pretending to have some kind of happy relationship going when we hardly knew each other." He trampled down the sudden urge to cry again. If he was going to go all the way with this thing, he couldn't spend a lot of time balling and whining.

"When I first began to really remember the dreams, Stephen and Carly were off the deck, between it and the pond. Then as they began to get clearer and clearer they seemed to get closer and closer. I've been thinking about it and I think that they were getting me used to the idea. You know?"

Ben looked over at Walsh. Walsh raised his eyebrows and shrugged his shoulders, wanting to believe.

"Shit, Walsh. I know what you're thinking without even lookin' at you. What the hell would dead people be doing in my dreams trying to get me used to the idea of dead people being in my dreams? Something like that?"

"Ben, you've got to agree this is pretty far out there. Not that I'm not with you on this thing it's just a little hard to take all at once."

"Well, if you want me to stop, say the word and we can get on down the road," Ben said, with a pale, flaming honesty that took Walsh by surprise.

"No, no. I want to go the distance. Getting old doesn't have too many highlights and if watching my best friend crumble under the pressure, so be it," he quickly winked and punched Ben in the arm to show no harm was intended. Ben smiled a cheerless grin and looked back out on the fairway.

"So it was like they were trying not to scare me into thinking that I *had* gone off the deep end, getting me used to the idea a little at a time. I guess it worked. At least I hope that it did. I don't think that I'm crazy."

They sat in the quiet morning, watching the mist burn off and the last of the dew evaporate. Another trio of golfers teed off. Ben had given up on someone undershooting his drive. Walsh waited patiently for him to continue.

"Like I said, they didn't say a lot at first, but as they got closer and I got more used to them being there, they began to tell me a lot more."

A cluster of sparrows flew so close to the front of the cart that it felt as if they'd flown through it. They watched the small birds settle in the upper branches of a Maple tree down the fairway.

"Walsh, my grandson, Blake, is in a lot of trouble."

"Blake? What kind of trouble?" Walsh said, much more alarmed than when Ben had suggested he might have some trouble with the Police. Walsh had spent a lot of time with Brenda and Blake and Stephen. Blake had always called him Uncle Walsh.

"Is it about that friend of his drowning?"

"No, no. Nothing like that. Although, that may be a part of it, thought I don't think I could ever make the connection. I'm having a hard enough time with my part of this deal."

"Then what is it?" Walsh asked. Ben noticed he finally had his complete attention.

"Well, I don't know for sure. But it has something to do with…with families. Not our family, but somebody else's family," Ben laughed with embarrassment. "I know that sounds like a crock, but I can't explain it any better than that. It's the way it was explained to me."

"He'd in trouble with somebody's family?"

"Well, sorta'. Stephen said—," Ben shot a quick glance at Walsh to see how talking about Stephen in the present up and walking around tense sat with him. If he was flustered he didn't show it. "—he was fucking around where he shouldn't be. You know something? I just realized that he sure has been cussing a lot since he's been dead. Stephen, I mean. Not that I think about it, just about every sentence he says if F'ing this and F'ing that. And you know what else? Carly just sits there and listens like he was pouring out the sweetest poetry you'd ever heard!" Ben laughed about it then realized how crazy he must sound to Walsh. Slamming down on that was the much heavier reality that he sure missed them. He missed them more than any other time since their passing from this Earth.

Walsh sat quietly as Ben worked it out.

"So, in my dreams, Stephen and Carly are telling me that Blake is in a lot of trouble with this family. But it's not the living family he's in trouble with. It's one guy. And he's dead." Ben wished the Earth and stars that he hadn't had to say that. If Walsh didn't think he was nutty as a peanut by now, that would surely do it. He glanced at him and was not too surprised to see him calmly nodding his head, urging Ben to continue.

"Did you hear what I said?" Ben asked, not sure he had.

"Sure. Just to bring me up to speed I'll run it by you. Let's see. You're having dreams about your dead wife and son. They've come back to you in your dreams to tell you that your Grandson—Stephen's son Blake—is in trouble with another family. Only that the guy he's in trouble with is also dead. Is that about it so far?"

Ben winced and shook his head. It had been stupid to even bring it up to Walsh. He should have just keep this mouth shut and gone on about his business. Crazy or not, it would have been easier.

"Yeah, Walsh I guess that's what I'm saying. Look, why don't we just forget about it and finish up our game. Just put it down to a lack of sleep lately. Okay? Let's just forget we spoke and finish up the game. Maybe I'll write it all down and when I'm dead you can read about it and then maybe you'll understand why I did what I did."

He wasn't mad with Walsh, just frustrated that Walsh wasn't able to understand what he was trying to share with him. But he certainly couldn't blame him. He was living it and it still sounded crazy as a purple moose in pink tennis shoes.

"Come on, Ben. You can't expect me to jump right in and swallow all of it at once. I'm really trying to keep up with you on it, but give me just a little room to poke at it. All right?"

"Sure. Okay. Just keep in mind that I'm not *fucking* around here. I'm telling you the truth, at least my version of it. There's no damn funny punch line at the end of this story."

It came out a lot rougher than he had intended, but he liked the results. Walsh quit fidgeting in his seat and seemed to settle in to the groove of the conversation.

"Your little up to speed summary sounds about right. I'll tell you though, I don't have the foggiest fucking idea about how all this came about, but I know for sure how it's going to come down. I've got to help Blake." Ben paused and decided to push through it. After all, if it came down to it he could deny he'd ever had this conversation with Walsh. "I've got to help him out of this mess he's in. The only way we can do it, according to Carly and Stephen, is to take away what they called the "contact point". According to them that'll get rid of this dead guy and Blake will be safe. Anyway, how it all works isn't something that I need to worry about. All I need to do is help Blake take away this…place and the guy will go away."

Ben refused to look at Walsh. *Absolutely* refused to look at his friend. He was living it and it still sounded like nut house prattle to him. If he was smiling or smirking he thought he wouldn't be able to help himself from socking him one right in the mouth.

"I wasn't ever able to get beyond my own needs with Stephen. I wasn't able to put him first. I wasn't even able to put Carly's needs before my own. Some husband, huh?" He hated to be down on himself, it wasn't like him to do it, but with the hindsight he had been given it was hard not to.

"I think that was the biggest part of my problems with Stephen. I wasn't ever able to give up what *I* wanted for what *Stephen* wanted. I had this mule head about what he should and shouldn't do and if he didn't fit into the frame I'd made for him, then he didn't matter. It wasn't important to me. Therefore, it didn't matter. The same with Carly, though she would just usually go my way on most things." Ben shook his head again and looked at the empty tee box. He felt like shit about how he had treated his only son and wife.

"I've got a way to fix that," he said, brightening. "I've been shone a route for redemption. A way I can put somebody else first and me last." He stole a glance over at Walsh and was glad that he was still listening with cold intensity, attentive and serious.

"How's that?" Walsh asked.

"Me and Blake and you—if you'll help us—have to take away the contact point from this other guy who wants to hurt Blake."

"What's the contract point?"

"It's '*contact*' point. It's a house."

"How are we going to take it away?"

Ben smiled at the unspoken, hidden commitment to help. He knew he could count on Walsh.

"I think we're going to burn it down."

*   *   *

Wednesday around ten in the morning Blake's Grandpa, Ben and his good friend, Walsh, were at this moment discussing the finer points of their earlier conversation and completing what Ben was fairly sure would prove to be one of the last rounds of golf he would ever play.

After Blake's close call with his mom on his first night of scouting he had been careful to put up a good front. He did all his chores around the house without being asked, mowed once a week and even had started weeding what had once been flower beds around the front and sides of the house. School had let out for summer break two weeks earlier so he'd had plenty of time.

His "scouting reports" had almost filled the spiral notebook. He'd made several attempts to fill in the ATTACK page without much success, but hadn't given up. His Dad had put the controls in his hands, and he was going to keep it straight and level until he found a way to land.

The monster hadn't returned to his dreams, but he could feel it watching and waiting. His Dad had been there sometimes. Sitting confidently in the pilots seat while Blake did the flying. Dark clouds swirling, the plane bucking and fighting to stay aloft. Other times he was alone in the cockpit, the monster somewhere in the back of the plane.

He slid the journal into his bottom desk drawer, and then went to the kitchen for a glass of water.

"What are you doing today, honey?"

"Garden beds. I'm almost done with the front."

"That sure is nice of you to do that," she said, polishing off the last of a bear claw for breakfast and staring at the TV.

He finished off the water and grabbed a couple of bear claws for himself.

"I'll be out front."

"Okay, honey."

He sat on the porch and slowly ate the sweet rolls. The day promised to be another warm one. He wondered what Tim was doing, down there in the ground. Had he started to rot? He wondered if it hurt but knew that it didn't. Tim was dead. Just like his Dad. They were both dead and gone.

A chill ran through him as the morbid thoughts came unbidden. Where would he be now if Tim were still alive? What if his Dad was still alive? Probably not spying on a monster and planing an attack that was for sure. He had begun to miss his Dad again. More than before. That faint spot that had died with his father had begun to ache very much now. Maybe it was the summer or maybe…maybe he just needed his Dad.

They had always taken a summer vacation together as long as he could remember. Usually just a long weekend trip to the tourist stops in Arkansas or Missouri. One time they had driven all the way to the Grand Canyon. Blake remembered seeing the Canyon. He had stood at the lookout with his Dad and looked out over the mile long drop.

It had been dusk and the sun was just tipping over the horizon. They were all tired and dirty with the stale odors of a long car trip. But for a brief moment, as they all stood looking out over the canyon, Blake felt everything come together for him. The bright prismatic light from the sun blazing across the sky, bathing the canyon in purple, pink, red and faint orange splashes.

His Dad was smiling at the view, his mother seemed to be relaxed or relieved, he couldn't tell which, and the world seemed to be a much more beautiful place than he had thought possible. The moment hadn't lasted, though. As the sun finally plunged over the horizon and the night set they piled back in the car and began to fight their way out of the canyon. The world he had always known came rushing back. He could almost hear it filling in the space that had just been pushed aside by the bright, colorful world he had only moments before seen over the canyon.

Yet it had left him with the feeling that he may one day find that same quiet beauty, not only find it but keep it as well.

A rusting older truck with a broken muffler rumbled by in the street and broke his train of thought. He had eaten all of one bear claw and half of the second. It suddenly didn't look as good and he stood up and walked around the side of the house. He tipped the lid off the garbage can and deposited the stale treat, then went back to the front of the house. After waiting for the water to run clear and cold he took a long drink from the hose, then dug into the flowerbeds.

His mother didn't take him on trips any longer. The last trip they had taken was the last summer of his father's life. He had been maybe eight or nine years old. It didn't really seem to matter now.

The grass was tough and didn't release the ground easily. The sun was beginning to blaze and before long he was sweating heavily. Using a shovel to loosen the dirt, he pulled out clumps of the tough foliage and shook the dirt loose. He took his shirt off and lay it on the porch. He got into the work and was thinking about nothing in particular when his mom came out on the porch. She looked a little worried.

"Honey, your Grandpa Ben's on the phone."

"Does he want to talk to me?"

"Yes, he does," she said, looking more worried still. It wasn't like Ben to call and when he did he usually kept the conversation limited to her. Blake wiped his hands on his pants and dried his sweaty head with his shirt.

The house had become shockingly cold compared to the early noon heat of the day and he was instantly chilled as he walked to the kitchen. The phone lay on the end of the counter and Blake picked up the receiver, curious as to what his Grandpa would want with him.

"Hi, Grandpa."

"Hi'ya yourself, Blake," Ben said.

There was an awkward pause as Ben tried to figure out a way to explain things to Blake. He thought that if he called, once he had him on the phone it would work itself out. He wasn't having such luck, however.

"How've you been doing?" he asked, just for something to break the awkward silence.

"Fine."

He hoped that Blake would expand a little more on the subject, but realized with a slight twinge of pain that Blake was uncomfortable because he didn't speak with his Grandpa much. That thought pushed him through his fear. He believed in the dreams enough to tell Walsh and though Walsh probably didn't fully believe him, he did believe enough to go along with it. At least for now he did.

Why should it be any different with Blake? There was only one way to find out if the dreams were a true reflection of reality and that was to spill it all to Blake.

"Listen, Blake, I was thinking that you might like to come out to the place for some fishing this afternoon. How does that sound?"

Blake had only been fishing a couple of times with his Dad, and never with his Grandpa Ben. He hadn't really enjoyed the brief experiences he had had, but it hadn't been something horrible either. The only thing he could remember catching were a couple of small perch.

He didn't have to think much about the offer. It was a welcomed change from the dullness the scouting had become. The monster wasn't going anywhere. He could spare at least one afternoon for some time off.

"I think so, let me ask Mom," he said, laying the phone down without waiting for an answer. Brenda was still out on the front porch, just standing there with her arms folded. Blake thought she looked more worried than before. She was wearing her pink shorts. The shorts were much too small for her and her white, thick legs seemed to be being squeezed from her shorts. She turned quickly as he came out the front door.

"Mom, Grandpa wants me to come over and go fishing this afternoon. Can I go?"

"Is that what he wanted?"

"Sure. He asked if I could come over fishing this afternoon."

"Do you want to go?" she asked, not liking the invitation but not knowing why. Maybe just because it was so unusual for Ben to call out of the blue and invite either of them to do anything. She supposed it was just her natural need to worry that was causing it.

"Sure! I'd like that. I can try and finish the front first if you want," he said, motioning at the flowerbeds and the pile of Bermuda grass he had already pulled. She suddenly felt bad for even questioning the invitation. Of course he would want to go over to his Grandpa's house and go fishing. She should have been more sensitive to his needs. With Stephen gone there wasn't a man around the house and she was sure he needed that influence, whether he realized it or not.

"Okay, go and tell him we'll be out in a little while."

"All-*right!* " Blake said, slamming back into the house, his worries about the monster and keeping up the front for his Mom gone.

"She says it's okay and that we'll be out in a little while," Blake said, barely getting the receiver to his mouth before gushing the information.

"Well, why don't you let me talk with her for a minute."

"Sure."

"Blake?"

"Yeah?"

"Be sure and wear some old clothes so you don't mess up your good ones."

"Okay, I'll go get Mom."

He ran back to the front porch and met Brenda coming in off the porch.

"Grandpa want's to talk with you and I'm gonna go change," with that he shot off, bumping the edge of the couch as he rounded the corner to his room. She couldn't help getting caught up in his excitement and her earlier worries began to fade.

"Ben?" she said into the phone.

"Sounds excited to me, what'd you think?"

"Yes, he does. What's the occasion?" she asked, then wished she hadn't. It had come out sounding trite and defensive, both of which she was not.

"I thought you might be wondering. Well, best I can tell you is that I…well, I guess I just got to thinking about Stephen," he said, trying to dance around the subject at hand. It had started with him thinking about Stephen, that part was true. The rest of it had come unbidden and with a frightening reality that he was just now getting used too.

"And I wanted to get to know Blake a little better."

He let that sit, thinking that Brenda was a smart egg and could fill in the rest of the blanks well enough.

Brenda thought she understood. Ben was nearly seventy and was having some serious thought about his past behavior on the family front. Stephen had spent a lot of time talking with her about Ben and a lack of closeness and clarity in their relationship. It didn't take a lot to connect that with Ben wanting to get close to Blake. If not his son, then his grandson. Almost the same thing.

"Well, he's certainly excited about it. I hope that you can do it more often," she said, knowing he would get the message.

"I plan to. Listen, I'm in town and it would be just as easy for me to come by and pick him up."

"Well, sure, that would be fine. Does he need to bring anything? Bug spray? A change of clothes?"

"Nope. Just be sure he's dressed for fishing. Oh, he might want to bring something to swim in, in case we get too hot and decide to cool off."

"Okay. We'll see you in a little while."

Ben hung up the phone and looked at it for a minute.

"Well?" Walsh said.

"No problem."

"He's coming?"

"Yup, he's coming."

"You want me to come out to your place later, see how things are going?"

They were sitting at the breakfast nook in Walsh's kitchen. Jennie was out. Just outside the sliding glass door off the dining room they could see the sixth green on the Hillcrest golf course.

Ben thought about Walsh coming out. But it could go both ways. If Blake was receptive to what Ben was going to tell him, letting Walsh into the picture might help his confidence. But if Blake thought his Grandpa was slipping a little, well, Walsh showing up would surely drive him off.

"Nope. Why don't you let me give you a call. We'll go from there."

"What'd you want to do it with?"

"What?" Ben asked.

"The house. What do you want to do it with?"

"Kinda' jumpin' the gun, aren't 'cha?"

"Well, if you sell it to Blake the way you sold it to me, the kid'll go for it. I am and I'm not even the one that's in trouble."

"You're sure that I'm not just growing something in my brain that's pushing on the wrong buttons?"

"Aren't you?"

"Shit if I know. But I'll tell you this, Walsh. It sure as hell *feels* right."

"Like I said. What do you want to do it with?"

" A few cans of gas and some rags should turn the trick."

"You think that maybe Blake has some ideas? You did say he was suppose to know something about this already, didn't you?"

"Yeah, I did. I guess we'll find out when I ask him."

*   *   *

Blake was sitting on the porch wearing denim shorts, a green T-shirt and a Dallas Cowboy's baseball cap. He was holding a gray duffel bag that fell from his lap when he stood up as Ben pulled into the driveway. He quickly snatched it up and ran around to the passenger side of Ben's truck.

"Hi'ya Blake. How'ya doin'?"

"Great, Grandpa! Thanks for taking me fishing."

"Well, you might want to wait until we see what we're gonna catch before you thank me," Ben said, feeling strangely guilty.

"Hi, Ben," Brenda said, following Blake up to the truck. She stood next to the driver's side door.

"How have you been, Brenda? Everything going well?"

"Oh, fine. We're getting along. Blake's been a real help around here lately. I guess he deserves a day off," she said, smiling at Blake.

"Well, I won't keep him too late. We'll call and let you know how it's going."

"Okay. Bye, honey. You have a good time."

"Bye, Mom. I will," Blake said, a little embarrassed.

They backed down the drive and were soon out on State Highway nine, heading toward Ben's farm. It was a quick drive to the front gate of his forty-acre spread. He and Carly had purchased the property when he'd retired from a management position with Cintron Oil.

"So, how've you been lately?"

"Fine. I've been doing a lot of work around the house to help Mom."

"Yeah, that's what she said. That's a big help to her I'm sure."

"Yeah," Blake said, then looked out the window.

Ben slowed and turned right off the highway. He sighed deeply and figured that there was no time like the present and he may as well get on with it. As he accelerated on the paved section line road he saw a blur of movement in the air to his left which was quickly followed by a loud *THAMP!* that seemed to come from near the front of the truck. A blur of white and brown feathers confirmed what Ben had thought. They'd hit some kind of bird and it wasn't a little one by the looks of all the feathers flying around. He got the truck stopped and he and Blake got out and looked back up the road. Right in the middle of the road was a tangled pile of dirty white and brown feathers. Blake thought they'd hit a chicken.

"Was it a chicken?" he asked, breathing hard. He'd never been in a car that had hit something before.

"Nope. Chickens can't fly. I think it's a hawk. Get in and we'll go take a look." They climbed back into the truck and Ben carefully backed up the side of the road. Blake turned around in his seat and watched the soft lump of milky feathers move in a swirling pile around the bird in the slight breeze. They pulled even to the bird and climbed out of the truck.

"Careful of cars, Blake. Why don't you help me and be my ears? I can't hear that well anymore."

"All right," Blake said, listening carefully then looking up and down the road. Seeing the road was clear he walked the short distance to where the bird lay sprawled on the road. Ben stood over it a moment then slowly kneeled down.

"Yup. Red-tailed hawk. See the tail feathers?" he said, pointing to some feathers that Blake thought looked more rust colored than red. The hawk was so broken up Blake couldn't tell which end was which until Ben carefully pulled it's head out of the maze it's body had become and gently laid the bird out. It was dead but still warm. Blake stared at the bright yellow eyes of the fierce looking bird and marveled at the sharp beak.

"Come on, we'll take it back to the house and bury it." Blake watched in awe as Ben picked up the bird by its legs, it's sharp talons no longer a threat to anything. He gently lay it in the bed of the truck then they got back in the truck. Blake turned around in his seat to watch the bird in the bed of the truck.

"Beautiful birds, aren't they?"

"Yeah. It still looks like it's alive."

"Deaths a funny thing sometimes."

"Yeah, I guess," he said, staring at the bird. "Where do you think the hawk is now?"

"What do you mean? Did it fall out?" Ben asked, slowing the truck.

"No, its body's still there, but I mean the hawk that was living before we hit it. Where do you think it is now?"

It took him a moment to realize what Blake was asking. If he hadn't been having the...well, he couldn't really call them dreams any longer, visions were more like it.

If he hadn't been having the *visions* about Carly and Stephen he would have given him the all around standard answer that adults gave kids about death. He would have told Blake that the hawk was now flying around Heaven and taking care of God's pest problems. But since he wasn't sure anymore that Heaven was a place you stayed very long—if at all—he didn't really know what to say.

"Well, I guess that it's gone some place else, besides here," Ben managed to put together.

"Oh," Blake said, turning back to look at the hawk again.

"Maybe it went where your Grandma Carly and your Dad went when they died."

"No. I don't think it did."

"Why's that?"

"Mom said that Dad and Grandma and my friend Tim were all in Heaven, looking down on us and praying with God."

Ben didn't think that he had said it with much conviction, however.

"Is that were *you* think they are?"

"I don't know. Sometimes I think that maybe they are still here, you know? Up here," he said, pointing to his head. "Other times I think that they aren't." He climbed off the seat and turned around to face forward.

"Well, I think that it may be a little of both, Blake. I wanted to talk with you about something today that I...well, I don't know how to say it. I invited you to go fishing so we could have a little talk." Ben was suddenly reminded of his talk with Walsh earlier in the day.

"What about?" Blake asked, his face open and honest. Ben hoped that if he had been wrong about all of it and that it turned out there actually was something growing in his head that wasn't suppose to be there, that Blake would be able to forgive him.

"Well, I guess it's about your Dad and me and probably Tim also, but I'm not for sure." Did he see Blake snap too just a little? Wasn't that just the slightest bit of a twinge Blake made at the mention of his Dad and Tim? He hoped that it was.

"What about them?" Blake asked, a new sharpness in his eye.

"Well, I've been having these dreams lately and in them…well, let's just say I know what you've been doing." There was a brief spat of surprise on Blake's face that he did a fair job of hiding. Ben sighed with relief. At least he may be partially right and the dreams of Stephen and Carly did carry some validity.

"What do you mean?" he asked, the open face gone.

"Don't ask me how I know, but I know that you're messing with a house and you're in a lot of trouble with some guy that has something to do with that house."

He glanced over at Blake and watched him carefully. His mouth hung open slightly and he stared straight ahead at the road. Ben looked forward and nearly stood on the brakes so as not to miss their turn. He overshot it a little and backed up the truck. They turned left onto a gravel road that ran back up a hill and into a stand of tall cottonwood trees.

Of all the things that he expected, Blake bursting into tears was not one of them. He had imagined several scenarios and all of them had centered on Blake thinking that he, Ben, was crazy. This was not what he had expected. He pulled the truck to a stop in the gravel road and put an arm around Blake. He cried all the harder.

They sat that way for a while. Ben didn't know how long and didn't really care. It felt good. It was the beginning of his redemption. He had never held Stephen close when he was crying about something or another. Carly had always done that.

After a moment his crying slowed and he pulled himself together. He wiped at his red and puffy eyes and slid back toward his side of the truck, looking at Ben.

"You want to talk about it?"

"I'm sorry I cried."

Ben felt an icy sliver drive through him. What the hell was so wrong with crying? Had he actually been such a bad father that Stephen had ingrained in his own son the idea that crying was not good?

"Nothing wrong with crying, Blake. It's sometimes the only way to get things out."

"Yeah, I guess."

Blake was looking at him closely, trying to figure out, Ben thought, just how he knew what he did.

"Let's get on up to the house."

He drove the remaining half-mile up the hill, then down into a little valley to his house. It was one of those log cabin homes you saw mostly in the northwest. With a wide walk around the porch and six-paned windows evenly spaced on the upper and lower floors of the home. Behind the house off in the trees you could just see the front edge of a cinder block barn.

Ben parked the truck next to the house and shut it off.

"Why don't we get on up to the pond, we can bury the hawk later."

"Okay," Blake said, climbing out of the truck.

Ben went into the house and quickly returned with two fishing poles, a small tackle box and a large pail.

"I thought we might get hungry up there," Ben said, smiling. He thought Blake looked relieved more than anything. If he could have read Blake's mind he would have been surprised at just how relieved he really was. Unlike most adults, children had a special knack of believing what they heard. When Ben told him that he knew about the house and not to ask how, Blake took him at his word.

"Let's get up there. Have you seen the new dock I built?" Ben asked, walking up the trail that led toward the cinder block barn.

"No, I don't think so."

Well, of course he hadn't. How long had it been since he had come out to the place? Six months? A year? Longer?

"Well, I built it for shade. Just right for summer fishing in the hot sun," he said, smiling back at Blake.

"Great. We'll need it today," he said, grinning and looking a little more recovered from his crying bout. Was he heavier than the last time he'd see him? Ben thought that he was.

They walked past the cinder block barn and through a little grove of small blackjack oaks. The ground ran down at a gentle slope and beneath the oaks they could see the small lake. It was more glamorous than a simple cattle pond, but at about six acres in size couldn't technically be called a lake, but they had always called it that anyhow.

The lake was free of brush on all sides except for the north end, which was choked full of cattails and a few small cottonwoods. They followed a well-worn trail through the high grass. The sun had become blisteringly hot at some point and the lazy *ZZZZZ-ZZZZZ-ZZZZZ* of the cicadas was at maximum throttle. Dry dust ticked at their noses as they reached the lake.

"Well, what do you think?" Ben said, pointing to the middle of the lake.

"Wow! That's really cool!" Blake said, his pains forgotten.

A gazebo was floating in the middle of the lake.

"How come it doesn't sink?"

"It's built on dock foam. It can't sink or drift. I've got it anchored in the lake bottom at all four corners. Come on, let's row out there and get after it."

They walked around the edge of the lake to the north end. Behind the cattails was an overturned rowboat. Ben set down his load and, with

Blake's help launched the small boat through a break in the foliage. Ben helped Blake into the boat then passed him all their gear.

"Now, sit right in the middle of the seat so we don't go for a swim," Ben instructed. "Hold on to the sides I'm going to shove us off." With a smooth gracefulness that beguiled his age, Ben stuck a foot into the little rowboat and pushed with the other foot against the bank. The little boat moved smoothly away from the shore and swung in a small arc as their momentum was spent. His hips were screaming with pain, but it had been worth it. He fell more than sat and after aligning the oars started them out to the gazebo.

"Well, Blake I suppose you're wondering just how it is that I know about the house," he said, facing Blake as he slowly rowed them toward the middle of the lake.

"Are you going to tell on me?" Blake asked. There was very little in the way of timidness in the statement and Ben found that somewhat comforting. After loosing his father to one of the worst kind of deaths their was, as far as Ben was concerned, the boy had found himself somehow and was doing well to stand on his own with such confidence. He felt a slight twinge of…pride? Maybe. But it didn't really matter. Whatever it was he felt didn't need to be defined. He knew that it felt good and that was enough.

"I think that I'm going to surprise you on this one," he said, looking at the edge of the lake receding as he dug another scoop of water and pulled for the gazebo. The boat glided forward.

"Nope. I'm not going to tell on you. In fact, I'm going to help you. But we've got some things that we need to get cleared up first. Okay?"

"You're going to help me?" Blake asked with more than just a hint of excitement.

"Yup. We're going to do this thing together. Just you and me and maybe, if we might need the help, Walsh. How's that sound?"

"Great!" Blake said, nearly bubbling out of the boat with excitement. "Are we getting close yet?"

"Not much farther. You need to move a little to the left. No, the other way. That's right. Keep going." Ben tried not to think about the pain in his hips as Blake guided them to the gazebo. Or the dozen other pains he was feeling. He was more thankful than ever that he had installed the swimming ladder on the gazebo. If there was a gun held to his head he didn't think that he could step up out of the boat. He thought he would be doing good just to get his legs over the edge.

Blake steadied the boat as Ben, hips still screaming, slowly executed the titanic maneuver of climbing out of the boat. Once out, his hips seemed to calm down. He was thankful for the little refrigerator Walsh had talked him into putting out here. Anchoring the electric line on the bottom of the pond had been a royal pain in the ass, not to mention the cost of waterproof cable. Yet, to sit out here on a hot summer night with your line in the water tight-line fishing for catfish and sipping an ice-cold beer just couldn't be beat. Walsh had been right, it had been a damn good idea. Especially now that he was really hurting and it was so hot out.

He was beginning to think that he should have waited a day to give himself a chance to recuperate from golf before he talked with Blake, but he knew he couldn't have. What if Blake had chosen this particular day to do whatever he had planned for the house? Unthinkable. A little arthritic twanging was a small price to pay for redemption.

He pulled up next to one of several director style chairs scattered about the gazebo. As he sat down in the comfortable chair, Blake nimbly climbed out of the boat and began to off load their gear.

"Better tie it down before you do that or you're gonna be swimming sooner than you think."

Blake looked at the boat and dropped the tackle box and a pole in time to grab it from drifting away.

"There's a rope in front and back. Don't really need them both, but what the hell. It makes it easier for Walsh and me to get in it." He neglected to add that the ease of climbing into the boat would be easier still without the aid of the several beers they would usually have. He watched as Blake carefully tied down the little rowboat fore and aft.

"Bring the poles over here and we'll get set up," Ben said.

The gazebo was built of decking lumber and had a high gabled roof. The wind moved it slightly, but not enough to be uncomfortable. Ben helped Blake with the poles, both of which were already rigged for bottom fishing.

"Look over there, see that little thing that looks like a big ring lying on the floor? Yup, right there. Pull it up."

Blake did as he was told and Ben enjoyed the look of surprise on his face as he discovered the refrigerator built into the floor. The foam on which the gazebo floated made for an excellent insulator. Again, it had been Walsh's idea. That Walsh could be quick as a whip when he wanted to. Maybe Ben should have been an engineer also. Too late now. It was too late for a lot of things.

"Grab that red bucket there. The one with all that black stuff sticking to the sides. Careful now, you don't want to spill it. We'll have catfish chopping up my nice new fishing pad."

Blake smiled.

"What is this stuff? It sure stinks."

"That, Blake, is the best stuff in the world for catching catfish. It's my secret recipe and maybe I'll pass it on to you. If you want it that is."

"Sure! Does that stuff really work?"

"Just wait and see."

Ben quietly baited their hooks with the foul smelling black paste and gently lowered the lines over the side.

"Trick is to feel for the bottom, then reel in about three cranks. That way it's right off the bottom. Right where they like it."

Ben began to see the man that Blake would become. Independent and probably a little somber. He wondered how it all would end. Dreams were one thing, reality another. He marveled at how old Blake seemed for just being eleven. Or was he twelve now?

"Blake, how old are you now? Eleven?"

"Yeah. Be twelve in January."

"Sure, that's right. I remember now. January eighth. I remember it because there was a big sleet storm that night and we all had a hell of a time getting to the hospital. Your Dad and I made it just about the same time. But by then you were already swaddled and in the cradle. Course, back then we didn't go in and watch everything like they do now."

Their lines reached bottom and they both cranked up a little on their respective reels.

"Up there, if you can reach 'em are a couple of pole stands. See these holes here?" Ben said, pointing to a line of small holes around the edge of the gazebo. "Those pole holders fit really snug in them. Do you think you can reach them?"

"Sure."

Ben watched as Blake slid around a chair and grabbed two of the pole holders. They fit them into the holes in the dock and lay the poles into them. Blake grabbed a pop for himself and a beer for Ben from the refrigerator gently let the door close the hole in the floor, then settled into a chair next to Ben.

"Well, I guess I've got some things to explain," Ben said. Blake nodded and sipped on his can of pop. He was watching the pole intently.

"Don't worry about your pole too much. The only kinds of catfish I've got in here are slow ones. It'll be awhile."

Ben looked out over the lake and sipped his beer. His hips were feeling better in the soft chair and he knew it wouldn't be long before he no longer noticed them. Blake was watching him.

"The best I can tell you is this, Blake. I've been having, well, dreams, I guess about your Dad and Grandma Carly. Though I like to call them visions because that seems more accurate. You know what that means? Accurate?"

"Sure. Like correct."

"Yes. Like correct. Anyhow, I've been having these visions about them. And in these visions they are telling me all about what you are doing because they are worried about you. They believe in you but aren't sure you know what you are up against." Ben sipped his beer.

"I...I don't know what, you know, to..."

"Don't worry about it. I've had my head checked out by a couple of people and so far nobody has said I'm crazy. But what'll prove I'm not is if you tell me what's going on. Are you messing with some house and some dead guy?"

"Yeah, but nobody believes me, Grandpa! At least until now. My friend Tim was killed by that monster and it lives in the old house on Cherokee and I thinking that if I take the house away it'll go away too. Then I was—."

"Whoa, whoa. Hold it a minute. Why don't you slow down and let me ask a few questions." Ben nearly tipped over in his chair. He was right. The dreams he liked to call visions had been real. Well, as real as something like that could be. The flood of relief he felt was overwhelming. He wasn't going to have to spend the rest of his life in some place called Shady something or another.

Blake seemed to be just as relieved to have somebody to share with. His babble of information proved as much. Ben slowed him down and began asking him detailed questions about the house. Blake relayed everything he knew about the house, Tim, his Journal—everything.

Ben was surprised the he seemed to take it all in fairly good stride. Children were amazing in that they didn't have all the preconceived ideas that adults had been burdened with. When Ben had shared what was happening with himself and the dreams to Walsh. Walsh had needed some convincing. He probably still wasn't quite convinced. But once he'd spoken with Blake, Walsh would come around all the way.

They sat quietly watching their poles. Blake had been through three pops and Ben the same number of beers. It was Blake that brought it up first and Ben was glad for it.

"Grandpa? Did you build a…ah…bathroom out here? I've got to go real bad."

"Nope, sure didn't, Blake. But now that you mention it, I've got to do the same."

"Should we row back to the house?"

"Nope. Me and Walsh just usually water the fish, if you know what I'm driving at."

Blake laughed and didn't hesitate to do so. Ben followed suit and wondered at how the world worked. If you had told him this was going to be happening a year ago, he would have offered to take you to the nut house himself.

Were he and his Grandson actually going to burn down a house to get rid of this 'contact point'? They put you in jail for that sort of thing. And if they decided you were crazy when you did it, they put you in the nut house. Well, crazy or not it felt good just to be fishing with his Grandson in the shade during a hot summer day. One day at a time, as had been said on many occasions, was sure as shit good advice.

"Now, as I understand it as it was explained to me, this house is what your Dad and Grandma Carly are calling a contact point. I guess it's something that this dead guy you're calling a monster can cling to, kind of like holding onto a float in the middle of the ocean. All we've got to do is take this contact point away and that'll be that."

Blake nodded, listening intently. He was secretly glad that he didn't have to do the thinking anymore. It felt better letting somebody else plan for a while.

"The thing that I don't understand is why you and this…monster are at odds?"

Blake explained about he club and initiation gone sour inside the house. Then again about the day Tim died in the run-off pond.

"I guess he's just pissed because I messed with his turf. I didn't know. He's a bad thing, though. I think that my Dad met him once that day…that day that he died. I don't want you to get hurt Grandpa. I don't know why, but I think I'm…that I'm…that he can't touch me any-more. At least it feels that way."

Ben thought that Carly and Stephen probably had something to do with that.

"Yup, but they wouldn't have told me about what you were up to if that was going to last, would they?"

"No, I guess not."

"Let's reel up and see what the deal is."

They pulled up their lines to find their bait gone. Ben showed Blake how to roll the stink bait into a ball and knead it onto the hook. They dropped their lines back down. Ben watched Blake reel the line in a cou-ple of turns. The kid was a fast study. Just like Stephen had been or *was* if you looked at it that way.

"Well, Walsh and I talked about it. Yeah, Walsh knows all about it. Don't worry though, he's on our side," Ben added as a look of alarm slid across Blake's face.

"Anyway, we talked about it and I think that we can get the job done. But you need to know that this isn't some game we're going to play. Burning down a house or any other thing is against the law. If we're not going to get caught, we're going to have to be smart and quick. We're going to have to think the thing through. All right?"

"Okay, Grandpa."

What kind of lessons was Blake learning now? How to break the law and not get caught? They had to wait and see on that score. Ben realized that he had not thought all the way through this deal himself. How could he reasonably ask an eleven-year-old to do so? What could this be doing to Blake? What kind of harm was it causing him? Making war plans with his Grandpa because his dead father and dead grandmother was telling his live Grandfather to do it because it's this science fiction sounding 'contact point' for another dead person? What kind of happy shit was that anyhow? It didn't make a lick of sense. Not one bit of sense. And though all that was true, every bit of it true to the bone, they were going to do it anyway. In the end, it really didn't have to make sense. Most of life didn't, so why should this?

Ben quit drinking after four beers and they fished for another hour without any luck. Ben put it down to the heat and that since they'd peed in the water it had scared all the fish down to the other end of the lake. Blake laughed at this.

With Blake's considerable help, Ben made it back into the rowboat after nearly spilling them both into the lake. He wondered briefly if he could still swim worth a shit, but didn't have any real desire to find out. Blake did his best to row them back. He had never rowed and was having trouble getting both oars into the water at the same point and pulling them simultaneously. Consequently he kept hitting the side of the boat and splashing Ben. They were both laughing and having a good time. One relieved to realize he wasn't crazy and was getting a shot at redemption, the other that he wasn't alone and that it was nice to have his Grandpa around again.

*   *   *

They made it back to shore without any major mishaps, though they were more than a little wet. They drug the boat up behind the cattails and turned it over on it's top, just as they'd found it. Blake followed Ben back up the trail, through the little stand of blackjack oaks, past the barn and up to the house. They leaned their gear against the side of the house and sat down to rest.

"Why don't we go get something to eat and then we'll go bury that hawk."

Blake had forgotten about the hawk and was back up looking in the bed of the truck.

Ben stood after catching his wind. He realized that he was going to feel this day for awhile, the deep fire in his hips and aching hands was just the beginning. No matter. It was good to feel something. Anything.

He wasn't going to have much longer to feel things on this level. He glanced back up through the trees to the cinder block barn. He could just see the front edge of the deck, looking just as it did in his dream. He wondered if he was going to dream about Carly and Stephen again, now that he and Blake were in cahoots. He thought that he might.

"It sure looks dead now, Grandpa," Blake said from where he was leaning over the side of the truck.

"Yup. I'm sure it does. Let's get something to eat. Are you hungry?"

"You bet! Starved!" Blake said, coming back around the truck. Ben thought that the boy could do with a few missed meals, but then so could he. He began thinking that they should eat something sensible and healthy, then laughed a little at his thoughts. What would a dying man want to eat sprouts and celery or a big unhealthy but tasty burger and fries? Or baked clams in white sauce? Or steaks rare, medium or well done?

Blake chose the burgers and Ben was surprised that he could match him burger for burger. They sat on the porch, the smell of fried burgers filling the whole house and beyond, both sipping iced water and waiting for their stomachs to settle. It was nearly six and the sun was just now beginning to get low in the horizon.

"Go ahead and give your mom a call, then we can go out and bury the hawk."

"Okay. What should I tell her?"

"Well, tell her that you'll be home after awhile and not to worry. Mom's like to here that if I remember correctly."

He went in the house and quickly called.

"She said Okay."

They buried the hawk at the top of the hill. Ben carried the shovel and Blake carried the hawk, now stiff and showing a streak of stiff, tacky blood on the back of it's head. They walked past the sandstone rocks that seemed to form a cave in Ben's dreams and he made no mention of them to Blake. There didn't seem to be any need to do so.

Besides, he found that he didn't want to share that small piece of Carly and Stephen he was given with anyone just yet.

Blake picked a spot that overlooked several miles of mostly flat Oklahoma fields and scattered woods. He dug a hole in the soft sand. Here and there over the land were fields rich with alfalfa and baled hay interspersed with patches of bright green trees that followed the snaky outline of a creek or small river, Blake didn't know which.

Ben helped him fold the wings of the once fierce and proud bird and Blake laid it gently in the hole that he had dug. They both pushed the dirt back into the hole, covering the hawk. There was a small mound of dirt left and they patted it down as best they could. Ben realized that the hole wasn't nearly deep enough to keep the coyote's and possums from digging up the bird, but Blake didn't need to know.

"Well, that's it," Ben said, turning back toward the trail. Blake hesitated a moment, the picked up the shovel and began to follow.

"You don't think that the hawk is cold, do you Grandpa?"

"What? Cold?" Ben asked, then he warmed to the greater question Blake was asking. He stopped in the trail and, though it caused him great pain, kneeled down next to Blake.

"Blake, everything dies—everything—that's just one of the laws of our lives. But when everything dies, it leaves something behind. Like a tree leaves its wood and leaves, or a fish its skeleton," Ben said, motioning at the woods around them.

"When that hawk died, it stopped feeling anything like cold or pain. It's gone to a greater world than this one. I don't know if it's Heaven, exactly, but I do know that it's not cold down there. That's just what it left behind when it died." Blake was watching him closely and listening intently.

"Do you understand?" Ben asked, wishing he had more of an answer.

"Yeah. I think so. Like when people die they're gone, but they leave their body behind…kind of like water leaving a cup?"

"Yes, that's the idea," Ben said, wishing he had said it. "Does that help?"

"Yeah. So I guess it's not cold down there."

"No, it's not. But if it was cold, it wouldn't be feeling it, because the hawk that flew into the truck today is long gone."

"Like Dad and Grandma Carly?"

"Yes, just like your Dad and Grandma Carly."

"Like water leaving a cup," Blake said, and for some reason Ben didn't understand, smiled brightly. After thinking about it most of the night, Ben thought that smile was meant to show understanding and maybe just a hint of relief. Once that water left the cup, it had to find someplace else to go; join a river, water a plant, somewhere. So in a sense, the statement was one of the rare truisms Ben had heard in his almost seventy years of living this life.

"Come on, let's get back and get you home. It'll be dark soon."

Blake trailed behind his Grandfather as they wound their way back past the sandstone rocks that looked like a cave and the cinder block barn.

He called his mom from the house and they piled into the truck and set out for town. Blake was asleep in ten minutes and Ben felt a deep warmth that he hadn't felt in a long time. It was his redemption taking hold and he welcomed it and tried not to think too much about the pay off that would be required.

SEVEN

…4

The Turtle hadn't moved from the beach. He blinked his eyes and rubbed his shoulders against the cold shivering through him.

He knew what was happening, of course he knew. But it was like seeing that you were going to smash the car in front of you and the full gas tanker truck behind you was going to smash you. You jumped on the brakes, fucking-off that pumping-the-brakes crap when the roads are icy and it was about a pebble past a peck until you impacted and you had just enough time to think that this was going to be one hell of a mess, but not long enough to wonder if you were going to survive it.

He thought he could come out of it. All he had to do was turn around and walk out of the lake…but he didn't really want to.

He had had enough. There was only so much the old sane-O-meter could take, and his had reached that point.

He moved a little deeper into the lake…

Marilyn showed up at six-thirty with a fruit salad and a small French loaf.

"Oh, not much has changed here," she said.

"Well, I wanted to leave it raw, you know? The way I remembered it. I wanted to capture as much of that time as I could. I thought it would help the book."

"Good idea. I like it," she said, walking down the hall. "Your office?" she asked, pointing to what had been his Dad's room.

"Yeah."

"How does that feel?" she asked, not opening the door. Had he closed it for a reason? He'd never closed it before.

"Fine. So Far," he said, laughing lightly. He turned went back to the kitchen. "I need to pull the chicken out. Are you ready to eat?"

"Sure."

They ate in silence, both taking the edge off their appetites.

"Do you remember telling me about the lake trip?" Marilyn asked, hoping that he did and at the same time that he didn't. He looked at her for a puzzled moment, and then nodded his head as his eyes cleared. He slowly chewed a large bite of chicken and tried to smile with his mouth full.

Marilyn thought that he was a handsome boy, especially when he smiled. His rough, marred face actually seemed to blend well with his black hair and those odd gray eyes.

"Do you remember if Ron was on that trip? You remember him, don't you? From the hospital?"

He nodded absently and she remembered he seemed bored with the conversation. Marilyn had been hoping for a better reaction than what she was getting. She'd actually hoped for a lot more, but he had acted like she was talking about a particularly uneventful trip to the grocery store.

"I remember him, but I don't think he was there," he said, shoveling another bite in his mouth.

She hadn't responded, choosing instead to let the subject die. She had only wanted to confirm what she had suspected. Even though the trip had never occurred, as far as she knew, Lane believed that it had. Even to the point of having specific, detailed memories about the trip. She'd checked around with the final hope that the trip had somehow taken place in her absence, but found what she'd expected to find.

Nothing.

No trip.

Period.

So it meant one of two possibilities. One—Lane was verging on another mental break. Two—Lane had something growing in his head that wasn't supposed to be there. She hoped for the latter.

After asking several times to see his work on the autobiography, hoping it may hold some clue, as Stan suggested it may, she'd given up. She had pushed him as far as she dared under the circumstances.

After dinner, they'd moved in to his rough living area for more casual conversation. They had ended up watching a PBS special on Sea Turtles. She left after the special. As she drove away, she had what at first she'd considered an absurd idea. But in the span of days from Monday to this afternoon, she had come to believe it was true. She was afraid of loosing Lane. Afraid of turning him back to the system.

If Litchfield prodded and probed him, he would surely find something wrong and back Lane would go. The state still had the power to rope him back in. Only this time, Marilyn would be out and somebody else would be in her place, beginning again. She would have failed Lane and perhaps herself also, though she usually didn't have such self centered thoughts. Or did she? Maybe this was all about *her* and *her* needs not to see somebody she had helped fall short. She could no longer be sure.

It all boiled down to getting Lane into the hospital for a look at what was happening beneath his skull, then if nothing turned up, Litchfield could take him. Yet, until he was run through a complete physical she would no longer pass along all the information she could to Litchfield. She wouldn't *lie* about Lane's situation to Litchfield, she just wouldn't take an active role in relaying information.

*   *   *

There was a remote brownish-gray hump on the horizon of this vast, mighty sea. High clouds surrounded the hump. He'd seen several sea birds. Two had been aloft, riding some invisible drafts, yet their height didn't prevent him from seeing the bright orange color of their plumage. They had appeared to be as big as gulls, maybe larger. The head feathers were a darker shade of orange, but he couldn't tell the color for sure. The only other bird he'd seen had been skimming over the wave tops. It was much smaller than the previous two birds and its plumage was a bright red, tapering to a shiny violet at its head and a dark shade of green at its tail. It flew with frequent wing beats as it circled him where he sat upon this great animal.

He thought the dark hump on the horizon must be the island on which these birds made landfall. The powerful strokes of the hard-shelled beast he rode had slowly shifted course to follow the red plumed bird. They began pulling toward the island. Yet it would be some time before it was reached.

At twenty miles on the ocean the curvature of the earth begins to block your line of sight. How high were the peaks of this remote island? How did that effect the distance equation? Was the distance fifty miles? Sixty? A hundred? Surely not a hundred miles, but easily more than fifty.

He sat comfortably and was satisfied to ride; watching, listening— the sounds were muted and slow—to the watery surroundings. It felt as if—.

"—not going to listen to me?"

"What?" Lane said, looking up from the computer screen.

Lester Hollie was standing in all his bulky grace next to his desk.

"I asked if you were all right? Are you?"

"Sure. Fine. Why?" Lane asked, looking at Lester. He remembered to put on a smile.

"Because you were just staring at your screen."

"Oh, yeah. I was just thinking about some things. Thanks for checking, Les."

"Sure, no problem." Lester slowly shuffled on up the aisle to the tables in front. On the way back, with a small pile of new paper work in hand, he smiled brightly at Tina and they chatted a moment. Lane felt a sudden and inexplicable happiness for them. It was gone as fast as it had come and he turned back to his work.

He turned back to the diagram currently hanging next to the terminal screen. Typing the last paragraph of directive, he slid the paper from its pressure sensitive holder and laid it in his much too small pile of completed sheets. Loading the next page he felt himself beginning to slip again into that strange sea. All fair sky, the beast he rode pulling hard toward a distant shore…another bird flying past…this one colored a bright—.

He shook his head, trying to rid himself of the vision. The dream had begun pressing him for attention Monday and it had been growing steadily more insistent with each passing hour.

It didn't feel bad, this waking dream of a sterile healthy paradise, not bad at all.

At night, the dream pulled him in toto with its raving finality of a clear, peaceful picture of what surely must be something nearing a deathly innocence. His waking from the dream the past few mornings was more a physical necessity than a conscious decision. He had always dreamt well and clearly, visions that he had put down in the book *Night Vision*, but those had not been dreams of a beautiful paradise. His dreams had always run along a macabre course that leaned more toward death and decay than life and growth. In fact, he had only had nightmares as long as he could remember.

The thought that it may be the return of Turtle (he knew beyond a doubt what he was riding in the dream, but had yet to admit it to himself) in a new and seductive disguise worried him, but not to a great degree. The dream was too soothing and too captivating a relief for him to be concerned about it's origins.

His writing on the autobiography had slowed to a near standstill. The yellow legal pads filled with notes remained scattered about his writing room, untouched and disorganized. He had left off at the third or fourth chapter, he wasn't sure which. He'd done roughly three hundred manuscript pages. The pages had been no more than a transcription of his rambling, discordant notes. Very little actual writing had been done. The plan was to work with the information once it was lain out. It wasn't working out that way.

He felt the same dull guilt he usually did when he wasn't writing as he should. The move and maybe the house—certainly his dreams— seemed to have taken the edge off. It was a simple case of writer's block. Like all the former cases he'd had, it would pass. It would have too. He didn't have anything else.

Five o'clock finally drug itself around and he did his best to get out without too much conversation.

"Hey, Lane!" He turned at the door and saw Williams calling him across the room.

"I whipped her ass today!" he said, shaking an envelope in the air. He was drawing a blank at the gesture then suddenly remembered, as if a box popped open and let the memory go.

"Great," he said, not much louder than a whisper. He turned and left. Once he'd hit the parking lot, he began to feel a little better, more himself. He was holding the vision at bay much easier, which would probably be a big plus once he'd started the drive back home.

He crossed the front drive and began to walk into the parking lot, he heard light footsteps behind him. He turned to see Foster Estroga keeping pace with him, his dirty blue baseball hat in place, his hollow eyes eating him up with their primitive intent.

"Hi, Lane. Got a moment?"

Where the hell did Foster come from? He fought the urge to speak his anger, then stopped walking and turned. Foster stopped with him.

"Sure, Foster. What's up?"

"I have dreams, too," he said, never shifting his gaze, never smiling. Lane would have thought him a mannequin if his eyes weren't blinking.

"What?" Lane asked, not believing what he'd heard.

"I have dreams, too."

"What the *fuck* are you talking about, Foster?" Lane asked. For the first time in his life he wanted the dark side of Turtle to bring his stinking self forward at high speed. He didn't want to hurt Foster, he just wanted to scare the piss out of him. He wanted him gone and out of his face. Then just as quickly he was inexplicably scared of this strange little person standing before him and speaking what seemed to be familiar incoherent bullshit.

"We're gonna dance. That's what going to happen. It's all gonna end with a dance. It'll be real ugly," Foster said, smiling a brittle grin. He reached out with his right hand and grabbed Lane's crotch, giving his penis and scrotum a hard squeeze. Then he turned and walked calmly away.

Lane watched him go, so completely blown away by the incident that he could do nothing but follow suit and walk to his car. He opened the drivers' door and slid into the seat, not noticing the suffocating heat. He started the Olds without thinking about it and sat, starring out at the parking lot.

What the hell had that been all about? What had he said? They would *dance?* What the fuck was that suppose to mean? He'd said it was all going to end when they danced. Wasn't that it? It was all going to end when they dance and that it would be ugly.

He reached out and clicked on the air conditioning. Still sitting and thinking about what Foster had said, it would be another half an hour before he felt able to drive home.

*   *   *

He woke immediately. One moment he was riding the now familiar beast, pulling toward what apparently was their island destination and the next he was wide awake. He was laying in bed, the sheets in a tangled confusion around his body, the dream no longer pressing itself upon him, but no less real for its absence. Had he driven home? What time was it?

He lay still, wondering what had wakened him so suddenly from his dream. The soft humm of the air conditioner kicking on reminded him of the waves lapping against the beast he rode and he began to fall back on the other side of wakefulness. His eyes began closing but a soft scratching brought them wide again. He listened closely, seeing if it would come again, if indeed he had actually heard it here in his room and not in the medium between sleeping and dreaming.

sccccreeeee...screeeee...screeeee...

Eyes wide, he sat up. Sitting on the edge of the bed in nothing but his white briefs, he untangled the sheets from his legs and listened.

One minute passed according to the glowing red digital clock—two-fifteen to two-sixteen in the morning. Two minutes passed and he'd heard nothing. Just as he was getting up to use the bathroom he heard it again.

screeeee...screeeee...screeeee

Standing, he moved to the open bedroom door, trying to locate the noise. It had a metallic ring to it, like a nail being drawn across a rusty metal pipe. He stood in the open door, needing to pee, and waited. At just past two minutes according to the clock, it came again.

screeeee...screeeee...screeeee

He walked quietly into the hallway, listening. It lasted no more than five seconds, enough time for him to tell it wasn't coming from the living room or the front of the house. He walked toward the back bedroom and waited, rubbing his arms against a chill, silently counting off the seconds to two minutes. At one hundred thirty-five seconds he heard it again.

Screeeee...screeeee...screeeee

It wasn't coming from the back room. He closed the door behind him and walked back up the hallway, trying to narrow down his choices. If not the front of the house or the back of the house, it must be coming from either the office or the bathroom. He settled on the bathroom and opened the door as he silently counted the seconds.

At one hundred three he heard it again. It sounded as if he were right on top of the strange noise, though it was probably only the late hour and the still night that amplified the sound into more than it was.

SCREEEEE...SCREEEEE...SCREEEEE

He reached for the light switch and hesitated, caught by what he saw in the gloom of moonlight filtering in through his bedroom window into the hall. The bathroom was the same as it had always been, more so in the soft glow of the moon. The peeling blue wallpaper with horizontal stripes of white, the un-vented gas stove that had worked in fits, the cracked, water stained hardwood floor, it's finish gone years before. The dirty white shower curtain had been replaced with a new one. He began to switch the light on, certain that he was just having some kind of memory jog, and then the noise came again.

screeeee...screeeee...screeeee

It had become small again, or weaker. Weaker? Where had he heard that before? He stared at the ghostly, wavering bathroom, wanting to flood the room with light to dispose of it and at the same time struggling to remember something that had happened in this room.

"Do you think it can get out?"

He turned quickly, banging his elbow against the door jam searching for the speaker of the voice. He quickly scanned the hallway. Seeing nobody, he steeled himself to go into the living room and confront the speaker. As he was turning, a faint glimmer of movement caught his eye in the bathroom. He focused on the spot he thought he'd seen the movement, but there was nothing there.

He turned from the bathroom again and this time was sure he'd seen a shimmering of something low on the floor of the bathroom, but as he focused on the spot, it disappeared once again.

SCREEEEE...SCREEEEE...SCREEEEE

The metallic scratching brought his attention fully around to the bathroom. If he turned his eyes to the sides and looked at the spot in the bathroom he thought he'd seen movement on the edge of his vision, he could just make out a form crouched on the floor. As he viewed it from the painful edge of his sight, he slowly recognized what the form was. It was his sister, Kristy.

He fought the urge to look away, and in so doing the scene in the bathroom seemed to gain strength and clarity from his resolve to experience it.

Kristy was crouched on the floor. She was fourteen, Lane thought, and was already pregnant but didn't know it yet. As the scene began to unfold, he saw a small figure crouched on the floor next to her. It was he, at the age of twelve, small, yet compact and strong for his age. Both the result of the punishment his father dished out.

"*I don't know,*" his long ago self told his phantom sister. "*I don't think so.*"

They were taking turns looking to the ragged end of a small broken pipe that protruded no more than an inch up from the bathroom floor. The pipe was possibly the remains of a bathroom vent, or an unfinished attempt at renovating the bathroom by some former owner. It was stuffed with a dirty piece of cloth most of the time. The bit of cloth now lay discarded at their feet. They both took turns looking into the small pipe.

Lane closed his eyes and felt something inside his head began to stretch beyond its capacity. Before the memory could break free completely, the flickering image of himself and Kristy on the floor demanded his attention once again.

SCREEEEE…SCREEEEE…SCREEEEE.

"*Lane, can't we do anything?*" the ghost of Kristy pleaded with her brother.

"I don't know. Maybe I can go under the house?" he said, more for something to say than with any real conviction to crawl into the dark guts of the house. Even for their pet now stuck down the pipe.

Lane stood at the bathroom door watching the scene unfold though he hadn't needed to stay much longer. The memory was coming on now and he couldn't stop it. As his mind was flooded with the incident, the image before his eyes slowly faded, then went dark as if staged on cues. He folded into his memory, standing in the doorway of the bathroom and willingly began to recount the history.

A sometime friend and classmate at school had given the small terrarium turtle to him. His parents hadn't allowed James to keep the harmless creature and he had offered it to Lane two weeks before, just as school had been let out for the summer. James had carried the animal in his pocket all day, keeping it wetted in between classes in the bathroom sink and offering it canned turtle food as it tried to breath in his cramped pocket.

Lane took the turtle, which had yet to be named, and the small can of turtle food home. He'd made a home for it in an old glass pie pan of his mothers dug from the confusion of old food, dirty counters and sticky floor that was the kitchen. He'd filled it with a little water and placed some gravel in it for atmosphere.

He had no way of knowing for sure, but he imagined the turtle seemed to be thankful it it's own turtle-ish way. Kristy had come home that day long ago and fallen for the small creature just as hard as Lane had. The intensity of the attention they had lavished on the animal for those short two weeks perhaps stemming from the reality of their bleak lives. Their mother was dead and their father had become a bully to one and a molester to the other. They had only each other to care for and the turtle seemed to become a third for which they both could share themselves with.

Lane slowly slumped to the floor on the hallway, relaxing into the memory, unable to stop it even if he had wished to do so. There was a wall that had been punctured to reveal a vast, unexplored mansion beyond and that small puncture had quickly grown to the removal of the entire wall. A flood of memories now clamored to be recognized and dealt with.

Playing with the turtle (still nameless, unless The Turtle counted as a name) in the bathtub after school letting it paddle the depths of its own small ocean. Then, with the shutter speed of a View Master toy, a picture flash of letting the turtle explore the reaches of his room as he braved the rare struggle with homework.

SHA–*Click!*—picking up the turtle late at night and gently comforting himself as Kristy's moans of pain and disgust reached through the walls of the house as his father laughed drunkenly at her struggles.

SHA-*Click!*—the mostly successful attempt to build a small pond for the turtle in the backyard using old boards, bricks and rocks picked from the various piles of junk strewn around the yard. Kristy helping as best she could, both of them not much in the way of mechanically inclined. The turtle paddling in the muddy water to the small sandy island they'd built in the middle. Warming itself in the sun as it lay on the sand, seemingly satisfied with their efforts.

SHA-*Click!*—his father smashing the small pond the next day, laughing as he stumbled through the flimsy world they had created on their own. Watching the demolition from the back door window, then running for cover when his father began to stumble toward the house. Hiding under the bed with the turtle. Being drug out by his feet, swinging wildly through his room, the sudden white stunning rush of his head crashing against the wall, then darkness.

SHA-*Click!*—the next day, or perhaps the day after, his father storming Kristy and he in the bathroom. Turtle turning lazy circles in the bathtub, unaware of the fate he was about to endure. Painful blows raining down on them both, Kristy being drug from the mayhem and tossed into the hall like the toy she had become for him, beating Lane back…seeing Turtle…laughing…picking him up…did he slip? Had he really meant to drop Turtle into the vent pipe? Yes, he had. Lane didn't see the actual end of the episode from his position in the hallway next to Kristy, but they had been there for the end…and beyond.

SCREEEEE…SCREEEEE…SCREEEEE…

Turtle seemed to mock his memories. He couldn't tell if the scratching of turtles toenails emanating from the depths of the pipe were from his memories, from the vision, or from the ghost of Turtle. It didn't really seem to matter. He knew what came next.

After three days, Turtle's scratching became fainter and fainter until it stopped completely. Another two days and the odor of Turtle's recent demise became prevalent throughout the house. It was anything but faint and no less pungent for Turtle's diminutive size. He smelled like rotten fish.

He woke to himself in the hall, the smell of Turtles putrefying corpse still assailing his senses. The ghosts of himself and Kristy had gone from the bathroom.

Silence now held the house in a soft embrace.

*   *   *

He woke promptly at seven Friday morning with only the vaguest memories of the night before. The dream of ridding a gigantic turtle in an ocean too beautiful to have ever existed outside of anyone's imagination was more prevalent in his thoughts. He smiled at the memory and felt himself looking forward to when he could enjoy it again.

He quickly showered and dressed in the haze of the long time early morning worker—a removed observer to the action—then grabbed an apple and banana for breakfast and headed out to Hubbard.

He opened the garage door and hesitated getting into the car. He could feel the coming heavy heat of summer as he walked outside. The sky was clear of clouds and of a deep, azure blue, unlike any sky he'd seen before. As he watched the sky, a flock of fifteen or twenty bright purple birds as big as pigeons peeled low across the roof tops along the street.

It must have been a trick of the morning light. There were no birds that were that purple, even parrots didn't radiate such a vibrant color. Let alone the fact that parrots didn't make it a habit to flock to Oklahoma. He rubbed the sleep in his eyes and when he looked again, they were either gone, or hadn't been there in the first place. He went back into the garage, got in the car and backed down the drive.

What should have been feelings of confusion over the incident last night and a lack of direction on the autobiography were somehow being funneled into a feeling of light elation. It was an almost expectant feeling, as if he were getting ready to give some kind of birth. There was a strange buzzing sound he could hear just beneath the general hum of life. The motor of the car, the soft whooshing of the vent struggling to push back the humid air the best it could.

He smiled at the morning as he turned off Cherokee Place onto Berry. Whatever he was feeling, it certainly wasn't bad. The low buzzing sound began to dissipate and was finally gone. As he pulled onto Highway nine, he again saw something that shouldn't have been there.

Out of the rising sun that was causing him to squint as it shone through his windshield, in the eastern sky came a rolling wave of color. He thought it was a another trick of the early morning light, or some kind of rare atmospheric condition.

As he accelerated onto the highway, he watched in confusion, as the wave of color became apparent. What he had thought was waves of color were in fact hundreds of thousands of tiny birds no bigger than canaries. There were colored in bright red, yellow, blue, fuchsia, purple, aqua and a dozen other colors. Their numbers had caused a slight optical illusion. Though while their multitudes could only be counted in the thousands, the distance he had perceived them from was no more than ten maybe fifteen feet above his car. The flock spread across the width of the highway by three or four times and ran to a depth Lane couldn't imagine.

He pulled to the side of the road, rolled the window down and carefully poked his head out to watch this apparent migration of tropical birds. They continued past him for what seemed to be at least a mile. As he watched the waves of color fly by, he looked to where they had gone and watched as the entire flock spun straight up into the sky and was turning back toward the tail end of the group. It looked like a living rainbow twisting up through the sky and back onto itself.

The last of the flock passed overhead and followed the same route as the lead had taken. He watched as they disappeared back into the southeastern sky. Not a feather had been dropped, not a single splatter of bird poop had marred the finish of his Olds. He watched the last few birds move over the horizon and noticed that no other drivers had stopped. He glanced at the morning rush hour traffic briskly plowing its way up and down highway nine, seemingly with a life of it's own. Not a single other car had stopped.

Maybe it had just been a migrating flock of sparrows or some other birds that had just *looked* like brightly colored exotic birds. Maybe. But a flock of purple pigeons followed by a…a mega-flock of rainbow colored canary-type birds? In the same morning? Some kind of weird shit was going on. He glanced in the rearview mirror and pulled back onto the highway, gaining speed in the flow of traffic.

Taking the earlier off ramp at the Ranch Gas-up, he slowed and pulled down the exit ramp, caught the green light at the intersection and turned back to the left, under the highway. He quickly turned back to the right onto the access road, still going east. Hoping to catch a glimpse of the flock of birds, he drove slowly down the access road. It was two miles to Hubbard and he hoped to prove or disprove the flock's existence before reaching it. Why he should think that the flock would still be visible or that it had lighted somewhere in the trees, he wasn't sure, but he wanted to know.

The ground dropped slightly away to the North from the access road and he had an unobstructed view for as far as he could see, which was maybe a distance of fifteen miles. There was no sign of the birds anywhere. He slowed down, then stopped on the road, looking as best he could behind him and across the highway back to the south.

Nothing. They were nowhere to be seen. He smiled, laughed and continued on to Hubbard still giddy by the experience of the morning. The vision of himself and Kristy suddenly came back to mind and his smile faltered, as he dealt with the painful memories it had awakened in him. There were so many that he had tried to forget. But his smile faltered only for a moment as he saw where the flock of tiny birds had gone.

Hubbard Electronics was nothing more than a warehouse for building the hundreds of products they produced. Being so, the majority of the buildings that made up the complex were not very presentable. They were built for function instead of architectural contemplation. That being the case, a line of screening pine and aspen trees had been planted along the access road and section where the five acre plant fronted the highway to act as a screen. Subsequently all that could be seen clearly from the highway was the front reception area.

The reception area was tripled paned glass and brick with a landscaped front lawn and three flagpoles. The flagpoles flew the Oklahoma flag, the American flag and a Hubbard electronics logo flag. The latter consisted of a picture of the Earth being orbited by what were suppose to be six electrons that were blue, green, yellow, orange, red and lavender. Above the earth with its orbits was the HE logo itself, something that looked rather like an H and an E intertwined in a biblical sense. The logo was Red and Blue.

Because of the screening trees Lane didn't have a clear view of Hubbard until he was at the reception area. When he pulled off the access road and into Hubbard Electronics front drive he found what he had been looking for. The flock of thousands had lighted on Hubbard.

Not just on a building or two, or the trees that lined the East and North side of the compound, but all of it. From the parking lot pavement to the flagpoles and every available wire, tree branch, building top, electric pole, parking lot light and curb they were perched.

The violence of color was painful to look upon. As he sat unmoving in the entrance watching the flowing carpet of birds, several began alighting on the new perch that was his car. He had a chance to see that the birds were not just singular in color, but many were multiple colors. From purple beaks and blue eyes to green eyes and bright blue feet, the variations seemed endless.

A horn honked behind him and he looked in the side view mirror to see a beaten, old Honda Civic waiting for him to either pull into the reception area turn around or move on into the main employee parking lot. The driver didn't seem to be concerned with the mass of birds currently finding his car a convenient roost.

The Honda honked again as Lane minds wandered back to the birds, the thousands and thousands of rainbow colored birds. He slowly pulled the Olds forward, hoping that the little guys would have the sense to hop out of the way or at the least fly over to another part of the lot.

The red Honda's engine wound up and the car shot past Lane on the right side. The birds seemed to respond in slow motion, as if they were suddenly part of a singular body with the ability to flow like water. The car parted them as if it was sloshing through a mud puddle; colorful birds simply rolled in a smooth, seemingly singular motion out of the wheel's path. He wondered if it looked the same in the front of his car.

He slowly drove on into the parking lot. It wasn't very full this early and he was able to find a spot close to the walkway. He pulled into the slot and watched the little birds hopping across the hood. Their tiny claws scratched lightly on the roof of the car. The driver of the red Honda had parked and was walking with a harried pace toward the side entrance of Development. Lane thought he recognized her from around Hubbard, but didn't know her name.

As he watched from inside the car, the same bizarre wave action took place; small birds rolling away from the path the woman walked, seemingly unaware of their presence.

"Unbelievable," he said, then laughed at the complete absurdity of what was taking place. A wave of nausea passed through him as a realization slowly began to form. He was beginning to believe, for whatever reason, that he was the only one who could see the little guys. In a vague sense he thought that he should be worried about that, but he smiled and soon forgot to worry. There were just so many of them!

He turned off the car and was shocked at the silence. Opening the door he expected to hear, at the very least, something that was nearly deafening, something that sounded like several thousand small birds chirping and singing and making little bird sounds. What he was met with was a silence that was not complete. While he could both see and hear the birds hopping on the cars, scratching through the tree branches and the rushing, windy clamor of small groups of them taking short flights, there were no verbal sounds from them. Not a chirp was to be heard. Not a single song was being sung. Nothing. Zilch. Nada.

Several of the little birds had gotten into the car in the short time he'd had the door open. Instead of trying to shoo them out, while more poured in (a job he quickly saw would be relatively endless as long as the door was open), he rolled down both windows half way and let them have at it. As he carefully stepped out of the car and shut the door, he remembered something else that wasn't right. There were no droppings accompanying the massing, neither a chirp nor a poop to be found.

"Shit," Lane said, finding none, as he looked around the ground. The car was beginning to fill up quickly as the birds began to find the available space. His cars interior had gone from a dull, rather muted gray, to a myriad of rainbows that were at one moment more purple than yellow and the next more red than green as the birds hopped and moved in a strange synchronized fashion across the interior.

Looking across the expanse of the parking lot, he could see the same wave like patterns of color shimmering and changing as the birds moved. Upon closer inspection, he saw individual birds opening and closing their beaks as if they were chirping and communicating with one another, but he still heard nothing.

More cars were entering the parking lot as nine o'clock approached. He watched the now almost familiar image of the wave of birds rolling away from the incoming cars.

"Hey, Lane!" he turned and saw Sheila, her long hair still damp from her mornings shower, walking toward him across the lot.

"Hey," he said back, smiling and watching the birds rolling in a smaller wave away from her heavily booted feet as she approached.

"Did I step in something?" she asked, following his gaze to her feet.

"What?" he asked, confused by the question. He guessed that she couldn't see the little guys due to the fact that nobody else was able to see them either, as far as he could tell. Why that should be the case, he didn't know. And, due to the strange feelings of warmth and calm he was feeling, didn't really care. The vision he'd had in the bathroom and the accompanying flood of memories it had triggered had opened a new door for him, or closed one.

"See something funny down there?" she asked again, her usual rough smile faltering slightly.

"No. Nice boots, though," he said, laughing lightly at the complete absurdity of the situation. He was now, quite sure that he was loosing his proverbial marbles. The only thing that was strange about it, besides the invisible birds, was that it didn't feel bad. There wasn't any pain, or confusion. He felt as it he had taken a long dive into a pool of warm, soothing water.

"You like?" she asked, lifting up her right foot to show them off. A solid red bird with a bright green head was perched on the toe of her boot. Lane watched and listened to the silence of its beak opening and closing. It's tiny chest heaved as if it were chirping.

"Yeah. What is that, snake?"

"Western Diamondback. Tough fuckers."

"Yeah."

"You going in?" she asked, her face showing that she was no longer questioning him.

"No, I think I'm going to wait until the last minute. Nice day out today."

Sheila looked around trying to see what the nice part of the day was. It was just another hot, muggy summer morning as far as she could tell.

"Cool. Are you betting today?" she asked, since he hadn't been in on the office pool lately.

"Counting your winnings already?"

"You got it!" she said, smiling and laughing her gravely warble.

Lane watched her rough face in the bright morning light. A splash of sunshine, shadowed slightly by some branches high in an asp seemed to lay it open for the briefest moment. There was a span of time that could only be measured in seconds that he saw something where her face had been that was pure white. It was flecked with flashing silver and brilliant to watch. Something in her face or eyes…then it was gone just as fast.

"See 'ya inside," she said, then turned and began to walk to the front office entrance. There was an employee entrance in the back of the building and the side door entrance Lane had watched the driver of the Honda enter earlier. The receptionist was a friend of Sheila's.

That she had chosen to take the longer route up to the front entrance instead of the shorter into the side entrance gave Lane another chance to marvel at the wave action of the little birds parting to let her pass. The wake was just like that of a small boat. After Sheila's passing, the birds flowed back to fill in the space she had emptied.

As he watched her turn the corner and disappear behind the front entrance, he wondered just why the little guys flowed out of her way like they had. If he was only seeing them, and they only existed in his thoughts, how could somebody harm them?

The thought took on some weight as the line of cars coming into the lot became almost constant, as nine o'clock got closer. Before he had put the thought completely together he looked at the dozens of birds hopping around and over his tennis shoe clad feet. Slowly, he raised his right foot, leaning his weight against the car.

It only took seconds for a pink and violet bird with a yellow tail to move into the space formally held by his right foot. He brought his foot down hard, not wanting to do it and at the same time fairly sure that the most resistance he would feel was the hard slap of concrete against the bottom of his shoe.

The bird didn't make any attempt to avoid his foot, or Lane was quite quick footed. The soft, muffled crunch of breaking little bird bones was what he felt, instead of the hard slap of shoe sole on years old cured concrete. For the first time he heard one of the little birds make a sound. It was the one that was currently crushed beneath his foot. A soft hush of air that was most likely it's air bladders and lungs letting go the suspending and life giving air.

Raising his foot, he had to shake it to dislodge the small animal. It landed back on the pink, blood stained spot with a wet sloppy sound.

"Oh, man," he said, shaking his head and looking at the mess of guts and blood and bone that had been a beautiful, if not quite real, bird. But he couldn't really say that the bird *wasn't* real, now. Here it was, dead and smashed. You had to be real to become dead and smashed, as far as he could tell.

The other birds around the killing zone began to cannibalize the remains. Lane watched with mounting horror as the birds in a circle around him began to enter what was quickly becoming a fray and grab their piece of the carcass. Bright rainbow feathers began to fly. The loose feathers were quickly picked off and devoured as well. He had to shield his head as the tight knot of flapping wings and scrambling legs worked it's way over him then back toward the side of Hubbard, following the carcass as it was pulled about.

Well over five hundred scrabbling, struggling, and fighting little rainbow birds no bigger than canaries or sparrows formed what looked like an epileptic cloud of color. Then as quickly as it had begun, it was over. Lane watched as the mob dispersed. Of the smashed bird, there was no sign. Even the splattering of blood on the concrete was removed. There wasn't a single feather or barb off a feather left. The little pink and violet bird that was his test of mortality was utterly and completely gone. It was the gone-est thing that he knew of and maybe had ever known.

These little guys were not something to fuck around with. Thinking that he glanced around at the mob. They had begun to settle down, once again hopping and chirping their silence around his feet. The majority of the birds in his car had taken part in the undoing of their fallen comrade and now were either taking up their former roosts or quickly being replaced by others.

"What is it? Rats, little fucking bunny's? What?"

He knew before he turned around whom he would see behind him and he was thankful that the car was between him and Foster.

"Get fucked, psycho," Lane said, turning to face him. Lane wasn't sure if Foster really did see something in the future for the both of them or if it was just part of Foster's head-trip. He didn't think that it could match what he had going on his own, though.

"Oh, don't worry about me. I've seen what's coming," Foster said, adjusting his dirty baseball hat and smiling his odd nasty smile. "I'll get a lot more than fucked when this thing is over with," he said, waving his hand in the direction of the buildings.

"You sure are talking some strange kind of shit lately," Lane suggested, now more afraid than before. Maybe it was the calm way in which he explained what he knew, or maybe it was that he, Lane, felt some of the truth Foster had to offer. Foster smiled and nodded his head knowingly.

"Tell me about them," he said, gesturing to the ground. "Tell me about what you're seeing."

Lane watched him roll his head slightly and tilt his nose up in the air.

"I can smell them," he said, more to himself than to Lane. "Whatever it is, it sure stinks."

Lane watched him, again willing Turtle to come out and begin to take care of business. But he sensed that Turtle was already here, that these thousands of birds were a greeting party of Turtle. It was the beginning of the showing of Turtle. They had finally reached that island on the horizon. But instead of finishing their journey across the ocean, enjoying the breeze and unchanging view, the island was coming to him.

"I don't have any idea what you're talking about, Foster," Lane said, bidding his time. If Foster couldn't see them, then he sure as hell wasn't going to inform him as to what he was seeing. He wasn't sure what his part was in all this, and he really didn't' want to find out either.

"You seem to be kind of edgy. Monday too soon for you?" he asked, moving around to the front of the car. Lane had the chance to notice that the birds didn't so much move wavelike in front of Foster, they scrambled in a panic to stay out of an area several feet around him.

"Foster, if you come any closer, I will kill you," Lane said. He didn't really mean it. He had wanted to say something that would stop him. It had the desired effect. Foster stopped instantly and stared at him with his cold, dead eyes.

"Cool. I'll see you inside then," he said, then walked toward the side entrance to Hubbard. The birds scrambled to be out of his path. There was no smooth flowing wave of retreat in the presence of Foster Estorga. The birds ran as if from a cat, pell-mell and uncaring. A few feathers were dislodged and were quickly devoured.

Lane watched the door close behind Foster. Something about their brief conversation had stuck out. What had he said? Something about Monday being soon enough? What the hell had that been about? Not to mention what the fuck was Foster trying to pull off? Suddenly remembering why he was at Hubbard in the first place, he checked his watch to see it was just minutes until nine. He'd missed the last minute crush of employees heading into Hubbard during his conversation with Foster. He quickly checked that the car doors were locked, then laughed. If he was going to leave the windows cracked, locking the doors would be…well, crazy, wouldn't it?

Sure it would.

The wave of little birds rolled away from him as he made his way to the side entrance. Stepping up the curb onto the sidewalk, he changed his mind and began walking up the sidewalk to take the longer route through the front entrance. The crush of the rainbow birds seemed to be thinning. There were now open patches of concrete in the parking lot where there had only been a moving mat of bird's moments before.

Though the high asp and cottonwoods trees hadn't shown the weight of the birds with drooping limbs, they had been colored and shimmering with the movement of thousands and the lack of that movement caused him to look up.

The trees were bare. Not a single bird was left in them. What birds remained were on the ground. They didn't appear to have been leaving. There just weren't as many now as there was before. They were still hopping around somewhat aimlessly. He paused at the front entrance to Hubbard. Glancing back just once to see their diminished numbers, he entered the glass and steel contemporary structure. As the door closed behind him he looked again. He stopped and turned to look out the glassed in front entrance. There was no longer a single bird in sight at least, none of the multi-hued, cannibalistic type. He had been standing longer than he thought, looking blankly out the windows.

"Are you waiting on somebody?"

He turned and smiled quickly at Dana, the receptionist. She smiled her

best you-might-have-a-shot smile that some receptionists seem to wear. The phone rang and she quickly punched buttons on the console in front of her, welcomed the caller to Hubbard and punched some more buttons, sending them off to their requested destination. She smiled back at Lane.

He opened his mouth to answer her when a raspberry-red lizard head the size of a grapefruit poked its snout above the rim of the reception area. If flicked a bright green tongue to test the air, then pulled its body up onto the top of the desk. It was about three feet long and looked like an iguana, with the only exception being the comb that ran from the top of its head down its back was of black feathers instead of skin. It slowly flicked its tongue toward Lane, seemed to dismiss him, and then began to crawl across the top of the desk in full view of Dana. She didn't seem to notice.

"Do you have any pets?" Lane asked. It was a strange subject change, but because she was trained to do so, she smoothly changed tracks.

"No. Do you?" she said, smiling. Lane thought that the brightness in her blue eyes dimmed slightly. The ringing phone stopped her again. He took advantage of the distraction to disengage from the conversation. He simply nodded his head and waved at her, then walked through the double door to the left of the reception desk. She smiled through her own conversation and quickly picked up two other incoming calls.

Lane watched the red lizard drop to the floor and scamper ahead of him through the doors as he opened them. It ran with a loping, twisting stride down the main hallway, then disappeared into one of the many copier rooms. He didn't follow it. Dana had confirmed that it had come from the same place the birds had. He decided not to mention anything else he saw.

He continued on down the hall to the far end of the building. Another set of double glass doors stood here and opened onto the plaza. The Data Input offices were just across the plaza, on the other side of the fountain. He paused and looked back down the hall.

Two raspberry-red lizards stared back at him from twenty feet back. He hadn't heard them following. The second lizard was completely identical to the first. In face, he couldn't have even guessed which was the one he had seen on the reception desk. They stared back at him, testing the air with their identical green forked tongues. Their eyes were like black, shiny marbles.

They pushed through the doors as Lane did and slowly swaggered their way across the plaza. They stopped and moved off the sidewalk as Lane walked past them. He wasn't afraid of the lizards, though they did present a more interesting challenge than the birds. Thinking that, he quickly glanced up at the edges of the buildings surrounding the plaza. There were only a handful of the rainbow birds perched about the roofs. He noticed a few more in the smaller trees in the park-like atmosphere of the plaza. Other than that, their numbers had been greatly reduced. By who or what he couldn't say.

He looked back at the lizards. The stopped moving again as his sight fell on them.

"Well, what are you waiting for?" he asked them, thinking that they were going to follow him no matter where he went. He held the door open and stepped to the side.

"Come on guys, we don't want to be late."

The lizards flicked their tongues, then slowly lumbered toward him. The stopped about five feet from the door and glanced around.

"Let's go, let's go. I sure as hell hope that you know what you're doing because I sure as shit don't."

They quickly scampered through the open door and on into the Data Input office foyer. Lane followed, then passed them in the hallway. They quickly took to his lead. As he turned into the doorway to the room where the work got done, the chimes rang out nine o'clock. There was a brief rush about the room as bodies made ready for another day.

He quickly walked down the aisle to his terminal, giving casual hi's and how's-it-going's along the way. William was sternly plugging away, bound and determined to give Sheila a run for the championship. Lester Hollie had managed to move his workspace opposite the aisle

from Tina. It appeared that love was indeed in bloom. Rachael squinted
at him with quiet suspicion and looked quickly away.

He sat, punched on the screen and terminal CPU, the realized that he
hadn't gotten any hard copy to input. He stood back up and had to hold
back a gasp. One of the lizards had managed to climb onto the tops of
the cubical dividers.

"You all right?" an older man with thin red hair and a pale, freckled
face asked from the terminal behind him.

"Yeah. Just tweaked my knee running yesterday. It' s okay now,
though," he smiled at the man and silently hoped that he wasn't a
runner.

"Perry Dover," he said, staying in his seat.

"Lane White," he said, pulling his face into a smile.

"Better get to work, huh?" Perry said, turning back to his screen.

"Yeah, forgot to get my data."

Perry nodded his head and then turned with a slightly apprehensive
look to his own work. Lane recognized it from the innumerable employees that had come and gone. Perry wouldn't last. He either didn't have
the patience or he wasn't creative enough to deal with the boredom.

He quickly gathered an armful of paperwork and sat back at his terminal. The red lizards continued roaming about the room. It was Friday,
after all. He just had to get through this day and he would be done until
Monday. Time enough to sort out this birds and lizards thing.

After thirty minutes he managed to put the lizards at least out of
mind if not out of sight (the one lying on the top of his partition was
sleeping as far as he could tell). In another thirty minutes he was in his
rhythm, never realizing that the strange beginnings to this day marked
one of the last four he had left to live.

EIGHT

...3

...and a little deeper.

"I don't think you should go with me, Walsh," Ben said.

Ben strode stiffly around the large, airy kitchen of his home, absently rubbing his back. He and Walsh had gone out earlier and purchased an aging blue ford truck that Ben had driven home. It was part of Walsh's every growing plans to take care of the house on Cherokee place. He'd come home to find Walsh had made them salami sandwiches for lunch. They'd eaten in silence. Though Walsh had asked how the truck ran. It ran just fine, Ben told him.

"What?" Walsh asked from where he sat at the butcher-block dining table.

"I said I don't think that you should go with me."

"Oh?"

"Yes," Ben said, picking up the last of the dishes and placing them in the sink. He'd managed to do enough of the house chores to keep the place from smelling, but that was about as far as it went. He hadn't grown up in the age of equality, and neither had Carly. He had worked and Carly had managed the house. That was that. No questions asked.

"Just how do you propose carrying all those gas jugs out of the truck and into the house? Those cans aren't light, Benny, not to mention breaking into the place and lighting it up. Yeah, go on and rub your back some more while you're thinking about it." Walsh grinned hugely and drained the last quarter of his beer. He swirled the foam around the bottom of the bottle contemplating another, then set the bottle back on the table.

Ben pulled his hand quickly away from his back, frowning slightly. Walsh had a point, and it wasn't a small one.

"Don't worry about it, Benny. There are maintenance people all over that neighborhood all the time. Nobody will pay any attention."

"No, not a first, but as soon as the fire gets heated up, their memories are going to get a hell of a lot better."

"Good point," Walsh said, picking up the bottle again. Ben joined him at the table and they sat in a comfortable silence, thinking.

Walsh quietly began to laugh his childish laugh.

"What?" Ben asked, smiling at Walsh's animated humor.

"No...no...your just gonna have to wait and see."

"See what?" Ben asked.

Walsh just smiled in response.

"Give me the keys to that piece of junk out there and you'll find out soon enough."

"Where are you going?"

"Ben, give me the keys. I'll worry about where I'm going and you worry about getting the lay of the house from Blake. He's still coming over tonight isn't he?" Ben fished in his pocket and tossed the keys on the table.

"Yup. I'm going to get him around five. Brenda thinks we're going to see a movie or something like that. I need to remember to watch one, just to cover our bases," Ben said, more to himself than to Walsh.

"Good idea," Walsh said, then looked at his watch. "Gotta' go if this is going to work," he said, smiling hugely. He stood and swept the keys off the table.

Ben smiled and shook his head, the movement of which seemed to fill it with a darker thought. Walsh seemed to catch the thought at the same time, or at least the darkness of it. The silence drew out and was broken by Ben.

"You know, Walsh, if this goes wrong, we're both going to be in a hell of a lot of trouble. I'm not just talking about a slap on the wrist. We both have contacts, but his kind of thing…they put you away for awhile."

"Yeah, I know. Don't sweat it though, I think I have the answer."

"Oh?" Ben asked.

"Yes. Don't worry about it."

Walsh left, still smiling despite Ben's concerns. Ben spent the rest of the afternoon thinking and getting ready for Blake's visit.

*   *   *

Throughout the afternoon the Data Input office had slowly evolved from the drab, functional space it had been. The ceiling, as if it had been fertilized and planted during the night, now sprouted a blue stringy Spanish moss. It hung down several feet and was still growing. The movement of it, which Lane had at first thought was caused by a draft of some kind, was the moss actually growing, moving and multiplying. Dime sized flowers with lime green petals grew in bunches throughout the moss, looking like Granny Smith apples floating in low volume, vertical seas. By noon the ceiling had become completely obscured, it's white tiles and fluorescent lights now backlit the somewhat translucent moss. It was around that time that the rust colored surface moss began to appear on his desk. It was a slowly spreading tea-colored stain that looked like living felt. It slowly took over his desk and framed his computer, surrounding the screen in a fuzzy, organic accent.

Lane continued to work with as much rhythm as he could, considering the circumstances. Taking a sidelong glance across the aisle, he watched Perry busily plugging along, apparently oblivious to the metamorphosis. He was talking to himself in a low voice and shaking his head; struggling with the keypad and the sometimes tedious task of deciphering scribbled notes and directives.

Perry suddenly looked up from his work and back at Lane. He smiled and shook his head side to side, as if to say he was trying.

"It gets a lot easier," Lane said, then turned back to his own mutated screen, but not before noticing that Perry's desk was being coated with the same moss.

Three more raspberry lizards had appeared. The one on top of Lane's partition wall hadn't moved since first arriving. The original second lizard had taken up residence on the wall that framed his workspace. The three new recruits had appeared in the aisle toward the front of the room. Lane caught sight of them in his peripheral vision. They looked like three lost puppy's, scrappy, just itching for trouble. They were smaller than the first two lizards and their feathered combs were light gray instead of the nightly black sported by Lizard One and Lizard Two. Lane watched as they swiveled their heads, taking in the room, then slowly waddled their separate paths.

Beetles began to appear on the walls and in the moss on the ceiling. Big beetles, as in BEETLES. Some as big as cantaloupe, with antennas nearly twice their body length protruding from in front of quarter sized black-marble eyes. Their bodies were a dark chocolate color. Lane noticed that several of the smaller ones had a bright yellow stripe running down the middle of their backs. They reminded him of gigantic June-bugs. He hoped they couldn't fly.

There had come a point, perhaps when he had first seen the two lizards, but he couldn't be sure, but it had been a definite point when Lane felt something in him give. It wasn't painful and it wasn't something that was dramatic. It was as it he had removed a small sliver of glass or wood that had been slowly working its way into his foot. The invasion being so slight that it wasn't really noticed until it was removed.

Though he couldn't pin point when that was, he knew it had happened. Something had given inside him. Some vitally important spur gear had been removed from the works, and he had felt it being pulled

out of the system. Turtle had been silenced…or he was here, now, playing this visual game for His own amusement. That wasn't clear and did-
n't matter. What Turtle did or didn't do no longer had any value for
him. Turtle either couldn't reach him here or had consumed him whole
and unbitten. Which seemed to make more sense, if sense could be
made of what was happening.

It came back to that small click he had felt. Just a slight twinge and
his world was being re-created for him and him alone as far as he could
tell.

"Getting a feel for it?"

Perry looked up from his screen and smiled at Lane.

"Yeah, a little."

Lane smiled. "You'll be betting in the pool by Monday."

"I don't think so," Perry said, smiling casually, his attention still on
his work.

"Looks like they changed out that bad light," Lane offered, looking
quickly up to the ceiling. Perry, as anyone would, followed Lane's gaze
to the ceiling. Lane was looking at blue moss, green flowers, beetles and
some kind of small birds, similar to the rainbow-canary's outside, that
had just recently decided to come join the growing group. There was
quite a lot to see, not to mention the bizarre fact that it was happening.
It was something even a very slow person would notice. Surely at least a
question would be offered, or a twist of the face that would indicate if
Perry was seeing something other than the bare, simple layout of the
ceiling.

It didn't happen. All Perry saw was the drab ceiling tiles and fluorescent lights where Lane was seeing much, much more. Lane quickly saw
the lack of recognition on Perry's face.

"Makes a difference when they go out."

"Oh?" Perry simply said, trying to ease back into his work.

"Yeah, looks fine now."

"Yeah," Perry agreed, offering a token glance back toward the ceiling.

The removal of the gear, whatever section of him it had been power-ing, must have taken more with it than he had thought. Realizing that he was, as confirmed by Perry, the only one experiencing this…change should have sounded, at the very least, some warning bells. Yet there was only a deep, quiet pool of calm in the depths of Lane White. It was not a false calm, either. He really actually *was* calm. Watching the new terrain unfold about and around him felt like watching a movie.

Foster Estorga rounded the corner at the front of the room and began to slowly make his way down the aisle. Lane watched him from the moment he appeared. He watched as Fosters small, dark eyes darted inside their sockets, trying to see everything at once. He looked scared or worked up, Lane couldn't tell. Since that bit about dancing together and grabbing his balls, Lane was more than a little sharpened by his approach. Foster slowed nearing Lanes desk and settled his dark, ill gaze on him.

"Yeah, what is it little fuck? Come back for another try?" Lane asked, finding the words in his mouth before any thought had been processed to say them. He had hissed them out. Perry was the only one that heard, besides Foster, and he was pretending that he hadn't. Lane's hands slide off the keyboard with a cold slowness that reminded him of his father when he was in a foul mood. That same slow movement always pre-ceded the punches, kicks, shouts and worse.

His hands found a temporary solace in his lap; they lay patient, wait-ing. All they had ever done was defend and run, they had never struck out intending to do damage. But they were now ready to do plenty if Foster so much as breathed funny.

Foster smiled a sad smile. The dark, thick nastiness of him seemed to be rolling off in sheets of pungent, smoky glass-like panes. Lane could feel them breaking across him into tiny pieces. Foster was, Lane decided, a dangerous, evil little person.

"What does it look like?" Foster asked, feigning a look about the room.

It was the last thing Lane would have expected him to say. He shot back, hoping that the surprise hadn't shown.

"What the fuck are you talking about?" Lane asked.

Foster's question had started a small glow of panic. How did he know? How *could* he know? Just like he asked about the birds. What had he said? I know you're seeing something but I'm not sure what?

"The change," Foster said, waving a solemn, somewhat dirty looking, pigment heavy hand toward the ceiling and room. "I can smell it, you know," he said.

"You're fucked, you little weirdo," Lane said, maybe a little too loudly. Perry was no longer faking ignorance. He'd stopped typing and was now looking at Foster and Lane alternately.

"True, true. Most of the people in this room are fucked," Foster said, looking up and down the aisle, as if he were taking a head count. "And they don't even know it. Not yet, anyway." He turned back to Lane and did something Lane was sure he had never seen Foster do. He smiled. Not the fake little how-can-I-screw-you smile he usually offered, but an actually happy guy smile. It was, Lane thought, only the second most disturbing sight he had ever seen. Lane felt his mouth moving, but could hear nothing coming out.

"That's cool, though. Everybody's got to take that trip sometime. I'll bet you didn't even know that you actually won't be the one that's here, did you know that?"

Again, Lane felt his mouth moving, but no words came out.

"No, you didn't. How could you? You're not—."

Red's office door opened at the front of the room. Foster stood quickly and looked up. It was only then that Lane realized just how close Foster had gotten to him. If he had had plans to make another grab, it was too late now. Red ambled to the front of the aisle and tilted his head back in a primitive form of recognition.

"Estorga, you having trouble finding your terminal?"

"No, sir," Foster quickly piped up. He shot a glance back toward Lane.

"See you Monday," he said, then winked. Lane watched him walk back up the aisle, say something quietly to Red, then disappear back to his cubical. Red nodded and smiled a tight, manly smile in Lane's direction, possibly showing him that he, Lane, had not committed any transgression. Lane managed to return the smile, then quickly looked back to his screen, attempting to look like he was working.

His conversation with Foster was quickly lost in the growth continuing around him. Some kind of plants that looked very much like Elephant ears had begun sprouting along the base of the exterior walls, the only difference Lane could see between them and the real thing was the stalks were a pastel magenta and the leaves a light pink. A confusing tangle of thick, gray, rough skinned vines sprouted beneath the magenta stalks and snaked out into the main room. Cherry sized berries were growing from the vine. Lane thought they would be sweet and fulfilling or bitter and deadly. He wasn't going to find out.

A soft, moist, pulpy crunch drew his attention to the far wall on the other side of the office. From what he could tell, a raspberry red lizard was doing it's best to eat one of the giant June bugs. He glanced around and saw another lizard stalking the beetles. But that didn't seem to be a problem for the beetles; they had more than quadrupled their numbers during his conversation with Foster. He closed his eyes and opened them slowly, hoping to see something different. If anything changed, it only got thicker, denser, livelier, or better still, more *alive*. The birds were now flying. They darted in and out of the moss in the ceiling and weighted down the Elephant ear plants with their small bodies. They appeared to be chasing their own food, but it was something too small for Lane to see. Faintly he could hear their high-pitched chirping, but he wasn't sure if that was imagined or not.

There was beauty in what was happening. The bright, alive rainbow colors in the plants and animals blooming all around him. The thick fertile smell of the—.

Smell?

He breathed deeply through his nose and, yes, there was a faint musty jungle smell about the room. It smelled of damp rotting leaves and fresh flowers, of earth and strange animal dung, or bugs and fungus and even the sweet, sick smell of the new life in animal death.

"You feeling all right?"

Lane jumped a little and looked up from his screen. Out of the corner of his eye he saw seven beetles appear on the wall. Two lizards took immediate notice and began to stalk them.

"Just a little tired, I guess. Ready for it to be Friday."

Sheila shook her head vaguely and looked at Lane with a question on her face.

"It is Friday, Lane."

"Oh, yeah. That's what I meant."

"I think you need to sleep through the whole weekend and start over on Monday, buddy. You're just a little out of it."

Lane smiled and thought that she had no idea of just how loaded that statement was. She laughed and walked back down the aisle to the break room. Lane watched as her feet drug through the thick growth of vines that had appeared on the floor. Her feet swung freely through them and didn't appear to affect them or be affected by them. It was as if the vines were being projected on the floor with a video projector. There was no substance to them. They were just the thought or images of vines; they were vines as vines would dream themselves to be. They didn't blur or shimmer or trip her up. They weren't really even there, or so it seemed.

He looked up to the raspberry iquana-ish lizard lounging on the top of his partition wall, thinking that it too must have a similar substance as the vines. That the red iguana would also appear to be just a vision and hold no substance. That it too was just perhaps the dream of some iguana out in the Galapagos Islands.

It would be a simple matter of standing up and casually laying his hand down where the lizard appeared to be laying. But what would he be accomplishing? Okay, so the lizards were also phantoms. So? The question quickly slid away. He was having trouble holding onto his thoughts. They were like thick, slimy eels that would quickly slip away the moment you grabbed them. What would it accomplish? Well, what wouldn't it accomplish? He was standing in a new world that was developing. Why shouldn't he explore it and find the boundaries, if there were any?

He stood, covering the action by stretching. It would be a simple matter of laying his hand casually on the top of the wall where the lizard lay watching beetles. Two more of the bugs had appeared on the opposite end of the partition. They were big ones and each had a violet stripe running perpendicular across their backs. The rest of their bodies were black as night and their eyes even darker.

He had forgotten about the bird in the parking lot. Forgot completely. Forgot how he had smashed its body against the cement with the heel of his boot. Forgot how the other birds had devoured the dead and misshapen body in a matter of seconds. Forgot the violent, thrashing mob of birds that had hungrily removed their comrade from whatever world they inhabited. Forgot right up to the moment he touched the dark feathers on the lizards' back.

The very instant his hand registered the sensation of the prickly feathers touching his palm (he was instantly glad that he hadn't slammed his hand down on the lizards back) the red lizard burst into life. It's feet scrambled madly for purchase on the partition wall. A single nail on a single toe on its back right hind leg found purchase, and it shot off the top of the wall and down into the cubical catty-corner to Lane's digs. He could hear the heavy thud of the lizard hitting something, then the mad scrabble of it's feet across the carpet.

He slowly sat back down and listened to the frantic scrambling of the lizard recede into the growing jungle.

"Everything Okay?" Perry asked across the aisle.

"Yeah, fine. Just a little tired, I guess," Lane responded, but thought that if there ever was such a thing as an understatement, that sure as shit was it.

Though time seemed to be lost to him, there was a period of several hours when he tried to ignore what was happening to the data input office and made a forced attempt at working. Yet, when the eight-inch long centipede creatures (he could see their tiny mouths filled with even smaller tiny dagger looking teeth) began to crawl around his fingers as they worked over the keyboard, it was too much. He lost his focus and for the rest of the afternoon he took in the view.

A thick tree with deeply grooved, chocolate colored bark appeared in the center of the room. It didn't grow into existence, like the rest of the flora, it simply wasn't there one minute and it was the next. It's thick, rambling branches had intermingled with the bright blue Spanish moss where the ceiling used to be. He could see small rust colored clover shaped leaves no bigger than fifty-cent coins flooding the tips of the branches.

Worms or small snakes were working their way throughout the branches. The birds had taken notice of them and were giving the inter-lopers hell about it. Whatever unseen prey they had been chasing was forgotten for this larger, more substantial sustenance.

One of the smaller lizards stalked through the thick vines that had taken over the floor. The vines were solid to the lizards, unlike Sheila's experience. He watched it methodically poking its snout into the tangle of vines, sticking its dark tongue out to feel the air, then moving on. Lane watched as it made a sudden, quick move with its head and swallowed something small and furry. Lane thought he heard a faint squeal, but couldn't be sure about it. He did note that if the vines were real to the lizard and the lizard was real to him, then the vines would impose a slight, but not unmanageable problem for him when it came time to leave.

The chocolate colored tree with clover shaped leaves began to sprout small, green nuts or fruits of some kind. They were shaped somewhat like a banana and grew in small bunches. The branches of the tree spread like a canopy over most of the room. There were several bunches growing just above his head. He watched as they grew from several inches long to nearly a foot and their color changed from dark green into a rich pastel orange. The growth seemed to stop there. They hung heavily on the branches, dragging them down to nearly touch the top of his cubical partition.

The day continued. But the time five o'clock sounded on the Muzak system (it sounded very distant and muffled) Lane couldn't see ten feet beyond his cubical though the growth. Animal sounds filled the room. Some were heavy and brutal, but most were the light chattering of smaller animals. He could hear a dozen different calls in the brush immediately around him. The soft squeaks and harsh chirps and deep rustling grunts were oddly tuned down, as if their individual volumes had been set low.

"Well, not bad for the first day," Perry offered, as he stood and stretched.

"Yeah, it starts to go faster," Lane said, watching one of the centipedes (this one was pale blue with black legs) chase something that looked like a pill bug across the landscape of his keyboard. The pill bug made good its escape by ducking into the gate for the disk drive.

Did it start to go faster? If this change were on slow speed, what would happen if it cranked up to high speed? It was quickly becoming physically impossible to fit anything else into the Data Input office. He could hear heavy, much larger animals moving in the distance. It was a distance that seemed to be beyond the known, measureable walls of the office. Which was something that was both possible and impossible. Impossible, because the room had a known dimension; possible because it was happening anyway.

"Well, I guess I'll see you Monday," Perry said, offering a smile that showed the yellowing teeth of a smoker. He offered his hand and Lane shook it from what seemed to be a great distance. He wondered if Perry could feel the birds that were perched on his head and shoulders.

"Sure thing, Monday," Lane said, again wondering how he was going to get through this forest to exit the building. Not to mention what he was going to find outside the door once he did make it out.

Through the brush he could see glimpses of people standing, they reminded him of pop-up targets in an arcade. He had closed out his computer terminal and was standing next to his chair, his arms full with work he hadn't completed. At the last minute, with no forethought, he shoved the unfinished work into the bottom of his completed work pile, then pushed his chair beneath his desk.

The thought of leaving the unfinished work in the completed pile wouldn't have been a consideration only a day ago. Now, it didn't seem to matter one way or the other what happened to it. When, in the short span of a day your world has…has…*gone over*, you don't sweat the small stuff.

There was a quick shift in the room, something that wouldn't have been noticeable if he had been looking at his desk, or anywhere else except into the thick jungle about him. It took him a moment to realize that there hadn't been a shift in the room, there had been a shift in where he was standing in the room. In less than a second he had moved from standing beside his desk to standing at the exit door in the front of the room. Red was standing in front of him and several other people where standing behind Red. He had the impression he had been spoken to.

"Excuse me?" he said, his voice sounding much stronger than he felt. It was a gamble, thinking that he had been asked something, but what the fuck. Very faintly, just beneath the growing din (it *had* become louder, hadn't it?) of the jungle, he could hear the old mantra, doing it's best to push through to him. But it was tired and worn and repeating mostly out of habit than anything else. It no longer worked, or it had worked too well. Yes, today was a new day and, yes, the past sure as hell was going if not gone, but just what kind of a new day was it becoming?

He noticed Red's mouth moving and watched as his thick eyebrows came together at the bridge of his nose in a worried frown.

"You all right?" finally reached through the thick, fertile noise of the growing jungle.

From what seemed to be a great distance, Lane could hear himself telling Red and the small gathered group, that he was fine. Red remained standing where he was. Lane watched as he folded his arms across his chest and tilted his head back slightly, waiting for any continued response that Lane may have to offer. He simply shrugged and turned to leave. He thought he could hear Red calling him back, but if Red was, Lane wasn't responding and he pushed through the exit door.

The stark nakedness of the hallway struck with an unexpected force, his breath began to feel pulpy and thick. There was nothing like the jungle growth that had become the Data Input office. There wasn't so much as a leaf or bug crawling across the floor. It was the same plain functional architecture it had always been. He stood just outside the door, tempted to go back into the office to double check what he had been seeing. But since that would mean talking to Red and the gang, he decided not to do it. He could hear their low voices talking just behind the doors. His name came up a couple of times, but he wasn't really trying to listen.

A sharp movement at the end of the hall by the bathrooms caught his eye. He didn't see anything, but then he understood why. He wasn't looking large enough. He was reminded of the one rare trip when his father had taken them to the zoo. He had stood in front of a small aquarium, looking for the captive inside. After five minutes, he still couldn't see what the placard had described as an Alligator Snapping Turtle. Then Kristy walked up and nearly screamed with surprise when she saw the huge, static animal. She'd pointed it out to him. He hadn't been able to see it because it was nearly as big as the tank of water it was in. That was what he was seeing now.

The entire wall at the end of the hall was slowly cracking open along its horizontal axis near the middle of the wall. It was more like a straight smooth seam opening up, then a splintering crack. Lane watched as the seam stopped spreading at about six inches wide. He waited for what may come. When it did, it was the last thing he would have expected to see.

*　　　　*　　　　*

"Hi'ya Blake!"

"Hi Grandpa!" Blake said, running up to the truck. Brenda slowly walked along behind him, then helped him into the truck, closing the door behind him. She placed a small, red suitcase into the bed of the truck.

"Give me a kiss, honey," she said, leaning into the open window. Blake obliged her.

"Three days of fishing? You sure you guys won't get tired of that?" she asked.

"No way!" Blake said. "We're gonna catch Wilbur!"

"Wilbur?"

"Yeah! Grandpa said theirs a gigantic catfish in the pond that breaks his pole every time he hooks him and we're going to catch him!"

"Oh he did?" she said, raising her eyebrows at Ben.

Ben shrugged his shoulders and smiled. Better he and Blake make up a bunch of crap about a giant fish than she know the truth of their three day get together. Ben had called a little while after Walsh had left his house and asked Brenda's permission for Blake to spend the weekend and the following Monday at his place. Just messing around, fishing, getting to know each other for the first time. She had readily agreed, her initial suspicion of his past aloofness now gone.

"Yeah! Didn't'cha Grandpa?" Blake asked, his eyes brimming with excitement. Though they both knew the truth of the matter, Blake's genuine enthusiasm for the little bit of fishing they had done was showing through the façade. Ben made a mental note to get some fishing in this weekend, then realized he wouldn't remember it. He flipped down the visor and wrote one word on the small pad of paper he had taken to keeping there. Fish. Then he turned back to Brenda.

"Well, I might have said something about it," Ben said, dropping a wink to Brenda when Blake wasn't looking. She offered him a genuine smile, one he thought he wouldn't have seen from her, at least not this soon in the game.

"Thank you, Ben. I appreciate everything you're doing."

"No trouble and no need to thank me. It's no chore to hang-out with your favorite grandson," Ben said, reaching over and mussing Blake's hair. Blake blushed under the attention and smiled self-consciously. Ben noticed a smear of dark red jelly at the corner of Blake's mouth.

"What time should I expect you back Monday?"

"Probably late afternoon. We'll stay in touch and let you know for sure."

"Okay, then. You guys have fun," Brenda said, kissing Blake's head and absently wiping off the smear of jelly.

They didn't talk about the impending event on the long drive out to Ben's place. Ben tried to keep the conversation light and away from the weighty decision of committing what he thought was, at the very least, a seriously destructive act. The implications of getting caught, especially with Blake being involved were too much to consider. Was his thinking actually going to weeds and he didn't know it? If it was, then maybe Walsh's was also and neither of them realized it. What if that was the case? What would happen to Blake then? And what kind of Grandfather would he be to his late sons' child from prison?

"Grandpa?"

"Hmm? Yeah?"

"I wondered if we could be able to really go fishing sometime? If we get finished with this," Blake said, lifting up a blue, tattered spiral bound notebook that he had produced from somewhere.

"What's that?" Ben asked, motioning to the notebook.

"My journal about scouting the monsters house. I thought it would help us figure out how to do it."

"You kept a journal about it?" Ben asked, a small stab of fear piercing his already troubled mind. Now wouldn't that be an interesting book for the wrong person to find? How long until Brenda ran across it while cleaning Blake's room? What then? Especially if she found it after they torched the house of Cherokee Place?

"Yeah," Blake said, looking confused. "I told you about it, remember? You asked me to bring it so we could draw a picture of the house?"

Ben was suddenly lost and wasn't sure where they were driving, then, just as quickly, the earlier conversation with Blake about his journal came back. He did his best to mask his confusion with a smile and a nod of his head. He managed to keep the brakes from locking-up as he nearly missed the turn off from the highway to the side road they'd hit the hawk a few days back.

"Yup, I remember now. I guess I've been thinking about too many things lately." He smiled again and watched as Blake relaxed.

When they reached home, Blake ran from the truck and let himself into the house. It did more to prove their relationship was growing than any one thing either of them could have said. It spoke of a familiarity that was unconscious and uninhibited. He realized that his outpouring of mental analysis regarding how Blake had run up to the house was more than likely steeped in the dark and unfathomable desire by Blake for a soda. Such was the ways of life, you're sure you've found an uncharted, unrecorded, unheard of fossil from the Mesozoic and it turns out to be some dried coyote dung.

He shook the bitter thought aside and smiled for no reason other than that he found sometimes that by just smiling, even when you didn't feel like it, it made you feel better.

It did.

*   *   *

A blue and gold river had begun to pour out of the slice in the wall. Then the river began to break up and disperse itself about the room. It looked like if was breaking up into its individual components of compounds and molecules and atomic structure. It began to fill the hallway. Lane stood rooted where he was, unaware of the group of people that had exited with him and were now staring at him with the same wonder Lane stared at the river of blue and gold. To them it was a blank wall.

He watched as this diffused, growing river of color and glittering motion slowly enveloped him as it grew to fill the hallway. Reaching up into the mass of color he realized that what he had taken to be shimmering water was in fact the beating of millions and millions of tiny blue and gold butterfly wings. At least, they looked like butterflies. They were no bigger than a dime and had the tubular bodies of butterflies, but something about them wasn't right. He couldn't pinpoint if and yet, they did seem to be....

"...out of it?"

He turned to find Red's meaty, sweating, cigar smelling face several inches from his. The shock wasn't the closeness of his face, nor the unclean smell that ran beneath the general river of stench surrounding Red. In another time and place he might have responded more quickly to Red, in subservient manner; mannerism that more bespoke an underling. In the beauty of the river of butterflies, Red's heavy, bloated face stuck out in horrible fashion. It seemed to float in the twinkling, flashing stars of insect life like a rotting whale beached on a tropical beach. Lane found he was smiling, which only caused Red to become a more appropriate and descriptive name than ever before.

There was the faint smell of something sweet over the stench of Red. Lane was reminded of the playground at Hock elementary. The wall on the far south end of the playground was covered in a thick wash of twisting, turning Honeysuckle. Most recesses had been spent sitting beneath and in their green, sweet-flowering embrace because his body was too sore from the punches and kicks he'd gotten at home to play with the other kids.

He could hear the lazy buzz of bees and whirlwinds spinning of hummingbirds accompany the thick, heady scent. His arm was gripped by an iron hand and he opened his eyes, only then realizing that they had been closed.

"You need a doctor?" seemed to flow like thick syrup out of the stench of Red's mouth. Lane jerked his arm away and said something that he couldn't quite hear; the animals had taken to making an awful din in the background. But whatever he had said seemed to have the right effect, Red and the few people that had stayed behind left the scene in a hurry. They were nearly tripping over each other to get back into the office.

Lane smiled to himself and vaguely wondered what he had said. Not that it seemed to make much difference at this point. The butterflies continued to fill the foyer to a density that was nearly complete. He felt them fluttering in his mouth at one point; they tasted like they smelled; thick, syrupy and sweet, sweet, sweet.

He blinked, time shifted or his view of it did, and he was standing by his car in the parking lot. In his hand he found the keys to the good old Olds, the lock key positioned just outside the lock, ready to go. There was no sign of the rainbow birds that had followed him to work. Not so much as a feather was in the parking lot. Not even a spot of birdie doo-doo on the car, but it did smell strangely when he opened the door. He couldn't quite mark it but it was familiar.

He slid into the car and as he was adjusting the rearview mirror, he understood the thick, gamy smell. The face of two red lizards stared back at him. They were perched on the back of the rear seat looking around in their casual lizard way, their black, feathery combs standing up straight. There were some feathers scattered around the back seat. Lane reached back and picked several up, they were brightly colored, blue, red and green. He noticed a tiny bird leg complete with toes lying on the floor. He didn't bother to pick it up.

"Having a little snack, boys?" he said, to the rear view mirror. The boys didn't respond.

"Well, we'll just head on home and see what's there, shall we?"

Nothing.

They continued to look around outside the windows. Lane started the car and backed up, then slowly pulled forward toward the exit. He could not longer see the lizards in the rear view mirror, but he could hear them scratching around in the back seat. He guessed that they were fighting over the remaining bird leg.

By the time they had reached the highway, the boy's had stopped fighting and were perched on the back seat once again. There were no flocks of rainbow birds, no gigantic tropical fruit trees springing to life in the middle of the highway, no titanic animals crashing off in the distance. Nothing seemed to be out of the ordinary. Lane was beginning to think that there might be some kind of gas leak in the office that had caused the illusion. Or that Hubbard was experimenting on some kind of electronic device that would affect perceptions, maybe a war device that they were under secret contract to carry out. At least, he was thinking along those lines up to the point one of the lizards climbed over the back of the seat and plopped down in the front passenger seat next to him.

They turned onto Cherokee Place and he slowly pointed the car up the street. The house looked normal except for the windows. They appeared to be fogged over from the inside. Better yet, it looked as if someone had dropped by with a sandblaster and frosted all the windows. He sat in the drive for a moment, looking over the situation, then shut off the car.

The second lizard clamored into the front seat and joined the first. They snapped and hissed at each other for a moment then resumed their stoic lizard staring.

"What'd you think, boys? Safe to go in?"

No response.

"Yeah, that's what I thought. Not much choice in the matter." He sat a moment longer and watched the house. Not really looking for anything to happen, but just waiting, watching, feeling. It wasn't everyday that you went completely fucking nuts, might as well slow down and enjoy it.

The lizards began to scramble up the inside of the door, trying to look outside the windows of the car.

"Anxious to get to it, aren't you?" Lane asked, not expecting a response this time.

"Well, what's it going to be boys? More jungle shit and fruit? Maybe something a little more?"

Another flash of time and he was standing at the door to the house, keys in hand, lizards at his feet. Standing there, he had a bright moment of clarity. A pure moment in which he understood that he had crossed an invisible line some point in his past that he would now not be able to cross back from. He had taken that last, final plunge into the future that would now dictate what the remaining time he had alive would be like. More drugs and needles, certainly. More therapy, not likely. The institutions that practiced the kind of therapy that was aimed at returning you to a functioning society would no longer take him after today. No sir, after that line had been crossed he had crapped out, was bankrupt, ladies and gentlemen Elvis has *left* the building.

He turned and looked out at the street, trying to remember what his life had been like when he had lived the hell his father brought down on them. The pain had been too constant for a duration that still had no visible end. Thirty-three years seemed to be a long enough time to take it. Times, they was a'changin', and though he didn't have any idea what was on the other side of the door, he knew once he opened it, there would be no return.

One of the boys clamored across his foot and poked a tentative tongue at the door jam. Lane thought he could hear a low level-humming coming from behind the door. The boys were getting excited. Now they both began to scratch in their lethargic, lizard fashion at the door jam, seeking entry.

"Well, boys," Lane said, turning away from the street to face the door, "I think the time has come…"

The low level humming behind the door suddenly stepped up several notches in volume and the lizards stopped scratching at the door. Lane could feel a faint vibration in his feet coming up from the floor of the porch. He slowly reached for the lock with the key. When he touched the lock the hum suddenly stopped. He slid the key home and slowly turned the lock free. The boys backed off a few steps and seemed to be cowering behind Lane's legs.

"I don't blame you guys, if I could stand behind somebody right now, I would."

He left the key hanging in the lock and slowly slipped his hand to the knob on the door. If felt warmer than it should have. He began to turn the knob.

*   *   *

"Star Wars?" Ben asked.

"Yeah! Yeah! I've seen that one a lot of times," Blake said. "It's a really cool movie."

"Won't your mom think that it's strange we watched a movie you've already seen?"

"Nah. I watch movie's over and over."

"Oh," Ben said, going with the flow. Neat stacks of videotapes lay about the floor of the den. Blake was lying on the floor scanning titles along with Ben who had pulled up a chair from Carly's old craft table. They'd decided to cover their tracks as best they could in case Brenda asked about the movies. They put the movie in and while Blake watched, Ben started some steaks and corn-on-the-cob for dinner. He was just putting the steaks on the Jen-Air grille when the phone rang.

"Hello?"

"Ben?"

"Yeah, Walsh, who'd you expect it would be?"

"Blake there?"

"Yup, we're making dinner. T-Bones. You coming out? I'll lay another out for you if you are."

"Sounds good but I can't make it."

Ben could hear loud crashing of machinery in the background and the shouts of men trying to speak over the clatter.

"Where are you?"

"What?"

"*Where are you?*"

"Oh, you'll find out soon enough," Walsh said, laughing.

"Well, did you call for a reason or did you just want to laugh at me?" Ben asked.

"Yeah, I called for a reason. Do you still have all that old lawn equipment you keep stashed in your barn?"

"Yes," Ben said.

"Well, get together a few mowers and rakes and other yard working stuff and I'll be by in the morning," Walsh said.

"What the hell for?"

"Ah, now, there in lies the rub, eh?"

"*What?*"

Walsh began laughing again but was interrupted by a voice intruding into their conversation. Ben listened as his end of the reception was muted.

"Gotta' scoot," Walsh suddenly said to him.

"What?" Ben asked again.

"I've gotta' get going, just get that lawn equipment together in the morning and I'll be by sometime tomorrow."

"Don't you think you're having just a little too much fun with this, Walsh?"

"Hey, if this is going to be the last act of a couple of old farts, why not?"

Ben didn't have a response and Walsh let the thought sit heavy and fertile.

"See you tomorrow Ben," Walsh said.

Before Ben could come back with a snappy reply, Walsh had hung up. He slowly laid the phone in it's cradle and stared at it's faded, white handle, his thoughts now trying to turn dower and old.

"Grandpa?" Blake asked.

Ben turned and found a smile on his face. Here was something he could be happy about. Something that he could say he had done; had given everything he could to do. But was this effort of atonement also a famous last act? He couldn't answer that question. His life had, over the past several weeks, become very complex.

"Yes?"

"Who was that?"

"Walsh."

"Is he coming out tonight?"

"No. He'll be out tomorrow though," Ben said, shaking off the thoughts that were trying to creep into the foundation of his being. It wouldn't do anyone a bit of good for him to worry. It might, in fact, considering what they were planning, get somebody arrested, or worse, killed.

*   *   *

Lane slowly pushed open the door. A thick rush of moist, cool air spilled from the door to greet him. It smelled of thick fertile dirt, years old decay and rebirth. The smell of sour flowers and sticky saps assailed his senses. He smelled the acidic sting of pine and an underlying stench he couldn't quite place.

A flurry of movement rushed before his eyes and then stopped. He squinted and focused on the dark path that lay before him. He was staring at a forest. Not the tropic jungle he had left back at Hubbard, but a thick forest of pine and granite. He was reminded of pictures he had seen of the Pacific Northwest, up around Oregon and Washington.

As he watched the light became stronger and the forest began to become clearer, lighter, more welcoming. The boys took off like slalom racers through the thick bases of the towering pine, bent on some destination of their own.

Lane looked down at his feet. His toes jut touched the door threshold. Behind him the day was still there, the street was still there, the car was still there. He looked back through the door to what used to be his house and was surprised to see the lizards were back. They had come back up through the trees and were looking at him. Lane realized that he was looking down a hill and that he could hear running water.

He turned to look back at the street behind him through the doorway and realized with very little surprise that it was gone. He had expected it to be gone at some point, but not this soon. There was nothing behind him now but trees and nothing ahead but more trees, the two boys and the sound of running water. There was no sign of the house he had only seconds before been standing in the doorway of.

He felt oddly numb to what was happening, shocked into a mild stupor. His mind slipped and sputtered, trying to find some basis on which to prop it up, however crippled and misguided it had become, his mind, at least, had the will to live.

"Well, boys, this isn't quite what I expected, but I guess it'll have to do, since I don't know what…," Lane paused and listened to a deep bass humming in the distance. It seemed to be coming from down the slope, in the direction of the lizards and off a little to the left. It grew in intensity until the trees and surrounding ground were vibrating with it, then it abruptly stopped, rolling off through the forest as if he were in a valley or depression.

Lane breathed deeply and looked around him. There was a chill in the air, he didn't feel comfortable in his light slacks and short sleeved shirt. He wrapped his arms around himself and rubbed them in a gesture that was more defensive than anything else.

Today is a new day the past is gone. Today is a new day the past is gone. Today is a new day the past is gone.

If there had ever been a time in his life the mantra was truer than it was now, he would be hard pressed to name it. This time, the past was *literally* gone. At least his past was. He wasn't so sure about the past of this place, or if it ran on the same laws of time.

The rumbling was beginning again. He focused on it and could hear more than a deep humming. It started as a slow vibration that worked up to a faster and faster pitch. There were more cycles per second or whatever passed for seconds in this place. It peaked then stopped abruptly, the sound rolling off through the forest.

Lane looked for the boys and was surprised to see them standing on their hind legs, tongues hanging motionless out of their mouths, their bodies in a stupor, save for them standing so rigidly. When the last of the vibration was gone, then individually dropped down to their normal position and continued flicking their tongues to test the air of their new surroundings.

"Is this new to you, boys?" Lane called down the hill. The lizards just stared at him, tongues flickering. His voice seemed loud and invasive in this large, strangely hallowed place. There were no animal noises in the distance, no birds flickering through the trees, no deer scampering through the woods, nothing that you would expect to see in a *normal* forest. Nothing that should have been there if he had been back in *his* world.

He looked around again and noticed a ridge of rock off to his right. It looked like the granite base of a mountain, covered here and there with plain old ordinary looking moss and fern growth. It was several hundred yards away and he couldn't see to the top of it because of the trees. The boys began to slowly twitch their respective tails in the pinecone and pine needle forest floor, seemingly impatient to be on their way.

"Are you waiting for me?" Lane called down at them. If anything they began to twitch their tails faster. He took a single, slow step in their direction and they scrambled quickly down the hill like a couple of puppy's anxious to play ball. He stopped and waited to see if they would come back. After several minutes with no appearance he began to step forward again when he noticed two red heads peering at him from behind the same tree off to his right.

"Caught me, boys. Okay, okay. If you've got something to show me, let's get on with it. I've had enough of this crap. Let's get to where we're going."

They scrambled back down the hill and out of sight. Lane could hear them crashing down through the thick underbrush. He followed them down the hill, stepping slowly and carefully across the forest floor, trying to keep a tight grip on the chaotic rambling of thoughts that his mind had become. The sound of running water was becoming louder as he carefully skirted around several boulders and rocks jutting out from the hillside.

The view opened up a little on the other side of the boulder and he could see what looked like a flat, black plain in the valley below. It seemed to be where the slope bottomed out. He could just make out pieces of it through the small gaps in the trees.

The slope was steeper on the other side of the boulders and he was forced to reverse positions and actually climb down the slope in spots.

The lizards kept popping into view every few minutes, checking up on him, or so it seemed. He stopped to rest at the bottom of the steep slope and looked back up to the top. From this vantage it looked more like a cliff than a hillside. If he'd had to climb up it instead of down, he wouldn't have though it possible.

The sky was growing lighter above the trees and it felt as if the day in this place was beginning, though the silence of the forest was disturbing. The rustling of the lizards drew his attention back down the hill.

"Give me a minute, boys. Just need a little breather," he told them from where he sat.

The low end rumbling was beginning again. It was louder now, or closer. He watched the flat, black plain through the trees and imagined that it was shimmering with the vibration of the humming. Shimmering? Maybe. It looked more like waves on a lake. Small waves. Little waves that you would see on a calm day at the lake. Not really waves at all, but ripples.

He watched as the lizards went through their standing stupor, tongue sticking out routine. He thought that he could push them over and they wouldn't feel a thing. They were that far-gone.

It began to taper off and roll away as before. The lizards slowly dropped to their feet and immediately ran up the slope, their tails slapping madly at the thick forest floor covering.

"Yeah, all right," Lane said, standing. He brushed his pants clean of pine needles and moss and continued down the slope. The boys raced ahead, crashing madly through a thicket of underbrush. Lane could see the ground began to level off several hundred yards below where he stood. He could hear the boys scrambling wildly down the slope and eventually saw them coming off the hillside onto the flat. They stopped there, waiting for him.

The rush of water was louder as he descended down the slope. It was off to his left. He began to walk diagonally to the slope in search of the water. As he skirted around a boulder the source came into view. It was a stream of what looked and acted like water, with the only exception being it was as black as road tar.

It rippled and moved over unseen rocks, flowing like poison, toxic wastewater. He looked down the slope for the boys but couldn't see them any longer on the flat. He looked back to the stream. It was only six or seven feet across and didn't look much deeper in the smooth flowing spots than three or four feet. He looked down the hill again for the boys and not seeing them, slipped his way down the steep bank to the creek edge.

There was only a faint acidic smell to the water, not the thick pungent odor he had expected. Standing on the edge of the stream he looked back up the hill and saw a fall about thirty feet high. The black water shimmered with a bright splash of colors as it fell and misted off. The pool was only as wide as the creek but it certainly must be deeper due to the falls pounding out a hole.

"Hi, Lane."

He spun so quickly that his feet tangled in the rocks strewn about the dark creek edge and he began to fall backwards into the creek. By shear will power alone he forced himself to fall off to the side of the creek. His thoughts a blind panic, he looked up the side of the creek bed and saw someone he had expected to see sooner or later.

NINE

...2

The deep rumbling of the Turtle's breathing, coupled with the gentle, washing water urged him to swim on in.

Though he still waited, knowing that he eventually would, but not yet. Like your first time off the high dive. Everybody watching, and the beautiful Lisa Myers is watching, and she looks great standing there in the hot sun, water glistening off her long blonde hair, a hint of the woman that she will become and you know you're going to do it...but not just yet. Not...yet.

He let his arms slip from his shoulders and lowered them into the black water at his side. The chill left him immediately. The water began to warm him. He stopped shivering and stood upright, the water now reaching up his forearms but not quite to his elbows.

The cleaning the house had undergone was only seen as a faint mirage, or a trick of what was left of his one good eye. To Duane Trammel White the house appeared as it always had, dark, old, crumbling. If he could smell, the house would have smelt of rat droppings and termite chewed wood, or dry rot and the oddly sweet smell of death. These things he could only imagine, however. But he did imagine them well, and now smelled with his mind instead of his nose.

He had patiently waited for his time to come and it had finally arrived. He would now reclaim what was his. As Lane was stepping through the doorway of the house, with his friends in the lead, Duane had been waiting to take him out of *this* world and into his own. The boy was the last piece of the White family puzzle and there wasn't anything that was going to stop Duane from bringing him back into the fold.

Lane stepped through the doorway of the house and felt a hot, piercing sledgehammer blow to his stomach. His belly was suddenly a live coal burning his guts without destroying them. As quickly as the pain was there it was gone. He heard a metallic *PLOINK!* as he let himself go and slipped into the green, fertile world beyond the house.

Duane watched the boy come through the door and, gathering himself, slammed into him, burrowing through the only access he knew, down the boys' old lifeline. He clawed, ripped and tore, raping his way into the vessel that had carried the boys' true self…only to find the boy gone. As he reached for him and began to feel the bright flash of their embrace, the boy began to slip away. He was there one moment and completely gone the next.

Duane found himself standing in the husk of the boy. He could feel the slick, electric life of Lane's body surrounding him like a warm, moist blanket. The surprise of finding the boy slip away from him was too sudden and quick to warrant anger on his part. The revenge would come later, he could feel the molten steel of it burning, smoldering waiting to come forth.

He would find him again, that wouldn't be a problem. There wasn't that many places he could have gone. Even in this world or the others that he knew of. He was connected enough to get the word around. It would just take a little more time and he was no longer bound by time.

If he couldn't have the boy now, then he would do what he could with the boys' body. It wasn't much, but it was all he was left with and he would make do. Some fun could be had, after all, what was the rush? He found the car keys in his hand and after a brief adjustment to the physical movement of his newfound limbs, he turned and left the house. He didn't have a plan, but he did have a place to start.

*   *   *

He withdrew five thousand dollars cash from the boy's bank account. When the perky young and firm teller asked if he was going away for the weekend—just doing her banking duty, chatting up the customers—he asked her if she wanted to go with him and explore all the wonderful aspects of oral sex he could show her. When she said pardon me, not sure she'd heard the man with the gray eyes and scared up face correctly, he'd told her he was hung like a bull and could go all night. Security managed to remove him from the bank with words only.

The gray Olds stood waiting in the parking lot, but he didn't feel much like driving. The security guy stood by at the doors watching him. Duane pulled up Lane's hand and waved at him. The guy didn't move. It had been a long time since he had been alive. He could smell the heavy spring day and the spicy warm foods the light breeze brought up from an oriental restaurant down the street. He was having trouble with his eyesight until he realized that his binocular vision had been returned with the two good eyes Lane had. He made a quick mental note to blind Lane's body before he was finished.

Smiling at the thought he began walking toward the restaurant smells. The car would be fine where it was, should he decide he needed it back. He felt loose within this new body, as if he would fall out at the slightest bump. He concentrated on setting himself better inside but couldn't really tell if it helped or not.

Driving had been an interesting experience. He found he could let the boy's body go through the motions and not interfere. Once he tried taking the wheel and managed to pull the car over onto the curb. He quickly let go. The traffic moved so much faster than he remembered and the newness of the car was fascinating. How long had he been dead? If you held a gun to his head he wouldn't have been able to tell you. Ha. Ha.

He saw a reflection of himself in the window of a used bookstore and stopped. Turning to look he was surprised to recognize so much of

Lane. He smiled at the reflection of himself in Lane and felt something that was akin to happiness, but it was an unhealthy happiness at best. A sick, pulsing emotion that tasted bitter and gave him an erection like polished granite. He laughed without smiling and continued on up the street.

Duane stopped Lane's body in front of the Wong Ho restaurant and smelled the heady scents with two good nostrils. The thick spices and bubbling sauces caused his stomach to rumble in anticipation. How long had it been since he had actually sat down and eaten? About as long as it had been since he had had a complete tongue in his mouth.

"Too fucking long," he said aloud, then stopped in surprise. It wasn't his voice that came out. Now why that should be a surprise, he wasn't sure. But he wasn't expecting to hear Lane's voice, though it made sense that since it was Lane's body, that's what would come out.

"Too long," he said again, testing he waters.

"Hello, Lane, you little fucker. Daddy's home!" he said with a laugh, then walked into the Wong Ho.

He stood in line then ordered a number seven with two beers. The food had to be mediocre oriental fare at best, but to somebody who hasn't tasted food in years, it was a roller coaster of taste sensations. The spices burning his tongue and making his eyes water. He added more pepper to the Hunan Chicken and laughed with his mouth full at the burning sensation. He was aware of people watching him, but didn't care. He only had a couple of days until Monday, then he'd be gone anyway. So, what the fuck? He drained the beers quickly and wanted more but forced himself to stop. It wouldn't do to get to drinking. He still had the rest of this evening and all of the next two days. Plenty of time.

*　　　　　*　　　　　*

"You could have done better than this, don't you think? At least something tropical," Foster said, smiling a waning smile at the surrounding woods. Lane stared at Foster, and slowly turned to face him. The massive change in perspective in the last few minutes had not phased him nearly as bad as seeing Foster. The low level humming began again. Lane glanced at the raspberry lizards to find them playing statues, tongues agape.

"What's that sound?" Foster asked, looking at the surrounding woods. There was a brief hint of fear in his eyes. Foster was not as all knowing as he wished to be, Lane thought.

"Why the fuck would you pick *that*? Shit, you should've at least gotten something you could screw," Foster said, nodding toward the lizards. There was a growing unease in Foster. This was good. He had no doubts what was going to happen and he was equally as sure that Foster was just as aware of what was going to go down. It was just the how that had him stumped.

The throbbing, low level humming stopped, and the raspberry lizards dropped to their feet. Lane stood by the black stream and watched Foster watching the lizards.

"Ugly fuckers," Foster noted. He spat in their general direction. The lizard closest to Fosters offering took several slow steps toward the spot it had landed. Its tongue flickering wildly, tasting the air for scent, it looked the devils hound on the hunt.

The other lizard came up the hill behind the first. Its pace was also slow and tentative, its tongue quickly biting the scents in the air. It seemed to frown and crouch lower to the ground, as it tasted Fosters' scent. It continued up the hill then stopped a few feet away from the first lizard. Lane was reminded of Komodo dragons he'd seen at the Zoo.

"Oh...no way, man. Uh-huh. No *fucking* way," Foster said. He looked at Lane with what was undeniably growing fear.

"Come on, not this. That's...*barbaric*, man.

Lane watched with confused detachment. Did Foster think that he, Lane, had something to do with the lizards? That he was somehow controlling them? He opted to be quiet and wait. Foster seemed to be gearing up for something. Lane watched as he took a couple of steps backwards, up the hill, away from Lane and his boys. Lane quickly decided that he was safe where he was, unless Foster had a gun, which was unlikely. He would have certainly at least shown it by now.

He had backed up the hill a little more, then seemed to stand his ground, quickly glancing between Lane and the lizards. It seemed that Foster was looking for a way out, but from what? The lizards? Sure, they looked savage but they really weren't that big maybe two or three feet long, most of that was their tail. What could they do but give a nasty bite, unless they were toxic in some way.

The low level humming began and both lizards stood up in their now familiar pose. Tongues hanging agape, propped on their hind legs, their front arms and clawed hands drooping, they looked like a dog begging for table scraps.

Foster was half way to the closest lizard before Lane realized that he was moving. He noticed for the fist time that Foster was clad in what appeared to be lightweight hiking boots, some kind of safari pants with at least twenty pockets and a plaid logger shirt. All the clothing looked new with the exception of the ever-present blue baseball cap. He looked as if he were running through the pages of an L.L. Bean catalog.

Foster reached the first lizard and stopped, hesitating only a moment before drawing back his right leg and kicking the lizard squarely in what Lane thought might be it's stomach. The lizard careened down the hill, the slope serving to elevate its otherwise horizontal flight. It tumbled end over end, remaining stiff, tongue agape. He lost sight of it through the trees but thought he heard it land with a crash of brush and a solid, meaty whack.

"Ha," Foster said, smiling his dark grin and looking at Lane. "One down, one to—."

The deep rumbling hum stopped. Lane noticed for the first time the rumble echoing off the surrounding hills and mountains. The remaining lizard dropped from its stance. Foster quickly turned his attention to it.

"Not so tough without your buddy, huh?" he said, smirking, then winked at Lane as if they were conspirators in the lizards demise. He ran straight at the lizard and swung a kick in it direction, aiming to send it after its buddy. Lane noticed what might have been a blotch of the airborne lizards blood on Fosters boot.

Fosters' kick missed as the lizard scrambled close to the ground, beneath the kick and came up quickly between Fosters' legs. It clamped its toothy jaws firmly to Fosters' crotch, encompassing his penis and scrotum both. Foster could feel his balls turn to mush between the lizards spiked teeth. He hobbled around the lizard, trying to find his feet or his voice, he lost his footing and fell toward the creek. At least Lane thought he'd fallen, but he may have done it purposefully. He now rolled over into the creek, submerging the lizard in the black water. Fosters' legs kicked madly, his hat lay on the edge of the creek, soaked with the black water.

"*Waaaaaaah! Waaaaaaah!*" he screamed incoherently. Lane watched from upstream as the black creek washed over the firmly attached lizard and Foster.

"*Le-go! Le-go! Le-go!*" he suddenly began chanting as he writhed in the water pumping his hips from side to side trying to get the lizard to let go.

Lane was beginning to think that the lizard must surely be drowned by now when the second lizard appeared on the creek bank. Its face was wet with blood and it was breathing heavily from an open mouth. Blood slowly trickled from its mouth and it tongue hung with an odd limpness as if it were not fully attached. Its ragged appearance didn't seem to affect it enthusiasm for the fun its buddy was having. Seemingly not affected by its wounds, it scrambled recklessly down the slight embankment to join the fray.

Foster was still thrashing wildly and screaming at the lizard to let go when the second lizard made the small leap from the creek bank to land on his back. Foster didn't seem to notice the lizard until it had made its way up to his neck and began biting and chewing methodically.

Lane watched, detached, mesmerized by the attack he numbly realized that he was going to bear witness to the death of Foster Estroga. He expected to feel something like sorrow or an urge to save him, but didn't. Perhaps it was the part of him that was his father that felt nothing. If so, then the part of him that was his mother felt nothing either. Why or why not he felt anything for Foster didn't seem to matter. It felt right and it was going to happen whether he tried to stop it or not.

Foster had given up on trying to drown the lizard that was firmly attached to his crotch. As Lane watched, he stumbled from the creek, no longer screaming, but panting heavily. His L.L. Bean clothing was thoroughly soaked by the black water. Somewhere along the way he'd lost his hat and his long, black hair hung in stringy, matted tangles across his face. Both lizards hung tenaciously to their respective holds.

He began a loping run down the hill. There was a thick slick of blood covering the back of his neck that he was smearing about his face as he made unsuccessful grabs for the lizard on his back. The lizard at his crotch was being battered from side to side from Fosters pumping thighs, but still hung on like a pit bull. Lane could see its eyes were closed.

Now panicked and perhaps realizing that his own death was eminent, Foster began running blindly down the hill. Lane stepped quickly from the creek and then down the slope, for some macabre reason not wanting to lose sight of Foster.

As the hill became steeper, Foster lost his footing, began to fall on his left side and managed to slow himself somewhat by using the left half of his head to grab a tree. It didn't work very well and he was spun quickly to his right, blasting a fine spray of blood through the air as he impacted. He left a dark blotch of blood on the tree.

His body was limp as he began his final fall over a small ledge of rock. The fall alone could have killed him. The added momentum that the slope induced served only to punctuate the point of his death as he impacted the rocks at the bottom of the fifteen-foot drop.

As limp as he became after hitting the tree, Lane thought Foster was at least unconscious when he hit the outcropping of rock. All he could see was Fosters' feet sticking from the rocks down the slope. He stopped and watched for him to move. After about a minute with no sign of movement, Lane continued down the hill.

He walked to the ledge and looked over the crest. Foster slowly came into full view. He was lying on his back on a bed of sharp, granite rocks the size of basketballs. He appeared to be very dead.

The lizard at his crotch had let go and was standing off several feet to the left. It was smeared with blood as if it had bathed in it. Twigs and bits of pine needles were stuck to the blood, making the lizard look as if it were trying to camouflage itself. Its right eye was matted shut with tacky blood and it was swiping at it with its right front foot. Lane could smell the heavy stench of sweat and death.

The lizard that had been at Fosters' neck lay partially beneath Fosters' prone body. Lane could see the lower half of the lizard protruding from under Fosters' shoulders. It wasn't moving.

Foster lay crumpled and broken on his back, his face was soft and caved in. It was composed mainly of a pulpy mash of blood. There were bits of pine needle stuck to his face and a pinecone had gotten stuck beneath his chin. It was drenched in thick blood. The scene reminded Lane of another he had witnessed so many years ago.

"Well, what now?" Lane asked no one in particular. The remaining lizard seemed to get the message and slowly plodded to where Foster lay. It took Foster's right hand in its mouth and began to drag Fosters' arm straight out. Once I had the arm straight out at a right angle to Fosters body, it began tugging at it trying to pull Foster.

Lane could see bits of Fosters' flesh breaking off at the edge of the lizards' mouth. It let go of Fosters' hand and slowly plodded down hill.

It stopped after several feet and began rubbing its head in the thick forest matte, trying to clean itself.

Lane looked down the hill toward the black valley, then back at the lizard that was methodically cleaning itself. Why hadn't the humming sound started again? He pushed the thought aside for later. The woods were silent, there were no birds, no rustle of animals foraging, no squealing elk, no squirrels; a perfect, vacuous silence.

He was beyond what had been, too far-gone to ever return. His thoughts about his past life were beginning to feel fuzzy and unhinged. He briefly wondered what had happened to his body when he'd stepped through the front door and into this world, wherever *this* was.

The by now familiar drone suddenly began again and the second lizard stood as expected. The lizard beneath Fosters' body didn't move, somehow confirming its death. Lane waited for the humming to stop and wondered what would happen next.

✳   ✳   ✳

Duane left the restaurant in the slight buzz of the beers and the heady sensation of the food. Now, with the warm night pressing in on him, holding Lane's body in a moist sensation just as Lane's body held him, he began wandering through the downtown area.

He was trying to remember where the little store was. It may have been moved or gone completely out of business by now. It had been many years since he roamed these streets. So far, nothing was looking familiar.

Thirty minutes later, still high from the beer, Lane—with Duane at the controls—walked into Pebbles Pawn. A very thin man with a sparse beard and even thinner mustache stood behind the counter. The shop smelled of bleach and some type of lemon scented cleaner.

"Sorry, we're closed," the thin man said.

"Door was open," Duane said, closing the door behind him. He felt himself loosely floating inside Lane and tried not to pay attention to it.

"Yeah? We're still closed."

"As long as I'm here we may as well do some business. Won't take but a minute. I just—."

"Look, bud, we're closed," the little man said, coming from behind the counter. There was a small caliber handgun in a slip-clip on his belt at his right hip. The guy was nervous or suffering from some type of facial disorder. Duane reached into his back pocket and began to pull out the stack of one hundred-dollar bills as the little man continued to advance.

Just as Duane was beginning to register the feeling of the thick stack of hundred on the fingers of his left hand, the nervous little man had drawn his gun, moved to Duane's right and stopped in a half crouch, gun aimed squarely at Duane's chest.

"Nope. Last guy that tried to rob me is dead and I don't need the hassle again." Duane didn't doubt him. The nervous tick was gone and the man looked rock solid, green eyes never wavering from his target. Duane noted that he had taken up position behind a shelf of power tools. They were neatly stacked and very clean.

"Easy…easy. I'm just going to pull out my money. Okay? Cash only, right?"

The man didn't move.

"Mister, if there is even the hint of anything other than greenery, I will shoot you."

"Fair enough. But I have to tell you, I've been down that road and it ain't that bad." Duane formed Lane's face into a beaming smile, causing his gray eyes to light up with the darkness that was in him. The thin man adjusted his stance, but said nothing.

He grasped the thick wad of bills and began to ease the five thousand dollars out of his back pocket. The shopkeeper slid further behind the shelves of power tools and watched carefully. Duane had no doubt that the man would shoot him if he pulled out anything other than the promised contents. Part of Duane wanted to try and disarm the little shit then spend the better part of the night beating him. He quickly pushed the thought aside, maybe later.

He slowly slipped the money from his pocket.

"Just pinch it with your thumb and index finger and come around real slow with it," the man said.

"No problem." Duane did as he was told and brought the thick stack of bills into view from behind his back.

"See? Just good old money."

"Uh-huh. Now turn around and keep your hands clear of your body." He did as he was told. The thin man relaxed, then slowly slipped his gun back into the clip at his belt.

"Sorry about that. In this business you can't trust very much."

"Yeah."

The man stood upright and seemed to be thinking.

"What was it that you needed?" he finally asked, perhaps having weighed the cash against getting home fifteen minutes late. Duane smiled and stuck out what was, essentially, Lane's hand. "Lane White," he said.

"Burt Lancaster," the thin man said, offering his hand. Lane shook it.

"No shit?" he asked.

"No shit. My parents were big movie buffs."

"You don't say."

"Yeah. Big time buffs. All kinds of memorabilia."

"That right?"

"Oh, yeah, all kinds. I never did go in for it much though."

Duane followed Burt over to the counter. Now that they had both relaxed, Duane had time to see that Burt wasn't really a sickly thin, as he had first thought. He had the slim yet taught build of a runner. They reached the counter, Burt babbling on some more about his parents. He began to laugh at something he'd said. Duane joined right in, never missing a beat. He still had trouble getting used to being Lane. The familiar resonance of his former voice was what he unconsciously expected to hear when he spoke and every time he didn't hear it, he was reminded of the situation he was now in.

He tried not to smile at his reflection in a small mirror set in the wall behind the counter. It was undoubtedly a two-way that Burt used when the need arose. He may not have the boy home yet, but for right now *being* the boy was just fine.

"Something funny?" Burt asked, the edge of suspicion creeping back into his voice.

"Just remembering a joke I heard," Duane said.

"Yeah? Let's hear it," Burt offered, the suspicion trying to leave but just not quite able to do so. Duane smiled and laughed, thinking he would remember some joke to fill in the ruse. He opened Lane's mouth and listened to the joke being told.

"What do you do with an elephant with three balls?"

Burt shrugged his shoulders and shook his head lightly from side to side.

"Walk him and pitch to the Rhino," Duane said, not really liking the joke much himself. Must have been one of Lane's. Burt laughed out of courtesy.

"Yeah, well, I guess it was funnier during the new day, since the past is gone."

Burt smiled and nodded as if he understood and continued to look mostly suspiciously at his customer.

"Guess we should get down to business so you can get home, huh?"

"Maybe," Burt said, visibly changing roles into shopkeeper. "What're you looking for?"

"Well, I've been needing a hand gun lately, and tonight seemed to be the night to get it," Duane said.

"Yeah? And I suppose you can't wait for me to get you through the mandatory waiting period, that it? Somebody is prowling the neighborhood and your worried about your wife? Should've worn a wedding ring if you were going to use that one," Burt said, gesturing to where Duane's left hand lay palm down on the counter. "Or have you got something new that I haven't heard before?"

"Yeah, maybe," Duane said, smiling. This wasn't going to be as easy as he'd thought. Whatever this waiting period was, Burt expected him to know about it. But when you've been dead for twenty years it's hard to keep up with the changes. He spoke before he'd thought to.

"I'm going to use it to kill a lot of people," he said, smiling. Burt froze; not sure what to believe, then his face slowly relaxed into a smile. He nodded and chuckled lightly.

"Yeah, you're right, I've never heard that one before." Duane could see that Burt was now trying his best to relax but there was something he sensed in the situation that wouldn't let him. Duane thought Burt to be one smart cookie.

"So? Can we do something here?"

"Maybe," Burt said. He walked around from behind the counter and went back to the front door. He flipped the sign hanging in the door so it would read closed to any possible patrons. He thumbed home two deadbolts, then turned to face Duane.

"How do I know you're not a cop?"

"I guess you don't."

"Well, there's one way to find out."

"Yeah?"

"Yeah. And if this little party is going to go any farther you have to do it."

"What's that?"

"Strip."

Duane liked the man's style all the more.

"Strip?" he asked, playing dumb. "My clothes?"

"Yeah. Otherwise you're leaving now," Burt said, moving his hand to rest on the butt of his gun. Duane wanted to mention that the door was locked and the closed sign turned out, but decided to play along.

"You're not going to try and fuck me, are you?" he asked, smirking. He began to pull off his shirt.

Burt didn't respond. Duane slowly stripped the clothes from Lane's body, aware of the everyday activity as a wholly new sensory experience. He stood naked it the bright, clean florescent light.

"Okay?"

"Turn around."

"Uh-oh, here it comes."

"You should be so lucky," Burt offered.

Duane did as requested, turned slowly in the light with his hands at his sides.

"Lift your arms up." Duane did.

"Okay, get dressed."

Duane did.

"See any wires?" Duane asked, pulling on his shirt.

"No unless they're somewhere I'm not going to look."

"If I said please, would you?"

Burt smiled, but didn't laugh. Duane could tell that Burt's opinion of him was quickly beginning to sour.

"Okay. We can do something. Here's the deal," Burt said, coming back behind the counter. "Any gun in this case," he said, waving his hand over the display.

"Yeah?" Duane asked, holding a tennis shoe in one hand.

"Three thousand dollars and you walk out of here tonight with nothing but the gun."

"That much?"

"That much," Burt said.

"What about the paper work?" Duane asked, simply because he thought he should.

"I'll handle it as part of our little deal."

Duane finished dressing, then pulled the stack of one hundred-dollar bills off the counter where he'd laid it. He peeled off thirty bills and lay them on the counter. Burt picked up the pile, counted it again, then quickly exited to the back room. He told Duane to look around and he'd be right back. A minute later he was back.

"See anything that might suit your needs?"

"Well, I'm going to have to lean on you for some help."

"You want something that can stop someone in a hurry, right?"

"Yeah. Something with some kick behind it."

He settled on a forty-five caliber semi-automatic pistol. It was the largest gun in the case.

"Do you think you could walk me through the gun?" Duane asked, doing his best to look sheepish embarrassed at his own ignorance. Burt smiled, ready to be the professional gunman to the willing pupil.

He showed Duane the routine of loading, locking and how to shoot the gun. Duane asked to be shown the loading sequence again, the once more after that.

"I still don't understand how the bullet stays in the…clip?"

"Yes, that's the clip. See this spring in here?" Burt said, pointing to the spring.

"Yeah," Duane said, all goggled eyed pupil.

"The pressure of that spring keeps the bullet locked against the top of the clip."

"And that's the next bullet to be shot?"

"Yes. After you chamber the load, this one will be next."

"Hmm," Duane said, still looking confused. He reached for the bundle of hundreds in his pocket, peeled one off, then lay it on the counter. Burst stared at it, confused.

"For the lessons," Duane said; trying to act slightly embarrassed.

"Do you think you've got it?" Burt asked, slipping the bill into his pocket.

"Well, if you had a bullet to put in there," he said, pointing to the clip. "Then I think it would clear up a lot."

Burt, completely into the mode of a gun lover educating another to the ways of the clan, lay the forty-five on the felt counter tray.

He walked down the aisle behind the counter, produced a set of keys, and bent down. Duane could hear the soft clinking of the keys on the chain, then the smooth swishing of a sliding door being opened. Burt closed his stash and returned with a box of what Duane assumed to be forty-five shells.

"Here we go," Burt said, smiling blissfully. He opened the box and produced a shell.

"Now, this is how it stays in the clip," he said, then demonstrated.

"Oh, yeah," Duane responded, not quite believing Burt was so fucking dumb. He thought of Kristy and the whores he used to buy. He began to get an enormous erection.

"Can I try it?" he asked.

"Sure. Here," Burt handed the clip with the single load over to him. Duane fumbled with the bullet then slid it home.

"Nothing to it," Burt said.

"Yeah. Nothing at all," Duane agreed. He quickly and smoothly picked up the gun from where it lay on the counter, slid the clip home, and then just as quickly chambered one of the two rounds.

"Heh...oh shit," Burt said. His eyes grew wide with fear, which quickly changed to calculation.

"I'm not even going to give you the benefit of trying," Duane said, smiling hugely. The roar from the gun was deafening. Burt's surprised face disappeared in a bright red spray. The wall behind him was thickly coated in blood and brain matter. Burt hit the wall and crumpled to the floor. Duane was reminded of his own death by the very hand that now held the forty-five. He stuck the gun in his mouth just for kicks, then pulled it out.

He took the box of shells off the counter, then went behind the counter and rummaged through Burt's pockets for the keys. The small cabinet beneath the counter contained the mother load. He looked quickly through the surrounding shelves until he found a plastic grocery bag. Filling it with about ten boxes of forty-five shells he stuffed the gun into his waistband and began to walk to the storefront. His erection had become the stuff of legend—true blue steel.

He stopped on his way out of the store and looked at the security camera mounted in the corner near the ceiling. A small red light was illuminated on the top on the camera, undoubtedly having captured the whole episode.

Still smiling, Duane pulled the gun out of his waistband and lay it with the sack of shells on the floor. With a quick glance to the street he slipped his pants down and masturbated for the camera, smiling the whole while. It didn't take long.

Burt wouldn't be found until Monday morning. Though the police would find the videotape of the crime, by the time they identified the criminal it would be too late.

Duane moved Lane's body out the door and into the night. He didn't bother locking up. He'd thrown the keys indifferently toward Burt's lifeless body on his way back out of the store. Shells in hand, gun back in his waistband and erection somewhat decreased, he headed into the night with only a vague idea of what would come next. It was a good night to be dead and living in your sons' body. A tune came to mind and he began to hum along with it as it played through his thoughts. He didn't recognize it but like it anyway. He walked on through the night, humming a nursery rhyme about a mockingbird.

*   *   *

Saturday, early morning, and Ben hadn't slept well. Not well at all. Though he was by now fully committed to the task that lay ahead and was faithful that his dreams had been telling him the truth, there remained a lingering doubt. Blake was following his grandpa's lead and Walsh was trusting and believing in a life long friend.

And what was it, exactly, that Ben Morrow *was* doing? His whole life had been spent dealing in facts, tangibles that you could lay your hands upon, add up, diversify. And this? This…this was *faith.*

He sat up in bed, poised on something like a revelation. The clock radio that he hadn't been able to set properly since Carly died showed the time to be a little past six in the morning. He must have slept some, though it didn't feel like it.

He pulled the covers back and slid his legs over the edge of the bed. Doing his best not to notice the pain in his body, especially his back. He had definitely wrenched something in there and it wasn't the least bit happy about it. With his feet now firmly on the floor he waited for the rest of his body to catch up.

He wore his usual boxer shorts and a clean undershirt to bed. During the winter he could add socks, but no more.

The quit sounds of the house waking with the day reminded him of Carly. She would have been up already and in the corner of the kitchen nook, sipping her strange teas and reading one of her fiction paperbacks.

Faith. No…FAITH.

It all came down to that one word. He had to believe. Not just his current dilema, but the whole crap shoot. Faith. You had to have it to get anywhere.

Ben stood, slowly stretching to his full height. His back began to cramp but gave in before it became too painful. Slowly shuffling along, he made his way to the bathroom and urinated a mostly clear fluid. This was good, he thought absently, getting plenty of water. Hie health had become more and more a consideration over the years, even more so now that he was preparing to undertake certain illegal activities.

He dressed then returned to the bathroom to shave and clean his teeth. That done, he checked the clock again: six thirty-two. Blake wouldn't be up for hours yet. Ben had fallen asleep to the dull murmur of Blake's television and he had probably stayed up till early this morning.

Even by trying very hard Ben couldn't capture the emotions and thought processes of his youth. The memories were there; pictures in black and white, caring parents, and a very traditional upbringing. All of these memories were there, clear as a bright winter day. But the *feelings* and the *enthusiasms* of his youth…he couldn't recall. Motivation had moved from what's fun to what will get us along financially to will it keep us secure?

He made his way to the kitchen, pausing only to look in on Blake sleeping deeply. The sun had already crested the horizon and the Blackjack Oak and Maples framed the bright orange morning sky. It was suppose to get into the mid-nineties. He hadn't seen the weather for Monday but it was more than likely going to be hot.

"A good day for a house burning," he said aloud, then smiled and thought some more about faith while brewing the morning coffee.

The squealing whine of a jet engine drew him out of his thoughts. It grew slowly louder. Since the house wasn't in any usual flight paths a low passing plane was an oddity. He casually peered through the kitchen window for the plane. The whine grew louder still. Windowpanes began to rattle as the jet approached. It seemed to take a long time to build, but once the jet passed over the house the roar seemed to double or treble in volume and intensity. Dishes in the cabinet nearly jumped out of the cupboard. Ben grabbed his ears as the jet blasted over the house, seemingly low enough to set the roof on fire. The plane pulled up and began to climb straight up into the morning sky.

"What the hell was that?" Ben asked the empty kitchen. He leaned over the sink until he'd lost sight of the jet and it was a distant roar. Probably some pilot out goofing off with a National Guard plane. A weekend warrior playing sky raider.

Ben reached for a coffee mug from the cabinet and climbed back into this thought when the deep whine of the jet began to grow again. He set the mug down unfilled and began to work his way to the sliding door just off the Den. As he reached the door and slid it open the jet thundered overhead, blasting seemingly treetop level then rocketing back up into the warm morning sky. He left the porch door open and walked out into the backyard.

Scanning the sky he spotted the jet moving East to West in the northern sky, appearing as a faint dot. He watched as it continued West, swung south, then came around again to the East. He was flying straight into the morning sun, which was at Ben's back. Ben thought it was odd, since he was performing low level flight maneuvers and the sun would be straight in the pilot's eyes. But it also made it much easier for Ben to watch the plane.

It slowly grew in the sky. Its angle of descent kept it fully in view as it dove toward the house. Ben watched, unsure of what to think. The whine of its engines slowly began to build to the coming scream. It began to level off, just off the tops of the trees and was going to pass on the North side of the property. It was so low and close that Ben could have hit it with a rock if he could have thrown a rock that hard.

As the plane neared the house it seemed to slow down, which was physically impossible. On the other passes the plane had been hauling ass, traveling every bit of at least five hundred miles an hour Ben would have guessed.

Yet now, as the plane began to pull even with his property line, on the other side of the pond, it rolled, tilting the cockpit toward the house where Ben stood. It did seem to be going much slower than even a light aircraft could fly. In fact…it was very nearly stopped, there, on the other side of the pond, just above the trees.

Roaring just as loudly as if it were moving the plane had actually stopped just above the trees. The cockpit cover had a gold tint to it and the entire plane was a bright pearl white. It was like, and yet unlike, any fighter that might be seen at an air show. But there was something obviously missing. Something that Ben could almost—there were no markings on the plane he suddenly realized. No tail number, no logos, no red or yellow and black warnings. Nothing. It was a pearl white fighter jet stopped in mid–flight above the tree line.

Ben scanned the plane again and realized that he could actually see the pilot. He squinted his eyes and adjusted his hand to better shield the glare coming off the plane. Just as he recognized whom the pilot *looked* like (not *was* he quickly told himself, *looked* like) the plane began to move again, blistering on across the tree tops, blasting across the sky. This time it didn't return.

Ben watched until the plane was a small dot high in the sky, then slowly disappeared in the distance. He strained to hear the whine of the engine, but couldn't. Had he really seen what he thought he had? It was impossible, of course, but then what he was planning to do Monday he would have considered impossible only a few weeks ago.

It was coincidence that was all, just simple coincidence. Nothing more. He shook his head and chuckled.

"You sure are one stubborn asshole," he said to the morning. "God or whatever's pulling the strings around here comes and slaps you in the face with it and you still can't let go and believe." Turning back to the house he saw the open porch door and wondered why Blake hadn't come outside. With all the racket the jet had made he surely should have waken.

Ben looked back to the morning sky. It was patchy with cottonish balls of clouds backed with a light blue. The jet wasn't anywhere in sight. Starlings were chattering in the trees and somewhere close by a mockingbird sang. Further away he could hear crows calling to one another.

No, it wasn't coincidence, or chance or a trick of the light. The pilot of the airplane had been Stephen. He felt it too much for there to be any other conclusion. The pilot had been Stephen in a new form. Something different from the body he'd used here in this place. Smiling, tipping his hand in a small wave, it *had* been him.

Did he need a clearer sign? Was there any question which way he should proceed? Now he no longer even needed faith. Here was his factual verification. Stephen—his body long dead yet his spirit thriving—cruising by in the true love of his life at close to Mach one.

His jet.

Why had he never nurtured Stephen's love of flight? He'd never thought Stephen could make it as a pilot, that he should stick closer to his own abilities. It was hard to get into military flight school, much less be picked as a pilot.

His thoughts trailed off. The drone of a small piston engine airplane hummed somewhere in the distance. Absently searching the sky for the plane, Ben realized that there was another underlying reason he'd never encouraged Stephen to fly. One very painful reason. Stephen would have outgrown him. He would have accomplished something greater than Ben Morrow would. At the time, that was something that Ben couldn't have taken. Now, he would easily trade the remaining years of his life so that he could have Stephen back. Just for an afternoon, that would be all. Just a few hours to tell him how he'd felt about him and why he'd done the things he'd done.

Then, that done, he would have gladly walked into that darkness that was death and given what years he may have remaining to Stephen.

He began to cry. Slow, steady tears of a life long regret. His son, his boy, Stephen, a suicide. He quietly cried out his caged and carefully groomed world of excuses and felt the hard pain begin to loosen, just a little.

Had it all been that easy? Something so simple as his pride or vanity? Several biblical quotes came to mind but Ben was no longer listening. He no longer needed to think about his actions. He'd been given a rare prize, a gift. One last chance in his life was being given to make amends, to be the father he never was and the grandfather he could be. The way was set, and though he didn't understand more than eighty percent of the how and nearly none of the why, burning down the house on

Cherokee place was going to happen. It would be the beginning of a kind of life he'd never thought possible, or the tragic dismal end he feared it could become.

He pulled out a clean handkerchief from his back pocket and wiped his face dry. Had he ever told Stephen he'd loved him? He wasn't sure, but thought that before it was over he may yet get that chance.

"Sure wish you were here, Carly," Ben said to the waking morning. He wanted to cry again but didn't. Blake should be up soon and it would put him off if he saw Ben crying. The jet had been for his eyes and ears only. He walked back into the house with a new resolve and poured his Saturday morning cup of coffee.

*   *   *

Marilyn rang the doorbell for the third time and added a knock on the door. She wasn't worried, yet. But her instincts were telling her something was not right. Lane's car was in the driveway, parked at an off angle as if he'd rushed into the driveway. That the car was even in the driveway was unusual. Lane had always been careful with his car and had always parked in the garage.

She struggled with maybe peeking in the windows just to see if he was lying dead on the living room floor. But if he was home and simply didn't want to be disturbed and he caught her peeking it would blow his trust in her. Probably not much, but maybe enough to change his mind about sharing something with her.

She reached out to ring the bell again then stopped herself. It could wait. There was no need to push right now. Monday they could discuss the doctor and physical testing, until then, maybe he would be better of left alone. It was going to be a sunny Saturday and she should really leave and take advantage of the coming day. He probably hadn't received her message; technology wasn't always foolproof.

She waited another moment, glanced at her watch and noted the time was almost eleven thirty, then forced herself to leave. Everything was fine. It could wait until Monday.

*   *   *

Duane didn't remember going to sleep. When he woke, he had a strange feeling of vertigo. There was a brief, yet sharp moment when he wasn't sure if he was in the boy or if the boy was in him. Had be become Lane? Was he *now* Lane? For a moment he was lost to himself. Then it was gone and he found old Duane Trammel White, ready to roll.

He wandered around the house, having no memory of returning to it the night before. It was new and strangely thrilling to see it through the boy's eyes. On the way down the hall he noticed a small smear of what looked like blood on the wall. He reached up with Lane's hand and touched the spot. It was blood. He'd seen enough of it in his former life to know. It was in the act of reaching up to touch the spot that he noticed Lane's hands and the damage that had been done to them.

The knuckles were bruised, swollen and the skin split in several places. His left hand was damaged also only to a lesser extent, he was right handed, the same as Lane. He moved the fingers and felt the pain in them, but it was distant. Where the skin had split and was trying to heal now opened and began to bleed freely as he flexed the sore skin, muscle and bone. He held his hands up and watched the blood slowly trickle down the back of them. They looked as if they'd gone five hard rounds in a bare-knuckle match and his opponent had been a brick wall.

He could have been in a fight, but that somehow didn't feel right. He thought back and could only remember eating, then something about explosions or fireworks...gun. He'd gotten a gun somewhere...then... here he was.

Instincts led him to the bathroom. He rinsed his bloody hands then dried them with a towel he found under the sink. A vast panorama of memory flooded through him; the times he'd played with Kristy in the shower, forcing her to entertain his desires, no matter how she cried. Her protests only amplified his desire to posses her in anyway he chose. She hadn't even been his daughter, no matter what that bitch Amanda had told him. He'd known she had been screwing around.

He caught sight of his reflection in the mirror and gazed through the eyes of Lane. The sudden memory of stuffing their damn pet turtle into the drain came back. That had been a mistake. The little thing had died and stunk up the house for nearly two weeks.

There was a sudden movement of darkness—a shadow passing across his eyes—then he was standing before a mostly demolished wall. He looked around the vaguely familiar room and slowly realized that beneath the fancy office shit was his old room.

Why had he come in here? He looked back at the crumbled and smashed sheet rock. There was a good deal of blood splattered on the wall, drops and small puddles of it on the floor mixed with the crumbled sheet rock. He looked down at his hands to find what he expected to see. If they had been raw and wounded from the pummeling they had taken some point last night; they were now more akin too freshly ground beef. He was dripping sweat, breathing hard and could smell his own foul breath and meaty stench.

He had been beating the wall with fisted hands. Beating it for all he was worth by the looks of things. Sweat ran freely down his face, his shirt was stuck to his back and soaked thoroughly and he was panting from the effort he had thrown into it. Holding his hands up he viewed them as if they had become disconnected from him. Why was he doing this? He had taken the boy, the boy was gone, Lane was no longer here…or was he? Here was only Duane Trammel White…and yet, this? Was there yet a part of the boy hiding in him at this moment planning the next move to screw his old Dad yet again?

The black out scared him the most. His hands bleeding and numb he slowly moved to the bedroom, lay down and was soon sound asleep. So deeply that he didn't hear Marilyn knocking and ringing the doorbell several hours later.

✶   ✶   ✶

"Who's that?" Blake asked, pointing out the kitchen window at the blue truck pulling up the drive. Ben recognized the truck he'd purchased the day before.

"Probably Walsh," he said. The truck looked washed and there appeared to be some stenciling on the door, but from where he stood Ben couldn't make out what it said.

Blake had appeared in the kitchen not long after the mysterious jet had gone. Ben had made no mention of it and neither had Blake. He hadn't heard the jet and Ben was convinced that he wouldn't have seen it, even if he'd been standing in the yard with him.

They had spent the morning quietly cooking breakfast as Blake slowly woke to the day and Ben cleared his thoughts. Brenda called around nine to check on the both of them. Ben tried to sound up but didn't think he did very well. His thoughts were confirmed when he handed the phone to Blake and began ladling pancake batter. He overheard Blake respond to Brenda in a quiet voice, telling her that Grandpa was fine.

They were just finishing up breakfast when Walsh pulled down the drive. Ben and Blake left the kitchen and met him in the yard just as he was getting out of the truck. A vague plum of dust stirred up by the truck settled over them all.

"Hey, Blake! How they hanging?" Walsh asked, dropping Ben a wink.

"Great," Blake said, smiling self-consciously.

As they came closer, Ben could see what was stenciled on the truck door. He smiled and thought it a marvelous idea.

"Well?" Walsh asked as they read the stenciling. Ben smiled all the more and began to actually feel good about their expedition.

"Where'd you get the truck?" Blake asked.

"Well, this truck kind of belongs to all of us, Blake. See what that says there?" Walsh asked, bending at the hips to be nearer Blake while pointing at the door.

"B.B.W. Lawn Care," Blake read aloud. Beneath that were a fictitious phone number and a picture of a riding lawn mower. Under the mower was the picture of a leaf rake. The stenciling was done in a light green color that stood out well against the dark blue truck.

"What do you think that means?" Walsh asked. He glanced at Ben and raised his eyebrows, throwing the question to him also. Ben shrugged, enjoying the moment. Blake thought for a moment, silently mouthing words that came to mind. None seemed to match.

"I give," Blake finally said.

"Ben, Blake and Walsh Lawn Care," Walsh said.

"Really?"

"Really."

"Cool."

"Here that Ben? We've arrived, now we're cool, man."

Blake laughed then ran around to the other side of the truck to look at the other door. Walsh stood up and looked at Ben, he didn't see what he expected to see in Ben's face and was glad for that.

"What?" Ben asked.

"Nothing. Just looks like you've had a change of heart or finally taken that crap you've been working on all week."

"Yeah? Well, maybe a little of both."

"Good. I was getting worried I'd have to do this job alone."

"Alone? You'd do that?"

"Sure. I believe you and I sure don't want to see anything happen to Blake."

"You're full of shit, Walsh."

"Maybe," he said, grinning hugely and winking.

Ben knew that he was serious and that if he, Ben, did have a last minute change of plans, Walsh would see it all the way through to the lighting of the match.

With that small exchange of words and glances, the deal was done, as far as Ben felt. He no longer had doubts that it was the right direction, but did that make it right? He couldn't answer that, at least not right now. Maybe later he could, but not right now.

There had been other things that Stephen had told him during the dreams. Other things that were a possibility of happening as a result of their little expedition. He hadn't shared those things with anyone, thinking that they would all be better off not having to worry about the maybes and getting on with their goal.

"Where'd you get it done?" Ben asked, quickly changing his thoughts away from the track they were taking him.

"Vera Creek."

"Long drive out there. Friends of yours?"

"Now do you really think that I'd do something like that? Hell, Ben, you are without a doubt the only friend I have to trust something like this with."

Ben simply nodded, knowing it was something Walsh would have thought of already.

"So, we load up the truck with a shit load of that lawn equipment you've got stashed and maybe get up some kind of uniforms and slip right in without a peep," Walsh said, nearly bursting with excitement. He couldn't withhold a chuckle that erupted into outright laughter.

"You enjoying this, Walsh?" Ben asked, doing his best to look somber and somewhat hurt. He couldn't keep a smile from creeping across his face, however seeing it, Walsh let the floodgates open.

"Hell yes, buddy! I've not felt this alive in…shit, I don't know, a long fucking time, I can tell you that!"

"Take it easy on the French there Walsh," Ben said pointing toward where Blake was exploring something in the brush at the edge of the lawn. Ben had long ago forgotten what a wonder the country was when all you've seen is the city. They both watched, as Blake appeared to be following something in the waist high grass.

The day was still and Ben could taste the dry dust the truck had kicked up. The cicadas and grasshoppers were already starting in on a long day of noise making.

"Yeah, okay, I just get excited by the whole thing. Reminds me a little of those Ross Wagner private eye books I used to read as a kid. Do you remember those?"

"Nope. Sure don't," Ben said, wondering what Blake was watching in the grass. Walsh, seeing Ben was out of the conversation, followed his gaze to where Blake was now crouched down in the grass, slowly shuffling along, intently following something on the ground. Crouched as he was, the grass nearly covered his head. They both watched for a moment longer, the day growing hotter.

"Why don't we go play a round later this afternoon?" Ben asked, breaking their gaze away from Blake.

"Today?" Walsh asked, instinctively looking at the clear, hot sky.

"Tomorrow, then?" Ben asked.

"Either," Walsh said. "If you want to, I'm available. Just seems that maybe we should get ready for Monday," Walsh asked.

"Yeah, I know. I'd just like to play one more round before then."

"Oh?"

"Yes."

"You thinking that something's going to prevent you from playing golf after Monday?"

"No, no," Ben lied. "Nothing like that. I just felt like getting out, try and take my mind off of all this for awhile," he said, waving his hand in the general direction of the truck.

"Well, if you think we'll have time I could—."

"Grandpa!" Blake yelled from where he was standing in the grass.

"Blake? Everything all right?" Walsh called back, alarmed. They both began to jog as best they could to where Blake was in the tall grass.

"Yeah! Fine!" he called back without looking up from the ground.

They both slowed their pace and tried not to breathe too heavily. Reaching the edge of the lawn they began to work their way through the tall, dry grass toward Blake. Walsh noticed the smell first.

"Smells like your pond is turning over, Ben."

"It's this!" Blake said, pointing to the ground where he was standing.

"Oh? What is *this*?" Walsh asked as they came upon what Blake had been following.

"My God!" Ben said, staring at the animal that was slowly pulling itself through the grass.

"Have you ever, I mean *ever* seen a turtle that big?" Walsh asked.

"Pretty big, huh?" Blake said, excited at their surprise but not realizing just how abnormally large the turtle was.

"Yes, on National Geographic when they do the Galapagos Islands," Ben said.

"It looks bigger than that," Walsh said.

The turtle began to slowly drag itself forward.

"Step back a little Blake," Walsh said, pulling gently on his arm.

"What'd you think? Four, maybe five feet long?"

"Your easily in the ballpark," Walsh said, staring in disbelief. The turtle lurched forward then stopped once again.

"Smells like dead fish," Blake said.

"Yeah. I wonder if it's sick? Look how dark it is, almost black. You ever see a black turtle?" Walsh asked.

"No. Not around here," Ben said, looking up and following the crushed grass trail of the turtle back to where it had come from.

"I'd say its heading toward the pond," Ben added.

Blake picked up a stick and gently poked the turtle on its back right foot. The foot had four toes; each with a long sharp claw attached and there was webbing between its toes. The turtle didn't respond to the prodding by Blake.

"Looks like it came from up there," Ben said, taking several steps up the hill.

"Yeah, sure does," Walsh responded without looking up, he stared at the turtle, still fascinated by its actual presence. If he put the turtle in a kids plastic swimming pool, the kind you get for five bucks at the local discount store, it would just fit if it tucked in it head and tail. The turtle began to lurch forward again, either unaware or not caring about their presence. Walsh stepped back a little further and Blake followed, now beginning to get the big picture.

Ben had followed the back-trail through the grass and up the hill and was now walking back down. Walsh glanced up as he approached.

"You know, it looks just like a regular snapping turtle," Walsh said.

"Except its black," Ben said.

"Yeah and on steroids," Walsh offered.

"Guess what else."

"What?" Walsh asked, forcing his gaze away from the turtle.

"The trail just ends inside the woods."

"Oh?"

"Yeah. It just...ends. Like it just appeared there, on the edge of the woods," Ben said, looking back at the trail. "No stirring up of dirt, leaves...nothing."

"Huh," Walsh said, not really paying attention.

"Shouldn't we call the zoo or something? I mean this thing is really unusual. It's not normal."

Walsh came out of his stupor at the suggestion.

"Oh? Get a bunch of people snooping around here? Maybe they can help us get ready for Monday," Walsh suggested. Ben nodded and the idea was dropped.

"Besides, we can always call somebody later, after we're finished," Walsh added.

It took the turtle another two hours to crawl to the pond. Walsh said a little prayer for the fish that would surely perish at the jaws of their new houseguest as they watched the anomaly slip into the red Oklahoma pond water.

Ben laughed only half-hearted as he'd spent literally thousand of dollars and well over ten years stocking and maintaining the fish population. He'd farmed the fish to a more respectable table size and now the uninvited guest would have a field day.

Walsh laughed all the harder.

"Don't worry, Ben, when he's done here he'll move on!"

Ben smirked at the comment and they went back to the house.

The remainder of Saturday was spent readying the truck and lawn equipment. The early evening was spent going over the plan. It didn't take that long, as it was not that complex.

They would arrive at the house around nine thirty and begin to service the lawn. One can at a time Ben and Walsh would move the gas cans to the backyard. From there they would find a way into the basement, pour out several cans of fuel, ignite it then be gone.

TEN

...1

He counted to three, plunged his head into the dark water, and then pushed back through the surface. The Turtle stirred, but didn't move toward the water. Even if It had, the distance wasn't far. He thought he could beat it across the lake before it even hulked into the water.

He began to swim.

Lane stood on the shore of a vast, dark lake. The stream he'd first encountered emptied into the lake at his side; the black water slid syrup thick into the lake. The shore was littered with quarter sized pearl white snails and white crabs as big as peaches with tiny pink eyes. He thought he could even see the occasional white fish swimming by, but the water was so dark it was hard to tell. It could have been a simple play of the odd sunlight.

The raspberry lizard stood on the bank fifteen yards away. Foster Estorga's battered, lifeless body lay just behind him. Not understanding why, but feeling it was the right thing to do, he'd drug and carried Foster's corpse to the lakeshore. At times letting it crash ahead down the steep drops as they made their way to the lake.

It had been much easier to do than he'd thought. He forced himself not to think about what he was moving and it had worked most of the time. The raspberry lizard that had remained slowly scampered ahead. The low end rumbling hadn't returned since just after Foster's death.

Lane now sat on a large rock at the lake edge. He wasn't tired from the experience of dragging Foster down the hill, not physically tired, but mentally, he was exhausted. His thoughts had become thick and vibrated as if his head were full of bees or wasps. As he'd descended the hill down to the lake it felt as if he were trying to remember something while pushing that same memory away. It felt as if he were being pulled apart in a precise, surgically methodical process.

When they'd reached the lakeshore (Lane tried not to look at the beating Fosters' head had taken from the ride down the hill) he'd looked across to the opposite bank. It was maybe a mile to the nearest shore. The length of the lake was impossible to gauge as he couldn't see either end.

As his increasingly disjointed thoughts had sporadic moments of clarity, he wondered if he'd died as he'd walked through the front door of his house, his body perhaps still lying there—legs sticking out the open door—waiting to be discovered. Several times he was sure he had died walking through the doorway and that this was his version on an afterlife, not quite heaven, not quite hell. Maybe he was in an eternal limbo for the sin he'd committed in his former life; the raspberry lizards his Angels; Foster an all to personal mentor gone mad.

Other times he found himself staring into the black, silty water gently lapping on the rock shore, staring; his mind a smooth, cooling blank. He wasn't sure how long he'd been sitting there on the rock by the shore, tossing marble sized pebbles at the white crabs. There shells weren't hard and the round, black pebbles struck them as if they were cups of cold vanilla pudding. Time didn't feel the same as it had…when? Before? He tried to imagine a time before and couldn't, though he was sure there had been something before this. All he had was here and at the moment, that seemed to be enough.

He breathed the pungent, fishy air of the lake and looked over to the lizard. It was crouched low to the ground its eyes half closed, breathing slowly, it seemed to be drowsing. Most of the blood was gone from its face, but its body was still splotched with the now dried dark fluid. The dark feathers along its back were matted and several were broken.

"Well?" Lane asked, looking to the lizard. The lizards eyes opened slightly, then they dropped to their former half closed indifference.

"Yeah…well," Lane answered himself, then was lost again in that blank, painless void, contemplating the black water and trying not to smell the bloody mess that Foster had become.

The next sensation was that of cool water gently washing over his waist. As his thoughts came to a whole he realized he was standing in the water. His clothes lay discarded on the bank. He could see them neatly folded by the rock on which he'd been sitting. His white briefs lay on top, his sneakers at the base of the rock with his white socks stuffed inside them. He could feel the crabs gently probing and caressing his feet, contemplating a taste. There were other things in the water with him. He felt their soft, willowy touch, as if he were being brushed with a feather duster; soft and fleeting, yet there.

Foster's body lay face down, floating stiffly next to him. He was holding the corpse at its right wrist. The lizard was back on the shore, pacing quickly up and down the bank, its tail whipping with anticipation, knocking crabs and snails about in the process.

Foster was also naked, though Lane didn't see any of his clothes on the bank. What he could see of his dark, bony body was bobbing up and down in the gently swelling water like some macabre buoy.

As he looked back across the lake, trying to see some detail in the distant shore, the low level humming began again. It seemed to be coming from everywhere at once and was much louder than before. The thick forest of trees perhaps having had muffled it on the hill. The lizard stood—mouth agape—propped on its hind feet. The water around Lane seemed to dance and vibrate with the deep droning. It sounded like a rusty fog horn and seemed to bring a sharp, acidic smell to the already pungent lake water.

As the humming stopped and echoed off through the valley, the raspberry lizard instantly plunged itself into the water. Like a snake, it whipped through the water and began circling Lane. It nipped like a puppy at his side then swam ten feet or so toward the middle of the lake.

"Going for a swim now?" Lane asked. The lizard continued to turn lazy circles then it came back toward him. It nipped his side again, hard enough to be painful, then swam back toward the middle of the lake. This time it kept going.

Lane stepped a little deeper into the water. He slowly drug Foster's body ahead of him then pushed it out into the water. It sank a little then bobbed back to the surface, floating lazily off to his left. He pulled his feet off the rocky lake bottom and began to swim, kicking hard to dislodge one persistent crab. When he reached Foster's body, he gave it another shove, watched it sink then slowly surface ahead of him, then swam out to it. The trio began to swim across the lake.

*   *   *

He tasted blood before he could smell the heavy, fertile odor. It was dark in the room. The digital clock glowing green on the bedside table was blurred in his vision, but he thought it was somewhere around three in the morning. Laying very still he tasted the thick blood in his throat and tried to pull things together.

Something was not right. He had planned to take the boys body and drive it into the ground, but it seemed that the boys body was doing well enough on its own. He carefully swung his legs off the bed and sat. A thick wave of nausea passed over him and he steadied himself on the edge of the bed. Through the one bedroom window enough of the street light shown through to illuminate his hands. They were misshapen and shiny with blood. He reached up to his face and felt it was wet.

He slowly made his way to the bathroom and turned on the light. In the mirror over the sink he looked at a face he wasn't sure he recognized. It was covered with blood that had come from several deep cuts about his eyes. There didn't seem to be any other damage, except for his nose, which had bled profusely. It was still giving forth a small trickle of blood.

The little finger on his right hand was bent at an odd angle and swollen to twice the size of his thumb. Every knuckle was split open in at least one place and both hands were nearly the size of softballs. There was an odd protrusion beneath the skin on the back of his left hand that he thought might be a bone and he wasn't able to close either hand without a supreme effort.

He had taken off his clothes at some point in the night. The boy's chest was splashed with blood from his face wounds and there was the track of dried blood down to his crotch. Duane looked back in the mirror and stared into the gore-streaked face of his son. He would continue to make him pay, or at least make his body pay, but no more of this self-indulgent shit. If he kept this up he wouldn't be able to do his job Monday. He had to keep that in mind. It all came down to Monday. After that, he could do what he wanted. After the boy's body was dead, he could continue the search for him elsewhere. Until then, he would have to get hold of the situation, and right away.

He washed in a cold shower and managed to stop the bleeding from the cuts above his eyes, his nose quite bleeding on its own. Without bothering to dry, he went back to the bedroom, turned on the light and clumsily went through Lane's clothes until he found what he was looking for. Loose fitting jeans, a tee shirt and heavy work boots.

Back in the kitchen he emptied the ice from the three trays in the freezer into a blue, plastic bowl then went back to the bathroom. He poured the ice into the sink then shoved his hands into it. The pain of the wounds and the sensation of the ice were registered remotely. If the boy's body failed him, he wouldn't be able to pull off his evolving plans for Monday.

He was buoyed by thoughts of the coming event. How would he approach it? Most likely be would just begin as soon as he arrived. No use putting off what you can do right now, he thought, smiling. It was then, smiling in the mirror, that he noticed the missing tooth. He ran Lane's tongue over the gap and could feel the jagged, sharp stump of the tooth. So it wasn't all missing, just broken off.

"Just the beginning, you little fucker," he said to the image in the mirror. "Just the beginning." A thin spray of blood from his mouth sprinkled the mirror. Duane sucked more blood through the ruptured tooth and spit it out. It ran down the mirror in a syrupy, red glob.

He kept his hands in the ice until most of it was melted. Then he gently dried them and went back to the bedroom. It was just past five Sunday morning. A little over twenty-four hours remained until Monday morning. He'd found that if he pulled back a little the boy was able to lead him where he wanted to go. His mind and thought patterns went through the motions as if the boy were still in charge. He'd done it when driving, though didn't realize it at the time. Still naked, hands bleeding in slow trickles, he went to the kitchen and after three attempts started the first of many pots of coffee.

*   *   *

The dark water began to warm. Not suddenly, as if he'd swam into a warm pocket, but slowly and steadily as he stroked his way across the lake. His short limbs and stocky body were more at home wrestling or boxing, swimming had never been his strong suit.

Pushing Foster along and taking an occasional quick glance up to the opposite bank, he'd covered more than half the distance to the other side. He paused, smoothly treading water, and tried to catch his breath. It was then he noticed the wave. Off to his left, there was a wave slowly moving across the lake toward him. It took a moment for him to realize the wave was actually a pressure wave caused by the movement of something *under* the water—something roughly the size of a semi truck. He suddenly felt very naked, there in the water, his penis floating out like a fish lure, with a large *something* in the water bearing down on him. The raspberry lizard was back at his side, circling around him. This time Lane didn't need to be nipped into action. Abandoning Foster's body, he began to swim as fast as he could.

The pressure wave slowly diminished as it drew nearer to him as whatever was in the water submerged. He continued swimming hard, the brackish water left a dusty fruit taste in his mouth and burned his eyes. He stopped and tread water after a hundred yards and looked back. There was no sign of the creature. It could be right under him.

The raspberry lizard was now behind him and was somehow standing on the water. He was ready to accept his latest happening when he saw Foster's head bobbing in the rippling lake water. The lizard was riding on Foster's back. Just as he turned to continue for the opposite shore, he saw the pressure wave of water return to the surface. Mesmerized, he watched as it bore down on Foster's corpse.

The wave grew until Lane could see the dark, black surface of the creature beneath the water. It was as big as a school bus and though he didn't know why, it looked vaguely familiar. It appeared to be the huge, domed half of a boulder pushing through the water.

When it was thirty yards from Foster's body, the lizard seemed to get the idea and plunged back into the water toward Lane. It should have been his own wake-up call, but he still stared at the creature bearing down on Foster.

When it was ten yards from him, a gigantic, bony head came up out of the water. In the front of the head was a single beak, behind which yellow eyes as big as car tires stared blankly out. Lane turned in panic just as the beak of the gigantic turtle opened and began closing over Foster. Trying to function with is mind one large tremor, he began to swim faster than he thought possible.

Within twenty yards his lungs were burning from the effort and his arms were beginning to cramp, but he didn't stop pulling as hard as he could. He wanted to look back, but that would mean stopping and he sure as hell didn't want to stop.

After another thirty yards he slowed just enough to see the opposite shore actually was nearer. At the same time he saw the raspberry lizard off to his left, passing him. As he turned back to his swimming, what he thought was the lake bottom brushed his feet; then the bottom moved beneath him. He could feel the slick, bumpy shell of the turtle passing just beneath the surface. The water pushed out of the way in its passing washed against him. Then it was gone.

With no hesitation he kept pulling for the opposite bank. In between strokes he watched the raspberry lizard ahead and to his left. It looked like a snake wiping through the water as a small, ineffective wake trailed behind in an ever-widening "V".

As he pulled through the brackish water, feeling a calm that was unnatural and somehow worse than panic as the behemoth cruised somewhere behind him he felt the muscles in his left shoulder begin to stitch, threatening to give up the fight and cramp completely. Then, as quick as he had thought it, in a rushing explosion of pain, his left shoulder and the muscles in his left arm cramped with a sharp, steady intensity. He was forced to stop, his left arm now useless, gripped by the cramp, it clung tightly to his side.

He looked after the lizard and watched, as the water seemed to sink in around it, then the same enormous beak protruded through the dark surface and sucked down Lane's odd companion. For a brief moment he was genuinely sorry to see it go.

He began punching his shoulder with is one good arm, now having seen his immediate future twice if he didn't get moving. He struggled to kick and managed a half-ass imitation of a dog paddle. There was no more than fifty yards to the shore and he expected to feel the sharp rocks of the lake bottom or the sharp beak of the turtle closing down on him at any moment.

Forty yards left and he was forced to stop and do his best imitation of treading water once again. The pain in his shoulder hadn't lessened and seemed to be getting worse, if that was possible. His arm was twisted against his left side and the muscles felt like they were tearing themselves apart in their hunger for oxygen. He kicked with his legs while lying on his back. Across the lake he could see the pressure wave building, coming toward him.

✳   ✳   ✳

Grasping a mug of hot coffee with Lane's numb, bleeding hands, Duane went back down the hall to what had been his room when he was alive. The door stood open several inches. There was the smell of dirt or dust in the hallway that he didn't remember being there before. He could see nothing in the dark slit the door presented. The thought that something from another place could have followed him here briefly held vigil in his thoroughly fucked up thoughts, then it was passed on as he opted for ignorance.

He nudged the door with his right elbow and it swung gently open, the light from the hall splaying across the devastation the room had become. The light partially drove back the dark and a mist of white dust hung in the air; a microscopic galaxy floating in dead, silent darkness.

The desk, chair and packed boxes in the room were scattered across the floor, impaled in the walls and spilled about like some adolescent giant's toys. The computer screen was imbedded upside down in the far wall next to the window. It's broken screen looked like a gaping mouth full of broken, jagged teeth. The one window in the room was shattered, what was left of the wooden frame and screen lay beneath it, as if it had been pulled into the room instead of being punched out.

Most the walls had been gouged and torn, the plaster and lathe handing in large chunks, the floor was covered with plaster, splattered blood, paper, books and crushed cardboard boxes. Duane looked at Lane's hands, then back to the damage that had been inflicted to the walls. He was lucky to still have them by the looks of the damage.

He sipped coffee, enjoying the burning hot liquid scorching Lane's tongue and throat, then began to close the door on the whole mess. He didn't care about finding any answers as to why this was happening. It was, so what the fuck? He just had to stay up until tomorrow morning and after that none of this shit would matter anyway because both he and the boy would be gone.

What stopped him from closing the door completely was a cardboard box sitting just inside the door to the left. It still held its contents, making it stick out like the proverbial turd in the punch bowl. The sides of the boxes, besides being stamped in black ink with a U-MOOVIT cow logo, were sprayed with blood and other dark spots that could be anything. He thought it must have been a hell of a destruction tour and wondered if he'd been too loud. The lid was open and he could see something was inside the box.

He took a large gulp of the coffee and laughed as he felt the burn all the way down to his stomach. He kicked at the door with his right foot and it swung back on it's hinges with enough force to stick the door knob into the wall behind it with a dull crash and splinter of wood as the hinges loosened their hold on the door jam. Absently tossing the half-filled coffee mug toward the shattered window—it bounced off the windowsill, landing with a dull tinkling unbroken against the baseboard, leaving a trail of hot coffee across the small room—he stepped over the box and looked into it.

The box was filled with neatly stacked piles of yellow legal pads, though Duane only registered the contents as paper with handwriting on it. He reached down to pull back one of the flaps for a better look, for some reason wanting to understand why this box had escaped his unconscious, destructive jag. There might be an answer to why he didn't have control of the boy in this box or even to where the boy went.

He pulled back the flap on the box, faintly aware of the acidic burning in Lane's stomach, and began to reach for the stack of tablets. There was a sudden whiff of something dead and rotting and a bolt of nausea ripped through his stomach that doubled over Lane's body. He stepped back from the box and stood upright, waiting to puke or for the sensation to pass. It passed, though slowly.

He stood watching the box for another ten minutes, grasping for something that was just beyond his reach. Once again he pulled back the box flap. As he reached for the tablets a blistering bolt of pain slammed into his stomach and doubled him over enough to drop him to his knees. He gasped for breath and fought to keep conscious, if he went on another wall pounding binge, he didn't think Lane's hands would be able to function, and that wouldn't do. The pain slowly subsided and he managed to stay conscious.

He stood and looked at the box. Three strikes and you're out. No, he didn't want anymore of that shit. Whatever was in the box, he wasn't suppose to see, or if he did, it would probably end in the death of the boy's body and he would be off again into the dark, frigid womb that was his own death.

"Stay," he said to the box, then went back to the kitchen for another cup of coffee.

*　　　　　*　　　　　*

His feet finally touched bottom. It was sandy and smooth and didn't move under his touch, something he at first feared. It really was the lake bottom and not the back of that thing undercutting him again. He dug his feet in and ran, fought and stumbled through the shallows toward the beach. His left shoulder and arm were a frozen and useless bundled of muscle, tendon and bone, his lungs vacant bellows screaming for air.

He fell again, still pushing toward the beach as he was falling. He watched as water began to roll up around him, pushing ahead in a surge as the turtle swam and crawled up the shore behind him. The pressure wave had reached him. If he turned now, he would see the turtle slowly pulling its bulk up through the sandy soil, it's dead yellow eyes looking down on him.

He fought his way to a standing position, forcing himself not to stop, not to hesitate, to keep pushing for the beach. He would feel the sharp beak of his approaching death any instant, of that he was sure. Where would he go from here? If this place was death from his past life, then what kind of hell awaited him down the road from this?

Fifteen yards to the beach, then ten and he stumbled in the soft soil again, landing in the shallow water face first. He almost didn't push himself out of the water, it would be so much easier to just breathe that foul, black water into his lungs and be gone. Yet, even as he began to inhale the vile brew, he found the stinking lake air rushing to fill his lungs. He pushed on.

The smell of the turtle reached him; it was a thick putrid smell. He imagined the cracks, crevices and folds of the Turtle would be filled with water ticks and dripping sores. He thought he could even smell the breath of the beast as it opened its mouth to engulf him. The rotting-fish stench of the thing was unbearable; choking out what little stale air he managed to inhale.

He pushed on, now crawling through the dark mire with his one good arm, digging his knees as best he could, the black water a backdrop to his impending demise. The ground trembled from the turtles ponderous shuffling in the wet sand. He was no longer imagining feeling its hot breath.

Knowing he was already dead (again?), he pushed on up the beach and began to pull himself through warm, dry sand. He vaguely registered that the shadow surrounding him was shaped like the head of the turtle. He crawled on for another fifteen yards and finally gave up, collapsing; his thoughts clapping shut just as his exhausted body quit.

He lay still—the only sign that he was living was the faint rise and fall of his chest—wondering if it would hurt.

The turtle hung back in the water, watching where Lane had fallen. Hundred's of small purple bugs the size and shape of golf balls fell from the animal's thick putrid skin. They hit the beach with a soft plop, most of them rolling themselves back to the water with their one leg, their round, soft mouths making sucking sounds.

There were no rough rocks on this beach, just smooth, soft sand. Several hundred yards back from the beach a stand of pines stood guard as the gateway to a forest. There was a sparse population of knee high grass that started at what must have been the high water mark and ran back to the trees. Beyond that it was anyone's guess. Lane saw none of this from where he lay.

The turtle slowly began to backtrack into the water. After several minutes it disappeared back into the lake, the only sign of its passing was a deep furrow in the beach and a lot of mostly dead stinking purple ball bugs.

*   *   *

Ben stood on the lawn and watched what may very well be his last Sunday on God's green earth begin. The sun was still just a hint of light in the East, but the birds knew it was coming and had begun their song. He stood amid the landscaping that had been Carly's doing. He never had an eye for it until it was done. Then he could tell you if it looked good or not. Now, however, it didn't look good. The Bermuda and weeds had choked out the bushes and flowers and shrubs (he'd never gotten their names down) that Carly had carefully chosen and placed. Ben had been the workhorse, enjoying the physical work without having to think just as he had enjoyed the lawn work when he was younger. Move this here, dig a hole there; he'd listened and did as he was bidden. He would enjoy the day, the sweat, the toil and the sounds, sights and smells of his beloved Carly.

He sipped his coffee and quickly changed his thoughts. It wouldn't do for Walsh or Blake to find him standing out here crying. This was to be a time of resolve, a time of strength, a time to decide if a lifetime was spent in a worthy cause or spent jacking off in a corner.

The faint, dull roar of a passenger jet underlay the bird song. He looked up and watched it coming out of the night and into the glow of the morning; several miles up, position lights flashing. He knew he probably wouldn't see Stephen again (God rarely gave second chances to grab on for the ride of your life), today at least, but he had wanted to make himself available none-the-less. He watched until the plane was a dot in the far sky.

The stars began to succumb to the day and the first bright arch of the sun was just becoming visible through the trees in the East.

"I love you Carly, with all my heart," he spoke aloud to the dawn. "I miss you dearly, but I'm sure you and Stephen know more than I about when I'll see you both again. I suspect it'll be soon now." He paused, swallowing another mouthful of coffee.

"And I love you Stephen. I don't think I ever told you that enough…or maybe at all. Yet, here we are and what's going to be done will decide what happens next. Either way, I'm giving it everything."

The sun had driven the last of the stars from the sky by the time Ben turned back to the house. He poured out the now cooled coffee and nearly dropped the mug when he looked up at the porch.

"Morning," Walsh said, a small smile creasing his large, bright face. Ben thought he looked ten years younger and hadn't he lost some weight? Maybe. He sat on one of the long benches that were placed about the porch.

"Morning," Ben said, hoping like hell Walsh had heard none of the monologue.

"Coffee?" Ben asked walking by him to the French doors that lead into the kitchen. "Or are you just sneaking around this morning?"

"How about a beer?" Walsh asked, smiling.

"What?" Ben asked, stopping.

"Why don't you grab a couple of beers and let's sit out here awhile," then, when Ben still hesitated, he added. "Go on, Blake won't be up for hours."

Ben shrugged and walked on into the kitchen. He returned with two opened bottles of Coors light, handed one to Walsh, then sat on the patio bench next to him.

Twenty minutes later and not a word had been passed between them. Walsh slowly raised himself and fetched two more. They drank in silence, watching the day begin. Nothing needed to be said; they both knew what they were going to do.

After another twenty minutes, Ben stared to get up for round three.

"Save your back," Walsh said. Ben settled back down in his chair, then looked to the sky. It was a clear, light blue with no sign of clouds.

"You still offering a round today?" Walsh asked, handing Ben his drink and settling himself on the bench.

"If we keep this up we won't even make it to the course," Ben said, taking a long sip. He should have eaten something. It's been a long time since he'd had a beer for breakfast. Still, the warmth that was growing in his belly and the numbness growing in his head felt damn good. He hadn't realized just how worked up he'd been over the past few months until now that he could see if from behind a few beers.

"Yeah, I suppose, but we might as well have a go at it. No telling what we'll be doing after Monday."

"All right, let's do it. Think we can get a tee time?"

"Already done."

Ben looked at Walsh, then back to the now risen sun.

"Planned it all along, eh?" Ben said, smiling.

"Planned it all along," Walsh echoed.

"What if I'd said no?"

"You wouldn't," Walsh said, draining his beer. Ben laughed. Walsh was right.

Blake woke around nine-thirty. Ben thought it was the smell of omelets and sausage that did it more than a fulfillment of sleep. They ate their fill (Ben and Walsh quit on the beer for the time being) then loaded up for the course.

*   *   *

He remembered the gun. He sat on the living room floor with the sack of shells in his lap and the forty-five in his right hand lying across his legs. The box of yellow legal pads filled with writing sat by the front door where he'd kicked it. What shades there were he'd tried to close, only small ineffective stabs of sunshine poked into the house and these seemed to be eaten by the darkness.

He'd made one other attempt to approach the box with even worse results; his nose had started bleeding heavily. His once white shirt was now blood stained. He hadn't bothered to clean the blood, other than the occasional swipe with the back of his hand. His face and hands were smeared with drying blood.

It was the box and the gun that now held his attention. What was in the fucking box and why couldn't he see it? He rubbed the gun with his hands and watched the box. It sat unmoving.

Staring at the box, his hands went through the motions of loading the gun as if they were someone else's. He chambered a round and fired three quick shots into the box. Cardboard flew in small puffs as the three rounds punched through the box and into the wall behind. The box remained relatively intact. Small wisps of smoke curled up from the holes and torn paper flew up. The sound was deafening and he immediately regretted doing it. He may have just screwed his plans for tomorrow morning. What if the police showed up? The thought was quickly lost in the view of the box. That fucking box. He stood, letting loose shells and the sack with the bulk of them drop out of his lap and roll across the floor.

Sticking the gun into the front of his pants he went to the kitchen and took out the last of the ice trays. For the past four hours he'd been drinking coffee and icing down his swollen, pulverized hands. They seemed to be getting better, but only a little. He'd found several bottles of painkillers and taken four or five for no particular reason other than he thought it might help the swelling go down. He was still able to shoot, that he'd just proven, so perhaps it would be enough.

He dumped ice into the plugged kitchen sink and stuck his hands in, vaguely aware of the sensation. His thoughts drifted to the next day and it helped to push away the worry about the box of paper. It was nearly noon. In a little over twenty hours he would be due at work. Nine in the morning if he was reading Lane's memory correctly, and he certainly didn't want to be late. No, that wouldn't do to be late for Lane's last day of work.

He began laughing and the box seemed a little further from his thoughts.

"Today is a new day, today is a new day, today is a new day," he said aloud, then let the thought run on in his mind as he rocked on the floor with the gun in his lap.

*   *   *

About the time Duane was pumping rounds into a cardboard box looking like somebody's bloodied up nightmare, Ben, Walsh and Blake were checking in for their tee time. Walsh rented two carts, one for him and one for Ben and Blake to share.

"We'll trade off as we need to," he told Blake, giving him a soft punch in the arm. "You'd better watch him, Blake, his eyes aren't what they used to be," he said, winking and pointing at Ben. "He ran over three guys just last week out by the eighth hole." Blake laughed and looked to Ben who just shook his head and rolled his eyes.

"How's your back today?" Walsh asked, as they loaded up their clubs. "Still sore?"

"A little tight, but I think it'll loosen up."

The first nine holes went quickly, thought not as well as either Ben or Walsh would have liked. They stopped for a quick lunch after the ninth hole then were out for the back nine. Ben would have been hard pressed to remember the incident with the gold cart and Stephen so many years ago. With all that was happening he was lucky to be fully clothed. But as they teed off on the eleventh hole and approached their respective lays, he slowly remembered.

Smiling at the thought he took a long pull on his beer then pulled himself out of the cart and went to the back where his bag was strapped to select a club. Blake sat in the passenger seat and happily washed down soda over his hamburger and fries.

"Why don't you slide over there in the drivers seat, Blake. I'm not feeling too good about driving this thing right now. Probably the beer."

Blake looked at him with wide-eyed excitement, yet still didn't move. Ben pretended to be deciding on a club and rummaged around his bag a moment longer, finally selecting a fairway wood.

"Problem?" Ben asked.

"No, I...just...don't, you know," Blake stammered out, looking at the wheel.

"Oh, I see," Ben said, then dropped him a wink. "The pedal on the right makes it go and the one on the left makes it stop. The wheel there takes you where you want to go." He had meant it to come out funny, a bit of humor to lighten the heaviness of the day, and to Blake it proba-bly did come out funny. Ben saw his face blaze into a thrill that only a pre-teen can muster and he could feel his own face crack into a smile.

Yet, in his heart, in a place he had yet to touch, there was a deep and piercing sadness, something that he had yet to reach in all that had transpired. And now, standing on the fairway waiting to make his second shot on the longest hole on the course, that spot had been reached. It had been touched and opened to either be resolved for life or forever fester until the day of his death.

If he elected to ignore it and go on, burying it for good, what of it? Well, nothing, really. It would just be there, unresolved. No big whip. Yet his life would have already peaked, his apex would have been reached and it would all be down hill from this point on. But if he chose to take it out, play with it, see if he could fix it, take his life to a higher level and if he couldn't, well, then at least dispose of it the best he could, what would happen then? He wasn't sure, but it was a hell of a lot better than giving up now. The commitment had been for all or nothing, and he was going to give it his all.

"Blake, I just want you to know that I wasn't a very good father to your Dad," the bright excitement on Blake's face faltered. "No, that's not it, I wasn't really even a father to him. I don't know why and that's not important now," he gently swung the club at a clump of grass, slowly working out that sore spot in his heart. "And I guess what I'd like to say to you is that I love you and I'd like to be the best grandfather I can be for you," he suddenly dropped the club and found hot, painful tears filling his eyes. He tried to fight back for control and almost won, but in the end he let it ride and the hurt poured out.

"I just wish I'd...I'd," he choked on the words and could go no further. He burst into a fresh flood of tears and began to cry out that last painful spot that he thought could never be reached. At some point he fell to his knees and hid his face in his hands, ignoring the sharp pain in his legs and back. He was lost to himself, completely gone with the flood of relief he now felt pouring out.

A hand gripped his right shoulder and he knew it was Walsh. He felt no shame, no embarrassment for his actions, only a deep and satisfying sense of relief. After he'd gathered himself, he got up with Walsh's help then sat next to Blake in the cart.

"Silly old fart, eh?" he asked, smiling his first real smile in years. He was finally clean and unburdened to face what they were to do the next day. There wasn't even the last bit of lingering doubt he had been harboring. It was their row, the three of them, and they were going to hoe it.

Blake smiled and shook his head, looking up at Ben.

"I love you too, Grandpa," was all he could say. There was more he felt, but wasn't sure how to express. It would come, in time, but for now, that simple statement would do. Ben reached an arm around him and gave him a hug.

"All right, we'll talk more about it later. Right now, we've got a golf game to finish," he said, pushing by Walsh and going back to where his ball and club lay.

They finished the round with clearer heads than when they'd started, though their hearts may have been a little heavier with the unknown looming closer. Walsh left them at the club after making sure the mowing truck would be loaded and ready to roll at first light.

"I'll get out sooner if I can, but if I can't we've got to get to that house right around eight or a little after. The earlier we can get in the better," he'd told Ben. Ben smiled and nodded, taking it all in and feeling none of it.

"You all right?" Walsh asked. Blake was sitting in Ben's truck, trying not to fall asleep.

"Walsh, old buddy, never better, never better," he said, clapping his friend on the shoulder then surprising them both by kissing him full on the lips. Ben laughed and marveled at how good he actually felt. It wouldn't be much longer and he would be with Carly and Stephen.

*   *   *

His hands still bled if he flexed them, but they were limber enough to get the job done. The morning was coming; he could feel it in the air around him, sheltered though he was inside the house. He could feel the morning wet dew and hear the birds singing to the new day that would be remembered for a very long time by the folks in and around Burkett.

Duane sat on the floor with his back to the wall, facing the front door and the box. That fucking box. He had been tempted over the last— what, ten, fifteen hours he'd been sitting here?—to just go over there and take another peek, but just didn't want to risk passing out and having all his plans go to shit. The now thoroughly dried blood had caked around his mouth and crusted to the front of his shirt. His eyes were set in deep bags of sleeplessness and jittered around the dawning room from the hours of caffeine he'd drunk with mechanical efficiency.

The gun was loaded—he'd replaced the three shells—and extra shells were stuffed in every available pocket in his jeans in addition to two full clips he'd placed in his back pockets for easy access.

He sucked air quickly in through his mouth and felt the sharp bite of the broken tooth shoot through Lane's head.

"Hush little baby don't say a word, Daddies gonna buy you a mockingbird and if that mockingbird don't sing, Daddies gonna buy you a diamond ring," he quietly sang. A manic grin plastered across his bloodstained face; his eyes lost to everything but the growing light of the day.

The slice of light moving across the living room floor continued to grow. He watched it with fascination, his time was quickly approaching. When he could stand it no longer, he got up and stretched Lane's cramped, tired body and marched it to the bedroom to check the time. It was just a little past seven, but not too early to begin. No sir, not at all.

"Let's rock and roll, children," he quietly whispered, caressing the gun. He watched two minutes tick off the digital clock, stuck the gun into his waistband and went back to the living room.

"All right motherfucker, I've got a place for you, so just sit tight a minute," Duane said to the box, pointing at it with false bravado. He rummaged through his pockets, making sure all his things were in place. Noticing the bloodied shirt for the first time, he went back to the bedroom and pulled on a clean short sleeve shirt over the stained one, thinking it wouldn't do to be seen all bloodied up too early in the game.

Back in the living room he went straight to the box and shoved it with his foot further away from the door. No pain, no bloody nose, nothing. So far so good. He checked his pockets for their loads once again, found the car keys in his hand, and then opened the front door.

Time suddenly slipped, as if somebody bumping the earth had skipped the light of the day. He had the instantaneous sensation of lost time. The light was of a certain brightness as he opened the door, then suddenly it became brighter, as if the day had progressed why he had been elsewhere. He looked at his hands fearing he'd been off on another blacked out rage, but they looked the same as they had; swollen, bruised and painful to look upon.

But there was something else, also. Something that he should know or remember, but wasn't quite sure about. It was a smell, the smell of something that, like the light, hadn't been there before, but was now. He pushed the thought back and turned to the box.

With his foot he carefully closed the flaps of the box as best he could. Expecting the worst, he stooped and picked up the box. So far so good. He supposed as long as he wasn't trying to see what was in there, he would be all right and he was.

He carried the box out the front door, to the edge of the front lawn by the street. The open sky and clear day made him dizzy and the fresh air made him sick to his stomach. Or was it the box? It was suddenly very heavy in his arms and he all but dropped it there on the edge of the lawn.

"There, you fuck. Get out and stay out," he said, giving the box another good kick. The side crushed in and a piece tore off.

Leaving the front door open he checked his pockets one last time, then got in Lane's car and drove away from the house, trying with little success to not watch the box.

As he reached the end of the block and was turning after the stop sign he remembered the smell. The smell he should have remembered when he stood with the door open was the everyday smell of gasoline.

✳   ✳   ✳

"Turn here," Blake said. Walsh coaxed the broken, old truck around the corner, something fell in the bed with a metallic crash, then fell again after they'd made the corner. They sat in silence; each lost in a world of questions upon questions about what they were about to do. Blake sat between Ben and Walsh and stared out the front window. He could feel the monster probing him, questioning him, reaching out to him and trying to find out why he was coming back. It was scared; he could feel it squirming as they got closer. Like a roach caught in the open kitchen by the light, it wanted to scatter for cover, but didn't have anywhere to go.

"It knows we're here," Blake said.

"Who?" Ben asked, with a nerve-induced quickness that made his voice rise to an unnatural pitch.

"Him. The monster. He knows we're coming. But he's scared, he doesn't have anywhere to go."

They drove on in silence. Nothing more needed to be said.

"Here. Turn up there at the stop sign and it's at the end of the street, on the left," Blake directed.

Walsh turned—whatever lawn tools had been crashing around finally settled—and began to slow down as they eased up the street.

"Don't slow down, we don't want to stand out," Ben quickly said, his voice still high and tense.

"Easy, Ben, I don't know which house it is, that's all."

But that wasn't entirely true. With all his talk of taking action and kicking some butt and getting this done for better or worse, he found himself scared. If nothing else then just the mechanics of burning down a house. There was enough gas in the back of the truck to burn them all to a crisp several times over. This was something real to be fearful of.

A small flicker of panic began to rise as he thought of the flames the fuel would produce. They would have to start somewhere and he realized it sure as shit wouldn't be with him. And why wouldn't the flames start with him? For the very simple reason that he—Mr. let's do this thing—didn't bring a lighter, or a simple book of matches.

"There, that's it, on the left," Blake said, breaking his train of thoughts.

"Just pull up in the drive and turn around, then park in front along the curb so you'll be facing the right direction," Ben directed, his voice still a pinched, nervous pitch. He was scanning the street and trying to look into the windows of the houses to see if they were being watched.

"Okay, okay, just take it easy Ben."

He pulled up the drive and dropped the clutch, letting the truck roll back down, then pulled up to the curb.

"All right, let's get out, we can't just sit here," Ben said, jerking the door handle hard enough to dislodge his grip.

"Whoa. Not just yet. You need to calm down," Walsh said, reaching across Blake and gently taking Ben's left arm. He had already grabbed the door handle and was trying to open it again, not feeling Walsh's grasp or hearing his words.

"Ben! Hold up!" Walsh said again, giving his arm a stiff squeeze in the process. Ben glanced at him as if he'd been stuck with a knife.

"*What?*" he shot back. His eyes were wide and scattered. Blake tried to melt into the seat between them, wanting to get on with it and wanting to run away at the same time.

"You need to hold on a minute. Just sit tight and collect yourself, okay?"

Ben took a deep breath and continued to scrutinize the houses around them.

"Yeah, okay. Just a minute, though," he said, taking several long breaths.

After a minute, he seemed calmed down.

"Better?" Walsh asked.

"Getting there, getting there," he said, drawing a final breath. He looked over at Walsh and nodded his head. Blake saw the old calmness in his eyes.

"All right, good," Walsh said, patting Ben on the shoulder. "Good, good," he continued. "Ah, there's just one thing I want to ask. Did anyone think to bring a lighter, or even matches?"

"What?" Ben asked, sure he heard him correctly but unable to comprehend the facts that they may well have forgotten something so simple as a lighter or matches. That he, Ben, the one whom started this whole expedition may well have forgotten to bring an ignition source of the six cans of gas in the bed of the truck.

"Did you bring any matches?" Walsh asked, unable to bring himself to look over at Ben. He knew what he was thinking and it matched his thoughts.

"Well, ah…fuck," Ben quietly whispered. "All this and we didn't even think to bring matches."

"I did," Blake said, holding up a small box of wooden matches.

"Well, Blake, you may have just saved all our asses," Walsh said. "Let's get to it," he said, pushing open the squealing old drivers' door.

They slipped out of the truck and began to unload the lawn equipment. Walsh had further surprised them with blue short sleeved work shirts that sported the same green rake/mower logo on the back and breast pocket. He had brought them with him when they'd met to load the truck this morning. If anything, they certainly looked the part of a lawn crew.

Walsh carried a weed-wacker around to the back in one hand and a can of gas in the other. He stuck it by the back door and walked back to the front yard with the same weed-wacker for another can. Ben passed him pushing a mower loaded with a can of gas on top. Walsh could see his back was hurting him.

"Take it easy. We don't need to get hurt here," he said as they passed. Ben just nodded and continued pushing the mower up the slightly rising lawn to the back yard. Blake struggled with one of the two mowers left in the back of the truck.

"Push it over here and I'll give you a hand," Walsh said. Blake struggled it over to the back of the truck and Walsh pulled it off and set it down, dropping it the last ten inches or so. He then reached for the gas can that Blake was scooting to the back of the truck. He put the can on the mower just as Ben came around the corner of the house.

"Take this on up to the front of the house, then carry the can to the back. I'll get these last two and get Blake started mowing the front." Ben did as he was asked, glad for something else to focus on.

"Get those other two gas jugs over here, Blake, then slide that last mower back." Blake did his best to move the heavy cans around. Walsh took the last two cans to the back yard and set them by the other four near the back door. Ben was standing in the yard looking down at a small window.

"We're never going to fit in that," he said, as Walsh walked up behind him. Walsh looked at the small window covered with rusted thin wire mesh and knew he was right.

"Nope, but Blake could probably get through it," he said, knowing that Blake would probably have a hard time getting through the window even if he was at a normal weight, but not with the belly he was carrying now.

"Uh-huh. Yeah, and maybe we can get Santa to drop down the chimney and open the door for us," Ben said.

Walsh smiled, glad to hear the old sour notes back in his voice. Ben was coming around to the task at hand.

"Well, let me get Blake started mowing the front and we can think about it."

Walsh left Ben staring at the small basement window and went back around to the front of the house. He found Blake with the mower at the top of the lawn. Blake bent and pulled the starter cord and the mower coughed to life.

"Got it?" Walsh asked close to Blake's ear. Blake nodded up at Walsh with a huge smile on his face.

"Good. Just start mowing and I'll let you know what to do next. If you finish, start in with the weed-wacker on the edging," Walsh nearly shouted above the metallic roar of the mower.

"All right!" Blake shouted back. As he turned back to the mower and began to position it, Walsh grabbed his shoulder.

"Have you seen anyone?"

Blake shook his head side to side.

Walsh nodded and turned for the backyard. He found Ben now kneeling at the basement window with his back to him.

"Everything all right?" he asked.

"Maybe. I think that I can get this window open. Do you have a smaller screw driver than this?" he said, holding up a flat tipped screwdriver.

"What for?" Walsh asked, taking the screwdriver from Ben. "Back away there, Grandpa," he said, dropping him a wink.

"What are you going to do?"

"Open this window like you should be," he said, then jabbed the sharp end of the screwdriver into the old glass and wire mesh. The handle of the screwdriver followed the tip right through the glass and the mesh was so rusted it pushed through and fell into the basement.

"Shit," Walsh mumbled as he jerked his hand back from the jagged opening. He was bleeding from several deep cuts.

"Here," Ben said, producing a handkerchief from a pocket. "Wrap that up and we'll see to it after we're done."

Walsh did as he was told.

"Where's the screwdriver?" Ben asked.

Walsh looked around where they were kneeling and didn't find it. "I must have dropped it in there," he said, nodding toward the window. Ben grunted a reply and pulled a small hammer from his back pocket and began tapping the remaining glass out of the window frame.

"What else have you got in there?" Walsh asked, trying to lighten the mood. Ben grunted something as he continued to work at the broken window.

"Sounds like Blake's got it under control out front," Ben finally said.

"He's going to start edging if he finishes mowing before we're done."

"Good. All right. That's done, what now?" Ben asked.

"I guess we should start dropping jugs in then pour out the last one and set if off?"

"You sound real sure about that, Walsh."

"Yeah? How many houses have you burned down, buddy?" Walsh shot back. Ben could hear the venom in his response and caught himself from adding to it with is own terse reply.

"We don't have time for this. I'm sorry."

"No problem."

"Drop them in then pour the last one out?" Ben asked.

"Sounds good to me. Once we get it going those other five are going up sooner or later."

"All right. Why don't you check on Blake and I'll get started," Ben said. Walsh pulled himself to his feet and began to go back to the front yard.

"Hold on there."

"Yeah?" Walsh said, turning on knees that weren't quite ready to be walking after kneeling so long.

"Look at your hand." Walsh looked down at his right hand. The handkerchief was soaked so thoroughly with blood that it had dripped a small trail from where he had been kneeling. There was a small puddle of blood by the window.

"Shit," he said, beginning to take the wrap off his hand.

"Hold it, leave that on there. Ben stood haltingly and produced another handkerchief from his back pocket.

"How many of those things did you bring?"

Ben ignored the comment. "Here, lift your hand up."

Walsh did. Ben retied the original handkerchief, then tied the new one over the first.

"That's more than tight enough," Walsh winced.

"You better hope so, if we don't hurry up and finish so we can get you to a hospital—."

"I'll be fine. We don't need to rush this thing and screw something up."

"Yeah? You think somebody might get hurt?" Ben asked, pulling the final knot tighter than he really needed to.

"I'll check on Blake," Walsh said, ignoring the comment. By the time he'd made it to the side of the house the second handkerchief was soaked through. Both his hands and forearms were smeared with blood.

*   *   *

Not all the plum bugs were dead. Maybe as many as a dozen the Turtle had left behind were still waving their single, long hooked legs and puckering their sucker mouths. They had no eyes and looked everything like a plum with a mouth and single black, spidery leg. Of the dozen that still lived, most went toward the water, trying to find their old host. There were a few that sensed a new host, higher up the beach, and started their jerking, rolling walk toward that host.

Though he was in a state that was as near death as he had been recently, there was a small path left from what was essentially Lane White to this world. And that path began to widen and glow until he could hear bits and pieces from the world. There wasn't that much to hear; water lapping on the beach, a soft wind rustling the tall grass that seemed to be warm and another liquid sound that he couldn't quite place.

There was a ripple of time and he realized that he could see. He blinked rapidly to try and clear sand from his eyes. One was stuck in the sand and the other was clear from where he lay on his right cheek. He could feel the heat of the sun in this world. It felt soothing and contradicted the brightness of the day. It should have been overcast, but the small sliver of horizon he could see at the far edge of the lake was clear and blue.

The same sucking sound washed into his thoughts, but didn't stay for long as his vision began to clear. He blinked rapidly again, his eye beginning to water furiously as it released most of the grit. Gently pushing himself off the sand he slowly turned over to lie on his back. It was then that he felt the tingling sensation along his left side and felt the weight of the plum bugs attached at several points along his sides.

He lay staring in a mild stupor at the bugs pulsing with his blood where they were attached along his side. There were three bunched together at his left waist, just above his hip, burrowing into the soft flesh next to his stomach. Two more were on his outer left thigh. There was a small trickle of blood from where they had attached themselves to his body.

By the time he had awaken enough to realize what they were doing to him, they had grown from the size of plums to that of oranges, and were still growing. The tingling became more insistent as he woke until he realized that what had been tingling was quickly becoming pain. He pushed up into a sitting position and with as little forethought as he dare put into it, and with as little imaging as he could, grabbed one of the bugs on his side and squeezed as hard as he could.

It felt like grabbing a puddle of thick, hot mud that had grown a skin. His fingers dug deep into the hide of the thing and didn't seem to be making a difference to the bug. By now he could feel what were teeth digging all the harder into his flesh and the sounds of their sucking mouths increase. Then with a small, fleshy pop the bug burst and a gout of his own still warm blood covered his side. He didn't hesitate. If he stopped to think about it, he wouldn't be able to do it. He let go the husk of the first bug and grabbed the next.

By the time the last bug had been popped his left side was completely covered in a thickening smear of blood and bug guts. The remains of the bugs clung to his side, until he stood and they fell away on their own. He looked to the black water with thoughts of rinsing, but not for very long. He could handle being bloodied for awhile. The wounds the bugs had left had already begun to clot and he looked over the lake for signs of the turtle.

"And then there was one," he said to the breeze and dark lake. Slowly turning from the lake—his side was stiffening and sore—he began to work his way up the beach through the tall grass, heading back toward the trees.

*   *   *

They were all fucked. Every last one of them. He may not have enough shells to do it, but he sure as shit had his fists and feet. This was going to be White's Last Stand and it was going to be good. He could feel a steely erection ridding point and it was all he could do to wait until he got to Lane's offices before the fun began.

"Hey, cunt," he said to the receptionist as he entered the offices through the front foyer.

"*Excuse me?*" he heard her say, but by then he was already through the entrance doors and down the hall. Lee immediately grabbed the phone to call security, but not fully realizing Lane's intent, took an incoming call, then another, then a third. By the time she made her call to security, the shooting had started.

He crossed the plaza, past the fountain, pulling the forty-five out of his waistband in the process. As he opened the entry door, Rachael

Simpson was coming out of the woman's bathroom down the hall. They met at the door to the Data Input offices.

"Hey, Lane," she said, then saw the gun he was holding by his right leg. He smiled, pointing the gun toward the ceiling. Smiling broadly, he raised his eyebrows and nodded at the gun. She stopped and looked at the gun again, mild confusion showing on her face.

"Is that real?" she asked, knowing it was, yet refusing to believe.

"Take your shirt off and I won't shoot you," he said, lowering the gun in her general direction.

"What?" she said, panic growing on her face. Her instincts took over and she began to back away, her arms spread out in vain for something to grab onto.

Lee heard the first shot as dull thunder from where she sat at the receptionist desk, she jumped at the crash. Lane heard it as a bright crashing clap and a quick snap in his wrist and arm. Rachael felt it as a sledgehammer blow to her chest, then felt no longer. She was dead before her body had collapsed to the floor, her heart having been mostly obliterated.

"Oh, God," Lane said, then Duane was quickly back in charge. The door to the offices slammed open and out stumbled Red and a dozen or so employee behind him, with the rest of the force pushing behind them.

"*Ladies and Gentlemen, welcome to the fun house!*" Lane said, raising his arms into a V above his head. The group held still a moment, mesmerized by the sight of him, until somebody (the name Sheila shot across his quickly deteriorating thoughts) screamed and shouted, "*He shot Rachael!*"

The paralysis broke and the group began to scramble back into the offices except Red and the all too large Lester Hollie. Lester had the deal figured on the spot and was having nothing to do with it. Lester was giving this shit the old fuck-off and heading as fast as he could for the door to the plaza. Red watched Lester then looked quickly back to Lane.

"Hold on now, its not too late. We can fix this, Lane. It's never too late," Red said, holding his hands up in front of his chest.

Today is a new day, today is a new day, the past is gone. Today is a new day, the past is gone.

Lane ignored the mantra.

"You're right there, tubby," Lane smiled, then pointed the gun toward Red. Red licked his ample lips and stared at the gun. Lester was almost to the door. Red glanced over quickly at him, then back to Lane.

"Take your pants off," Lane said to Red.

"*What?*"

"Wrong answer."

Quickly swinging the gun to the left, he pulled the trigger twice and Lester Hollie crashed into the plaza doors, shattering the right one and partially opening both of them. He lodged himself on his right side, wrapped around the center doorpost. Both bullets had caught him in the back; one had severed his spinal cord. Lester felt no pain. He lay silent, growing pools of his ample blood supply spreading around him. The last thing Lester heard was the faint wail of sirens.

"How about now?" Lane asked Red.

Red was staring at Lester, his face a pasty white, his mouth hung open, and his eyes were blinking rapidly. There was a dark stain spreading at his crotch.

"Hey, dick-fuck, over here."

Red turned his gaze from Lester back to Lane.

"He's dead," Red said, then looked at Rachael and the blood stains on the wall behind her.

"Yeah, enough to scare the piss out of you, huh?" Lane said, motioning with the gun to Reds pants.

Red didn't notice as he continued to stare at Rachael. He was quick for such a large man and nearly had the gun before Lane knew that he was moving. He shouldn't have underestimated him. He may be a hillbilly redneck bigot but he was a fast and hard hillbilly redneck bigot that much was for sure.

"*RRRRWWAAAAAA!*" Red yelled as he lunged for the gun, Lane or both. There were no heroic thoughts behind his actions, no thoughts of honor or medals or long speeches being bestowed upon audiences for his benefit as he soaked up the warmth and glory for his deed. Nope. Nothing as grand as that. All Red wanted to do was save his own ass from being killed and he very nearly did it. But not quite.

Lane sidestepped the charge and with momentum carrying his bulk beyond his original destination, Red tripped over Rachael's lifeless body and went sprawling across the low wear-ever carpet.

"Sorry, fuck-head, not today." He punched three bright red flowers in the back of Red's shirt, then turned for the door to the office.

*   *   *

"Is that the last one?" Ben asked, taking the canister of gas Walsh offered. He pushed it toward the basement window.

"No, one more. Are you going to pour it out down there?" he said, pointing to the window.

"Yeah. None of these have burst yet," Ben said, shoving the can through the window and watching as it dropped to the floor. It landed with a loud, hollow bang and softer clanking as it tumbled over the other cans, looking for a place to settle. Walsh nodded and went for the last can. The weed-whacker engine started in the front yard.Ben sat back on his bottom and leaned up against the house. His back throbbed mercilessly and he wasn't sure he would be able to stand after they dumped in the last can. That wouldn't be for at least another five minutes, an eternity as time was going today. He rested, confused, wired and ready to leave. By his watch they hadn't been on site twenty minutes. The weed-whacker engine stopped and he could hear Walsh and Blake talking in the front yard.

There was something about this that wasn't right. Something beyond the obviously fucked up thinking that got them all here. He believed, by the Heavens he believed. And if this activity wasn't having faith, then he didn't have the right definition of the word. He'd never felt as close to Carly and Stephen as he did now. Yet, beyond that, beyond all of it, there was a small, nagging, forgotten task. Something they were *all* overlooking. He wasn't able to get hold of it, no doubt due to the situation they found themselves in. It was right there and if he had just a minute more he'd be able to tell what it—.

"Hey, Grandpa," Blake said, coming around the corner of the house. His work shirt was already grass stained and soaked with sweat. He was carrying the weed-whacker with both hands, the strap slung around his shoulder.

"Hey," Ben said as the thought he almost had slipped from his mind. He tried to appear calm. Walsh came behind Blake with the last can of gas.

"Well, here you go," Walsh said. He looked ready to run for the street at any minute.

"You okay?" Ben asked.

"Yeah," Walsh said with little conviction.

"I see you got the bleeding slowed down," Ben said, point to his hand. Both handkerchiefs were soaked through, but it wasn't dripping.

Walsh looked at his hand hanging from the end of his arm like an abnormal growth he had just noticed, but said nothing.

Blake stood between them, listening to the conversation. His eyes were alive with the adventure. Ben wasn't sure how he was going to react to the actual fire, and he hoped he wouldn't be around long enough for any of them to see it.

The dull rumble of a car coming up the street broke his thoughts into tiny shards of razor thin glass.

Ben tried to get to his feet, stammering to say something, just what he wasn't sure.

"Ben! *Ben! Stay there!*" Walsh said, holding him by the shoulder more to hold him down than to get his attention. He looked up, panic spread across his face.

"All right?" Walsh asked. He didn't wait for an answer and turned for the front yard. Before he could reach the corner of the house, the car turned around the cul-de-sac. He went back to where Ben was sitting with Blake standing by him.

"Come on, let's do it and get out of here," Walsh said, his patience gone.

"I can feel it," Blake blurted out, his face drawn down into a thick frown, his eyes shutting slightly.

"The monster?" Ben asked.

"Yeah. It's really mad. But it can't...can't quite get to us, I don't know why." He paused, lost in thought. Ben looked up to Walsh and shook his head side to side, shrugging his shoulders slightly.

"Is it gone now?" Walsh asked, placing his good hand on Blake's shoulder.

"Yeah...but it's waiting...for something...to happen."

"All right. You just sit tight and we'll take care of it," then to Ben, "Do it."

Ben screwed the cap off the gas can and began to tip the volatile liquid into the basement window. It was then, as the first cup began to trickle down the old, brick wall of the basement, that he remembered. Most people put a furnace in the basement and most of those furnaces were fired by natural gas and the ignition source for the natural gas was usually a pilot light. He hoped that the light had been put out for the summer.

By the time the thought had been processed, a fourth of the fuel was out of the can and fumes were spreading into the closed area of the basement. So he kept pouring, then the next thought struck him. Even if the furnace pilot light had been doused, there was always the hot water heater. As that thought was being sent and received, the fumes of fuel ignited.

The secondary explosion of the five other cans of gas did the most damage, pulverizing the house into thousands of splinters of wood, glass and metal two blocks away.

Walsh, Ben and Blake went with it.

*   *   *

The television screen went blank, then cut to a familiar face.

"This is Chad Stephens, Channel three action news with a breaking story. According to sources, there is a developing hostage situation at the Hubbard Electronics plant East of Burkett. For more we'll go live to Leslie Mouton. Leslie?"

The screen cut to a young woman with short brunette hair and sharp, chiseled features. She was holding a microphone close to her mouth. The Hubbard plant could be seen in the distance behind her. It was nearly half a mile away. Yet, even at that distance, the unmistakable outline of police cars, vans and trucks could be seen surrounding the complex. The wail of sirens could be heard and several other reporters and camera people walked in and out of the shot.

"Chad, I am just West of the Hubbard Electronics plant at the top of Chandler Park Road. As you can see below (the shot zoomed past Leslie and the Hubbard plant encompassed the screen) the plant is surrounded by local police and, we're told, a hostage negotiating team is in position. Details are sketchy at this point. All we know is that a gunman entered the Hubbard Plant this morning, shots were fired, and that the gunman has not come out of the plant."

"Leslie, are there any reports of deaths?"

The camera pulled back and encompassed Leslie again.

"Steve, at this time we have no confirmed reports of deaths. The local police have told us the plant has been evacuated with the exception of the wing that the gunman is in. We are still hearing an occasional sound that could be gunfire and if you—there! Are you picking that up?" A muffled *pop-pop-pop* carried up the hill. The screen shot zoomed past Leslie again to show several policemen hunkered down behind their cars, then panned to a team of police suiting up with the modern day version of armored plating.

"Leslie, is that gunfire we're hearing?"

"Yes, Steve, we believe so."

The camera shot stayed with the police suiting up.

"Any word on the gunman or a motive?"

"No, Steve, at this time all we're being told is that the individual inside is suspected to be an employee of Hubbard."

With nothing much else to watch, Leslie turned it back to the Studio and Steve. Steve went on to explain that Channel Three Action News would keep the public informed. He also added a note to stay away from the area, to those of the listeners that weren't already on the way out to Hubbard.

*   *   *

"*Quack, quack, quack, come on out little ducks!*" Lane sang out in a stage whisper, walking slowly down the aisles and rows of the data input offices. He held the gun at his side pointed to the ground. At some point he'd taken off his shirt. His nose had begun to bleed again due to someone tossing a chair in his direction. He'd blocked it well enough with his face, but it had hurt non-the-less.

How many were left? He wasn't sure. Some had gotten out by breaking windows while he was in the hall outside. Maybe none were left. No matter where he turned, or stood, he could see at least three or four bodies. The gore and fluids of death seemed only a macabre painting or a bit of theater to him. They were just playing, after all, Duane knew that. There was a lot more beyond this life, one *hell* of a lot more.

It had been a long time since he'd heard movement, he was sure he'd gotten everyone that hadn't made it out but wanted to make certain. Some that didn't dive through the broken windows had made it out the front doors as he'd circled the offices in pursuit; shooting, yelling, watching them fall, glass windows shattering, lights bursting overhead, computer terminals cracking and exploding as the bullets raped and tore through the bodies and office. His nose was full of the dull iron smell of blood and the sharp scent of gunpowder; his hands were screaming in pain. He'd done some shooting of a more personal nature during the melee and the front of his pants showed it.

"Come out, come out, wherever you are," he called again. There was a quick, heavy movement behind him toward the front of the office.

"Hello? Anybody there? *Daddies gonna buy you a mockingbirdy!*" he called again, drawing the gun toward the sound.

The door to the office crashed open and he could see a blur of black figures rush into the room, he dropped to the floor and scrambled back into a cubicle. He pulled up under the small table in the cubicle and listened to them spreading out into the room.

"Lane White?" a rather pissed off, amplified voice rang out.

He didn't answer. Those that got out must have spilled the bean as to who was causing the ruckus, Duane thought.

"You have one minute to show yourself and lay down your weapons."

Duane didn't answer, he could still hear them moving about the office, behind the cubicles and along both walls. There was the sharp smell of ozone and he noticed smoke rising to the ceiling from some terminal terminal. He laughed out loud at that one and was rewarded with the rustling of the black clad figures heading his way.

Then he began to feel himself split. Lying on his side, tucked under the table, most of his bullets spent and his body nearly worn out, he began to let a bit of the reality in. Not all at once, he didn't want to turn the gun on himself, but he let enough in to taste the bitterness of it.

He must have been seven or eight and Kristy was probably ten or so when it happened. He wasn't sure why they'd done it, the memory of the day was all he had. For some reason the ill fated White clan had taken to Woodland park—picnic and all—on a bright, sunlight, perfectly scripted day one spring. There were greasy burgers from the drive through at the Burger Stop, pop and a bag of licorice nips for dessert.

His Mom had smiled most of the day and he remembered catching a glimpse of a much younger, healthier Duane Trammel White pulling that mostly hard, stony face into a grin that wasn't sour and mocking. The smiles that day were genuine as he enjoyed a day at the park with his young bride and their children.

It had already been a rough road for them; Duane had developed a taste for drinking and liked it more all the time. His bride had her days where the first thing she reached for in the morning was an ice pack before her morning coffee. He and Kristy already knew to stay out of arm length when he was ranting on about one thing or another, though it was nothing compared to what was to come.

It had been a day unlike any he'd experienced in the few years of his young life. As they were leaving the park—the sun trailing low in the sky, their bodies tired and dusty—his Dad suddenly picked him up and perched him high up on his shoulders for the long walk to the car on the other side of the park.

He held tightly to Duane's thick, rough hands and saw the balding spot on the crown of his head. He could smell the thick, oily scent of his hair tonic and the honest sweat of a workingman. On that long walk, looking down at Kristy, his Mother smiling up at him as she shyly nudged Duane for the unusual antic, he felt as if he would burst with the love he felt for his Dad. If he'd had a way to bottle that day—that precise moment in time—his life would have turned out much differently.

He could have taken that bottle out and uncorked that long ago beautiful day and be reminded of what life could be. But it was too late for all that and all he was left with was as room full of dead bodies and several live ones that wanted him to cut out the shit and give it up.

The black clad figure was before him in an instant, short, dark gun raised. He said nothing. What was there to say? He was, beyond any shadow of doubt, seriously fucked. He raised the pistol but never got off a shot.

The bullets struck him in the left side and worked their way up to his chest.

ELEVEN

...0

...and the goose walked on.

What had been was faded from his thoughts at best and at worst, was gone completely. He slowly worked his way through the dunes and tall grass; naked, still bleeding from the purple bug attack, beach sand stuck to the drying blood along his side, hair hanging in tangled confusion, eyes red and swollen from the brackish water. He stopped at the edge of the grass and looked at the still distant trees.

The air was fresher away from the lake and he could smell the first tinge of pine needles and sap. He began to move again, then stopped, looking back at the edge of the trees. Was there movement there? He looked closer and, yes, he could see some people standing and walking about the edge of the forest. They noticed him at the same time and began to wave, but didn't leave the edge of the trees.

Wasn't there something familiar about a couple of those figures in the trees? A certain bend in their stance that he knew; an intimate angle to their posture? A familiar kink in those waving arms? There sure was. He raised his arm and waved back.

He began to cry with relief as he did his best to sprint for the trees, anxious to embrace them.

*   *   *

"Please come in, Mrs. Duran, I'm Sgt. Beck, but please call me Syd."

"Thank you, Syd," Marilyn said, briefly shaking the offered hand, then sat. Her eyes were swollen from lack of sleep and her thoughts were not the best she'd had. Losing Lane had been almost more than she was able to take. It was the last thing she'd expected to happen. It had all been going so well. It had seemed the right thing to do. She had seen something coming, but didn't think it would be this bad.

Henry and Linda wouldn't return her calls, but Stan Litchfield told her on the side that Linda was searching for a way to sue her for something, anything. Thanks, Stan, bring me up a little more. No matter, he'd told her, there was no case.

It was just one of the many alley's of thought she was running down.

"Well," Syd said, sitting back down in his chair. His office was functional, drab and very neat. Everything was in its place, from his simple white shirt and dark blue suit to his pencil and penholder. It was an office designed for function and nothing else.

The sun was still in the early sky and cut through the windows, despite the drawn shades. Behind the door she could hear the hustle and bustle of a medium sized police department waking for another day of crime fighting.

"I guess we don't need to discuss why you're here."

Syd was tall and thin with a thick stir of brown hair atop his head. His eyes were brown and his face was somewhat doughy for such a thin person.

"Actually, I've given several statements to several different officers, so I'm not sure why I'm here. You have access to all Lane's records with the state. I'm sure you have read my statement."

Syd nodded, hands folded together on his desk.

"Yes, I did," he said, leaning back in his chair. "It all boils down to this—and correct me if I'm wrong here. Mr. White moved back to his childhood home to pursue his writing career by writing an autobiography on his own life experiences, of which we are all aware," he nodded at

Marilyn again. She nodded back, already bored and thinking through the incident for something she may have missed.

"Somehow or another…things went wrong and we had the incident last week out at Hubbard Electronics."

"Yes," Marilyn said, cringing at the word incident. Where had she missed it? Where had the one thing that would have led her to bring Lane back been? How could she have missed it?

"I have something further that I hope you can help me with," Syd stood and went to a door in the back of his office. He pulled out a cardboard box that smelled of smoke and had a picture of a cow on the side. There were also several holes in the box that might have been made with bullets, but she wasn't sure. Syd placed the box on his desk.

"The fire department found this box on the lawn when they arrived. Quick thinking, they saved it as evidence for what has turned out to be arson after all. Did they tell you how the fire was started?"

"At the house?"

"Yes."

"No, I'm not sure how it started."

"We found the remains of gas cans in the basement. We think he set them up on some kind of time delay fuse."

"Oh," Marilyn said, still not interested in how it happened. The box held her attention and she leaned forward in her chair for a closer look. Syd noticed her lack of attention to the fire story.

"In any case, the house was a total loss. They just watched it burn and controlled the fire as best they could."

Marilyn looked at him and smiled. Syd sat down on the front edge of his desk, next to the box.

"Then they find this," he said. Reaching into the box he pulled out a handful of yellow legal pads. Marilyns heart skipped as she recognized the handwriting on the tablets. She stood and pulled several more tablets from the box. Syd stood and went back to his chair as Marilyn began reading.

"Now, nobody knows about this box, except for the fireman that turned it over. Yet, their interest ends there. I'm not sure why I'm sharing this with you other than that I felt you'd want to see it. Since you've been working with Lane since the incident with his father, I thought it might help give you some answers."

Marilyn didn't answer, she was reading through the tablets, scanning, searching, and hoping again to find that answer she'd missed. It would surely be in here.

"I've read through all of them. There are sixty-three tablets that are more or less full. The story is quite good."

"Story?" Marilyn asked, no looking up from her reading.

"Yes. It's about a Grandfather and his grandson. In the end they burn down the house at Cherokee Place. Lane's house."

"The characters in the story?"

"Yes. That's the common theme, the house on Cherokee Place. His father even makes an appearance as a monster of sorts. But I'm sure you'll read through it. It's a hell of a case. I've never seen anything like it."

"Does anyone else know about this?"

"The stories?"

"Yes."

"No. And as far as I'm concerned, they're yours. There's nothing more that can be done. There is nobody to prosecute. My only reason in calling you is that I thought having the writing might help in some way."

"I see," Marilyn said, reluctantly laying the tablets down.

"The story is on only about half the tablets. Did you read any of the others? They're on the bottom of the box," Syd asked, calmly sitting in his chair.

Marilyn pulled out another handful of tablets and lay them on the desk. Revealing the tablets beneath. She fought back the swelling in her soul that threatened to spill out in tears as she read what Lane had written.

"I guess he figured he was writing this autobiography when all that was being put down," Syd offered.

Marilyn didn't respond for fear of letting go the tidal wave that was building in her. She placed the tablets back in the box and thanked Syd for his thoughtfulness in contacting her.

"He didn't have the best penmanship, but that does say what I think it does?" Syd asked.

"It says 'I love my daddy,'" Marilyn managed to choke out.

"I thought so."

He walked Marilyn back through the maze of desks to the front entrance.

"Well, I hope this can help you in some way," Syd said, setting the box in the trunk of her tired, old Maverick. He offered his hand and she quickly shook it.

"Maybe it will, Syd, maybe it will," she said, then paused, looking down at the closed trunk of her car.

"Sometimes life isn't what you think it is," she said aloud, searching for something to hang onto. She didn't have her own mantra, not yet anyhow.

"I find that most everyday," he said, then put his hand on her shoulder. "Let me know if I can help," he said, turning back to his office.

"Thank you," she said. He raised his hand in reply as he was walking away, already into the rest of his day's schedule.

She stood by her car for over an hour. When she finally left she knew she couldn't bring herself to read through the box of Lane's writing. Not now, maybe not for some time to come. It would also be some time before she could get her head back on straight enough to perform her duties, if ever.

But for now, she was going home and fixing something for lunch, and that was enough.

0-595-20218-7